BEST KEPT *Secrets*

DANIELLE BAKER

Dedication

This book is for all those that felt "Me Too".

You are Invincible.

You are Unbreakable.

You are ENOUGH.

Me Too.

Content Warning/
Trigger Warning

Dear Reader,

Before reading this book, please note it may have triggering scenes and themes for some readers. It references sexual assault in the past (not on page), PTSD flashbacks, anxiety disorders, mention of homicide (not on page), and references child abandonment (not on page). Please proceed with caution.

Your mental health matters.

ONE

Breathe.

Inhale. One. Two. Three. Four. Five.

She hated the smell of cinnamon.

Breathe.

Exhale. Six. Seven. Eight. Nine. Ten.

Zoey Chandler opened her eyes at the end of the exhale. She glanced over her shoulder to see if anyone had noticed the minor anxiety attack she'd just had. When the other shoppers in the aisle just went about their business, she forced her shoulders to relax, to unclench the fists her fingers had made on the shopping cart handle. Her knuckles were white.

She hated the smell of *artificial* cinnamon, she amended to herself. Candles, potpourri, those stupid cinnamon scented pinecones that seemed to be everywhere in the stores once November arrived.

The smell of Fireball Whisky.

Before that thought even completely registered, she shoved it down, blocked it out. Used the techniques she'd been learning in therapy to stave off the crippling panic attacks she'd been living with for over a year.

Unconsciously, she reached for the small keychain of mace on her purse, holding it in her clammy fingers for just a moment before letting it dangle back down. Not that it would do much, she admitted, but it was still better than nothing.

No one is going to do anything in a brightly lit, bustling grocery store, she reminded herself, her own inner monologue tinged with annoyance at herself. She had more than herself to worry about, now.

Smoothing a hand over her five-month-olds rounded back where she slept peacefully against her chest, swaddled snuggly in her favorite baby wearing contraption, Zoey breathed as calmness settled over her. She was not in any harm. Nor was Verity.

Zoey smiled down at that peaceful little face, the best thing to have happened to her.

She'd once worried that peering into that tiny face would be torture. Worried that when she'd been born that she would look like someone else, a constant reminder of a chilly fall night, of a dark-haired, brown-eyed guy that she'd considered her friend, one that reeked and tasted of cinnamon flavored whisky as he'd shoved his mouth on hers, stifling the screams she tried and failed to deliver, the drug he'd slipped into her drink making her mind a densely fogged nightmare.

But, to Zoey's immense relief, her child had been born with the same blonde hair and indigo eyes as her mother. No trace of that asshole lay in the perfect face she stared at now.

Zoey was thankful the infant was sleeping, though she knew the tiny terror against her chest would awaken soon, hungry, so she rushed to complete her shopping. Thanksgiving was just a few short days away, and Zoey still needed to find a turkey.

It was her first full Thanksgiving meal she'd ever prepared and cooked all on her own, and the nerves had started to set in. It was also the first Thanksgiving she would have without her mom.

That familiar wave of grief settled over her, and she let it linger for a moment as she studied the frozen turkeys in the meat department, unsure what weight to get. It would just be the six of them, herself and Verity, her brother Tommy, his fiancé Shauntelle, who happened to be her childhood best friend, and her father. And his new lady friend.

Zoey's lips thinned at the last thought, dispelling the grief that had swept over her. They had barely just laid her mother to rest when Thom Chandler had announced that he was dating a woman he'd met at work. Zoey... had not taken the news well. Her brother Tommy hadn't seen the issue with the announcement, stating that their father deserved to grieve in whatever way he needed to. That woman had been the first in a steadily growing line of new lady friends that had come along.

Zoey hadn't been particularly nice to any of them. She also didn't bother to learn or remember their names. They didn't last long enough to be worth the effort.

It had been... a difficult year.

As Verity began to squirm inside the ring sling against her breasts, Zoey knew she had precious little time before the squirming turned into a full out meltdown. Verity would be ready to eat in minutes, and though Zoey was extremely pro breastfeeding anywhere at any time, she hadn't had the courage to try it herself. Having survived being left, half-naked for anyone to see in that parking lot thirteen months ago, she closely guarded her nakedness now. Even if that meant that Verity would have to wait a few extra minutes to eat.

Quickly pushing the grocery cart with one hand and patting Verity's back soothingly with the other, Zoey was nearly running out of the store as Verity's first wail erupted. She groaned, as she knew any moment what her body's response to her infant's cry would mean.

Dumping the groceries into the back hatch of her car, she jumped into the backseat, grateful for the heavy tinted windows as she crooned soothingly, then sighed, leaning her head back against the seat rest as Verity went quiet at her breast.

TWO

Tommy met her at the car as she pulled into the driveway, and Zoey thanked him profusely as he helped carry in the groceries as she carried Verity in, buckled securely into her infant car seat.

Zoey had barely made it through the door before Tommy was taking the car seat out of her hands, already crooning to the now wide-awake baby. Verity babbled up into the face of her uncle, waving her hands wildly around herself in excitement. He set the car seat on the counter and with quick, nimble fingers unbuckled her, pulling her out with a grunt.

"Good gravy missy, you're getting heavy," her brother chuckled. Zoey took pride in the rolls on Verity's chunky little thighs and arms, and she swatted Tommy's arm in reproach. He laughed again, hiking the infant higher in his arms. "I didn't say it was a bad thing!"

As Zoey began unbagging the groceries, she watched her brother as he carried her daughter through the kitchen, talking to her gently. Verity's hands clamped over his lips and she held tightly in her little fist, the other reaching up to touch his hair.

"That looks like quite the spread," he said to Zoey then, the words muffled around the tiny hand still clutching his lips, motioning with his head to the pile of groceries on the counter now.

Zoey shrugged. "I didn't know how much of everything I would need. I'd rather have too much than not enough. Mom would have known how much to get."

Tommy nodded, gnawing on Verity's fingers with his lips pulled over his teeth, making Verity belly laugh, and the sound helped cut through Zoey's anxiety. "It'll turn out great."

Zoey turned and began putting groceries away, canned goods in the pantry, cold items in the refrigerator or freezer. She had moved back into their parent's house after the attack, unable to remain living in the dorm rooms after dropping out, her anxiety crippling in the beginning. It had felt safer at home. She had been hired at a dental office as a receptionist, and the job was simple and safe and worked with her during her pregnancy. When their mother had passed, Tommy had moved back home, too, insisting that he needed to be here to help Zoey with Verity when she was born. Zoey had been grateful for her brother's presence, especially at night. She hated being alone with Verity in the house at night, her anxiety and fear seemingly heightened. Just knowing he was down the hall made her feel better, since their father was rarely there, either working or staying with whichever new lady friend he was currently on.

She looked around the small kitchen and beyond to the living room. It looked the same as it always had growing up, though many of her mothers' personal belongings had been put away, packed into boxes and stacked in the back of Zoey's closet upstairs.

"So, hey," he said then, juggling the wriggling infant in his arms again, "I was wondering if it's not too much trouble to invite one more on Thursday?"

"Sure, who?" Zoey asked, pausing to look at him.

"Chase."

Zoey's eyebrows shot up. "Is he home?"

"He will be," her brother said. "He gets in day after tomorrow. I wanted to talk to you about letting him crash here for a couple nights. He's moving back, and his new place isn't ready until next week."

Zoey's throat closed, panic rising instantly.

Breathe.

Inhale. One. Two. Three. Four. Five.

Breathe.

Exhale. Six. Seven. Eight. Nine. Ten.

"If it's too much—" Tommy began, his voice tinged with concern, but Zoey shook her head.

"Of course it's not too much," Zoey said, forcing an easy smile, though anxiety still thumped at her chest. "I don't want you to feel like you can't invite your friends here just because of me, Tommy."

"I know," he hedged, his brown eyes worried, "but I don't want to take away your safe place. I know... I know you still struggle... around men."

"It's Chase," Zoey said and smiled again, as the anxiety faded, slowly, but faded nonetheless. "I'll be fine, I promise."

Tommy nodded, though his eyes were still crinkled with worry. He hefted Verity into a football hold and headed from the kitchen, saying, "Phew! Girl, you stink."

THREE

Chase Manning gritted his teeth, sweat pouring from his brow as he pushed up, again, again, again. Resting the dumbbell bar on the hooks, he exhaled as he sat up, letting his body relax after the rigorous set. He reached over and grabbed the water bottle to his left, taking a long pull, then splashed some over his face, pushing the black lock of hair back that had fallen over his brow.

The gym was about half full, a smattering of men and women on different work out machines throughout the long room. He rested his elbows on his spread knees, hands holding the water bottle dangling between them. His upper body was completely bare, having taken off his shirt an hour ago. He rolled his shoulders, stretching the muscles there, before pushing himself to his feet.

He crossed the room to a leg press machine, added weights, and then sat down. He was halfway through his first set when he realized a young woman was staring at him fixedly in one of the many mirrors that ran along the entire back wall of the gym. She had faltered on the treadmill as she watched him; thigh muscles bunching, calf muscles straining, as he counted out his reps. When she caught him staring at her, she quickly averted her gaze, the ponytail her blonde hair was in swinging over her shoulder. He chuckled to himself. She was pretty.

When he'd finally managed to make it through the rotation of machines he typically used, he was sweating, his breathing none too steady. He did a series of cool down exercises, and then made a beeline to the locker room, removing his gym shoes, where he pulled on a pair of grey sweatpants overtop of his shorts, then tugged a long-sleeved black shirt over his head. He stuffed his feet into his street shoes, before exiting the locker room.

The woman that had been watching him earlier was just outside the locker room door, and she made a show of bumping into him to catch his attention. He grinned down at her, from a long way up. At six foot five, he was taller than the average man, let alone the woman that couldn't have stood taller than five foot seven.

He let her apologize coyly, again flashing that grin he knew was disarming, before excusing himself from around her and heading toward the exit and out into the November cold.

Maybe he'd see her there again.

He'd only been in town a couple hours, but had needed to get a workout in before meeting up with his best friend, the brother he'd chosen for himself after having gotten a gaggle of little sisters instead. All of whom had tried their hand at setting him up with their friends, or friends of friends.

Busy bodies, all of them.

The chill in the late November air felt good against his flushed skin. He could have gone to the station, he supposed, gone in and gotten acquainted, but he'd welcomed the old, familiar gym he'd frequented years ago.

He climbed into his Jeep Rubicon and shut the door, tossing his gym bag into the back seat, and digging his keys out of his pocket. Starting the Jeep, he adjusted the thermostat to defog the windshield before setting off into the familiar streets.

It was a short drive through town, and it wasn't long before he pulled into the driveway of the house. He turned off the Jeep and climbed out. He had just reached into the backseat to grab the duffel bag with his street clothes when the front door of the house opened and Tommy stepped out, coming down the concrete path toward him.

Chase grinned, straightening, and extended his right hand. Tommy grinned back, taking that hand in his own and they drew together to lightly bump chests, their own way of embracing. Tommy stood several inches shorter than him, and his sandy blonde hair was cut short, almost buzzed. "What's up, dude?"

Chase rolled one shoulder in a shrug as he hoisted his duffel bag over it, letting it hang over his back as they started the short walk back to the house. "Just livin' the dream."

Tommy shot him a side-eyed glance. "Is that why you moved back? Livin' the dream?"

"Meh," Chase muttered and rolled his shoulder in that same casual shrug. "Needed a change of scenery."

As the two of them made it to the door, Tommy stopped and turned toward him. The wind whipped around them, stirring up a pile of fallen leaves and twirling them in a mini tornado around their feet. "I know you're gonna want to give Zoey a hug when you get inside," he said, and Chase narrowed his eyes on the shorter man as he continued, "but I need you to give her some space, okay?"

"Sure," Chase said slowly, eyeing Tommy uncertainly. "Is she okay?"

"She's fine," Tommy said, a bit unevenly. Chase knew his friend, and trusted his professional instincts, enough to know something was up. Tommy put his hand on the doorknob and opened it, saying roughly, "I know you haven't been home in a while. A lot has... changed."

As they entered, Chase couldn't help but smile at the familiar kitchen, smaller and a bit more cramped than was comfortable, but cozy and bright. He remembered the first time he'd banged his head on the hanging light from the middle of the ceiling; he'd grown several inches one summer and hadn't realized just how tall he'd gotten until he'd tried to walk under the light as usual and had caught the top of his head on it as he walked by. He'd been all gangly arms and legs for months.

When his eyes fell on a small pamphlet pinned to the door of the refrigerator, he cursed under his breath. Of course.

"I'm sorry I didn't make it up to say good-bye to your mom," he said solemnly, nodding with his chin to the funeral program with a black and white photo of their mother, Lena.

Tommy glanced at it and nodded. "It's okay. She would have understood." He crossed to the fridge, opening it. "Want a beer?"

"Absolutely," Chase said, accepting the cold beer Tommy held out to him. "Can I bum a shower though? I stink."

Tommy nodded around a drink of his own beer. "You know where it is. Bedroom at the end of the hall has been made up for you, too."

"Thanks," he said and ducked his head through the low archway that led from the kitchen to the living room, and the stairs to the second floor. He climbed them two at a time, easily finding his way to the bathroom. He glanced at the door that used to be Zoey's when they'd been young. She was six years younger, just a kid when they'd graduated and he'd headed off to the police academy downstate.

Shutting the bathroom door, he quickly shucked his clothes, turning on the shower taps to get the water heating. He dug out a towel from the cabinet in the far corner, then stepped into the steaming shower that was much too short for his six five frame.

Setting the beer on the window sill after taking a long drink, he ducked his head under the spray and rinsed his hair, lathering it with shampoo and washed his body of the sweat from his workout.

Ducking his head under the too short shower head again, he rinsed his hair. Cut short on the sides but left long on top, too long, he was sure he'd be informed it needed a cut before next week.

Tommy had asked him why he'd moved back. He wasn't sure he was ready to tell that story, not yet.

Nightmares still haunted him, sometimes even when he just closed his eyes. He could still see her. He hadn't been able to save her, and it had haunted him ever since. He'd needed to get away, start fresh.

Finishing the beer in one swallow, he climbed out of the shower. Drying himself, he realized he'd left his duffel bag down in the kitchen. He slung the towel around his hips, securing it by tucking the end in. He exited the bathroom and was halfway down the hall when he realized Zoey's bedroom door was open, cracked about six inches. The sun had set and beyond the windows of her bedroom the sky was darkening, the only light in the room one dim lamp. As he made to walk past, his head turned and he peeked into the bedroom just for a heartbeat, but what he saw stopped him in his tracks.

Zoey was sitting in a padded gliding chair that had been positioned in the corner of the room. Her legs were crossed, one over the other, her top foot dangling, the other rocking gently, pushing against the carpeted floor.

But what had stopped him dead was the golden head that lay against her bare breast, a tiny hand that flailed in the air, as if trying to grab a hold of something invisible hanging above it. Zoey's dark golden hair fell in a curtain across her face, obscuring her, as she crooned softly to the babe in her arms.

Chase wasn't sure if he'd made a noise, but her head whipped around, as if sensing his presence. Her eyes went wide, but she didn't move.

Chase nearly tripped on himself as he rushed away from the door and down the stairs, stumbling into the kitchen, still naked save the towel slung around his hips.

Tommy looked up from where he sat at the small dining table. When he saw Chase's face, Tommy opened his mouth to speak, but Chase was quicker.

"She had a baby?"

Tommy nodded, standing.

"With who?" Chase demanded, that same old protective instinct he had with all of his sisters kicking in.

The look on Tommy's face was pained. "Some douchebag." Chase's mouth tightened, but he waited for Tommy to continue. "She was assaulted, Chase. Some dickhead college kid."

Blood roared in Chase's ears. "She was *what*? When?"

"Last year," Tommy said, sliding his hands into the pockets of his jeans. "Like I said... a lot has changed. She's changed. She's... still healing. Mentally."

Chase scrubbed a hand over his face, blowing out his breath. "What happened?"

Tommy shook his head. "I only know the bare minimum; she hasn't wanted to talk about it. I haven't pushed her. I'm not sure I want to know the details." The skin on Tommy's face went taut and paled slightly.

"What the fuck," Chase breathed, dropping his chin almost to his chest. When he did, he realized he was still in a towel, and swore again. "Is she... is she okay? Physically?"

Tommy nodded, shrugging one shoulder. "She doesn't have any permanent injuries, if that's what you're asking."

"Why didn't you say anything?" he asked, while he rifled through his duffel bag until he found a pair of sweatpants, pulling them on under the towel before hanging it over the nearest dining chair. He pushed his fingers through the longer locks on the top of his head, pulling the still damp strands away from his brow. He squeezed his eyes shut, but quickly opened them, memories assailing him.

Tommy crossed the small kitchen to the refrigerator, opening it, and grabbed two beers out of it. He held one up to Chase, who shook his head no. Tommy put one back, but opened the second.

Again, Chase asked, "Why didn't you say anything?"

Tommy opened his mouth to speak, but a small voice from behind him answered.

"Because I asked him not to."

FOUR

Chase whipped his head around to where Zoey had appeared in the arched doorway between the living room and kitchen, and she sucked in an involuntary breath when his electric blue eyes met hers.

He wore a pair of gray sweatpants that rode low, impossibly low, on his narrow hips... and nothing else.

Zoey's eyes flit over him, only once for a half of a heartbeat, and then raised them back to his. His upper body was bare: torso, chest, shoulders, arms. All of it carved with muscle. She'd forgotten how incredibly tall he was as he stood in their small kitchen, making it feel smaller.

She had dressed for bed before he'd peeked into her room, and she wore a pair of comfortable navy-blue lounge pants and a thin, lilac purple robe tied closed at her waist. The color complimented her skin, almost made it appear to glow.

Chase's eyes never left hers, and if possible, he raised his chin higher, before asking, "Why?"

Zoey crossed her arms over her middle, her indigo eyes never leaving his. Her dark golden, caramel blonde hair swayed around her shoulders, and she reached up to tuck one side behind an ear. "Shame, at first. Later, I just didn't want to have to explain it over and over again. Even to... family."

Zoey faltered on the last word, unsure how to label Chase. Sure, they'd grown up together, kind of. He was her brother's best friend, had basically been another big brother to her as a kid. She'd been in high school when they'd made a trip downstate and had stopped in to visit him. She'd seen him, wearing his uniform, and hadn't been able to think of him as a brother since that weekend.

Now, he stood in her kitchen, half naked. A year ago, she would have drooled over the sight of him; impossibly tanned skin, chiseled muscles, his dark hair that continued to fall over his brow even as he pushed it back with his fingers. Now, his nakedness and proximity made her throat close with anxiety. Even knowing this man would die to protect her, she feared him. Couldn't stop the dread from clawing at her chest.

Breathe.

Inhale. One. Two. Three. Four. Five.

Breathe.

Exhale. Six. Seven. Eight. Nine. Ten.

"Can you—" Zoey whispered, her throat closing, "—can you put a shirt on? Please."

Chase looked startled, then reached for his bag, pulling out a clean shirt and tugging it on over his head. She breathed easier once he was covered.

"I'm sorry," Zoey said in an exhaled breath, hugging herself around the middle tighter. She gave him a sad half smile that she knew didn't reach her eyes. "It's not you. I promise."

"Are you—" Chase began, but stopped, thinking. "Did he—"

Zoey pushed the memories down, even as his words registered, without even asking them fully. She shook her head, eyes closing, taking those five seconds to inhale, and five to exhale again. She could feel the edge of her robe fluttering against her chest as it rose and fell rapidly. "I don't... I don't like to talk about it."

"I'm sorry," Chase murmured, and she knew his apology was genuine. His electric blue eyes were pained as they stared into hers. He turned to Tommy then, sparing her from those incredible eyes. "I wish there was something I could do to help."

"It is what it is," Zoey said, straightening her shoulders slightly. Then, she gave them each a smile that tilted one side of her mouth as she quipped, "You two have a good night. I'm going back up to bed. Try not to get too crazy down here, there is a baby sleeping upstairs after all."

Chase's eyes cut to the stairway that led upstairs. Zoey smiled gently, touching the door frame as she stopped on her way out. "You can meet her tomorrow."

"A girl?" he asked reverently, his blue eyes wide. He grinned over at Tommy.

Zoey nodded, her heart tugging at the instant adoration on Chase's face. The same adoration he showed to his niece and nephew that belonged to his sister.

"Her name is Verity," Zoey murmured, smiling. "It means '*Truth*.'"

FIVE

Zoey sat upright in bed, her heart hammering in her throat, and took several deep, clawing breaths. She glanced over to the other side of the room to Verity's crib, where she could see the outline of her little body through the protective rails. Throwing her legs over the side of the bed, she padded over to the crib, leaning over just far enough to place her hand on the baby's back, where she could feel the gentle rise and fall of her breathing. Zoey exhaled, calmness settling over her again.

She glanced at the clock on her nightstand, which read 5:17 am, and she sighed. Pulling on the same lilac colored robe over her tank top, she chose to leave her pants where they lay on the floor beside the bed. She was over-warm anyway.

On silent feet, she crept out of the bedroom, careful not to wake the baby, as she tiptoed down the hallway to the stairs. She made it to the darkened kitchen, turning on the dim light over the stove, casting the small room in just enough light to see. Zoey filled the kettle and put it on the stove to heat. She would start coffee later, when she knew Tommy would be awake. She had always preferred tea. As she waited, she ran down her mental notes to herself on all the different dishes she would be making throughout the day.

A noise behind her, an almost silent rustle of clothing, made her spin around, hand flying to clutch the folds of her robe closed over her chest, her eyes wide.

Out of the shadows of the living room, Chase appeared, stepping through the archway into the dimly lit kitchen. He hadn't seen her yet, as his face was obscured by a t-shirt that he was in the process of pulling on over his head.

Each individual muscle moved, rippling with the movements of his arms over his body as they twisted inside the shirt.

And those gray sweatpants did nothing to hide the lower portion of his body.

His face appeared, his eyes meeting hers instantly, and he stopped mid-step, arms still half suspended in the air, the hem of the shirt stalled at his torso. He blinked rapidly at her in the semi-dark.

"I uhh—" he stammered, tugging the shirt the rest of the way down his torso. "I didn't realize anyone was awake yet. I'm sorry."

Zoey swallowed hard, tamping the panic back down until it settled. "It's okay, I couldn't sleep. Do you want some coffee?"

"Desperately," he chuckled, and took a wide step around her toward the coffee pot. It was still in the same spot it had always been, the fixings in neatly labeled canisters beside it. She watched him as he filled the coffee pot with water at the sink, stepping back to pour it into the reservoir. He plunked a filter into the basket and then measured out coffee grounds using the spoon that had been shoved into the canister. Zoey made a face; it would be strong, she could tell.

Her teakettle began to whistle, and she pulled it off the stove before it made too much noise. She poured the piping hot water over the tea bag, letting it steep. She turned toward him and was shocked to see him standing with his hips leaning against the countertop across from where she stood, watching her as one hand massaged the back of his neck and one shoulder. The way his arm was raised, it pulled the hem of his shirt up slightly, revealing several inches of his abdomen and side. His gaze was intense in the semi-dark. It made her nervous.

Not that she didn't find that swatch of bare skin attractive. Or the broad, muscled chest she knew lay beneath the shirt.

He must have sensed her nervousness, as he lowered his arm and crossed them over his chest, as if to shrink himself. The only noise in the small kitchen was the sound of the steady dripping of the coffee as it perked. He rolled his head across his shoulders again, stretching.

"Was the bed upstairs not comfortable?" Zoey asked into the quiet, removing the steeped tea bag and adding a dash of cream, motioning to his movements.

"Most beds aren't quite long enough, I usually end up hanging off one end or the other," he admitted with a rueful smile that tilted up one corner of his mouth.

"I'm sorry," Zoey murmured, turning with her cup of tea. She nodded to the coffee. "I think it's ready." Indeed, it had stopped dripping. "There's milk and creamer in the refrigerator, sugar on the counter."

"Black is perfect, but thank you," he said over his shoulder as he poured a generous cup. Even his back was muscled and lean. Good lord, she could see through his shirt as those muscles rippled with each movement he made. Zoey snapped her eyes back up to his when he turned back around. "Thank you for letting me join you for dinner today and giving me a bed to crash in for a few days."

Zoey sipped her tea, crossing her ankles, one over the other. Her bare feet were chilled slightly against the linoleum floor. "Tommy says you have a new place that won't be ready for a few days?"

"Mmhmm," he murmured around a drink of his scalding coffee. "I was lucky to snag it when I did. It's small, but it will work for just me."

Zoey heard a small, mewling cry drift toward her ears from the stairwell and stood up straight, turning to set her mug down on the counter behind her. Chase's eyes went to the doorway, where he too, could hear it. Chase's body stiffened.

"I'm sorry," Zoey murmured, already walking to the door. "I promise she doesn't fuss often."

The skin across Chase's cheekbones was taut, and paler than she'd seen. Her brows furrowed together. He shook his head, as if clearing it, and said, "No, it's not that. She's fine."

"She's just hungry," Zoey explained lamely as she made it to the door. Verity let out a cry in earnest. Zoey rushed out, not only to get to her fussy infant, but to escape the haunted look that crossed Chase's face at the sound of the baby's cry.

SIX

Chase scrubbed one hand over his face, taking a deep, restorative breath.

He finished his coffee and headed upstairs, looking straight ahead as he passed Zoey's closed bedroom door. Chase quickly stuffed his feet into a pair of running shoes, pulled on a long-sleeved shirt, and then headed back down the stairs and out the door. Ear buds that played music linked to his cellphone drowned out the sounds of the early morning and the occasional car that passed by, though it did nothing to silence the thoughts that ran through his head.

The sky had lightened from ebony black to a muted grey as the sun began its ascent along the eastern horizon. It was cloudy, the wind a touch too biting, but he didn't care. He did several minutes of stretches, then took off down the street at a brisk jog.

The music and the steady cadence of his breathing, along with the pounding of the asphalt beneath his feet, finally worked to clear his mind, and he had covered several miles before turning around to head back to the Chandler residence. His brisk pace kept his blood flowing, and he didn't even feel the cold anymore.

He passed by a shallow ditch, brambles and overgrown saplings making it difficult to see through to the other side. A flash of white, tangled in the brambles caught his attention. It looked just like when they'd found—

His breath hitched and he stumbled to an abrupt halt, leaning down to brace his hands on his knees as he heaved in lungful after lungful of air. He stared into the ditch, his heart hammering. He scrubbed his hands over his face, pushing the long locks of hair away from his brow where they'd fallen.

It had been six months; six months and he still couldn't get the images out of his head. Nightmares haunted him, and despite the mandated therapy his captain had ordered, it hadn't done much to alleviate them.

And that sound, the mewling, needy cry that had drifted down to him from the baby upstairs, had rocked him to his core. He wasn't sure he would ever get that sound out of his head, what it did to him, or be able to explain why it affected him so deeply.

By the time he made it back to Tommy's, the sun had risen behind dismal gray clouds. A light, fluttering snow had begun to fall, whipped around in the wind, but it didn't stick to the pavement or the patches of near frozen grass that lined the small yards on either side of him.

Stretching through a short cool down, Chase let himself back into the house, stepping into the tiny kitchen. He was drenched with sweat despite the chill outside, and headed immediately to the arched doorway to head up the stairs for a shower.

Before he made it through the door, though, he was brought up short when Zoey stepped down off the bottom step, that little golden-haired bundle cradled in one arm.

He beamed a smile down at Zoey, who smiled back shyly. She adjusted the infant in her arms, hiking her higher against her chest before spinning her around to face outward. He laughed out loud when the chubbiest little thighs he'd ever seen started kicking excitedly, equally chunky arms flailing wildly. Two tiny teeth along her bottom gum peeked out when she looked up at him and gave him a wide smile.

She had the same indigo eyes as her mother, not quite blue, not quite violet. And a curly, golden mop of hair sat atop her head, a large orange hair bow was secured there with a clip.

"Oh my gosh," he breathed, stepping forward, bending his knees slightly. He reached out his hands, but looked to Zoey and asked gently, "May I?"

Zoey laughed, holding tighter to the squirming baby, but held her out to him. "I think she'd riot if you didn't."

Chase's hands covered Zoey's briefly, lightly, as the infant exchanged hands. It was Chase's job to notice the little things, and he didn't miss the way she stiffened, sucking in her breath involuntarily. The way those blue-violet eyes shuttered in panic before opening once more, clear.

The sight of her distress made him quake with inner rage. Whoever this bastard was, he would find out.

He made sure his face was once again calm before she raised those eyes to him, so heartbreakingly wary, but he could see she was fighting–fighting for the squirming little thing in his arms. He could tell she would fight like hell.

So he bounced the baby higher into his arms, one forearm beneath her diapered and clothed rear, the other hand splayed wide across her back, that felt so much tinier now in his hands than how she looked in her mother's embrace. She wore a white onesie with the words 'Cutest Pumpkin' on it, and an orange and yellow plaid bum-cover skirt.

"If you aren't the sweetest thing," Chase murmured, his voice low. Verity studied him, reaching one tiny hand up to grab a fistful of his hair. Chase yelped in surprise and Zoey laughed, stepping forward. Chase hunkered down so that she could reach the hand ensnared in his hair, slowly loosening each miniature finger until he was finally free. He chuckled, "You're a sour patch kid is what you are!"

He glanced at Zoey, and his breath halted in his throat when he realized his face was inches away from her breasts, the way he'd lowered his tall frame for Zoey's hands to reach Verity's bringing them close. Her breath fluttered the knit of the sweater she wore, the caramel color almost the same shade as the hair that lay in loose waves around her shoulders. This close, he could smell just a hint of lilac and lemongrass. He swallowed with difficulty.

As he straightened to his full height, Zoey looked up at him, her indigo eyes sparkling, as she laughed, "You'll learn to watch those hands at all times. And she knows they're lethal."

Verity claimed his attention again at that moment, using that same hand she'd fisted into his hair to pat his face excitedly.

"Where did you go?" Zoey asked then, motioning to his attire. He'd totally forgotten about his sweat-dampened clothes.

"Just a quick run," Chase said, bouncing Verity in his arms as he glanced down at her.

"How far did you go?"

"I usually do three to five miles depending on the day. Today I did seven; I know I'm going to need it after the food," he laughed.

"Do you run often?" Zoey asked as they passed back through the archway into the kitchen.

"Every day. I also hit the gym several days a week," he said, sitting down at the tiny table, holding Verity in his lap. Zoey raised her eyebrows in surprise as she began rifling through the cupboard, pulling out ingredients and supplies for the huge meal. He shrugged, continuing, "In my line of work, it's important to stay in shape. It could mean life or death for not only myself, but my fellow officers, and others, if I'm not."

He watched Zoey's face as he said it. It was the truth, a terrifying truth. He knew the risks his line of work came with.

It was part of the reason he'd never let his sisters or friends set him up with any of their single friends. It was an unfair request to make of someone.

Zoey had turned to the refrigerator, pulling out the turkey, which she had brined overnight. He watched his friend's sister, who he had known for almost her entire life. He and Tommy had met in sixth grade, when Chase's family had moved to the new city. They had bonded almost instantly over the San Francisco 49er's jersey Chase had been wearing that first day. The pair of them were rarely seen without the other for the remainder of their school years until graduation, when Chase had moved downstate for the police academy.

"How have you been? Other than..."

Zoey shrugged, her back to him as she worked at the counter, chopping vegetables for the stuffing. "Fine, I guess. It's been a tough year."

"I'm sorry about your mom," Chase said, adjusting Verity in his lap. "I wanted to make it for her service."

Zoey took a deep breath and let it out slowly, smiling at him over her shoulder. "Thank you. She always loved you."

"She was a wonderful lady," he said. "I can't imagine how tough this has been on you."

She shrugged again, dropping her shoulders quickly. "I just wish she'd been able to meet Verity.

Mom passed just a couple weeks before she was born. She was so excited."

Chase looked down into the happy face of the baby he held. "I'm sure she would have loved her."

But Zoey waved her hand in dismissal, and he sensed her grief. "Today is hard. All these firsts without her."

"How is your dad?" he asked.

Zoey laughed then, though it wasn't exactly a pretty sound, and he was surprised at the tone. "He's fine. Moved on like we didn't just lose Mom."

"I'm sorry," he murmured genuinely, but again she just waved that hand dismissively. "Will he be here today? I haven't seen him."

Zoey nodded, concentrating on what she was doing. "He will probably stop in for a bit. He moved out after... He left the house to Tommy and myself, and he got a small apartment on the other side of town."

"Ahh," Chase breathed, his dark brows shooting up, which made Verity belly laugh, so he did it again, wiggling and bobbing his eyebrows.

The front door opened then, a bluster of cool November air whipping through the room, and Chase grinned when he recognized Shauntelle Kendall as she came flying through the door, a store bought boxed pie in her hands.

"Well, I'll be damned," Shauntelle laughed as her eyes lit upon Chase where he sat holding Verity. She set the boxed pie on the counter and he smiled broadly and stood, reaching out to embrace the woman hard. Shaun and Zoey had been friends since kindergarten, and Shaun had spent as much time chasing after the guys wanting to join them in playing flag football as she had spending time with Zoey herself. Chase had known years ago that Tommy had a crush on the girl and had razzed him terribly for it. She had gotten more beautiful as an adult. Her long legs were encased in tight jeans, a pair of black converse on her feet, and a Carhardt hoodie covered her upper body. Her long, curly brown hair was tied back into a long French braid that ran down one side of her neck. "How are you?"

"I've been good," he said and grinned again as they pulled apart. Spotting the sparkling diamond on her left hand that signified their engagement, he nodded toward it. "I hear congratulations are in order."

Shaun fidgeted with the simple ring, smiling herself. "Thank you. I can't believe you're here! Tommy didn't even say anything."

"It was pretty last minute," he said, adjusting the wiggling baby in his arms, who was flailing her arms in delight at the newcomer.

"I see you've met the newest addition," Shaun laughed and looked at Zoey, reaching for and taking the excited baby from his arms. She held the infant up high, making her scream in delight, those chunky arms and legs never stopping their wild kicking. "Yes, I see you my little bug!"

Chase glanced over at Zoey, who was smiling warmly as she watched the three of them. "You're early," Zoey said to Shaun, who had tucked the infant into her arms like a football. "I didn't think you'd even roll out of bed until noon."

Shaun made a face at Zoey and Chase laughed. It was the same as it had always been, and the familiarity eased the tension that seemed to live buried under his skin.

Family.

He had missed this, he realized, and sat back down to enjoy it.

SEVEN

The small kitchen was filled with so much laughter that Zoey couldn't help but relax. Tommy had joined them downstairs moments after Shaun arrived, and the four of them made the already small kitchen feel entirely too cramped, but Zoey loved it.

Tommy had missed his best friend, and the familiar banter between the two took her back to her childhood.

Chase had excused himself to shower after his run, and when he came back down Zoey was once again struck by how handsome he was. He wore a pair of dark wash jeans that fit extremely well to his incredibly long legs, hips, and... other things. She blushed furiously at the thought. He had pulled on a gray sweater over a plain white t-shirt, but quickly pulled it off over his head, the heat in the kitchen from the multiple dishes cooking, along with the four bodies crammed into the small space making the room uncomfortably warm. Zoey regretted the thick caramel colored sweater she wore, sweating slightly as she worked.

Shaun reached over the sink, sliding the window open to let the chilly November air cool the room slightly. Zoey thanked her with a smile from where she stood at the stove.

Eventually, Tommy and Chase migrated to the living room, beers in hand, and turned on the big football game. Zoey smiled as she listened to them from the kitchen.

Shaun had carried the small platter of snacks out to the coffee table, and the guys munched as they watched the game, though Zoey did call out, "Tommy, don't you dare try to give her any of that!" and she rolled her eyes when Tommy's hand dropped from Verity's mouth where he'd about to let her try a pickle.

Shaun hung out at the arched doorway, leaning against the doorframe, half watching the game on the tv, and half talking to Zoey. Verity had been passed from one set of hands to the next, and she was currently cradled in the crook of Chase's arm as he sat on the couch.

"We root for the scarlet and gold team," he was telling Verity, in all seriousness, "*not* that nasty green and white team."

Zoey laughed out loud, which caused Chase's dark head to turn from where he sat on the couch and grin at her, his electric blue eyes crinkled at the corners. It nearly knocked the breath out of her.

Verity started to squirm, and Zoey knew that she had just a few minutes before she started to fuss in earnest. It had been several hours since she'd eaten, and with the excitement she had refused a nap as well.

"Will you keep an eye on the turkey?" Zoey asked Shaun, wiping her hands on a dishtowel. Shaun nodded, though she was paying attention to the tv. Zoey squeezed past, walking through the living room to where Chase sat on the couch. She extended her hands, palms out, for the infant that was steadily getting fussier. "She's hungry. I'll take her upstairs."

The words were out before she could stop them, and as she watched, his eyes dropped from her eyes to her chest, for the briefest of moments, before they swung back up to hers. Zoey blushed to the roots of her golden hair, reaching up and tucking a strand behind her ear.

Chase sat up straighter, rolling off his spine, bringing Verity with him. He extended his arms, raising the baby upward toward Zoey's waiting hands. It was nearly impossible to grab hold of her without touching the backs of Chase's large hands, and when her skin met his she couldn't breathe.

But it was as if Chase knew, and quickly removed his hands after placing Verity in her arms.

She practically scrambled up the stairs to the bedroom, closing the door behind her.

Sinking into the padded gliding chair in the corner as Verity's first indignant cry sounded, she quickly adjusted her clothing. Verity's fist thumped her breast as she latched, and Zoey sighed, leaning her head back. She rocked them gently, pulling a disgruntled Verity off long enough to switch sides. When the baby's mouth finally went slack, Zoey knew she had lost the fight and had fallen asleep.

She stood, stepping over to the changing table and stripping the infant of her skirt and onesie, changed her diaper with deft fingers, and redressed her into footed pajamas before laying her down in the crib for her afternoon nap.

Zoey glanced at the clock, mentally doing math. The turkey should be done soon, she thought. Still no sign of her father. No surprise there.

Returning to the first floor, she sniffed the air. It smelled heavenly.

When she took the final step into the living room, she laughed when she saw her brother and Chase on the edge of their seats, avidly watching the game unfold on the tv.

"Come on, that was a bullshit call!" Tommy grunted, taking a drink of his beer. Chase was shaking his head angrily, then raked his fingers through his hair in frustration. Shaun stood next to Tommy where he sat, arms crossed as she watched, her mouth hanging open in dismay.

As she watched, Tommy slid his palm around the back of one of Shaun's thighs, his fingers curving in around the inside of that thigh, and he squeezed lightly. Zoey's face blazed and she whirled away, nearly running to the safety of the kitchen.

Her cheeks were still flaming as she checked the boiling potatoes with a fork. She turned when she heard Chase, as he was ducking under the archway into the kitchen. He grinned at her, winking, motioning over his shoulder behind him. She didn't need to look; she knew what he meant.

He wandered over to the refrigerator, taking a beer out. He held one up, asking, "Do you want one?"

She shook her head, no, but she smiled. "No, thank you. I don't drink."

"Oh?" he asked, replacing the one he'd just offered before uncapping his own.

Zoey's cheeks flamed again, and she stuttered, "Because of Verity."

"Oh," he repeated, understanding. He coughed lightly to cover his own discomfort. Why couldn't they stay away from the subject of her breastfeeding?

Tommy appeared in the doorway, his phone in his hand. "Dad just called. He's not going to make it. Said something came up."

Zoey's shoulders dropped, though she wasn't surprised. "Oh well," she said on a deep breath out, shrugging her shoulders. She turned back towards the stove. "Dinner should be ready soon; I just have to whip the potatoes together. I can do that if one of you want to get the turkey out and start carving."

She saw Tommy nod out of her peripheral, though she knew he was analyzing the look on her face. He stepped forward and began the process of getting the turkey on the platter. Zoey had arranged dinnerware on the small table earlier, and she directed both Shaun and Chase on where to set the finished dishes in the center of the table, family style.

When they all sat at the table together, Zoey smiled around at them before they all dug into the deliciousness before them.

Chase went straight in for the flaky, buttery rolls and dunked it in his gravy, rolling his eyes heavenward when he took the first bite. Zoey beamed before digging into her own plate.

As they finished the meal, Zoey moaned, patting her stomach. "I should have worn my maternity pants."

Tommy howled with laughter and Chase choked on a bite of green bean casserole. Shaun thumped him on the back hard as she laughed.

"Ohmygod," Shaun breathed. "I don't think I can eat another bite."

"Everything turned out great," Tommy said appreciatively to Zoey. "Mom would be proud."

"Thank you," Zoey said with a small smile. He reached over and squeezed her hand gently, just for a moment, before sliding his hand away. "I didn't have the heart to attempt her pecan pie, though."

"I think this was a great start," Chase said and smiled over at her.

Then Shaun heaved herself out of the chair with a groan, taking her plate and Tommy's to the sink. Zoey stood too, reaching for Chase's plate, but he stopped her.

"You cooked all day, we'll clean," he said, shooing her hands away, picking up their dishes and standing.

"I can't—" Zoey started, but he glared at her with those electric blue eyes of his and she laughed, conceding. "Okay. Thank you."

"Go sit down," he said and pointed with his chin to the living room. "We've got this."

Zoey shook her head but didn't argue, drifting to the living room. She laughed as she listened to the three of them in the kitchen, noisy and cackling to themselves at whatever was being said. They found her in the recliner chair half-an-hour later, a soft chenille throw blanket pulled up over her. "I don't think I can move," she whispered, chuckling.

Tommy and Chase both sank into opposite corners of the couch, and Shaun lowered her tall frame to the floor, lying flat on her stomach. She rested her cheek on her stacked arms, yawning broadly. "I'm so full I can't think."

Zoey's eyes met Chase's where he sat on the couch and he smiled gently before tipping his beer to his lips and taking a drink. Tommy slapped Chase's knee, which made those blue eyes swing from hers over to her brother. "Who's ready for pie?"

A chorus of vehement groans erupted throughout the living room, but he just laughed.

Shaun fell asleep on the floor, her breathing slow and deep. Zoey remained curled into the corner of the recliner, letting her eyes drift closed as she listened to the soothing, low cadence of the two men as they talked.

EIGHT

When she woke, the sky out of the windows was dark. She listened for a moment, realizing what had woken her, and she sat up. Chase lay on the couch on his back, head propped on the arm of the couch. Verity sat on his stomach, her back resting against his raised knees. Her little hands clapped excitedly, babbling softly.

He turned his head toward her, grinning. His dark hair fell over one brow before he flicked it away. "She woke up so I got her changed and brought her down here. I hope that's okay."

"Of course," Zoey mumbled, stretching slightly around a yawn. "I'm sorry I fell asleep."

"I don't mind. You had an early morning," Chase said softly.

"So did you," Zoey reminded him.

"I'm used to it," he said and shrugged. When he did, Verity's body wiggled and she belly laughed. "We've just been hanging out."

Zoey looked around the room, the only light from the tv. "Where are Shaun and Tommy?"

Chase's eyes flicked up to the ceiling, and Zoey blushed scarlet. Indeed, over the noise of the tv, she could hear the unmistakable sounds from Tommy's room above them.

"I'm so sorry," Zoey stammered. "They're terrible."

But Chase grinned, shrugging again. "It's normal. They're in love."

Zoey's face fell and he must have sensed the shift in her, because he looked at her then.

"I'm sorry," he murmured. "That wasn't a dig at you, I swear."

"I know," Zoey whispered, hugging the throw blanket to her chest. "I know I'm not normal."

Chase rolled to a sitting position, bringing Verity with him, throwing his long legs over the side of the couch until his feet hit the floor again. "How you feel after what happened is totally normal, Zoey."

"I know that, too," Zoey said, her lips tightening slightly. "My therapist says everyone heals differently. This is how my body has adjusted to the trauma. I don't like that I make them feel like they can't show affection to each other because of something I went through."

Breathe.

"I miss... I miss being hugged, sometimes," she whispered. His brows pulled over his eyes, and she hated the pity in them that shone there. "Most of the time, the idea of such an embrace is terrifying. But sometimes... I wish I could. That's what makes me the angriest, I think. Is that...he took so many *normal* things from me. I can't even imagine *that*..." she whispered, motioning to the ceiling, where the sounds had tapered off at last.

Chase swallowed hard and she smiled sadly, lowering her eyes.

Breathe, she instructed herself.

"I'm sorry," she said then, looking back at him. "That was... obscenely heavy."

"You don't need to apologize for your pain," he said gently. "I wish there was something I could do."

"Therapy is helping," Zoey murmured as she watched her daughter playing with Chase's chin. "She said it could take a while."

They were quiet for a time, Verity content to sit with Chase.

Zoey sighed and smiled, then said, "I should probably feed her." Chase nodded and Zoey stood. She was just reaching for Verity when the noises above them started again, heavier this time, and Zoey paled. She knew she couldn't go up there now.

He knew. Somehow, he knew, and said gruffly, "I can go to the kitchen so you can..."

Zoey nodded. "Thank you."

Chase stood, handing the squirming baby over, and then he disappeared through the kitchen door. As she settled into the recliner, Verity began to fuss, ready. She quickly adjusted her shirt so she could latch. Zoey could hear Chase rummaging through the drawers in the kitchen, then the zip of a cardboard seal being ripped open. She laughed. "Pie?"

"Heck yeah," he called back, chuckling too. "Do you want some?"

"Pie sounds amazing, actually," she said. "She should be done in a few minutes."

But as she sat in the chair, she laughed out loud at the noises he was making from the other room, and she smiled when she realized he was doing it to cover the sounds coming from upstairs. "Sure you want to wait? There might not be any left when I'm done."

So Zoey adjusted her shirt so that the briefest bit of skin was visible over Verity's mouth, and said, "You convinced me."

When Chase came back into the living room, he was walking backward, arm outstretched behind him. She laughed again. "Turn around before you fall!"

He did, but kept his head averted slightly as he handed her the small dessert plate with a hefty slice of pumpkin pie, and he had topped it with a generous spritz of whipped cream. His eyes slid to hers for the briefest of seconds when she looked up at him, before turning away again, respecting her privacy. "Can you do this one handed?"

Zoey rolled her eyes. "I got very good at doing things one handed."

Chase's eyebrows shot up and Zoey blushed. Good Lord!

He lowered himself to the couch again, facing away from her as he ate his own pie, and she dug into hers, the plate balancing on the arm of the recliner. When she was ready to switch sides, he turned his dark head away as she adjusted herself and Verity.

They ate in silence for several minutes, and as Verity's mouth slackened, Zoey pulled her away, covering herself once more. The two upstairs had once again quieted. She adjusted the baby up to her shoulder, one hand under her bottom, the other patting her back gently. Chase looked over, laughing at the fast asleep baby against Zoey's shoulder. "Milk drunk little thing."

Zoey smiled, nuzzling her nose against the curls at the back of Verity's head. "I work hard for that," she chuckled, and her eyes met Chase's over the top of that little golden head. "I should get her to bed."

Chase nodded, standing as Zoey did. He took the now empty dessert plates and headed toward the kitchen doorway as Zoey walked slowly to the stairs.

"Hey, Zoey?" Chase called softly. She turned as she took the first step up, looking at him over Verity's head. He touched the doorframe, curling his fingers around the rough wood beam.

"Yeah?" she asked, her voice quiet, so as not to wake Verity. Those electric blue eyes were intense as he stared at her.

"I see what you do. Those breathing exercises," he murmured. One side of his face was illuminated by the blue light of the tv across the room, the other half shadowed slightly from the darkened kitchen. She nodded. "Can I add something to them?"

Zoey looked at him inquisitively, but said, "Sure?"

"When you tell yourself to breathe..." he said quietly, "do me a favor and tell yourself to 'inhale courage, exhale fear'."

Zoey's eyebrows shot up in surprise. And dammit to hell, but her nose stung with tears. He smiled at her, gently, before ducking his head and disappearing into the kitchen.

NINE

Chase tossed and turned on the too small bed, his neck aching from being cramped. He sat up, rolling to the side of the bed, where he let his feet touch the floor. He braced his elbows on his knees, hanging his head until his chin almost touched his chest.

Pushing himself to his feet, he crossed the dark room, pulling the door open silently. He didn't bother to pull on the sweatpants he'd left on the floor, instead padding quietly down the hallway only in his boxer briefs. He was almost to the top of the stairs, taking the corner to go down them when his body slammed into another in the darkness.

Instinctually, he wrapped his fingers around the arms he found in the inky blackness, holding tightly and spinning to keep them both from tumbling down the stairs. In the spin, his hands pulled the small form against his naked chest, and he lost his balance slightly.

"D-don't touch me!" he heard Zoey's terrified voice through the dark, and he immediately dropped his hands, stepping away from her. But she stumbled against him at the sudden loss of stability, and he couldn't stop himself from grabbing hold of her again to keep her from falling. The breathing he heard from her was ragged, terrified. "Stop!"

"Zoey, it's just me," he said into the dark, but she was shaking, twisting out of his grasp violently. Tiny fists pummeled at his chest, and he stepped away again. "Zoey, honey, you're okay—"

The bedroom to their left opened and the light came on, illuminating the hallway. Chase's chest caved in at the undiluted terror on Zoey's face as she cowered against the opposite wall, trembling from head to toe. Tommy and Shaun spilled out of the bedroom in varying states of undress, rushing toward her.

Zoey sobbed brokenly as Shaun took hold of her arms, but she slid down the wall to the floor onto her knees, soul wracking sobs pouring out of her as she covered her face. Tears stung his own eyes as he watched, helpless to fight the demons she was facing.

Because he'd frightened her.

"Come on, sweetheart," he heard Shaun murmuring to her, the tall brunette's voice thick with unshed tears. "It's okay. You're okay, I promise."

Tommy touched his shoulder then, motioning for him to follow down the hallway, as Shaun finally got Zoey to her feet. Shaun half carried a still hyperventilating Zoey into Tommy's bedroom, closing the door. Chase stared at the closed door for a long time before following Tommy back to the bedroom he'd just walked out of moments ago. Or had it been a lifetime? He wasn't sure.

Tommy's eyes were suspiciously wet when Chase flicked the light switch on. He crossed the room and picked up his pants, shoving his feet into them roughly. "You didn't do anything wrong," he heard his friend say.

"I scared the hell out of her," Chase snarled through clenched teeth. "She thought I—" he broke off, his throat closing over the words. Fury and self-loathing washed over him, roiling like a wave. He could still hear her crying, though it was lessening. Heard Shaun telling her to breathe. *Fuck.*

"It wasn't your fault. I've done it, too," his friend said, but it didn't help. "She knows you would never... Her mind just can't tell the difference sometimes."

"I want to tear that bastard apart piece by piece," Chase snarled again, pacing through the room, his chest heaving. "No one should have to live with fear like that. God dammit!"

"I agree," Tommy murmured from where he stood at the door. "I've never known pain like I have had from watching her go through this. It tortures me."

"There *has* to be something, anything, that we can do to help," Chase said raggedly, stalling in his pacing. He raked his hands through his hair. "I hate this."

His best friend nodded solemnly, but there was a light in his eyes that Chase recognized and immediately shook his head firmly. "Whatever you're planning; no. Just no."

Tommy looked behind him, down the hallway to his still closed door, before taking a step into the bedroom and closing the door to Chase's room. He stepped forward. "But what if there is."

"What if there is what?" Chase ground out.

"What if there is a way we can help," Tommy whispered roughly, his voice low.

"Whatever you're planning, I already said no. I won't be an accessory to premeditated murder," Chase snapped, waving his hand in a wide arc. "Anything else you say, I absolutely cannot hear it."

Tommy made a face and said, "What the fuck? You think I'm talking about murdering the bastard?"

"I know that look," Chase snapped again, pointing to his friend's face, the look in his eyes.

"*No*," Tommy whispered, shaking his head in confusion, before stepping forward again. "Chase. *Marry her*."

Chase's entire body went deathly still as he stared at his friend as if he'd just sprouted a second head and dressed in drag. "*What?*" he ground out through clenched teeth. "Are you high? Jesus, never mind, I don't want to know that answer, either."

Chase spun in place, pacing away from Tommy, before turning back to him, hands on his hips, mouth open in astonishment. Tommy's face was lit with that 'eureka!' moment he assumed Thomas Edison had had when inventing the lightbulb.

"You've got to be kidding me, man," Chase finally whispered.

Tommy shook his head. "No, I'm not. She needs someone to take care of her, to protect her—"

"She is a grown woman who can make those decisions herself, and she doesn't need someone to take care of her," Chase snapped. He couldn't believe he was hearing this!

"The therapist even said if she were to open up for a relationship, a real relationship, she thinks it will help the anxiety, the panic attacks," Tommy whispered, throwing a glance back at the bedroom door that was still closed behind him.

"So let her find a boyfriend, don't shove a *husband* at her for Christ's sake!" Chase bit out incredulously.

But again, Tommy was shaking his head before Chase could finish. "She's too scared to even try. She won't even consider the idea. And she needs someone permanent, not some tool bag fuck boy...I'll pay you."

Chase placed his hands together, palms pressed together as if in prayer, index fingers running vertically along his lips, and stared at his friend over them. "*Bro*. Respectfully, this is *the dumbest* idea you've ever had in our lives. And I was there for all the dumbest ones! You cannot *pay* someone to marry your sister."

"She needs someone good, someone trustworthy."

"Not a good enough reason," Chase snapped, pacing again. "I'm not that person."

"I don't trust anyone else with her and Verity," Tommy continued as if Chase hadn't spoken. Chase thought his head was going to explode. They'd had more to drink throughout the day than he usually imbibed on and was feeling the effects. "You're my best friend."

"And she's like my little sister!" Chase exclaimed in a heated whisper. "Did you think about that? Oh my god, I'm not having this conversation." He pointed through the walls toward the bedroom where the two women were. "You're engaged, dude. We all know what comes with a relationship. Are you telling me you want me to fuck your sister?"

Tommy faltered at that, blinking rapidly.

Chase breathed, "You cannot ask me to do this. I won't do that to her. That girl in there, that beautiful girl that has had *horrors* shoved on her, deserves the world. Deserves to make her own choices. And I refuse to be part of taking that away from her. I can't do it, Tommy. I won't."

Tommy opened his mouth to speak, but a soft knock sounded on the door and Chase jumped as if he'd been shot... Which he had been, once.

Shaun showed up in the doorway then, tear tracks drying on her cheeks. "She's calmed down, back in bed."

Tommy nodded, taking her hand in his and rubbing the back of it with his thumb. "Thank you." He was staring at Chase, who refused to meet his gaze.

But Shaun smiled sadly, and then she turned to Chase and said quietly, "When she was doing her breathings, she said you told her to 'inhale courage' and 'exhale fear'." Chase nodded grimly, blood pounding in his ears. His head ached.

She nodded back, and said, "This is the quickest I've seen her come out of one of these. You helped her more than you know."

Chase hated the smug look that crossed Tommy's face before the two of them disappeared back down the hall.

TEN

Zoey was sitting in the kitchen at the table, mug of tea in her hands, when Chase came in from his run.

He stopped mid-step, freezing on the threshold. His eyes were wary as they met hers, and his breathing was ragged from the workout. She smiled gently, though she knew her face was paler than normal, purple shadows under her eyes a testament to the crying she'd done the night before. He closed the door quietly, taking a step into the kitchen.

"I'm sorry," she whispered into the dusky gray blue of the room. The sun had barely begun its ascent and had only lightened the kitchen by degrees.

Chase took another step, shaking his head. "I told you that you don't need to apologize to me. I'm the one that should be sorry."

Zoey's mouth tilted up at one corner. "You didn't do anything, Chase. I knew better than to walk around in the dark in the middle of the night—"

Chase was already shaking his head, and dropped into a crouch in front of her, so that they were closer to eye level. She flinched slightly at the sudden

59

movement, but didn't move away, instead staring steadily into those electric blue eyes that were so haunted. His cheeks were tinged pink from the cold. He didn't touch her, though she could tell he wanted to reach for her hands.

"Listen to that sentence, Zoey. You should not have to worry about walking around in your own house at night," he whispered emphatically, still shaking his head. That single lock of hair that didn't like to stay back fell over his brow as he shook his head. "I'm sorry I frightened you."

Zoey set her mug down on the table, letting her hands rest in her lap, turning slightly so that her legs were facing where he crouched. "You didn't, I promise you."

"I did," he whispered miserably, his eyes tormented as he stared up at her. Zoey's heart ached. She knew it had been a bad one and was both embarrassed and upset that she'd let Chase see that part of her.

"You didn't," she whispered, and without a thought reached up and lightly pushed that errant lock of hair back over his head. Zoey froze at the same time that she was sure Chase quit breathing. She lowered her hand back to her lap, slowly. "It was just really dark, and my mind plays tricks on me at night. In here—" she laid her palm flat against her chest, over her heart, "—I knew it was you. I knew the hands on me were there to help me, not hurt me. But here—" she whispered and pointed to her head, "—I was trapped."

Her eyes were sorrowful as she beseeched him, "I know you would never hurt me, Chase."

He squeezed his eyes shut, but she saw the pain in them before he did. "I hated seeing you so scared, Zoey. My job is to protect people like you, and I have no idea how to help you."

"I know it doesn't seem like it, but I am getting better," Zoey said in a wry half-laugh. He opened his eyes and she wrinkled her nose at him, a teasing smile tilting up her lips. "You stink."

Chase laughed out loud, nodding his head in agreement. "Yeah, I'm sure I do." His eyes scanned hers for a long moment before he said, "Are you sure you're okay this morning?"

She nodded. "Yes, I promise."

He stood then, straightening to his full height, which towered over Zoey where she sat. He took a couple steps backward, and she breathed easier. "I'm gonna go shower. What are everyone's plans for today?"

"I have the rest of the weekend off. We won't open again until Monday," she said, picking up her tea and bringing it to her lips. "Tommy and Shaun are still asleep, but they'll be gone for the day."

He nodded and then headed for the door to the kitchen. "So it's just you and Verity home today?"

"Mmhmm," Zoey murmured.

"Is it alright if I hang out here for the day, too?" he asked from the doorway.

"Of course," Zoey said and smiled. "Stop worrying. And go shower."

She heard his low chuckle drift down the stairs as he climbed them.

ELEVEN

Chase bared his teeth and pushed up, again. Again. His arms straining, shaking, torso screaming at him. But he did it. And continued, until his arms gave out and he slung the weight into the cradle, letting his arms dangle on either side of the bench while he sucked in his breath.

'Marry her.'

He sat up, chest heaving. Tommy's voice had haunted him all day. He rested his elbows on his widespread knees and hung his head.

I can't. I'm not... not good. Not for her.

Sweat dripped from his brow, down his neck, his back. He was pushing himself too hard, but he didn't care. Anything to drown out the words.

He stood and crossed to another machine, adjusting the weights, then sat down and started chest presses until he was shaking.

I don't trust anyone else with her and Verity.

He started another grueling set, grunting through each one.

You're my best friend.

And dammit, if it wasn't bad enough that they'd even discussed it, if you called what happened last night a discussion, he hated himself more for letting a tiny kernel of consideration to pop open in his traitorous mind.

We all know what comes with a relationship. Are you telling me you want me to fuck your sister?

Chase shoved that thought down, refusing to acknowledge that he'd even voiced it aloud. It was preposterous. It was *Zoey* they were talking about. He wasn't even sure he was attracted to her like that.

He'd rushed upstairs to take a shower after that grueling run, shucking his sweaty running clothes onto the floor and turning on the taps. He was just rinsing the shampoo out of his hair when he'd heard that tiny cry from across the hall. He'd let it go, sure that Zoey would be to her in an instant. But as the minute got longer and that pitiful cry got harder, he had jumped out of the shower, barely taking the time to sling the towel around his waist, before crossing the hall and entering Zoey's room.

Verity was crying in earnest, and the sound of it had nearly undone him. The memories of that car... He'd pushed those thoughts down as he reached into the crib, scooping the infant up and cradling her against his chest, bouncing her gently, crooning soothingly. Her cries had softened just as Zoey ran into the room, out of breath. She stopped short when she saw him, dressed in nothing but a scant towel around his hips, dripping water onto her carpeted floor.

"I...uh... I just stepped outside to take the garbage to the road," she said lamely, tripping over her tongue. If he hadn't been so lost in his own thoughts he might have laughed at the look on her face.

"She's okay," he said, both to Zoey and Verity, the latter of which was using one teeny tiny finger to explore with the rivulets of water that ran from his soaking wet hair down his neck, and further down his chest. "Right? We're okay."

When he looked back at Zoey, he had gone still. Her eyes were huge in her face, though they weren't wide with fear, but something else that closely resembled adoration.

Chase had panicked, stepping quickly to Zoey to hand her the infant, before rushing back to the bathroom. He'd left the house without saying goodbye, heading straight to the gym. He'd done a punishing, hilly eight mile run that morning, but he needed more.

Now, he grabbed his water bottle and took a long pull. Setting it back down, he glanced around. He'd been there for over an hour, pounding the machines as hard as his body would allow him to, praying that it would exhaust his mind as much as it did his body.

"Can you spot me?" a soft, feminine voice from behind him said, and he turned.

It was the girl from the other night. He smiled, though he was still slightly out of breath. "Sure, I'm done with my set," he said and stood, following her to the pull up bar. Her long blonde hair was pulled back into that ponytail again. He smirked from behind her. She raised her arms over her head, and he obliged, lifting her when she jumped to reach the bar above their heads.

The majority of her upper body was bare, the only swatch of fabric covering her was a barely-there sports bra, which he assumed was more for looks than practicality. She wore a cock teasingly short pair of exercise bottoms that cupped and delineated her ass cheeks, but left her toned legs bare. And of course, it was right at his eye level.

She crossed her ankles and pulled up, then lowered herself, repeating it several times. She started to struggle after the sixth one, and he stepped forward, placing his hands on the slope of her hips as she dangled with her ass in his face. She pulled up again, struggling more, so he assisted by giving her a slight boost. If he hadn't been so distracted, he might have enjoyed watching that rounded ass rise and fall in front of him.

After number eight, she tapped out, and he gripped her waist as she dropped. She turned, thanking him with a coy smile, which he returned with a grin.

He could feel her watching him as he walked away, toward the locker rooms. Before he got close, she was there, handing him a folded piece of paper. He grinned again, knowing exactly what would be written on that small slip of paper. He winked, then turned to walk away.

As he got closer, a neon yellow sheet of paper with little pull tabs caught his eye and he stopped, reading quickly.

He smiled and gripped one of the pull tabs, ripping it from the sheet, and put both slips in his pocket.

TWELVE

"Brazilian Jiu Jitsu?"

Chase nodded, grinning widely down at her. Zoey pulled her eyebrows together in a deep furrow, her eyes filled with apprehension. She juggled Verity in her arms, the infant more excited to see him than Zoey would have expected after such a short time.

He must have seen it, because he reached for the wriggling infant, taking her out of Zoey's arms and cradling her against his chest, crooning softly, "Hello my little sunshine."

Zoey crossed her arms over her middle, biting her lower lip. "I don't know about that, Chase."

"It's a great self-defense program. It works with your own body strength and agility, while teaching both escape maneuvers and offensive exercises, too. We wouldn't start with partnered drills," he said gently, reading the worry on her face. "I would not put you on a mat with another person until you are one hundred percent comfortable with it. First thing we would need to work on is strengthening your body as a whole." He reached out and pointed to her bicep, though he didn't touch her. "Your arms are surprisingly strong, but then again lugging this tank around all day long—" he said and held the squirming baby, belly up, to his mouth and blew raspberries into that tummy, making her squeal with delight before lowering her back to his chest, "—will build those muscles pretty well. But you need a strong core, too." For reference, he patted his own rock-hard abdomen with one hand, and Zoey's mouth went involuntarily dry.

When Zoey only looked up at him, wariness clouding her indigo eyes, he sat down at the kitchen table, putting Verity in his lap.

"Do you want to be able to defend yourself and her—" he asked, nodding down to the golden-haired infant in his lap, "—in the future if necessary?"

"I would kill anyone that touched her," Zoey said through clenched teeth.

"I believe it," Chase said softly, watching her. "Will you let me help you, give you the tools that I pray to God you will never need to use again?"

"Can I think about it?" Zoey hedged nervously.

"Of course," he said, smiling. "Take all the time you need."

And then he stood, taking her daughter with him as he ducked through the arched kitchen doorway to the living room, tucking her into a football hold. "C'mon goldie, you're going to learn how to clean a handgun."

Zoey spluttered a protest and he laughed out loud, calling back, "Just kidding, Momma." She rolled her eyes and sighed, then heard, "We're starting with the shotgun first."

"Chase," she growled, though a smile tugged at her lips.

She walked to the doorway and put one hand on her hip as she glared at him. He had sunk into the recliner chair, rocking gently with Verity in his arms. He peeked at her through his dark lashes and pressed a finger to his lips. "Shh. We're trying to nap, here."

One corner of his lips twitched and she watched as he looked down into Verity's face. "She's still staring at us," he whispered loudly enough for her to hear. She rolled her eyes again and headed back into the kitchen, where her tea kettle had begun to whistle shrilly.

"Tommy should be home in an hour or so," Zoey called from the kitchen, then walked back into the living room a few moments later with a mug of steaming tea, and sank into one corner of the couch. "Dinner is just leftovers from yesterday, I hope that's okay."

"I love a Thanksgiving leftover sandwich," Chase said as he continued to rock himself and the now dozing Verity in the recliner. "Best part of a holiday meal, if you ask me."

Zoey stacked her feet beneath her, holding the mug of tea in both of her hands, which were chilled. "When do you start work?" she asked.

"One week from Monday. I have some final paperwork that needs to be done, physical that needs to be filed, that sort of thing," he murmured, and she was surprisingly content to watch him watching Verity sleep. "I find out next week who my new partner is, get sworn in, all the fun stuff."

He looked up at her then, and she was once again stunned by the brilliance of the blue of his eyes. Something on her face must have worried him, because he asked, "Are you alright? After last night?"

"Of course," she said, smiling. "I told you this morning, I'm okay. I promise." Then, she said softly, "Are you okay?"

He nodded. "I still feel awful, but yes. I'm okay."

The front door opened and Zoey peered over the back of the couch into the kitchen, surprise making her mouth fall open. She sat up straighter, standing. Chase looked over his shoulder from where he sat in the recliner, his own brows shooting up with surprise.

Thom Chandler, Zoey and Tommy's father, came into view. He was an average height, average build man, with sandy blonde hair that was dusted with silver, and his brown eyes matched his sons. He'd always been a gentle soul, almost too gentle, if Zoey admitted it. He was soft, and somewhat easily manipulated, much to his children's dismay.

Zoey rounded the edge of the couch, a smile on her face as she headed toward her dad. She stopped just shy of him, and he nodded awkwardly, as if he didn't know what to do.

Chase stood then, heaving himself out of the recliner, Verity still cradled in one arm. Thom beamed a smile. Chase had always been welcome in their home, and she remembered many nights and weekends that Tommy and Chase had spent on the couch watching football with her father. Thom extended a hand, and Chase took it, shaking it firmly.

"Chase, how are you son?" Thom asked, his brown eyes gentle as they stared up at the younger man.

"Good," Chase said and smiled back. "It's good to see you, sir."

Zoey smiled, but then it disappeared when the door opened again, and a woman with shoulder length, box black hair walked in. Thom turned at the sound, and said, "Ah, there you are. Tanya, this is my daughter, Zoey, and I told you about my granddaughter," he said, motioning to Verity still sleeping in Chase's arm. Tanya's eyes slid up Chase's body, her crystalline blue eyes appreciating what she saw. Zoey's hackles went up; she had to be twice Chase's age, and on her father's arm.

Zoey stepped closer to Chase, until her shoulder almost touched the arm that held the still sleeping baby. He glanced down at her, *lord was he tall*, she thought dazedly for a moment, before he extended his hand to the woman.

"This is Chase, my son's friend from school," Thom introduced them, oblivious to the covetous looks his new lady friend was giving the younger man. Zoey thought she would be sick.

"Tommy should be home soon," Zoey said, tight-lipped, crossing her arms over her chest.

"We just wanted to stop in for a quick minute to say hi," Thom said softly. Zoey couldn't stop the roll of her eyes.

"It was nice to meet you," Zoey murmured quietly, if a little stiffly to the woman. She turned to her father, "There's leftovers from yesterday in the refrigerator if you'd like some."

"Oh, no thank you, kid," he mumbled, glancing over her head to the far wall, the photo wall, and beyond to the closed bedroom door. His brown eyes were sad, but only for a moment. "We're going out to eat, but we appreciate the offer." Sticking his hand out to Chase again, they shook hands once more. "Chase my boy, it was good to see you."

Thom stepped forward, running one stocky, callused finger down Verity's cheek where it lay close to Chase's chest. And then with a gruff goodbye, the two were gone.

When the two had let themselves out, Chase whistled low, turning his incredulous eyes to her indigo ones. "I take it you don't agree with your father's new lifestyle?"

"He can do whatever he wants, he's a grown man," she snapped, rounding the couch once more and sinking into it, picking up her tea. Chase lowered himself back into the recliner. Verity had remained asleep through the whole interaction, which Zoey was grateful for. She'd been a holy terror all day, refusing her mid-morning nap. "But no, I don't agree with it. Mom's only been gone six months. I guess... I just can't understand how a person can move on that quickly after spending almost thirty years with someone."

She glanced over at the wall of photos. Her father had wanted to take them all down, but Zoey had refused. She wouldn't shove every last reminder of her mother into a box to be forgotten. He had announced that he had found an apartment and was signing over the house to Zoey and Tommy just a week or two later.

When she looked back at Chase, he was watching her, silently, those blue eyes so intense. He murmured quietly, "Maybe... maybe he's lonely, Zoey. Everyone grieves differently, you know that."

Tears stung her nose, and she crossed her arms over her chest again, cradling the cup of tea near her chin. "I just really miss her. I miss my mom."

Chase's eyes were gentle as they looked at her, which made tears fill her eyes. "I know. You know he does, too, even if he doesn't show it how you think he should."

Zoey tipped her head back against the cushions of the couch, exhaling deeply. "You and Tommy and my therapist all sound the same."

Chase chuckled, and it rumbled over her. "Maybe we're all onto something, then."

She rolled her eyes at the ceiling. But when she brought her chin back down, he was staring at her again.

"He's letting you heal how you need to," he said softly. When her brow furrowed slightly in confusion, he continued, motioning to where they'd stood before, "He knows you are not comfortable being touched, and he respects that, even if it kills him not to be able to hug his daughter." Her lip wobbled, just the tiniest bit, at his words. "And even though it hurts him, he would rather take that pain alone than to do something he knows would hurt you, more. Let him heal without hurting him more, Zoey."

As Chase watched tv, Zoey lost herself in thought. Cooking the Thanksgiving meal, her mother's favorite holiday, where she'd gotten to cook a feast for the people she loved the most, had been emotional for her.

She wondered if the idea of eating that first holiday meal without her mother was more painful for her father than she'd realized.

She'd been angry, so impossibly angry, that he never came by anymore. But seeing that look of pain on his face as he'd looked at the pictures of her mother on the wall, to the now empty master bedroom, she finally understood. It was more painful for him to be here, in the home he'd built with the love of his life, than it was to stay away.

THIRTEEN

Chase and Zoey were sitting at the kitchen table when Tommy returned the following evening, having spent the night and most of that day at Shaun's. Chase avoided his friend's eyes as he walked in, leaning down to press a kiss to the top of Verity's golden-haired head where she sat strapped into her highchair, before saying hello to the both of them.

Zoey stood, going to the refrigerator, and said over her shoulder, "I made turkey noodle soup with the leftovers, it's ready in the crockpot if you'd like some."

"Thanks," he said gratefully and grabbed a bowl from the cupboard before ladling himself a hefty portion of the steaming hot soup. He sat in the chair directly beside Chase. Chase could feel his friend's eyes on him, but he refused to look up, to meet those brown eyes. They hadn't spoken since Thursday night, when Tommy had made that absolutely ludicrous proposition.

That absolutely ludicrous proposition that Chase had given more and more thought to as the day had progressed. He and Zoey had spent the entire evening Friday together, just the two of them with the baby, after Thom and Tanya had left. When Tommy had called her to let her know he was staying with Shaun, he had been both terrified and elated. Dammit.

Saturday morning Chase woke early, sneaking out quietly to get his run in. When he'd returned, Zoey was waiting for him in the kitchen, a pot of coffee ready for him.

Zoey was sweet, funny, and pretty. He watched her throughout the day, when she wasn't looking. She was a loving, gentle mother to Verity, who very clearly adored her. Chase couldn't stay away, stealing the baby from Zoey as often as he could. This tiny little thing had weaseled her way into his heart and already had him wrapped around her tiny little finger.

They laughed, much as they had done as kids growing up. She was hilariously funny and kept him rolling with laughter.

Today, her shoulder length golden hair was loose around her shoulders in waves, and she kept tucking one side behind her ear every so often as it fell into her face. She wore a pair of black leggings that molded to her shape, and today had pulled on an oversized wine-red sweater that looked incredibly soft to the touch, the tail dipping low to cover her bottom. But she'd given him several unintentional shows; as she'd been resting on her shins sitting back on the backs of her legs, hunched over on her forearms as she blew raspberries onto Verity's naked tummy after a diaper change. Her sweater had ridden up, revealing her rounded ass, and Chase had had a hard time pulling his eyes away. Or when he'd walked into the kitchen and she'd been bent at the waist, picking up the baby toy Verity had thrown to the floor in a fit.

And when she'd gotten too warm and pulled that sweater up and over her head, he'd been sure his eyes were going to pop out of his skull when she'd just been in a tight white tank top, her breasts small but round against the thin material. He'd coughed to cover the slight groan that had escaped him, excusing himself as he took the stairs up to the second floor two at a time. He closed the bedroom door, staring at it for a long time.

There was no way, *no way in hell*, that he had a damn erection for *Zoey*.

Oh, but he did. And his cock ached between his legs at the thought of what her breasts would feel like in his large hands.

He blamed Tommy.

If he hadn't come up with such an asinine proposition, Chase would never have even thought about Zoey's breasts, about her ass, about how soft her skin would feel against his fingertips, against his lips...

Cursing his friend, he strode to the dresser across the room, and he unfolded that slip of paper he'd forgotten about until he'd emptied his pockets after his shower. He picked up his phone and sent out a text message, short and to the point.

She didn't disappoint. And minutes later he was back down the stairs, saying a gruff goodbye to Zoey.

"Are you going to work out?" Zoey asked softly, holding Verity in her arms.

No, he wanted to say, but didn't. He was headed out for a totally different kind of workout. But she didn't need to know that.

"Yeah," was what he said though, because it wasn't a complete lie. "I'll be back later."

She nodded, smiling at him, and he hated Tommy for putting these thoughts into his mind in the first place. He didn't smile in return as he walked out the door.

Shay was her name, he found out as he drove to her apartment. She wasn't looking for anything serious, she said. Just sex.

He could do that.

It was quick and hard, just what he'd needed. No frills, no kissing, no cuddling afterward. Just a satisfyingly deep orgasm, a way to scratch that itch. She pulled on an oversized hooded sweatshirt afterward, walking with no pants on through the tiny apartment as he dressed and tossed the used condom in the trash. She merely winked at him as he'd let himself out.

He'd driven back to Zoey and Tommy's house, sitting outside in his Jeep for a long time, guilt crushing him. He wasn't sure why it ate at him so much, but as he finally walked in through the door and Zoey had smiled at him through the arched doorway from the living room, he knew he was in trouble, and hated himself for it.

Because it hadn't been Shay that Chase had envisioned as he'd fucked her from behind, wrapping his hand around that blonde ponytail and pulling tight; but Zoey.

Now, sitting across the table from her as she resumed her seat and smiled at him warmly, with her brother sitting beside him still staring between bites of his soup, he knew what his answer would be.

And he hated himself all the more for it.

When Zoey looked at him then and said, "Okay," he nearly choked on a spoonful of his soup, terrified she'd somehow read his mind.

FOURTEEN

"Okay."

Chase looked up from his soup and speared her with those electric blue eyes, and she almost lost her nerve. He'd been... strange... today. Intense and broody and quiet.

"I'll do it," she said softly. Tommy looked between them quizzically and she watched as Chase's eyes widened slightly. "I'll do the lessons. Teach me how to protect myself."

Tommy's eyes bounced between the two of them, but she didn't take her eyes from Chase's as her words registered, and that look disappeared from his eyes, replaced with surprise.

"Are you sure?" Chase asked, leaning against his forearms, that he rested on the table. "It's not going to be a picnic."

"I don't expect it to be," Zoey said simply, leaning back in her chair slightly. "I have rules, though."

"Of course," Chase said, one side of his mouth tilting up.

"No one touches me unless I say so. Doesn't matter what it's for. Even you. Agreed?" she said.

"I promise," he said sincerely, and she knew he meant it. "Not a soul will touch you when you're training with me, unless you specifically say otherwise."

"If— if I have a panic attack, you can't make fun of me," she whispered.

"Why on earth would I make fun of you?" he asked back, his tone one of bewilderment.

She shrugged but kept going. "I refuse to wear those skimpy outfits the other girls wear at the gym."

He smiled then. "You can wear whatever you're comfortable in. Within reason. Loose clothing runs the risk of getting caught on machinery, and that can lead to serious accidents and injuries."

Zoey nodded. "I'll keep that in mind."

"Does someone want to tell me what's going on?" Tommy asked finally.

Zoey looked over at him, finally pulling her eyes from Chase's. He seemed happier than he had when he'd come back from his workout earlier, which made her glad.

"Chase has offered to give me self-defense lessons," Zoey explained, taking a bite of her soup.

"Self-defense?" Tommy repeated. "Why?"

"So she can protect herself," Chase murmured, his voice low, and Zoey watched as his eyes slid over to her brothers. They stared at each other for a long time. She wondered if something was going on between them, almost as if they'd had a fight.

Which was nothing new, she admitted. They often bumped heads, as best friends and brothers typically did.

But then Tommy shrugged his shoulders and said, "Cool," and dropped his gaze to his soup bowl, taking a bite. Zoey smiled over at Chase, though that tightness she'd seen earlier had returned to his eyes. When his eyes met hers, they softened slightly, and he returned her smile.

"So when do we start?" Zoey asked.

Chase scraped his spoon across the bottom of the bowl, taking the last spoonful of a bite before saying, "Whenever you're ready. I have the next week off, I can work around your schedule. We can work something out once I get my schedule ironed out next week."

"How often are we talking about?" she asked, a worried frown marring her forehead.

Chase laughed out loud then, winking at her. "I was thinking three times a week, keep it simple. Once we get into Jiu Jitsu, we will do strength training for two days and Jiu Jitsu drills for two days as well." Zoey nodded slowly and watched as Chase's grin widened. "Like I said, we will start slowly. Stretches and floor exercises to start. Going too hard too fast can cause injuries."

Zoey's face flushed scarlet at the same time that Tommy choked on a bite of soup, coughing to clear his windpipe. Chase chuckled, though she saw a hint of a blush tinge his own cheeks at the realization of what he'd said.

"Coupla' teenagers," he teased. "Shame on you both."

To cover her sudden awkwardness, Zoey stood and cleared hers and Chase's dishes from the table while Tommy finished eating. She stood at the sink, washing the few bowls and spoons, her back to the two men. She heard Chase unbuckle Verity from her highchair, recognizing the high-pitched squeal of delight she seemed to save just for him.

Over Verity's excited baby sounds and the spray of water in the sink she could hear Tommy and Chase whispering heatedly between them, though she couldn't make out what was being said. She glanced over her shoulder and Tommy stopped talking, quickly lowering his eyes to his food. Chase shifted in his seat, his mouth tight as he stared at her brother. Zoey's brow furrowed; there was definitely something going on between the two friends, she was sure of it.

She swallowed and turned back to the sink, anxiety clawing at her chest. As sure as she was that something had happened between the two men at the table, she was also sure it had something to do with her.

FIFTEEN

Zoey glanced nervously around the crowded gym, her eyes taking in all the different machines. She felt her cheeks brighten, sure that every pair of eyes in the place were on her.

As if they knew she was fresh meat.

Chase sensed her hesitation, stepping closer to her and leaning against the counter that they had stopped at to get signed in. "You will get used to the company. Pretty much anyone that comes to the gym is here just to get a workout in, not for socialization. Most gyms aren't like what you see on TikTok. I won't let anyone bother you, I promise."

Zoey blushed again, thinking about how he'd caught her looking up gym workouts on TikTok, and when he'd asked her what she was doing she'd stuttered a lame excuse about 'research'. He'd chuckled and let it go, but she'd blushed crimson at being caught watching the videos of scantily clad women and buff, half naked men.

She nodded now, clutching the small duffle bag that was slung across her chest, the strap cutting in between her breasts. She worried the strap in her fingers anxiously, once more glancing around nervously. He ducked his head so that he was more on level with her, and she raised her eyes to his.

"You don't need to be nervous. And we won't be starting on any of these machines right away," he said, and waved to the sea of machinery before them, reminding her of their conversation the night before. He pointed to the back wall, where she could see a sign that was suspended from the high ceiling that read 'Locker Rooms'. "You can put your bag in one of the lockers, or you can carry it with you. We will be starting super simple today, Zoey. Just stretches and a warmup that only uses your body for resistance, and then a cool down."

She nodded again, choosing to follow him to the back, to the locker rooms. He disappeared into the one on the right designated 'Men' and she stepped into the door on the left that read 'Women'. She took off her street shoes and put on her sneakers, then put her belongings into one of the small lockers and exited to find Chase waiting for her. He smiled encouragingly down at her and some of her nervousness fluttered away. She had chosen to wear a pair of black leggings with extra support at the waist, self-conscious of the softness of her belly from carrying Verity. A tight sports bra kept her breasts strapped in, though she was worried one wasn't enough. She had stolen one of Tommy's oversized t-shirts and had thrown on a loose sweatshirt as well for good measure. She felt better when she was covered in loose fitting clothes, another trauma response her therapist had told her that she was unaware that she was doing. She wanted to make herself as invisible as possible, she'd been told. She fidgeted with the cuffs of the sweater where they fell past her hands.

Chase led her toward the back corner, where a portion of the large room was empty of machines, instead lined with yoga mats, a rack of light weight dumbbells, and a selection of color-coded elastic resistance bands.

"First, we need to stretch. I'm stiff as a board from sleeping on that too small bed," he said and winked. She wrinkled her nose and he grinned. "Stretching is a great warmup; it's low impact, gets your blood flowing, and limbers up those muscles and joints. Stretching is also a great way to minimize the chance of injury."

He demonstrated a series of stretches, and she copied him, though her face was blazing with embarrassment. She kept glancing around, nervousness making her cautious.

"Zoey," he murmured, getting her attention. His eyes were serious as he stared at her. "Are you sure you're okay to be here?"

Zoey nodded, swallowing her nervousness and giving him her full attention. "Yes. I'm sure."

"Okay," he said, then continued, "alright, show me what you've got."

Zoey copied the moves he did, but he made them look effortless and easy. She was much more uncoordinated than he gave her credit for. She fell over several times, and he chuckled before stepping toward her. He knelt next to her, pointing to her left foot. "See here? You're standing on the outside of your foot. Your center of balance is going to be off until you correct that. It's from carrying Verity on your left hip, your body is adjusting for that shift in your center of gravity, but you're continuing it even when you're not holding her."

Zoey's eyes were wide. She hadn't realized just how closely he was paying attention to her–from how she stood to how she held her daughter.

So she straightened her foot, planting it more securely on the floor. She immediately felt the difference and gaped at him in awe.

"Good," he murmured and grinned, then stood. She continued, and again he stepped forward saying, "Don't hunch your back. Straighten your spine... yes, just like that. Good."

The huskily spoken words did something to her insides. She swallowed hard.

After they had gone through several stretches that were surprisingly tough, he grinned over at her lightly, her breathing already ragged.

Chase walked over to the wall and grabbed a blue foam yoga mat, unrolling it onto an open spot on the floor, and Zoey hesitated only a second before doing the same. He lowered his tall frame to the mat, sitting on his bottom, knees bent and heels on the floor. Zoey copied him and watched him expectantly.

"Okay, next we're going to do some floor exercises," he said and rolled until he was on his stomach. He raised himself onto his elbows and toes, holding his body off the mat. She heaved a sigh and did the same. "We're going to hold this for thirty seconds, go down for fifteen seconds, then repeat for thirty seconds again."

"Ooof," she groaned as she felt muscles in her stomach that hadn't been used since before her pregnancy. She panted, letting her head drop between her shoulders, her back shaking.

Chase chuckled breathlessly, then said, "Okay, go ahead and go down for a rest." She did, groaning. He laughed again. "It's only thirty seconds!"

"You carry an almost nine-pound baby and tell me how well your abdominal muscles recover!" she snapped, out of breath, and he laughed out loud. She glared over at him as he hitched his chin up, and she exhaled as she pushed up, holding the plank shakily.

"Don't let your back arch," he said, his own speech ragged. "You're not Quasimodo."

The glare Zoey sent his way was withering, and he huffed another laugh before they lowered to the ground. He made her do it two more times, and by the end of the fourth one, sweat was shimmering on her brow, and she deeply regretted the thick sweatshirt she'd pulled on.

"If you get too warm, take that off. And drink water," he murmured as if reading her mind. He'd sat back on his haunches, reaching for the two water bottles he'd brought with them, handing one to her. She thanked him, uncapping it and taking a long drink before recapping it. She pulled the sweatshirt over her head and tossed it aside, adjusting the loose t-shirt she had beneath it.

"You tricked me," Zoey grumbled, and he grinned over at her as he took another drink of his water.

"We're just getting started," he chuckled. "This is child's play compared to the workouts we will progress to for Jiu Jitsu. I told you, we need to build your strength and endurance before we move into that. If we tried doing Jiu Jitsu drills right off the bat, you'd probably pull a muscle or throw your back out. A strong, stable core is going to be the most important thing to condition."

They moved through several floor exercises, each one only using her own body for resistance, but by the end of the hour she was sweating, shaking, and exhausted. He coached her through a series of cool down stretches, and when he called it for the day, she flopped onto her back on the foam mat and panted.

He lay on the mat directly beside hers, and he turned his head to look at her, grinning broadly. He reached out a hand, palm out, and she slapped it lightly in a high five. The contact made her hand tingle, electricity zinging through her. "You did great for your first day, Zoey."

He had continued to express his praise for her throughout the workout, and each time he did, a little light had glowed inside her. She didn't want to disappoint him. But more, she didn't want to disappoint herself. She was doing this for her. For Verity.

It had been tough; her body was soft, not used to the workouts he'd put her through. She knew she would sleep like the dead that night and would probably wake up sore as hell in the morning.

But when he grinned over at her, those electric blue eyes alight as they met hers, she didn't care how sore she'd be.

Chase stood, picking up the yoga mat and rolling it. He reached a hand down to her and she stared at it for an extended heartbeat, panic setting in at the thought of his hand on hers. He must have sensed her hesitation, as always knowing what was going through her head as if he'd read her mind, and he winked, saying gently, "Hand me your mat, I'll take care of it for you."

Zoey nodded, pushing the panic down, and heaved herself off the floor, grateful that he understood she'd not wanted to put her hand in his, even if it was just to help her to her feet. She handed him the mat after rolling it, and he walked away to place them in the used bin for disinfecting later.

Sweat had made his shirt damp and it clung to his skin, delineating the muscles of his back as he moved. He was outrageously, unfairly attractive. Mind-altering attractive. Zoey watched him as she took another drink of her water, wishing that the sight of any male body didn't trigger that chest clawing dread like it did.

When he turned back toward her, he hitched his head toward the doors of the locker rooms. "I'm going to change; meet you back out here in a few minutes?"

She nodded, following and walking into the women's locker room. She hated the idea of putting her sweaty sweatshirt back on, but the thought of stripping naked and showering in a public shower was enough to send her into another panic attack that she quickly squashed. There was no danger here, she reminded herself calmly. And Chase was only feet away, he wouldn't let anything happen to her.

She changed her shoes quickly and exited, smilingly shyly up at Chase when she saw him waiting for her just outside the door of the locker room.

"You did really great," he said again as they walked together toward the door. "Make sure you take a hot bath tonight; you're going to be sore."

They walked briskly through the late November cold toward their vehicles. Chase made sure she got safely into her Subaru before climbing into the Rubicon. He had offered to drive her, but she'd insisted on driving herself. She knew he had to go to the station after their workout to submit paperwork and she didn't want him to have to drive her all the way home. She waved as he pulled out of the parking lot.

SIXTEEN

Chase stepped inside the station, snorting a quiet laugh when the smell of burnt coffee assailed his nostrils. Someone had left a pot of coffee on the burner in the breakroom, he could tell. He walked through the small station toward the office he'd been told was his new sheriff's.

Mitchell Bradley was a man in his late forties, shorter than Chase by four or five inches, but built like a brick house. His light brown hair was buzzed short, his face clean shaven to reveal a jaw that seemed to be cut from stone. Intense hazel eyes raised from the sheaf of papers littering the top of the desk to meet Chase's. When Sheriff Bradley saw Chase, he stood, rounding his desk.

"Hello, sir, my name is—"

Sheriff Bradley extended his hand and said gruffly, "I know who you are, Officer. We're honored to have you join us from Metro." He nodded to one of the uncomfortable looking chairs in front of the desk. "Have a seat."

Chase lowered his tall frame into the chipped vinyl covered chair as Sheriff Bradley rounded his desk and sat down. His brown uniform was pressed and clean, though his tan colored tie had been taken off and hung on the edge of his chair, the top button of his uniform shirt left undone at his throat. His badge glittered in the fluorescent light above where it was pinned to the left side of his chest. He reached out a hand and Chase extended the file he'd brought with him.

Bradley flipped through it briefly, not stopping on any page in particular before setting it down on the desk. He leaned back in his chair and Chase waited.

"We've heard about your work down in Metro," he said, and Chase knew what was coming next, and had been counting on this coming up. "What made you decide to transfer?"

Chase shifted in his seat, but when he spoke, his voice was clear and steady. "As I'm sure you've heard, I was assigned to the Holly Vines case. After that was closed, I needed a change of scenery, sir."

Bradley was silent for a long moment and Chase realized he was chewing on a toothpick that was almost completely hidden in one side of his mouth. "News of the Vines case made it up here. It was tragic what happened to her and those children. I understand needing a palette cleanser after something like that."

Chase nodded once. He hated talking about it. Hated the reminders that they'd been too late to save her, all they could do was convict the bastard that had tortured her before leaving her mutilated body in that ditch and had left her children without a mother. Life in prison didn't seem like justice enough to Chase.

"It won't affect my performance, if that's a concern, sir," Chase said then.

"Your background check and psychological review came back clear. You wouldn't be here if that were a concern," Bradley grunted, and Chase nodded his appreciation. Bradley motioned over Chase's shoulder and he turned to see a tall, blonde haired deputy step through the door. "You'll be partnered with Deputy Graham Beckett. Six weeks of FTO for observation, after that you'll be in your own squad car for patrol. Rosie will give you your schedule on your way out, along with all your effects."

"Thank you, sir," Chase said and stood at the same time that Bradley did. They shook hands again before Chase moved toward the door.

Deputy Graham Beckett was a tree of a man, Chase thought as he walked toward him. Chase was tall at six feet five, but Graham stood at least two inches taller than him. Chase could tell the man was solid muscle beneath his uniform. Shrewd green eyes made a sweep of Chase, then the mouth that had been pulled into a stern line tilted up at the corners. Dark blonde facial hair covered the lower portion of his face, though it was trimmed short.

"So you're the guy that put away Ray Malcolm," Graham said, extending one large, tanned hand. Chase took it, shaking it firmly.

Chase nodded. "Among others."

Graham raised his golden blonde brows and grinned then. "Glad to have someone who knows what he's doing."

"I do my best," Chase said. "You been here long?"

Graham shrugged his wide shoulders as the two walked toward the front of the building. "I transferred about five years ago from Marquette after my dad died. Moved Mom down here to be closer to family, decided I liked it enough to stay, too."

"So you're a Yooper?" Chase asked, grinning.

"Sure am," Graham chuckled. "Born and raised. You?"

"Born in McHenry, Illinois. My parents moved us up here when I was twelve, and I was here until I graduated high school. From there I went straight to the academy, then hired in with Detroit Metro. Now I'm home again," Chase said, giving the abbreviated version.

As they stopped at the front desk, a short, squat woman with strawberry blonde hair sprinkled with silver shuffled over to them. Graham leaned against the counter and flashed a grin at the woman, who was easily in her mid to late fifties, crooning, "Heya Rosie."

Rosie swatted one hand toward him and shoved his elbow off the counter, snapping, "Get out of here with that, you heathen. Don't you have a report to type up? I told you last week I'm not your mammy, boy."

Chase laughed. He could already tell he was going to like Rosie. No nonsense, straight to the point. He'd bet anything she was the one that kept this department in line.

Graham grinned and slapped the counter with his palm. "Nice to meet you. Don't let Rosie scare you off."

"Get," Rosie snapped, though Chase saw the fondness in her brown eyes as she stared at the young officer. "You must be the new deputy. I've got your things here." When Chase didn't move around the counter, she muttered, "Well come on, we don't have all day."

"Yes, ma'am," Chase said with a chuckle and followed.

Rosie shouted back over her shoulder to Graham as he walked away, "And which one of you left the coffee to burn? I can smell it all the way out here!"

Chase chuckled when Graham's eyes widened slightly, then disappeared around the corner. As Rosie handed him his new effects, he glanced around at his new home away from home, and for the first time in a long time, he felt good.

SEVENTEEN

Zoey swiped at the tears that leaked down her cheeks when she heard Chase's Jeep pull into the driveway, followed moments later by his door closing. She had just seconds before he came through the kitchen door, carrying a heavy garment bag that was hooked on one finger over his shoulder, and a file box in the other. He juggled the box, closing the door behind him from the cold, then draped the garment bag over the back of one of the dining chairs and set the box down on the table.

He turned to her and she angled her face away, at the same time doing her best to dry her face without him seeing.

"Hey, how was your evening?" he asked lightly, stepping widely around her toward the refrigerator, taking a beer out and cracking it open.

She swallowed past the lump in her throat from her tears, trying to sound cheerful, "It's been great, how was your meeting?"

When he didn't respond right away, she dared a glance over her shoulder at him. He was staring at her, his electric blue eyes narrowed with worry. She turned away quickly, returning to the dishes.

"What's wrong?" he asked, stepping toward her.

She shrank back instinctively, then hung her head in defeat, dropping her hands into the soapy water as more tears tracked down her cheeks.

"Zoey, what's wrong?" he asked again gently, though he didn't make another move to come closer.

"I don't know," she whispered miserably, sniffling back tears. "I was fine, but after the gym... I'm just struggling in my own head today. Some days are harder than others. Seeing all those people going about their lives, doing *normal things* like going to the gym and not being terrified of every single stranger in the building. *Normal things* like going to the store by yourself and not glancing over your shoulder the entire time. *Normal things* like holding someone's hand. *Normal things* like not flinching every single time someone walks toward you..." Zoey shook her head, her breath catching as she cried. "I hate what he did to me. I hate what he took from me. I hate being this scared, pathetic shell of a person."

Chase set his beer down on the counter and took a small step closer, leaning his hand on the counter several feet away from where she stood. "Look at me," he said gently, and Zoey shook her head, sniffling again. "Zoey. You are not pathetic. You have gone through something extremely traumatic. You have to give yourself some grace, and time to heal."

"I want to be normal again," she whispered miserably.

"You are normal," Chase whispered back. "What you went through is not normal. But the way you're handling this trauma is."

Zoey pulled her hands out of the water and reached for a dishtowel. Turning toward him, she dried her hands angrily. "Chase, I can't even watch a rom-com anymore. I can't read a book with sex scenes in it. I went to a bachelorette party and they watched *Magic Mike,* and I hid in the bathroom so they wouldn't know I was having an anxiety attack. My brother and my best friend are getting married and have to hide from me when they want to show any kind of affection. How does that sound normal?" She threw the towel down on the counter, crossing her arms over her chest. "I nearly had a panic attack today because you offered me your hand *to help me stand.* How is any of that normal? I want to be hugged, I want to—to be kissed... I'm twenty-freaking-two for crying out loud! I want to be able to go out on a date and not be terrified that some douchebag is going to roofie my drink! I want to *have* a drink; a glass of wine, or a beer, or a cocktail... but nope, can't have that either because the feeling of being drunk makes me remember what it felt like to not have control over my body. Being just aware enough to know what was happening but not being able to *do anything* to stop it!"

Zoey drew a shaky, trembling breath. She hadn't spoken about this with anyone except her therapist, and only one time. She had a vague memory of telling the police what she could remember of that night while sitting in a cold, sterile hospital room, and had been forced to recount it in court, a hell she'd never imagined as *he'd* sat across the room, staring at her. She had begged her family to stay out of the courtroom during her testimony; she knew it would have destroyed them to hear. She preferred to keep the details of that night to herself under lock and key, her best kept secrets.

Chase's hands were balled into fists at his side. She shook her head sorrowfully. "I'm sorry. I—"

"Come here," Chase said gently, motioning toward one of the dining chairs. Zoey eyed him warily but stepped forward, sinking into the chair that he had pulled out for her. He moved around the kitchen, and Zoey watched as he readied the tea kettle to boil, then grabbed a mug and a tea bag. When the kettle whistled, he poured the piping hot water over the tea bag, letting it steep. He stirred in a dash of honey and squeezed a hint of lemon, then brought it to her, sitting down in the chair kitty-corner from her. Their knees nearly touched.

"Thank you," Zoey whispered despondently. "I don't know what's wrong with me today. That wasn't fair to you."

She knew she was being irrational and highly emotional, but she wasn't able to help it. Her body ached, her breasts were tender, and she'd been crying off and on all day. Verity had been a doll and had even gone down for her afternoon nap without a fuss. Tommy had left for Shaun's for the day and Chase had been gone. Which had left Zoey too much time to think.

Chase leaned his elbows on his knees, clasping his hands together as he ducked his head to look at her. She swiped at the tear tracks down her cheeks, painfully aware that she probably looked like a hot mess.

"I know you feel like you're lost in this right now. Like you're never going to come up from it. You're already fighting, Zoey, don't you see that? Every single day, you're fighting, and doing a helluva good job—"

Zoey made to protest weakly, but he shushed her and she eyed him skeptically. He smiled gently.

"You took a huge step today. You pushed yourself out of your comfort zone and I am so insanely proud of you for it," he whispered, and tears filled her eyes again, making her nose sting. "Please give yourself time."

"It's been a year," Zoey mumbled, fidgeting with the handle of the mug she held in her hands.

"Healing isn't linear."

"Speaking from experience?" she whispered drolly, only half serious.

"Yes," he stated simply.

Zoey brought her eyes to his, seeing in those electric blue depths his own torment. She wondered what traumas he was still healing from but respected him enough not to ask.

"My job can be heartbreaking," he said, his lips pulling into a tight line. "But I push on every single day because I know that it's worth it. Can you do that for me? Keep pushing every day?"

Zoey nodded slowly, her eyes never leaving his. Her chest ached for the pain she could see in his eyes. He wasn't the boy, the teenager, she'd grown up with. This was a man that had seen awful, horrible things. If he could fight, so could she.

From above them, Zoey heard Verity begin fussing upstairs. Lowering her eyes from his finally, she set her cup of tea on the table next to her and made to stand. Before she could, he stopped her, rising to his feet.

"Drink your tea, I can go get little Miss Sunshine," Chase said and stepped around her, making his way to the arched doorway that led out of the kitchen. She smiled gratefully and heard him take the stairs two at a time.

When Chase came down the stairs several minutes later, Verity had been given a diaper change and was cradled contentedly in one of his muscled arms. She clapped her tiny hands excitedly, cooing all the while.

"I don't know her cues yet, is she hungry?" Chase asked, and Zoey blushed before she could help it. She didn't know why it was so difficult for her to talk about that with Chase.

"She doesn't seem to be right now, but give it ten minutes, or when she sees me," Zoey said and smiled. Chase whirled Verity around to face into the living room, making both Verity and Zoey laugh.

"Enjoy your tea, we'll be in here watching NFL Redzone," he called over his shoulder. "Remember, we don't like that nasty green and white team!"

EIGHTEEN

"Oh good, you're home," Chase said the second Zoey walked in through the door. She laughed at his giddiness, shifting Verity's car seat on her arm as she closed the door behind her. Chase stepped forward and took Verity's car seat from Zoey, moving through the kitchen to set her on the counter, where he quickly unbuckled the squirming infant. He lifted her out, smiling widely at her excited squeal. "Yes, hello to you, too!"

Zoey pulled the diaper bag that she'd slung across her body over her head, placing it onto one of the dining chairs and took off her jacket, laughing at the two.

"How was work?" Chase asked, looking at her over Verity's blonde head.

"It was... a Monday," Zoey chuckled dryly. "I don't know what it is about holiday weekends, but it always feels like the Monday after is pure chaos."

Verity was squirming in earnest, and Zoey took her from Chase, careful to avoid contact with

Chase's skin. She took her into the living room, lowering her to a playmat with a mobile suspended over it for sensory play. The infant began swatting at the hanging rattles, cooing contentedly. Zoey turned back toward the kitchen to find Chase fairly bouncing on the balls of his feet.

"What on earth has gotten into you?" she laughed as she came around the couch toward him.

"I have something for you," he said as he stepped aside to let her enter the kitchen and pulled something out of his pocket. "This," he said, showing her a narrow, ridged metal instrument approximately four inches long, with one end angled into a point, "is a tactical kubaton. It's more commonly known as a glass breaker for cars, but it is an extremely useful tool for self-defense, as it's great for pressure points."

He patted his chest with one hand, indicating for her to place her hand on the front of his shirt. Zoey stared at that spot for a long time before raising her eyes to his, her breathing uneven.

"I promise you I will not hurt you. I won't even touch you, just let me show you how to use it," he murmured, as always sensing her hesitation.

Zoey nodded, reaching out her right hand and placing it, palm down on his chest. When she did, he pantomimed bracing his empty hand on the inside of her forearm, though he didn't touch her, and placed the point of the kubaton at the outside of her elbow, pressing lightly against the sensitive spot there. She gasped sharply before dropping her arm quickly. He grinned knowingly. He patted his chest again, and she eyed him warily before replacing her hand on his chest. Again, he pressed the pointed end, this time into the back of her hand, between the bones in her hand, and she was again startled by the bite of pain. She didn't pull away this time as he flipped it lengthwise, showing her how to press the hard ridges across her knuckles on the back of her hand as well. It was surprisingly effective.

He flipped it in the air lightly, catching it, then held it out to her. As she took it, he dug into his pocket again, pulling out a leather wristlet keychain, dangling it out to her as well.

"I want you to put the kubaton on this keychain. Whenever you are out in public, you wear this on your wrist, and the kubaton will always be within your grasp. It is an outrageously simple self-defense tool that doesn't require brute strength to be effective." She took the wristlet and he continued, "The spray mace you have is effective for keeping an attacker at bay; but if they get close enough to get their hands on you, this will give them enough pause for you to get out of their grasp. Then you'll use other techniques if necessary. Typically though, when this is brought out and used properly, an attacker is going to back off. You're no longer an easy target with this. They're usually looking for the least resistance."

"You did this for me?" she asked quietly, stunned.

"Of course," Chase said, smiling gently as he backed away a step. He shrugged his shoulders, and Zoey was once again reminded how *broad* he was. "You mentioned last night how you get worried going out by yourself. I wanted to give you something that would make you feel a little safer doing those normal things again."

Tears threatened Zoey's eyes, and she blinked up at him, shaking her head. "Thank you," she said simply, her throat tight with emotion. She shook her head mentally, wishing she could get a handle on whatever was happening to make her so emotional the last two days. She gripped the cool metal and the leather wristlet in her hand and smiled self-consciously. "This... is incredibly thoughtful."

Again, Chase shrugged and ran the fingers of one of his hands through his hair, pulling it away from his brow before smiling down at her. "I told you I wanted to help. I will help in any way I can, Zoey. Even something as simple as this."

Zoey attached the kubaton to the wristlet by the keyring, placing it on her wrist. It felt awkward hanging from her hand, but she felt better having it there. She smiled radiantly again. "You're amazing, you know that?"

Chase waved one hand at her, though a shy grin pulled at his mouth. He turned away, crossing to the refrigerator, pulling out a bottled water. "I'm just a big brother and cop at heart. This is what I do."

"Well, thank you, Deputy Manning," Zoey said with a smile. She took the wristlet off and placed it on her purse, where it would be easy access when she was ready for it. The door opened and Tommy walked in, closing it quickly behind him. He waved to both of them, as Zoey said, "Speaking of which, how did yesterday go?"

Chase leaned his hips against the counter, ducking his head to look through the arched doorway toward Verity, and Zoey could see that she was still playing contentedly. "It was basically just a meet n' greet. I met the Sheriff, my new partner, got my schedule and effects, that sort of thing."

"Are you nervous?" Zoey asked, leaning against the opposite counter. Tommy sat in one of the dining chairs and started unlacing his work boots, watching them as they talked.

"Nah," Chase said, crossing his arms over his broad chest. Once again Zoey's attention was brought to his body. His arms bulged out of the short sleeves of his shirt where they were crossed, making them look more defined than normal. "I actually get to go check out the new apartment tomorrow. I'll be out of your guys' hair soon, I promise. I appreciate you letting me crash here."

"Oh," Zoey murmured, her eyebrows raising slightly. "I forgot you were still waiting on the apartment. You've made yourself so at home, it just felt... normal."

There was that word again, she thought. Normal. It did feel normal to have Chase here. Every morning when she got up, he was out on his run. She had coffee ready for him when he got back. He joined them for dinner every night. Verity had grown quite attached, too. Zoey was shocked to find an ache had formed in her chest at the thought of Chase leaving.

"You know," Tommy said then from where he sat at the table, having taken off both boots, "I wanted to run it past Zoey first, but if it's okay with her, you're more than welcome to stay here indefinitely. We have the extra room, especially since Dad moved out, and with me and Shaun getting married sometime, Zoey would be left here alone. You can stay as long as you want."

Zoey swallowed hard, lowering her gaze to the floor as she blushed. He'd said exactly what she was thinking.

When she raised her eyes, she saw a look pass between Chase and her brother, again wondering what had happened between them.

"I'll give it some thought," was all that Chase said, his body stiff and his tone shorter than she would have expected.

"I don't mind if you stay," Zoey heard herself say. His electric blue eyes met hers once again, and she was shocked by the intensity in them. "I mean, if that's what you're worried about," she said shyly. "I just want you to know, I don't mind if you want to stay."

He nodded and Zoey was grateful when Verity let out a 'I'm hungry' fuss from the living room. Zoey dashed through the archway, picking up the baby and disappearing up the stairs to feed her. As she sat in the gliding chair with Verity at her breast, Zoey couldn't believe the words that had come out of her mouth.

NINETEEN

"Dammit Tommy," Chase snapped, once he'd heard Zoey's bedroom door close upstairs. "I already told you my answer. I'm not going to do this. You have to stop."

"I just suggested that you stay here instead of paying for an apartment that you'll rarely be at," Tommy said, standing and crossing to the refrigerator, taking a beer out and cracking it open. He held it out to Chase, who took it with a grudging thank you. He pulled a second can out and opened it, taking a long drink. "I know the hours you're going to be pulling, and it seems ridiculous for you to pay rent on a place you'll be at only to sleep in. We have the extra space. It would be helping us out just as much, man."

Chase eyed his best friend warily, taking a drink of his own beer. "I don't believe a word that's coming out of your mouth, but I can see what you mean."

Tommy's brown eyes crinkled at the corners when he grinned. "I don't know what you're talking about."

"Lying sack of shit," Chase muttered. "*If* I agree to stay, you have got to stop this hairbrained scheme of yours. You can't do this to her. I won't be a part of it, man."

Tommy held his hands up, palms out. "You can't be mad at me for trying to take care of my sister, Chase. I'd sell my soul to the devil himself if that meant I could take this away from her."

Chase thought of his little sisters, admitting to himself that he would do the same for them. Novalee wasn't quite a year younger than he was, Irish twins he thought it was called. She had moved out of state to pursue a teaching job working with underprivileged kids in Chicago. Krissie was next at twenty-four, she'd stayed around northern Michigan working at one of the largest resorts in the area as a bartender. Bree was the baby of the family, not quite twenty-two, and she was a junior in college downstate studying criminal law. The thought of the same thing happening to any of them as Zoey made his chest ache.

"I get it, man. I do."

"Just think about what I said," Tommy said before exiting the kitchen.

"Which part?" Chase called.

Tommy was silent for a long moment before saying quietly, "Whichever part you think I'm talking about, Chase."

Chase opened his mouth to offer a retort, but his cell phone began to vibrate in his pocket. He dug it out as Tommy disappeared through the door and headed up the stairs. Chase recognized the number as the one for his new landlord and answered it quickly, saying, "Hello?"

"Yeah, hi, this is Greg from that apartment here in Petoskey. I hate to have to tell you, but I've got some bad news," the rumbly voice on the other end of the line said, and Chase sighed quietly.

"Oh? What's that?" he asked.

"Well uh, we had a water pipe burst in the apartment above yours, but we didn't realize it was leaking until today... There's uh, a significant amount of water damage and it's not going to be ready for probably several more weeks, son," the landlord muttered apologetically.

Chase heard footsteps on the stairs and turned as Zoey came into view, holding Verity on her hip. When the five-and-a-half-month-old saw Chase, her little face lit up and she started swinging her arms and legs wildly. Chase brought his eyes to Zoey and then said into the phone, "Yeah, I understand, thank you for calling me, Greg. I actually won't be needing the apartment after all." Zoey's eyes widened just the slightest as he took several steps toward her and Verity, who began to squeal in excitement. Tucking the phone between his ear and shoulder, he reached for the infant and Zoey handed her over without hesitation. Their eyes held as he continued speaking into the phone, "I think I'm good where I'm at. Thank you again."

Holding Verity with one arm, he reached up with his other hand and pulled the phone away from his ear, ending the call and sliding the phone back into his pocket. Zoey continued to stare at him, and he whispered quietly, "Are you sure you're okay with this?"

She was silent for an extended heartbeat, and just when he began to question his decision, she nodded, smiling, then said, "Yes."

TWENTY

Zoey made quick work of emptying the room Chase had been occupying for the last several days, removing everything except the bed, dresser, and nightstands. Tommy had been strangely gleeful when he had heard the news, and another strained glance between the two men had Zoey convinced something was going on with them. Not necessarily an argument, but definitely something that had put tension on their friendship. They acted fine when around her, but it still felt off... She shook her head, sending the thoughts from her mind as she stripped the bed of the sheets. They were big boys; they could figure it out on their own.

Chase carried the last of his things inside and up the stairs, depositing them in the freshly emptied bedroom. He had surprisingly few belongings. When she mentioned it, he shrugged his broad shoulders and said, "I work too much to have time for anything else. I don't need much this way."

"Will it be different up here than it was downstate?" Zoey asked as she pulled the pillowcases off the pillows, tossing them into the laundry basket by her feet.

"Oh absolutely," Chase said, turning to look at her as he opened the closet to hang a row of shirts that had been left on the hangers. Zoey had laughed when he'd carried everything in from his car that way. "Metro is much more fast paced, more cases of breaking and entering, petty thefts, more murders."

A look passed across his face and Zoey wondered if that was what had brought him home after so many years. But then his mouth pulled up at one corner and he shrugged again.

"Petoskey hasn't had a murder in years. Something like that rocks a community like this. It doesn't happen often," he said after a moment, straightening the row of hangers he'd just hooked on the bar in the closet. "I'm okay with that."

"Won't you be bored after such intense cases?" she asked, shaking out the sheets Chase handed her, then took to tucking in one side of the fitted sheet. He worked on the other side of the bed. He looked over the mattress at her where he stood half bent.

"I think it'll be an adjustment at first, sure. But I needed a break from that," he said, smoothing the corner out before straightening.

"So, you think you'll go back, eventually?" she asked quietly, stilling as she was trying to put the pillow into a clean pillowcase.

He glanced at her and shrugged. "I can't say it can't happen eventually. For now, no, I have no plans to return to a metro area police department.

It's not easy to transfer. I don't have any interest in doing this again anytime soon. Besides," he said and smiled, "I think Verity would riot if I left now."

Zoey laughed out loud, nodding in agreement, then placed her hands on her hips as she surveyed the freshly made bed. "I think you're right. I don't know what kind of magic you cast on her in such a short amount of time."

"I'll never give away the secret to my magic," Chase said seriously, though his eyes were alight with mischief. "And I'll swear Verity to secrecy, too."

Zoey rolled her eyes and grinned. "Right, because she's so loquacious at five-and-a-half months old."

Chase laughed. "Hey, how do I know you two don't have some kind of telepathy that we don't know about?"

She bent at the waist and picked up the laundry basket, heading toward the door. "You don't. I *am* her mother, after all."

His laughter followed her down the hall as she walked away. Once downstairs, she started a load of laundry and then crossed to the kitchen, opening the refrigerator and taking stock of its contents. Chase walked into the kitchen and she glanced over her shoulder. "Any preferences for dinner? I think I'm turkey'd out."

He reached around her and grabbed a beer from the shelf, close enough for their clothes to whisper against each other. Zoey sucked in her breath, and he backed away instantly. "Ah shit, I'm sorry, Zoey."

Breathe out. One. Two. Three...

She turned and one side of her mouth tilted up; the panic attack was already passing. "It's okay, I promise."

He backed away and leaned his hips against the counter, his typical stance when in the tiny kitchen. "I'm sorry," he said again, his brow furrowed.

"It's okay, I mean it. That was super fleeting. I swear," she said earnestly, smiling reassuringly at him. "Dinner ideas?"

Chase wrinkled his nose and took a drink of his beer, and she could tell he didn't quite believe her. She was surprised herself at how fleeting it was.

"I haven't had *Mighty Fine Pizza* since I left for the academy," he said and groaned, as if the thought of the local pizzeria was making his mouth water. "A *Northman* sounds fantastic. If you and Tommy are game?"

"I don't have to cook; that's a win for me," Zoey laughed. "Though I may have to do an extra work out tomorrow to work it off."

Chase chuckled, though he pointed a stern finger at her and said, "I don't want you counting calories or carbs or whatever else you women get all in a tizzy over. I still expect to see big ol chunky thighs on that baby."

She blushed to the roots of her hair. How did they always circle back around to her breastfeeding? Zoey groaned internally. She drew an X across her chest and said dramatically, "I cross my heart, I won't jeopardize Verity's meals for weight loss."

He laughed out loud, throwing his head back. "Good," he said and grinned at her. She reciprocated his smile, though she knew her cheeks were still flaming with embarrassment. They turned as Tommy entered the kitchen, showered and dressed in clean jeans and a fresh t-shirt. He sat down and started stuffing his feet into his boots.

"Are you leaving?" Zoey asked. "We were about to order pizza."

"Huh? Oh, yeah, I was gonna go to Shaun's," he said, though Zoey could tell he was distracted. "You guys go ahead."

"Thanks for the permission," Zoey said, her tone snarky, but he wasn't paying her any attention.

"Yeah, have fun," he said and was out the door seconds later. Zoey looked at Chase.

"Is there something going on with him lately or is it just my imagination?" she asked. "He never stays at her place this much."

Chase dropped his gaze to the floor and shrugged. "I think he's had a lot on his plate for a long time. I think maybe it's finally catching up to him and he just needs a bit of a break."

Zoey's face fell when his words registered, her chest tightening painfully. She hadn't dared to say out loud that she'd felt like a burden to Tommy, instead letting those feelings fester inside her for months. Chase had only been here for a few days and had said what she couldn't bring herself to. Tears stung her nose and she turned away. Damn these rioting emotions all of a sudden!

"Chase, I— I actually don't think I'm that hungry," she said around the lump in her throat. "I may just go up to bed early with Verity."

"Oh," Chase said from behind her, and she could hear the disappointment in his voice. "Yeah, okay. Are you alright?"

"I'm fine," Zoey said, forcing her voice not to waver, keeping her back to him as she moved around the kitchen. "It was just a long day, and we have an early day tomorrow for the gym..."

"Okay, sure," she heard him say. As she made her way toward the door, he called to her, "Good night, Zoey."

She paused at the arched doorway and risked a glance at him over her shoulder. "Good night, Chase."

TWENTY-ONE

Chase woke to the sound of Verity fussing, though it wasn't more than twenty seconds before it ended, and he heard the soft rustlings of Zoey moving around the room next door to his.

He tossed in bed, stacking one arm behind his head as he stared up at the dark ceiling. Every once in a while, a car would pass on the road and the headlights would cast slivers of dancing light beams across the wall and ceiling, then would disappear as the car moved out of range.

Glancing at the alarm clock on the nightstand, he sighed. It was nearly five in the morning, just minutes before his alarm would have woken him up anyway. Verity, he had learned, was like clockwork when it came to her meals, and he grinned in the dark at the thought.

Then his thoughts drifted back to the blonde woman in the room next door and how she would be feeding that precocious little thing that he'd grown to adore. When he thought about Verity feeding at

118

those breasts, he couldn't stop as images of Zoey came to him; her leaning over Verity in those black leggings that had delineated her bottom and thighs, the way her tits filled out the soft sweaters she wore, how he ached to tuck that one strand of blonde hair behind her ear that never seemed to want to stay out of her face.

He cursed Tommy again, over and over. If he hadn't brought up that stupid, moronic idea, he wouldn't be thinking about Zoey the way he was right now. The way he had been for the last three weeks since he'd moved in.

He wouldn't be thinking about how proud he was every day she pushed herself in the gym during their workouts and how adorable she was all flushed and sweaty afterwards.

Or how he had imagined kissing her lips as she'd smiled radiantly at him after she'd completed her first sixty second plank.

Shaking his head to clear the thoughts that never seemed to be far from his mind, he rolled to a sitting position and swung his legs over the edge of the bed, rolling his neck and shoulders. He'd ordered a new, bigger bed; something that better fit his tall frame. He and Tommy had fought like hell to get it up the narrow staircase and around the corner to the bedroom. Zoey had stood, laughing at the two of them bickering like an old married couple. When she called out, "Pivot! *Pivot!*" he had nearly dropped the mattress when he burst out laughing.

He yawned and stood, crossing the room to dress in his running gear. Ready for a normal morning. Their version of normal, anyway.

They had all settled into an easy routine. Each morning, except for his night shifts, he woke around the same time as Verity and Zoey. While he could hear Zoey feeding the cranky infant, he dressed and got ready for his run. Depending on who made it downstairs first, either he would start the coffee and Zoey's tea kettle to warm, or his coffee would be ready when he came downstairs if she beat him to it.

After his run, Zoey would drop Verity off at daycare and the two of them would meet at the gym for their work out before work. Chase could already see a change in her even if she couldn't see it herself. They were still doing simple body resistance workouts, but she was more agile and much surer footed than she was even just three weeks ago. She worked hard, pushing herself each time.

He was two weeks in, still doing Field Training Observation for the next two months before he would be on his own. He and Graham had formed a quick camaraderie, and Chase was grateful that he had been partnered with someone as solid as Graham Beckett. He was a stickler for rules but ultimately a very fair and well-liked deputy.

The following week would be his first scheduled shift for the night shift and he wouldn't get out of work until seven in the morning. They had agreed that they would go for their workouts before his shift started in the evenings, after her workday had ended.

He knew it would take time for his body to adjust to the rotation in day and night shifts. Four day shifts on, seven am to seven pm, four days off. Switch to three days on, three days off. This week would be the toughest one for him to adjust to; four night shifts on, seven pm to seven am, four nights off, switch to three nights on, three off.

Rinse and repeat.

Sneaking down the hallway now, he could still hear Zoey in her bedroom with Verity. He made it to the kitchen, the light over the sink the only light in the room and started the coffee to percolate. He had just turned on the back burner of the stove to heat the tea kettle when he heard a noise at the door a moment before Tommy stumbled in through it.

Chase raised his eyebrows at his friend and sniffed the air. "You reek like vodka. Long night? You didn't drive, did you?"

"No, Deputy Manning, I didn't drive," Tommy muttered sourly. "I got a ride home."

Chase chose to ignore the dig, pouring a cup of coffee and holding it out to his friend. "Were you out all night?"

"What are you, my mom?" Tommy snapped grumpily and Chase rolled his eyes. There was no point talking to him when he was like this.

"Take this coffee, go on up to bed," Chase said dryly as he watched Tommy kick off his snow-covered boots. "Sleep it off, bud."

Tommy offered a sarcastic and improper salute, muttering, "Yes, sir."

Tommy had just disappeared up the stairs when he heard Zoey coming down them. He leaned his hips against the counter as she appeared, holding Verity on one hip. "Is he drunk?"

"That was my guess," Chase sighed, then held up his hands. "I'm not here to judge. As long as he is safe, I don't care."

Zoey chose a tea and turned just as the kettle began to whistle. Chase plucked the tea bag out of her hand and clucked his tongue at her and reaching to turn the burner off. When she glanced up at him curiously, he motioned with his chin to one of the empty chairs, and said, "Sit. I'll bring it to you."

She murmured a thank you and sat down, and he turned to fetch a mug out of the cupboard, setting it next to the stove. He watched her out of the corner of his eye as he readied her tea, plopping the tea bag into the hot water. Chase turned, carefully setting it on the table in front of her before reaching for Verity, who was happily bouncing in her mother's arms, not so patiently waiting for his attention. He chuckled as Zoey passed her off to him, the tiny baby's fingers going straight for Chase's longer locks at the top of his head. He ducked just in time to avoid those superhuman strength hands of hers.

"You're getting quick," Zoey murmured after she took a sip of the hot tea, smiling.

"I just learned how mean those little fingers can be," he chuckled again, turning Verity in his arms and settling her in one arm, football style. He poured himself a cup of coffee and then leaned his hips against the counter. He was growing quite adept at this one-handed thing.

"Do you want breakfast?" he asked after taking a drink of his coffee, turning his head the opposite direction so Verity's flailing hand didn't knock into it. He tsked the infant, laughing, "You're going to burn yourself if you knock this out of my hands."

Zoey shook her head and said, "No, I don't like to eat before we workout. I've been taking a light breakfast with me that I eat at work. But thank you."

He nodded and glanced at the clock then, and it was as if Zoey read his mind, setting her tea down and coming toward him to take Verity. He pecked a kiss to the top of Verity's curly blonde head before slipping her into Zoey's arms. He pulled out one of the dining chairs and sat, quickly lacing his running shoes, and was out the door moments later.

As he stretched out in the cold, pre-dawn inky blackness, he sighed. Stepping out onto the snow-cleared road, he started a fast, grueling pace that he kept up for most of his run, only slowing the last half mile back to the house.

Zoey was waiting for him when he walked inside, dressed in her workout clothes, her work bag with a change of clothes ready by the door. He smiled at Verity, who clapped her hands excitedly when she saw him. Zoey handed her to him and he made quick work of buckling her into her car seat, bundling her against the December cold. Within minutes Zoey and Verity were loaded into her Subaru, and he climbed up into the Rubicon.

He made it to the gym before Zoey, as she had to drive across town to drop Verity off at daycare. Chase sat down at the chest press machine to get in a circuit before Zoey got there, and was surprised when Shay sidled up to him. He hadn't seen her since the day he'd gone to her apartment.

"Hey," she said with a coy smile. "You haven't been here in the evenings lately. I see why, now."

Letting go of the press, he nodded as he took a drink of the water bottle next to him. "My work schedule changes week to week. I try to fit workouts in when I can."

Dragging one finger down his bicep as he lifted the water bottle to his lips again, she said quietly, "I can think of another workout that we can fit in whenever you're available. I'm just about to leave, if you want to join me for a different kind of morning workout."

He should say yes to the invitation, he thought as he looked her up and down. Get it out of his system again, since thoughts of Zoey seemed to haunt him every day all day. He grinned, his only response, and took another drink of water.

He choked then and coughed roughly to clear his windpipe as he watched Zoey walk in the front door. Her eyes found his immediately and he swallowed hard.

Shay must have sensed his distraction, turning to look at what had caught his attention. Zoey signed in and started toward them, and Shay turned back to Chase, whispering harshly, "Is that your girlfriend?"

"No," Chase said, though the condescending tone in Shay's voice pissed him off more than he cared to admit. As Zoey got closer, he stood, stepping around Shay. "This is my roommate, Zoey. Zoey, Shay. She's a usual here."

Zoey smiled kindly at Shay and Chase could sense the animosity radiating off the other woman. "You're roommates?"

Zoey nodded, still smiling, blissfully ignorant to the other woman's hostility. "He's my brother's best friend. Moved in because his apartment flooded. Awful, right?"

"Right," Shay muttered, and any attraction Chase had felt for her dissipated. A fierce protectiveness washed over him, and he stepped closer to Zoey. "Well, I'll let you guys get to your workouts. You look like you need it."

Zoey's mouth opened in a silent 'o', and her eyes immediately lowered to the floor. Shay smirked at Chase as she moved toward the locker rooms. Chase moved so that he was standing in front of Zoey, who wouldn't meet his gaze. He bent at the knees, bringing himself eye level with her.

"Hey," he said and her eyes skittered to his for just a moment before flitting away. "Zoey, don't let her get in your head. You've just started working out after having a baby. She's just an unhappy woman with nothing better to do with herself." When she finally brought her eyes to his for longer than a few seconds, he murmured, "You know how proud of you I am, right?"

She nodded just the barest bit, and he reached out a hand to touch her shoulder, but pulled back before he made contact. He sighed. "You're doing great, Zoey. I promise you."

"I want to start on the machines," she said, and his brows shot up in surprise.

"Are you sure? I'll teach you, but I don't want you rushing yourself just because some ornery biddy—"

"I'm sure," she said, lifting her chin. One corner of his mouth tilted up. He knew she was nervous based on the way her fingers clutched at the strap of her duffel bag as it cut across her chest, but he nodded in agreement. "I know I'm not ready for the heavy weights yet—"

He chuckled then, turning and sweeping his hand forward for her to walk ahead of him. "We'll start you with baby weights and work our way up. Properly."

"Slowly, you mean," Zoey mumbled, giving him a sidelong glance. He laughed.

"Yes, slowly. Like I promised. I won't let you hurt yourself because you're a stubborn cuss," he said and winked at her, which finally made her laugh. "Alright, come on. Let's see what you're made of."

As Chase got Zoey situated on one of the benches and showed her how to choose weights properly, he saw Shay exit the locker room with her bag over her shoulder. While Zoey was turned around looking at the different weights, Shay shot him a questioning look, to which he shook his head. She mouthed 'Whatever' and rolled her eyes, walking out alone.

He turned his attention back to the sweet blonde in front of him just as she looked up at him expectantly, her indigo eyes wide with unfaltering trust. He couldn't help the smile that tugged at his lips as he shifted to show her the correct form.

This was where he was supposed to be, anyway.

TWENTY-TWO

"How is it almost Christmas already? Wasn't it still November like last week?" Shaun grumbled as Zoey pushed a grocery cart through the crowded aisles.

Zoey laughed, eyeing her best friend through her lashes. "I don't know where you've been, but this month has felt excruciatingly long. Then again it might be the gym days, I swear Chase is trying to kill me sometimes! My legs hurt so bad after this morning's workout." Shaun snickered and Zoey whipped her head around. "What?"

Shaun pulled her face into one of innocence, but a grin threatened to crack. "Nothing. I just... different kind of workout than I'm used to."

"Oh my god," Zoey groaned, turning the corner with the cart. "I don't want to know about your sex life with my brother. Please!"

She wasn't sure when it had happened, but she was slowly, day-by-day, sometimes minute-by-minute, getting stronger. Not just physically, but mentally, too. Perhaps it was the close proximity of having Chase living in their small home full time, or the three-times-a-week workouts they did together, or the fact that she'd finally started to open up and begin to process her trauma in therapy, but Zoey had noticed a change in herself. She was starting to feel... almost normal.

Chase was gone a lot, his new work schedule was grueling with the back and forth of day shift to night shift on rotating weeks, all the while not missing a morning or evening run or one of their workout sessions. Zoey was amazed he could still function. She was exhausted, though she was pleasantly surprised at the changes in her body as well as her mental health. When she had zipped into a pair of jeans she hadn't fit into since before her pregnancy, she had whooped and hollered so loudly that Chase and Tommy had come running from downstairs, panicking that something was wrong with her or Verity. She had blushed to the roots of her hair when she'd had to explain that nothing was wrong... she had just been too excited to contain herself.

Tommy had huffed off, grumbling something about giving him a heart attack, but Chase had held his hand out for a high five, which Zoey had given enthusiastically. His fingers had folded around hers gently, briefly, before letting go and dropping his electric blue gaze from hers. "You're doing great, Zoey. You're working your butt off. Literally."

Zoey had laughed, turning around to look in the tall mirror propped in one corner of the room. Spinning to look at her bottom in the tight jeans, she had been grinning when she met Chase's eyes in the mirror. Her smile froze at the way he was staring at her, her heart tripping in her chest.

It wasn't fear she felt tightening her chest, but attraction.

Chase cleared his throat roughly and mumbled something unintelligible as he'd ducked out of her room. Zoey turned back toward the mirror, raising her shirt to just below her breasts, admiring the slimness of her waist and the flatness of her stomach. He was right; she was working her butt off. And her mommy tummy.

"Switch me," Shaun said then, and Zoey took Verity from her as Shaun started pushing the cart. "She's giving me a cramp in my arm."

Zoey laughed, hiking Verity higher on her hip. "She's just a growing girl!"

Shaun stopped at a display of men's body wash gift sets, picking up several to do smell comparisons. Zoey continued forward, stopping at a row of Christmas stockings, choosing a white one with royal blue trim for Chase. Verity clasped it close, burying her face in the faux fur trim.

It was then that the hair on the back of Zoey's neck stood up, that gut feeling of being watched so strong she almost felt ill. She scanned the crowd around her, until her eyes landed on a woman possibly in her early fifties with shoulder length brown hair that was streaked with grey. She was staring at Verity, and when the woman noticed Zoey's attention, she quickly ducked around a corner, disappearing from sight.

Zoey glanced behind her, thankful that Shaun was still close by, carefully debating which body wash set to choose for Tommy. Zoey walked back toward her, at the same time gripping the cool metal of the kubaton suspended from her wrist. It made her feel better, even just slightly.

"You look like you just saw a ghost, are you okay?" Shaun asked, looking Zoey in the eyes. "What happened?"

"Nothing, I think," Zoey said softly, holding Verity closer. "I just don't like crowds is all."

"I think I'm done anyway, how about we head to check out?" she asked, glancing around the busy store. "Is there anything else you needed?"

"No, I don't think so," Zoey murmured. "I think I have everything."

The two women made their way to the front of the store, stopping in one of the many long lines. Zoey had started to breathe easier when she saw the same woman get into a lane several down from them. She didn't have anything in her hands and wasn't pushing a cart. Panic started to claw at her chest when the woman kept glancing their way.

She was grateful that their line moved swiftly, and just minutes later they had checked out and were headed out to the dark parking lot. She had insisted that they park beneath one of the tall light posts closest to the store. As Shaun loaded their bags into the trunk, Zoey quickly buckled Verity into her car seat and started to warm the car.

Shaun strode off with the cart to return it to the cart coral, and as Zoey rounded the back of the car, she gasped when the same woman from earlier appeared at her side. Gripping the kubaton tightly, she stared at the woman who stood within arm's reach.

"You're Zoey Chandler," the woman said, her voice wavering.

"Yes," Zoey said hesitantly. "And you are?"

The woman glanced around her and anxiety made Zoey feel faint. "Is that your baby?"

"Who are you?" Zoey demanded sharply, not taking her eyes off the woman. Shaun had to be on her way back, right? she thought frantically.

Again, the woman glanced around before turning back to Zoey and saying, "My name is Norma. I'm Robby Patterson's mom."

Zoey felt her eyesight blurring as undiluted panic set in, her chest too tight to draw a breath.

"That's my granddaughter," Norma said, handing her an envelope. "I want to see her."

TWENTY-THREE

"No," was all that Zoey could manage, her throat seizing on the word, even as her fingers closed around the envelope. "What is this?"

"Hey," Shaun said loudly then, as she came around the corner of the car. Zoey watched hazily as Norma backed away quickly saying something about mistaking this car as her own. She disappeared from view and Shaun grabbed hold of Zoey's shoulders, "Hey, what happened? Talk to me."

Zoey was shaking violently, tears threatening to spill over her lashes. "I want to go home. Please. Get Verity home. I need Chase."

Zoey didn't remember getting into the passenger seat, or the short drive home. Zoey carried Verity inside the house in the car seat, fumbling fingers unbuckling her quickly. She was hyperventilating by the time she had Verity out and clutched her to her chest as sobs wracked her. Shaun stood in the kitchen staring helplessly as Zoey sank into one of the dining chairs.

She barely registered the sound of another car pulling into the driveway before the door opened again and Chase barreled in, still wearing his uniform. Shaun whirled around when Chase barked, "What the hell happened? Zoey?" and Zoey half heard Shaun try to brokenly explain what she'd seen. He dropped to his knees in front of her, his hands hesitating before resting on the edge of her chair. Zoey continued to cry wretchedly, holding the now squirming and overstimulated Verity close. "Zoey, sweetheart, what happened?"

Zoey hiccupped miserably, tears continuing to track down her cheeks. Her lip wobbled and all she could manage to whimper was, "Chase..."

"What sweetheart? What happened? Talk to me," he pleaded, reaching up and swiping his uniform cap off, tossing it onto the table beside him. Verity twisted in Zoey's arms, trying to wriggle free to get to Chase. Zoey's hold slackened slightly and she allowed Verity to reach for Chase, who took her without hesitation. With his free hand he reached up and swiped the tears off her cheeks.

Zoey froze, she dared not move or even breathe. After a heartbeat, she closed her eyes and tilted her head just the slightest, resting her cheek in his large hand. She took a deep, shuddering breath in and opened her eyes once more, staring into the blue depths of his. "Talk to me, sweetheart."

"That woman," Shaun said from beside Zoey, "who was she? What did she want?"

Zoey lifted her cheek away from Chase's hand and reached up to swipe at the wet streaks her tears had left. "It was... *his* mom. She said Verity is her granddaughter and that she wants to see her."

"What the hell!" Shaun exclaimed. "Is she on crack? Absolutely not going to happen!"

"Was he convicted through a trial?" Chase asked Zoey gently.

"Yes," Zoey whispered, then swallowed. Her fingers shook as she opened the envelope she'd put on the table earlier. Panic clawed at her anew as she read the subpoena requesting a hearing to determine visitation with Verity and her paternal grandparents. "Upon conviction all of his rights were forfeit. I should have recognized her. She was in the courtroom." She held Chase's stare. "She can't take her away from me, right? She can't force me to let her see her?"

"Of course she can't!" Shaun muttered, pacing.

Chase opened his mouth and closed it, before saying quietly, "I don't know, Zoey. I'm not a family lawyer. Each state is different."

"I have a restraining order against him, but I didn't think to add his parents," Zoey whispered brokenly. "They can't take her. They'll let him see her."

"They're not going to take her," Shaun snapped, still pacing. Chase shot her a look but she just sighed and kept pacing back and forth.

"This says it's not until the end of February, well past the first of the year. We will call a lawyer and get this straightened out," Chase murmured, still kneeling before Zoey as he glanced over the formal court order. "If anything, they'll be lucky to get supervised visitation. They're not going to get custody, if that's what you're thinking, sweetheart. I won't let anything happen to you or Verity. You know that, right?"

Fresh tears started at his words, but Zoey nodded somberly.

"I have to go back to work, but I'll be back in an hour. Why don't you go upstairs and take a bath, let Shaun watch Verity for a few while you take time to calm down. You don't want to stress Verity out, right?" he asked gently, and she nodded again. "Okay, I'll be back as soon as I can. Do you want anything when I get back?"

Zoey shook her head as he stood. "Thank you, Chase."

"Of course sweetheart," he said and smiled. He handed Verity over to Shaun and motioned with his chin toward the doorway to the living room. "Go on, go relax for a few."

He extended his hand to her where she sat. She stared at it for a second before placing her hand in his and allowing him to raise her to her feet.

His touch zinged across every nerve ending in her body, and her eyes flew to his. He squeezed her fingers gently before releasing them, stepping away toward the door, and then he disappeared out into the cold night.

Shaun shooed her up the stairs, reassuring her that she was more than capable of watching the little miss. Zoey made it to the bathroom, turning on the taps and running a hot, bubbly bath. The bright light stung her eyes after her tears, so she crossed to the hall closet, digging out a handful of jar candles from a basket on the top shelf. Placing them throughout the small room, she lit them, then turned out the overhead lights. As the water became deep enough, she turned it off and shed her clothes.

Leaving the bathroom door cracked open just a hair to hear in case Shaun needed her, she lowered herself into the hot water, breathing a sigh of relief. She rested her head against the sloped edge of the bathtub, closing her eyes.

Thoughts started to run through her, and with it the panic all over again, but she forced it back, instead thinking of the way Chase's hand had felt against her cheek, how warm and gentle and soft it had been. How his eyes always seemed to see right into the deepest parts of her, as if he knew what she needed before she knew it herself. How his fingers had felt wrapped around her own and that jolt of electricity that coursed through her whenever his skin touched hers. How incredibly sweet and handsome he was.

Zoey opened her eyes, watching as the candles cast a fluttering light across the darkened bathroom walls. She wasn't sure how long she was in the bath, long enough for the water to begin to cool. She hadn't heard anything from downstairs. She let some of the water drain and then turned the taps back on, refilling it with more hot water and bubbles.

Zoey had just turned the taps back off, reclining again when she heard footsteps on the stairs, then heavy footfalls down the hallway, where they stopped at the bathroom.

"Zoey?" she heard Chase say from just outside the door. She slid deeper into the water, thankful she'd just refilled it with fresh bubbles to cover her nakedness. The door was still cracked open just slightly. In the mirror she could see his shadowed outline through the slit in the door. "Are you alright?"

"Yes, I think so," she said softly, running her hands along the bubbles on the surface of the water. "How are Shaun and Verity?"

"Fast asleep on the couch," Chase chuckled, and the sound sent more butterflies skittering through her belly. "Do you need anything?"

"No, I don't think so," she said quietly. She held her breath, unsure what she was waiting for next.

"Call if you need anything, Zoey," he said after a long moment, and then his heavy, booted footsteps faded down the hallway. A moment later she heard the click of his bedroom door closing and released the breath she had been holding.

TWENTY-FOUR

"I want to try a weighted squat."

Chase's eyebrows raised in surprise, but she held his stare. He shrugged and spread his arm wide to allow her to lead the way. She stopped at the machine and watched as Chase adjusted the weights. She needed to keep her mind occupied, and lifting heavy weights seemed to work the best. All she'd thought about for several days was the envelope Norma had handed her. Tommy had immediately called their lawyer the morning after; they had a meeting scheduled for after the holidays.

Drawing her attention back to the here and now, she watched as Chase stepped beneath the bar and demonstrated how to position her feet, shoulders, and arms, wrapping his large hands around the metal bar that was resting lightly on the top of his shoulders, behind his head. He took a breath in, standing straight up and taking a small step forward to take the bar out of the cradle.

Zoey watched, transfixed, as he dipped into a squat before rising again. He talked her through everything he was doing, though admittedly she was struggling to remain focused on what he was saying when the muscles in his arms and back rippled the way they did under the thin fabric of his shirt.

He did several reps before stepping back and replacing the bar in the cradle, stepping out from under it and turning to her. "Ready?"

Zoey swallowed hard, second guessing herself for a moment. He made everything look so damn easy, she thought mulishly. But then she pursed her lips and nodded. "I'm ready."

Chase adjusted the weights for her, making sure her safety came first. When the weights were ready, he said, "I know this looks light; it is. I want you to master the motion before we move into heavier weights." When she nodded, he said gruffly, "Okay, show me where to stand."

Zoey stepped forward, placing her feet shoulder width apart just as he had shown her, ducking under the bar and letting the cool metal rest against the back of her neck. She wrapped her fingers around the bar, adjusting them until it was comfortable.

"Okay, you're going to use your core muscles to lift this out of the cradle, not your arms," he said from behind her, and out of her peripheral she could see his hands outstretched slightly, just beneath the bar on either side of her hands, ready to catch it if necessary. "When you're ready, Zoey."

She nodded, then lifted the bar and weights, taking a tentative step forward. She lost her balance, the added weight on either side of her throwing her off more than she'd anticipated. His hands were there immediately, steadying the bar until she regained her balance and footing.

"You alright?" she felt more than heard his quiet murmur, his breath stirring the hairs at the back of her neck. She nodded, and he said, "Okay, show me what you've got."

Zoey exhaled as she dipped into a squat, inhaling as she came back up. She did three, though on the third her knees wobbled slightly as she raised into the standing position. Gritting her teeth, she lowered into a fourth, but she'd dropped too far down. Panic filled her as she struggled to rise, and Chase's hands gripped the first thing he could to keep her from going down, which was right beneath her arms. He raised her into a standing position, but Zoey stiffened involuntarily at the contact.

Chase removed his hands straightaway, closing his hands around the bar instead, directing her back so they could lower the bar into the cradle. As it settled, she dropped her chin forward, letting out a pained exhale. "I'm sorry."

"Don't be sorry," he said gently, stepping away from the spotter hold he'd been positioned in behind her. "You do not apologize to me. I'm the one that should be apologizing."

Zoey shook her head slightly and said, "You're doing what you promised. I'll get better." She straightened her back, stepping back into position. "I want to try again."

"Are you sure? I don't want you going too hard," he murmured, and she couldn't stop the blush that spread over her. She nodded, glad he stood behind her so she didn't have to meet his gaze.

Holding her posture like he'd shown her before, she tightened her hands on the bar, then heaved the weights up and out of the cradle. She dipped for her squat, exhaling on the down before raising up.

"Good," Chase said from behind her. "Keep your hips open, knees parallel to your shoulders... good. Good, Zoey."

She fairly glowed under his quiet praise and did another, her thighs starting to burn.

"Can you do another?" Chase murmured from behind her. She nodded, exhaling. Out of her peripheral she could see his hands outstretched on either side of her, ready in case she needed him. But he didn't touch her.

She repeated the motion, breathing through it. He had started her out with a lighter weight than she would have chosen for herself, and she was grateful. Just the bar and the two plates on either end were enough to make her sweat.

She breathed through another squat before rising.

"Give me one more," his voice was closer; he had stepped forward just the slightest as she hesitated, her legs, core, back, and arms straining. She nodded, her teeth gritted, before dipping again, letting out a grunt as she straightened. His fingertips brushed the undersides of her elbows as he guided her back into the cradle and she sucked in her breath as electricity coursed through her at the featherlight touch.

She ducked from under the bar and her breath stalled when she realized just how close he was behind her; she could almost feel him against her back. He backed up quickly, and she was surprised at the disappointment that skittered through her. "That was great, Zoey."

She turned to look up at him then, her gaze meeting his. He was breathing unsteadily, his lips slightly parted as he stared down at her.

But he dropped his gaze quickly, bending at the waist to retrieve the water bottle he'd set on the floor earlier. He took a long drink, and she reached for her water as well. "You're doing really well. I just don't want you pushing yourself too much. I know it's easy to lose yourself in a workout to... drown out other things."

It never failed to amaze Zoey how he could read her thoughts so easily. She shrugged then, shifting her weight from one foot to the other. "I just don't want to think about... that. If I let myself start thinking about it, I can't stop myself until I'm in a full anxiety attack."

"I know," he said gently. He nodded toward the locker rooms then. "We're just about out of time, I need to hit the shower before we take off." They headed in the direction of the locker rooms, and he stopped her just as they made it to the doors. Shay, that ornery blonde, was standing several feet away.

Zoey refused to glance in her direction, though she could feel the heated stare she and Chase were receiving. As if he could sense the other woman's stare and Zoey's change in mood, Chase just chuckled, notching his chin toward the women's locker room door. "I'll see you at home in a little bit, roomie."

"Right," Zoey breathed, wishing the floor would open up and swallow her whole. "Roomie."

Zoey disappeared into the locker room, showering quickly to rinse off the sweat. She changed clothes and was out within just a few minutes. Chase stood off to the side, his back to her as she exited. He was leaning one shoulder against a machine, Shay standing directly in front of him, and as Zoey hurried past, she watched as the blonde laughed at something Chase said, then placed her hand on his bicep.

Chase turned his head in the opposite direction for a moment, and Shay looked over at her, their eyes meeting. A smug smile tilted her lips, and then the hand still clutching Chase's bicep slid down his arm nearly to his wrist.

Jealousy ripped through Zoey like a freight train, and she stumbled, tripping on her own feet.

Pushing through the door to the sidewalk outside, Zoey hurried to her car, clambering into it. Her heartbeat roared in her ears, anger and jealousy warring in her. She shook her head to clear it. There was nothing going on between herself and Chase. She had no excuse to be jealous of that woman.

At least that's what she told herself as she started her car and pulled away from the curb.

TWENTY-FIVE

Zoey rolled over in bed, sighing into the darkness. Verity was sleeping soundly in her crib across the room, but Zoey had been awake for hours, unable to sleep.

A realization had dawned, crystal clear in her mind, as she'd pulled away from the gym earlier that morning. She wasn't entirely sure when it had happened, but without a doubt in her mind, she knew it to be true: she had developed a crush on Chase.

A really, *really big* crush.

Actually... that wasn't entirely true. Because Zoey feared it was far more than a simple crush. She had caught feelings. *Big feelings.*

For her brother's best friend.

Closing her eyes, she imagined him as he had been earlier, his fingers touching her arms, feather light, or how she had *wanted* him to lean in and kiss her... Butterflies seemed to take flight in her belly at the thought of Chase's lips on her own, of what he would taste like against her tongue... When

145

she thought of how Shay put her hands on him, it made her chest burn with a possessiveness that was alarming.

She wanted to know what it would feel like to have him touch *her*, every part of her. Her body flushed hot with the desire to touch and be touched overwhelming. She hadn't expected to feel that again for a long, long time, but here it was beckoning to her.

Perhaps Robby hadn't broken her completely after all.

Zoey regretted the thought as soon as it popped into her head; anxiety immediately began clawing at her chest, her throat closing, vision narrowing. She sat up in bed, clutching the fabric of her shirt and pulling it away from her neck, but the suffocating feeling didn't subside.

Nearly tripping on her own feet, she raced to the bedroom door as quietly as possible, tripping over her feet as she rushed across the hall. She made it to the bathroom just in time, vomiting into the toilet. Trembling violently, she sat back on her haunches, hands gripping the edge of the commode as she attempted to suck in lungful after lungful of air.

Tears started then, stinging her nose and then falling in tracks down her cheeks, and within several heartbeats she was sobbing, burying her face in her hands to stifle the sound. She was still so *angry*.

Robby had been her *friend*. Someone she trusted.

He had been in one of her college classes, and he'd introduced himself on the first day of class. By the end of the first week, he'd become a fast friend. He was charming, funny, and boyishly handsome.

It became a ritual of sorts for the two of them to meet each other in the cafeteria for lunch between classes several times a week.

Squeezing her eyes shut, Zoey panted into the darkness of the bathroom, not having taken the time to flip on the light as she'd sprinted to the toilet. Memories continued to roll through her.

Robby had said he was headed out with his two housemates and had invited her to a small dive bar a town away. While his two friends played billiards across the room, Robby and Zoey sat at the bar, laughing and flirting for hours. After downing a shot of fireball whisky, he had leaned in and kissed her, making goosebumps flash across her skin. She could taste the cinnamon flavored whisky on his tongue, and she could smell it as he leaned in close.

When he'd released her lips, she had smiled shyly and admitted that she hadn't been kissed in a long time, to which he had grinned and done it again, kissing her until she was breathless. This kissing was vastly different than the fumbling, awkward kisses her high school boyfriend had given her. Something new curled through her middle, a sensation she wasn't used to, but knew it had to be desire. She liked kissing Robby and let him do it again.

She came back from the restroom to a fresh drink—a long island, she was informed—and the first several sips were sickeningly strong. She pushed it away, claiming she didn't like it, but Robby had insisted she keep 'giving it a try'. Halfway through, Zoey could barely hold her head up, and she knew something wasn't right. She asked Robby to take her back to the dorms, because she didn't feel well. He agreed, paid their tab, and within minutes they were out the door.

It couldn't have been more than a twenty-minute drive from the bar to the dorms, but it felt like a lifetime to Zoey as she sat in the passenger seat, alert enough to know roughly where she was and who she was with, but her body wasn't cooperating; her hands wouldn't work, her head continually lolled to one side, and she struggled to form sentences.

She was grateful when Robby turned them into the familiar parking lot of the dorms, she could tell by the lights at the front door. He had helped her out of the car, but instead of walking her to the door, she'd been pushed into a darkened corner, sheltered between parked cars. Shoved onto her stomach on the cold, ice frosted pavement, she had tried to struggle; at least, her mind was screaming at her to fight, to kick, to bite, anything, as he'd pulled her clothes off.

She tried to scream, she wanted to, but nothing happened. Her face was ground into the pavement by one of his hands, and she felt the skin of her cheeks and temples tearing against the rough asphalt beneath her. He held her hands tightly behind her back, not that they would have been any use to her, whatever drug he'd slipped into her drink was enough to incapacitate her completely. His chest was pressed into her back, his face hovering over the side of her face as he moved over her, doing unspeakably vile things, and the smell of the cinnamon whisky on his breath as he panted above her made her gag uncontrollably.

Every particle of her being ached for the strength to stop it, to stop him, but she was helpless, trapped inside her own body. He was her friend. Her friend... the one that she had liked. Friends don't do this. Tears slid down her face, pain and fear all mixed together as he took her, hurt her, used her.

And then left her in the darkened parking lot, half naked in the cold and unable to move, when he had finished with her.

She remembered shivering uncontrollably, her muscles aching at the cold; it had snowed for the first time that day, leaving a dusting on the ground. She didn't know how long she lay there before someone found her, drifting in and out of consciousness as the police and EMTs arrived. She was loaded into an ambulance and transported to the hospital.

Zoey sat back against the wall of the bathroom, stretching her legs out in front of her as memories continued to roll through her in waves. Her sobs quieted, the whole-body tremors lessened, and eventually the tears slowed.

Breathe in. One. Two. Three. Four. Five.
Breathe out. Six. Seven. Eight. Nine. Ten.

Her family had been notified by the police and had stormed the ER room. As the drugs wore off and she became more lucid, she heard the doctors tell her mom and dad that they believed she had been drugged and that it was imperative that they perform a rape kit. Unable to stomach the agony on her parents' faces, she had insisted they remain outside. The next several hours were torturous, recounting the events over and over again for countless hospital staff and police officers.

It wasn't until one of the doctors touched her knee, patting it gently, innocently, that they would find out that the trauma would manifest through panic attacks. A psychiatrist was brought in to examine her, and she was diagnosed with PTSD.

After Zoey made her formal statement and made the decision to press charges, Robby was arrested, though was released on bail just a day later, his housemates had pooled their money to bail him out.

Her dorm room was vandalized, and she was made out to be a liar and a tease. His friends made sure to tell anyone that would listen how she had gone with them to the bar and had kissed him willingly. Zoey had made the decision to withdraw from school and moved out of the dorms to go back home.

The day she'd found out she was pregnant was the hardest day she'd lived through, second only to the day her mother had passed. Her mom had held her as she cried endlessly, smoothing her hair away from her face as she'd told her she would support her in any choice she made. She would have loved Verity.

Verity. Her beautiful, innocent baby girl. How had she gotten so lucky to get such a perfect baby out of such an ugly situation?

Zoey stood, flipping on the light and blinking through the sudden, blinding brightness. She splashed cold water on her face, washing away the tear tracks down her cheeks and chin, before patting it dry. Staring at her face in the mirror, she closed her eyes, breathing deeply and slowly.

"Inhale courage," she whispered.

Opening her eyes, she exhaled long and low.

"Exhale fear," she breathed out a sigh.

She reached for the light switch and turned it off before exiting the bathroom, moving blindly through the sudden darkness of the hallway after the brightly lit bathroom. She closed her bedroom door quietly, padding silently over to the crib on the other side of her room. She stared down at the sleeping, golden haired angel there. Her sweet, innocent child.

Zoey smoothed the rioting curls away from Verity's face, her tiny, rosebud mouth puckering slightly at the intrusion to her dreams.

She would be damned before she would let anyone harm her or let anyone take her away. She would fight like hell.

TWENTY-SIX

Chase leaned his head back against the wall, listening to the muffled sounds of Zoey's wracking sobs from inside the bathroom.

He'd lain awake for hours after getting them home, unable to shut his mind off, to forget the way Zoey's eyes had searched his, the way the softness of her arms felt beneath his fingertips.

Or how he'd never thought more about kissing someone than he did in that moment. He wondered what she would taste like against his tongue, what that impossibly soft hair would feel like between his fingers as they tunneled through it, bringing her mouth more firmly against his own.

And then Shay had been there, and he couldn't help but notice the way Zoey's mouth tightened every time the other blonde would come into their line of sight. He might have imagined it, but he liked to think maybe there was just a hint of jealousy in Zoey's indigo eyes. He admitted to himself now that he liked that thought. A lot.

Shay had cornered him while he waited for Zoey just outside the locker rooms, and when she'd let her hand slide down his arm to his wrist, he'd pulled away, in no uncertain terms telling her to keep her hands to herself as he turned away, just in time to see Zoey's caramel blonde head disappear out the front door. It was no guess that she'd seen the interaction between himself and Shay. His jaw tightened in annoyance. Shay was becoming a nuisance.

When he'd finally pulled into the driveway, most of the lights in the house were off, though he could see a dim light in Zoey's window.

He'd gone inside, heating up the dinner Zoey had left for him and hating himself for not rushing home, though he wasn't sure what he would have said if she'd still been in the kitchen when he'd walked in. When he'd finished, he headed up the stairs to the bathroom to shower quickly, then padded down the hallway, closing his own bedroom door and sliding in between the sheets, stacking his hands beneath his head as he stared up at the dark ceiling.

His imagination had begun torturing him again, imagining Zoey's sweet, soft body entwined with his own, her caramel hair hanging down on either side of her face, tickling his skin as she leaned over him, his hands spread wide on her waist as she moved... He groaned in the dark, palming his aching erection, drawing his hand from root to tip, wishing it was Zoey instead, knowing the futility of that wish.

Those violet eyes...he remembered the way she'd looked at him earlier, her eyes telling him everything he needed to know in that moment, and he swore beneath his breath as he fisted his cock in his hand and gave himself the release he desperately needed.

As his breathing settled and he cleaned up, he couldn't stop thinking that Zoey deserved better.

It was then that he heard her door open, and his heart skipped a beat before it sank into the pit of his stomach as he realized she was crying wretchedly. He slipped out of the bedroom door silently, padding down the hallway to stand just outside the door that had been left open just a hair.

Tears stung his nose at the sound of her weeping; sobs that seemed to come from the very pit of her soul. As he listened, he could make out whispered, broken words every so often. *"You were my friend"* and *"I hate you"* and *"You took everything from me"*.

Turning, he leaned against the wall, letting his head fall back and squeezing his eyes shut. This sweet, amazing woman had been through so much, and he didn't know half of it.

All he knew was how deeply he felt the need to protect her. It lived in him, completely, and he doubted it would ever go away.

He wanted to knock, to let her know she wasn't alone, that he was there if she needed him. He turned slightly so that he was angled toward the door, and he raised his hand to tap on the door but hesitated. He knew how private she was and doubted she would want to know he had heard her in a time as vulnerable as this.

As her crying slowed, he took a deep breath, mimicking one she made from inside the dark room.

He panicked for a moment when the light turned on, a tiny sliver casting outward into the hallway across the floor. He heard the water turn on and the unmistakable sound of splashing water on her face.

He held his breath as he listened, ready to move toward his bedroom, when he heard her quiet, reverent whisper, "Inhale courage... Exhale fear."

He was frozen in place when the light shut off and the door opened a heartbeat later. She crossed the hall quickly, shutting the bedroom door behind her. She hadn't seen him in the darkened hallway, and he used that time to pad silently back to his own room, closing the door as quietly as possible.

When he slid back into bed, he couldn't help the smile that tugged at one corner of his mouth.

He was so damn proud of her.

TWENTY-SEVEN

Christmas Eve dawned cold and crisp, and Zoey was happy when the sun made an appearance. The sunlight shone on the frost covered snow, making it glitter like diamonds. Even the branches of the trees were frosted, shimmering in the sunshine.

Verity awoke early, hungry, though she fell back to sleep as soon as she was done nursing. Zoey lowered her back into the crib and slipped back into bed herself, falling asleep and not waking until the sun had started to rise.

Slipping out of bed, she crossed to the door and made her way down to the kitchen. She glanced at the clock and then padded to the coffee pot, setting it to percolate so it would be ready when Chase got home from his night shift. They'd hardly seen each other in two days, as he'd been gone for a run when she'd woken the following morning, for which she was grateful. She knew her face had been pale, and her eyes were red rimmed and gritty from crying, and she didn't want to have to explain. As a rest day from the gym, she knew he wouldn't be waiting for her before work that morning, and they'd barely passed each other the night before as she'd rushed in from work and he'd been heading out the door for his night shift.

Turning on the stove, she waited for her water to boil for her tea.

As she was sitting down with her cup at the small dining table, she heard Chase's Jeep in the driveway and her heart began thudding in her chest. Those stupid, annoyingly possessive thoughts still clambered through her every time she remembered that the way Shay had put her hands on him made her hot with jealousy.

Her memory flashed to the way Chase had looked at her, those blue eyes hot on her mouth... and it made her flush for a different reason entirely.

The door opened and he ducked through it, closing it quickly against the bitter cold. Zoey held her breath as he caught sight of her at the table.

"Good morning," he said, his voice a low rumble as it reached her.

The sunlight filtering through the kitchen window danced in rays across the floor and opposite wall, casting the room in a golden glow that was a wonderful break from the bleak gray of winter that they had endured the last few weeks.

"Good morning," she whispered, her voice slightly breathless. His brown slacks fit exceptionally well to his long, muscular thighs, but his upper body was covered by his uniform jacket, thick and not well fitted. He took his patrol hat off, brushing his fingers up through the longer locks that fell over his brow as he took it off, then placed it on one of the wooden pegs next to the door. He shrugged out of his jacket, hanging it up next to the hat. With his back turned to her, she was afforded the luxury of looking at his backside without him knowing. His pants fit well there, too.

Zoey swallowed hard as he turned back toward her, his electric blue eyes meeting hers. "Uhh—" she stammered on a whisper, "I have coffee ready for you, if you'd like some."

"It smells amazing," he said with a tired smile and walked on heavy boots toward the opposite counter where the coffee had perked. Plucking a coffee cup from the cupboard, he poured a generous helping and took a swallow, making a *hasshhh* sound at the scalding temperature. Zoey's mouth went dry when he untucked his uniform shirt from the waistband of his pants, and scratched lightly, revealing several inches of his hard abdomen, before letting the untucked tails fall around his hips. "How did you sleep?"

Zoey blinked rapidly, stammering, "Huh?"

His cobalt blue eyes crinkled at the corners as a fleeting grin tugged at his mouth, and she sucked in her breath at the heat that blazed in those eyes momentarily. He stepped forward, touching just one strand of her hair that had fallen out of the bun on her head, tucking it back behind her ear. At the graze of just the tips of his fingers against the softness behind her ear, she shivered, her eyes fluttering closed.

Oh God... she liked that.

"I asked if you slept well," he repeated quietly, his voice low and husky.

"Oh," she struggled to say, nodding instead. She swallowed hard again as his fingers fell away from her. She was grateful he hadn't heard her anxiety attack the other night. She didn't want to have to talk about it. Not with him so near. Making her feel things. Delicious things. "I slept better last night. Verity was up early, hungry as a bear."

He chuckled lightly, "Is she still sleeping?"

He stepped around her chair and sank into an empty one kitty-corner to her own. He groaned lightly, and she could see the exhaustion on his handsome features. He was still adjusting to the back and forth of day shift to night shift. She couldn't imagine how difficult it was on one's body.

"She woke early to eat and then zonked back out," she said, shrugging. Now that he wasn't quite so close she could breathe easier, though when she looked at him for too long, she seemed to forget to breathe all over again.

"She must be going through a growth spurt," he said on a heavy exhale, and he scrubbed his hand over his face before taking another large swallow of coffee. He extended his legs out in front of him, his feet nearly touching hers under the table, and rolled his hips down, leaning back against the chair.

"You're telling me," Zoey laughed softly, shaking her head. "It's a good thing you've got me working out, she's turning into a tank."

"Good," he chuckled. "My little sunshine needs more rolls on her legs."

When his words registered in her mind, her eyes flashed to his, her heart thumping hard in her chest. She liked the way he made it sound like Verity was *his*.

She doubted that's how he meant it. But, she still liked it.

He coughed awkwardly and she dropped her gaze quickly, fiddling with the tea bag still in her mug. He rolled his spine so that he was sitting straighter in the chair, pulling his legs back toward his body.

"I should go for a run, but I'm afraid I'll fall asleep while running," he said and then yawned broadly.

"Go to bed," she murmured, her heart tugging. "I'm sure your run can wait."

He pushed himself to his feet by bracing his hands on his knees, groaning as he did. He took a step away from the table, and before she knew what he was doing, leaned down to press a kiss to the top of her head.

She froze, as did he.

Zoey could feel the expulsions of his breath as they fanned over her hair before he straightened. "I'm sorry," she heard him murmur. "I didn't—"

"It's okay," she said, raising her chin to look up at him. "I— I didn't mind."

She watched his Adam's apple dip in his throat as he swallowed. "I'm gonna go shower and then try to sleep for a while," she heard him say, and she nodded. He turned on his booted heel and made it to the arched doorway of the kitchen before he stopped. "Zoey—"

Verity's cry from upstairs halted whatever he'd been about to say, instead he turned away, glancing up the stairway to where the sound came from. Zoey stood, placing her cup beside the sink. She walked toward him, and he pressed against the doorjamb to allow her to pass.

Feeling bold, she placed her hand against his forearm, feeling the muscles beneath the fabric of his shirt jump at the contact. She squeezed lightly, smiling up at him shyly. "Go get some sleep."

Then, before she could melt into a puddle of embarrassment, she fled up the stairs. She was in the process of changing Verity's diaper when she heard Chase's footfalls down the hallway. She held her breath as he seemed to pause outside her door for an extended heartbeat before his footsteps faded down the hall, his bedroom door clicking shut quietly behind him.

Zoey turned to stare at the door for a long time after he'd retreated down the hallway, almost wishing he would come back.

She was in big trouble.

TWENTY-EIGHT

"You look refreshed," Zoey said as Chase descended the stairs to the living room. She graced him with a glowing smile that made Chase's footsteps falter. His heart thudded erratically in his chest at the brilliance of it.

He rubbed one hand over the back of his neck and returned her smile with one of his own. "I feel refreshed. The last couple nights have been tough. I guess I needed the sleep."

He had been appalled when he'd woken to find that it was after five in the evening. He'd slept for almost nine hours. Disappointment had engulfed him when he'd realized he would only have an hour or so with Zoey and Verity before he would need to be back to work for another night shift.

"Merry Christmas Eve, by the way," she said, standing from where she'd been kneeling on the living room floor, arranging a few presents under the Christmas tree that stood in the corner. She was dressed in black leggings that fit her snugly, delineating her curves. A hunter green, long-sleeved top brushed her thighs and hugged her chest and abdomen. She'd started wearing more form fitting clothes in the last few weeks, a testament that she was feeling more confidence in her body.

He both loved and hated it.

On the one hand, he loved seeing her body outlined by her clothes. On the other hand, it made it difficult not to stare, and when he did that, his cock would start to throb, for it seemed to have a mind of its own.

Her caramel golden hair fell in soft waves around her shoulders that begged to be stroked. He ached to sink his fingers into it, could imagine his hand cupping the back of her head as she leaned in to press her mouth to his, her tongue sliding past her lips to meet his—

A groan started to form in his throat, and he coughed to cover it before she could hear it. She tilted her head to look at him curiously, which made him think he hadn't hidden it as well as he'd hoped.

"I have dinner ready, if you're hungry?" she asked as she stepped around the couch, coming toward him where he stood, stalled, by the door of the kitchen. "It's not much, I didn't know if you'd eat before work, and Tommy is at Shaun's..."

"It smells wonderful," he said, following her into the kitchen. He felt awkward and gumpy as he trailed behind her, his heart still hammering in his chest, his dick halfcocked in his jeans. It got worse when she bent at the waist to reach into the oven, pulling out a sheet tray. He hated himself for thinking of her this way.

"Pot pies from scratch," she said proudly as she placed the hot tray on a heating pad, turning to beam a smile at him. "Mom always made them Christmas Eve, since they were easy and filling. She always had a huge feast for Christmas Day, and never wanted to spend the entire day in the kitchen Christmas Eve as well. I thought I'd give them a try."

Chase tamped down his unruly thoughts and stepped forward, leaning down to sniff at the golden-brown pastries. "They smell amazing, Zoey."

"Thank you," she breathed and beamed up at him again. She wrung her fingers around a dish towel in her hands. Sadness crept into her eyes for a flash, before she smiled once again. "I'm trying my best not to be sad. I know today and tomorrow will be hard, but I want it to be happy for Verity. It's her first Christmas. I don't want to be a downer for her."

"You're allowed to grieve, Zoey," he murmured, straightening.

"I know," she said and nodded, still wringing the dish towel between her fingers. "Dad came by earlier, while you were sleeping. I think I understand more now, that being here is too hard for him. I was too angry at him for how he was choosing to grieve, and that wasn't fair to him or myself. I needed to let go of that anger." She took a deep breath in and let it go on a long exhale. "Once I did that, I felt better. I'm still sad, and I know I'm always going to miss her. But I have so much to be grateful for."

He thought his heart was going to pound out of his chest when she looked up at him then, those violet eyes searching his. "I have my dad, Tommy and Shaun, and Verity. And you."

She blushed at her admission, and he liked the way her cheeks flushed pink. She waved the dish towel and shrugged self-consciously. He watched as the tip of her tongue darted out to wet her lips before she swallowed hard, and he felt his cock twitch at the motion. "Anyway, sit down, and I'll get you a plate."

He sat down at the table, watching her as she flit around the kitchen, plating the pot pies before placing one in front of him. "Do you want a beer?"

He shook his head as he picked up the fork she'd brought him. "No, thank you."

"Right, you work tonight, I don't know why I forgot," she rambled softly, laughing at herself. "How about a soda? Water?"

"Water is fine," he said and smiled. "I can get it, Zoey."

"No, no," she rushed to say as he made to stand, skirting around where he sat to fetch a large glass of ice water. "I said just sit there. I got it."

When she placed the water in front of him and lowered herself into the chair opposite him, she smiled shyly before dropping her eyes to her own plate in front of her.

"Where is Verity?" he asked before digging into the potpie with his fork, a tendril of steam rising from the middle. He blew on it lightly before taking a bite. He rolled his eyes heavenward. "Well, this is amazing."

Zoey sent him another one of those beaming smiles that made his chest feel warm. "She's napping."

He nodded around another bite, getting lost in the deliciousness of the meal in front of him. He hated to admit it, but he liked this. This easy, comfortable routine that he and Zoey had slowly morphed into. Almost like they were more than just roommates. That gut gnawing guilt always came back to haunt him, though.

She wasn't his.

But she could be. If he stopped fighting it.

He shook his head, dispelling the thought as soon as it came to his mind. He couldn't do it. He wouldn't do it.

Oh, but he wanted to. Lord did he want to.

"Shaun's parents invited us over for Christmas dinner tomorrow afternoon. Shaun said you're included in that invitation," she was saying, though he was barely able to pay attention with the direction his wayward thoughts had gone again. She pursed her lips and blew on the forkful of potpie she held, and he nearly catapulted out of his chair at the innocent eroticism of it. His cock jumped painfully.

Nope. Don't do this. Don't, he warned himself fiercely. *Don't look at her mouth.*

"Chase?" she said softly, pausing with her fork on her way to her mouth.

"Uhh," he stammered, shoving another bite into his mouth. Once he'd chewed and swallowed, he nodded and said, "That's very kind of them. Of course I'll go."

Again, she graced him with that smile that took his breath away, and he admitted to himself he was in far more trouble than he'd given himself credit for. If she would continue to give him that smile, he would do just about anything.

Zoey chatted animatedly throughout the remainder of their meal, and he was surprised when he realized the time. Disappointment flooded him; he didn't want to leave.

As he stood and took his dishes to the sink, rinsing them before placing them in the dishwasher, he watched Zoey.

He wondered if they would have gotten here on their own one way or another, even without Tommy planting that seed of possibility in him. He'd always liked Zoey, cared about her; but it had been platonic, like a big brother for a sister. After so many weeks of being around her, getting to know her as more than his best friend's little sister, he liked her in a different way.

He liked the way her hair glistened in the sunlight when it would filter in through the windows. He adored the way her head would toss back with tinkling laughter, when her smile would be wide and free of all the fear and anxiety and grief she seemed to be burdened with constantly. He liked how she cared deeply for her friends and family and how incredibly kind her heart was. She was a loving and gentle mother to Verity and a fiercely loyal friend and sister.

He had become obsessed with the way those deep violet eyes would watch him, sometimes with curiosity, sometimes awe, and he knew he had seen desire in them just that morning.

Now that he had seen glimpses of the desire she couldn't completely hide away, he wanted to see more of it. He'd give his left leg to see her flushed with arousal for him.

But more than that, he enjoyed spending time with her, at home, at the gym. She was funny and sweet and unintentionally sexy.

He found that he craved her company when he wasn't around her in a way that he had never experienced in any of his past relationships. Just relaxing at home, laying on the couch watching tv or a movie with her in the recliner beside him, was enough. They talked endlessly, and he'd learned so much about her that he'd never known before. She had a massive celebrity crush on some guy named Taylor Lautner, and something about *Team Jacob*, whatever that meant. *Friends* was her guilty pleasure tv show, and she admitted to having an unhealthy addiction to mini M&M's, and a ridiculously large stash of lilac scented candles hidden in the closet upstairs.

He had also learned that she absolutely adored hot bubble baths and tried his best to make sure she got to sneak away for one every few days.

When she told him she volunteered once a month at the local women's resource center to help other abused women, his heart had melted. She admitted that some days were harder than others, as it brought back her own traumas, but she would push through in order to assist the women in need, because she knew how badly they needed it.

He'd been floored by her courage and heart.

Again, he wondered if they would have ended up here without Tommy's outrageous plan. Looking at her now as she wiped her hands on the dish towel after clearing the table and counters, turning her face to smile over at him, he could admit that they just might have. She had wiggled her shy, cautious little self into his heart, irrevocably.

TWENTY-NINE

When Zoey's phone dinged just after midnight, she picked it up and opened it, smiling when she saw that it was a text from Chase while he was on duty.

> Merry Christmas, Zoey.

Typing a quick response, she hit send.

> Merry Christmas, Chase.

It wasn't long before another ding sounded, and she opened it, stifling a laugh so she didn't wake Verity as she rolled her eyes.

> You should be asleep.

Typing quickly, she sent:

> I was, but there is this guy that won't stop messaging me.

Waiting, she giggled when his response was swift.

I can have him arrested for you.

She sent back:

That's not necessary, I have
a friend that's a cop.

Before he could respond, she sent another.

Shouldn't you be working? Or is
someone bothering you?

When no response came right away, she set the phone down, turning onto her side. She was almost asleep when it dinged again, and she rolled over to grab it quickly.

It's a quiet night, and my
roommate is texting me while
she should be sleeping. But
I don't mind. She's kinda like my
best friend.

Zoey's heart pounded in her throat, and she half sat up, as if she needed a different position to better read the text. He thought of her as his best friend?

She stared at the text for a long time, then let it fall into her lap as she let out a breath that she didn't realize she had been holding. She swallowed past her dry throat, and then her shoulders drooped as she reread the text.

"Of course he only sees you as a friend, you dummy," she whispered to herself in the dark of the room. She flopped back down onto the pillow. Holding the phone above her, she reread it over and over. Did she even want Chase to like her as more?

Typing out a message, she hit send.

> Well, your roommate sounds like she needs to get a life and leave you to your work.

Almost immediately a new message popped up.

> Sounds like my roommate needs to get some sleep. I can still arrest this dude for keeping you up late. He sounds like a douche bag.

Before she could respond, another message bubble popped up:

> I just wanted to be the first one to say Merry Christmas. Give my little sunshine a snuggle for me when she wakes up.

Zoey sighed into the darkness of her bedroom. She rolled her head to face the window, where a sliver of pale moonlight filtered in through the panes. Snow had begun to fall outside, and Zoey could see the big, fat flakes that drifted slowly to the ground.

Her phone dinged in her hand.

Look outside.

Clambering out of her bed none too gracefully, she rushed to the window, pushing the curtains aside. Her heart thudded erratically in her chest and she let out a silent huff of laughter.

She watched as the window of the police cruiser rolled down, and his handsome face appeared in the window, his left arm resting on the ledge. He waved, and a smile split her face as she waved back. She could see his phone lit up in his other hand as he typed. Her phone dinged again.

Go to sleep. I'll see you in the morning.

She shook her head, another silent laugh escaping her as she read it. She typed back quickly before he drove away.

You're bossy.

Seconds later, he replied:

She waved once more, smiling ridiculously to herself as she typed:

Her phone dinged one more time, and she read:

The blue and red lights on top of the cruiser flashed briefly and she saw his hand wave one more time toward her before the window slid up and he slowly pulled away from the curb. She watched out the window until his taillights disappeared down the street before padding back to bed and climbing in under the covers.

With that same ridiculous grin on her face, she was asleep as soon as her head hit the pillow.

THIRTY

Zoey woke early, as if her body couldn't stand to be asleep for a moment longer. Like a kid on Christmas, she was eager for the day to start.

But she was more excited for Chase to come home.

She was giddy, heart racing, butterflies fluttering crazily in her belly. Hoping she had enough time to shower before Verity woke up, she slipped across the hall and showered as quickly as possible. She was just wrapping her hair in the towel when she heard Verity begin to fuss and raced back across the hall to her before she could turn into a flailing, hangry gremlin baby.

Once Verity was satisfied, Zoey got them both dressed quickly and headed downstairs. Setting Verity in the pack-n-play in the living room with a handful of baby toys, Zoey fairly skipped into the kitchen. In minutes she had the tea kettle on to warming and Chase's coffee pot on to percolate. Once those were started, she began prep for her mother's homemade cinnamon rolls.

After mixing the ingredients for the dough, rolling it out on the counter was cathartic and gave her tumultuous mind the space it needed to wander.

Was she crushing on Chase simply because he was here, around every day? 'Close proximity' and all that jazz? Or...was it more? Could it possibly be that something inside her was being healed? That she might be ready for something?

Slicing the dough into strips, she set them aside and started mixing together the softened butter, brown sugar, and cinnamon for the filling. Her mother always insisted on a healthy dash of vanilla, so she added that as well. Using a spatula to spread the gooey brown mixture on each slice of the dough, then painstakingly rolled each one, placing it in a glass baking dish.

Once all the cinnamon rolls were placed into the baking dish, she put them in the oven. Dusting her hands off, she walked into the living room and crooned, "Are you ready for some breakfast?" to Verity, who had rolled onto her belly and had managed to climb up onto all fours, rocking there excitedly. "You're going to be crawling before we know it!"

Scooping Verity up, she snuggled her close, letting her nose rest in the crook of her little neck. She inhaled deeply, her baby smell soothing. Verity smacked Zoey's face with her little hands and turned her face toward Zoey, placing her slobbery mouth against Zoey's cheek. She laughed and hugged her close again as she walked into the kitchen, pulling out the highchair and quickly strapping her into it securely.

She had just finished mashing a soft banana to spoon feed Verity when she heard Chase's Rubicon pull into the driveway. Sitting up straighter in her seat at the dining table in front of Verity's highchair, she held her breath, waiting for him to come to the door. Would things be different now?

Why would he want that? she asked herself sadly, dropping her gaze from the door and picking up the baby spoon, air-planing a spoonful of the mashed banana toward Verity's waiting mouth. *He thinks of us as roommates. That's it. He's made sure to remind you of that multiple times, Zoey. Stop wishing for something that's not going to happen.*

But when she heard his heavy footfalls just outside the door, she couldn't help but wish that just maybe that it would.

The door opened and he walked through, turning to close it quickly when he saw the two of them sitting at the dining table, making sure not to let cold air in to reach Verity. He sniffed appreciatively in the air, his eyes going to the oven.

"Cinnamon rolls?" he asked, his dark eyebrows raised in surprise.

"Homemade, from scratch," Zoey said with a smile, before turning back to Verity and spooning another glob of bananas into her mouth. She spit the bite out, which Zoey picked up with the spoon against her chin.

"Like the ones your mom used to make?" he asked, stepping into the kitchen after hanging his patrol hat and jacket on the hook by the door. He stepped toward her and Verity, standing about a foot away.

Zoey nodded, glancing up at him—a long way up—and she blushed to the roots of her hair when she realized her face was level with his lap, which was close enough that if she moved her elbow outward, she would bump him.

He didn't notice though, his attention was on the baby in the highchair. He bent at the waist, kissing the top of her golden, curly topped head. Verity slapped the tray of the highchair in excitement, her little face turning to beam a mostly toothless grin up at him.

"Good morning, my little sunshine," he crooned, then turned his head to look at Zoey, and she caught her breath at how close he was. His cobalt blue eyes found hers, and he murmured low, "Good morning, Zoey."

"Good morning," she whispered, her throat going dry. Butterflies erupted in her belly and chest as she dropped her gaze to his full lips. *Oh boy.*

"How was your night?" he asked, dropping into a crouch beside her and Verity. His left hand rested on the back of Verity's highchair, his right hand draped between his knees, his elbow resting on his bent knee. "Did that guy ever stop bothering you so you could sleep?"

Zoey blushed again, twisting her gaze from his handsome face back to the plate of mashed up bananas. Digging another small scoop up, she held it out to Verity, who gobbled it up eagerly. "I think this one cop scared him off."

His eyes crinkled at the corners and one side of his mouth tilted up in a grin. "Is that so?"

"Do you do that often?" Zoey asked before she could talk herself out of it, pushing the banana around on the small plate. Her heart was fluttering in her chest.

"Do what?" he asked, his voice low.

"Drive by the house at night?" she whispered.

Peeking at him through her lashes, she couldn't stop the flush that erupted across her cheeks and chest. He was staring so intently at her, she was worried he could see all the way inside her head.

"Yes," he said simply, and she raised her eyes to his again. "Especially if I know Tommy is at Shaun's for the night. I just... I like to check in."

"Chase..." she whispered, though she didn't know what she was going to say after that. It trailed off her lips, hanging in between them. She swallowed hard, then let her gaze fall back to his lips. Then, as doubt filled her once again like a bucket of ice water over her, she mumbled, "Umm, I should check the cinnamon rolls..."

He stayed crouched next to her for a moment longer, and she could feel his eyes on her face, watching her, before he stood and backed away. She breathed slightly easier, though frustration at the realization that he would never want her the way she wanted him crashed over her.

She stood, crossing to the oven. Pulling an oven mitt on her hand, she opened the oven and checked the rolls, before pulling them out, satisfied with how they looked. Carefully placing the hot baking dish on the stovetop to cool, she took the oven mitt off and set it aside, turning to glance at him over her shoulder.

When she did, she froze.

The expression on his face as he stared at her was one mixed with longing, desire, and torment.

His hands clenched and unclenched at his sides, as if itching to touch something he knew he shouldn't.

Zoey rotated to face him, her breath coming in soft and quick puffs. "Chase..." she whispered huskily, and those incredibly blue eyes of his found hers, spearing her to the floor.

And then he was gone, striding through the arched doorway to the living room, his booted footfalls sounding on the stairs as he climbed them quickly.

Zoey clutched the fabric of her shirt over her chest, disappointment choking her.

THIRTY-ONE

He couldn't get away fast enough.

Chase fairly ran up the stairs, taking them two at a time. He closed the bedroom door, tearing at his uniform until he'd stripped his shirt off. Running his hand over the bulge behind the fly of his pants, he groaned miserably.

He was running out of excuses not to do exactly what he had been fighting against. He had told Tommy he would never do it. He had told himself he would never do it.

But lord, when she looked at him like that, with those big, violet eyes, her lips parted slightly and looking so goddamn kissable... he wanted nothing more than to lean in and taste just how soft her lips were against his.

Every single particle of his being ached to go back downstairs and pull her to him, bury his fingers in her hair, and press his lips to hers. Her eyes said she wanted him to, but he wouldn't lay a finger on her until he heard the words come out of her mouth.

She had to tell him exactly what she wanted before he would touch her.

Chase scrubbed one hand over his face, pushing his hair back off his brow as self-loathing coursed through him.

You're not going to touch her, ever, he told himself ferociously. *She deserves better than this. Than you. Enough of this, of harboring any thought of the possibility. Enough!*

Tamping down the raging erection he still sported, he called himself every filthy name he could think of. She was everything good, innocent, and sweet.

He was not.

He was tainted, broken, and damaged. He had no right to want her the way he did.

If Tommy hadn't put this stupid, moronic idea in his head... he wouldn't be having these thoughts. Not about Zoey. He'd be fine booty-calling Shay any time he needed a quick lay.

And then he dropped his chin to his chest. Because he knew it was a lie. After the last month, being near Zoey, he knew he would be doing the same thing. He wanted her, even without the proposition her brother had offered him. He would still be thinking about kissing her, touching her, aching for her.

"God dammit," he snarled into the empty room even as he released the fly of his pants, palming his aching cock.

Gnashing his teeth together, he growled low as he stroked from root to tip, and it didn't take long before he felt his orgasm climbing steadily, starting at the base of his spine and radiating out until he came with a groan.

As his breathing came back to normal, he stiffened, and then clenched his eyes shut tight as he heard soft footsteps retreating from the other side of his door.

"Fuck," he whispered brokenly, knowing without a doubt that she had heard everything that had happened on this side of the door.

THIRTY-TWO

Zoey backed away from Chase's door, her heart thundering so loudly in her ears she couldn't hear anything else. She felt hot, so hot she pressed her hands to her cheeks, convinced they were on fire.

The noises coming from inside Chase's bedroom were carnal and sexy and forbidden. His deep growling moan and labored breathing told her everything.

Was he thinking about me? she wondered, her own breathing choppy and uneven as she slowly melted down the hallway, careful to be silent. She shook her head then, berating herself. *Of course he's not thinking about you, you idiot.*

Slipping back down the stairs to the living room where she had put Verity in her pack n play for her morning nap, she walked on trembling legs into the kitchen. Her body was on fire, desire pooling between her thighs. She squeezed them tightly together, gasping at the sensation.

She... wanted Chase.

Badly.

She stopped trying to deny it, letting it course through her fully. She wanted Chase. She liked him. He was outrageously attractive, but beyond that, she liked how comfortable she had become with him in the last weeks. He was making her feel things she hadn't felt in a long time, possibly ever.

Because what he had been doing upstairs... was *hot*.

She flushed again when she thought about watching him, wanting to see all of him, every last inch of his glorious body. She had been a virgin until Robby... *No,* she snapped to herself. She liked how this felt, and she wasn't going to let *him* take this, too. She wanted to see Chase, wanted to press her hands to his chest, run her fingers over the slope of his ribcage down to where it cinched at his narrow waist, wanted to press her lips to the hard ridges of his back, wanted to see *that*.

She wanted to touch him. Everywhere.

Again, pressing her thighs together tightly, she nearly moaned out loud. She had never felt desire like this, and he hadn't even done anything to her. Hadn't touched her. All he had to do was touch himself, from the privacy of his own room, and she was a puddle.

Shame crashed over her thinking about how she had invaded his privacy. She would have been mortified if he'd done the same to her.

And then she flushed hot all over again when she thought about Chase listening as she touched *herself*, and her knees almost gave out beneath her.

Fanning herself, she wondered what the hell was wrong with her.

Or, was this... *normal?*

She was woefully inexperienced in the sex department. Her high school boyfriend had been awkward and fumbling and had kept his mouth closed when they kissed. She had liked Robby kissing her, it had felt good, stirring a new kind of awakening in her that she hadn't felt before.

But this... This made her feel like a live wire had been touched to her skin. She felt shaky, but it wasn't fear or anxiety that made her tremble. Was this how true desire was supposed to feel? This, she wasn't scared of. In fact, she craved it.

Again, she clenched her thighs together against the onslaught of arousal she could feel curling in her middle, and for the first time since the attack, she wanted to touch herself, to ease that ache.

No. She wanted *Chase* to touch her.

Burying her face in her hands, she leaned her hips against the counter beside the sink. She felt like she was on fire, her body flushed and hot, her breaths still coming in short, quick puffs through the gaps of her hands. When she shifted her tightly clenched thighs, her tight leggings rubbed against her clit and she bit her bottom lip to keep from moaning at how good it felt.

Zoey jumped as if she'd been stung when she heard Chase's footsteps coming down the stairs. She turned to face the sink, angling her face away from the doorway as he stepped through. Her face flamed scarlet, knowing what he'd just been doing and praying that he couldn't tell how she'd worked herself into a fine frenzy at just the thought of him.

He stepped wide around her, making sure not even a thread of their clothing brushed against each other as he passed. He picked up one of the cinnamon rolls and brought it to his mouth, but she cried out, "Oh! They don't have the icing on them yet!"

His hand stopped just shy of his mouth and he turned those incredible blue eyes on her. He raised his eyebrows in surprise and Zoey reached for the bowl of homemade cream-cheese icing she'd whipped together. Dipping a spoon into the bowl, she waited until he lowered the cinnamon roll away from his mouth to drizzle some of the gooey icing over the top.

She could feel his breath against the top of her head as she leaned close to him, and when a drizzle of icing landed on her knuckles, she raised her hand to her mouth. Sucking the icing off, her eyes raised to his and she stopped breathing entirely.

His eyes were blazing hot and trained on her mouth, where she'd just licked off the white icing, and she realized with a flash of heat down her body what it looked like. Butterflies taking flight in her belly like a tornado, she licked her lips and took a shuddering breath in.

As if in slow motion, his eyes raised from her mouth to hers, and a shiver of anticipation erupted over her, making gooseflesh break out over her skin. Squeezing the icing bowl in her arms, she pressed it against her middle as if clutching to a life preserver. Her head tilted in the opposite direction as his as his head lowered, again, as if in slow motion, toward her.

The fingers still holding the spoon slackened and the metal spoon clattered to the linoleum floor at their feet, but they barely noticed. Blood roared in Zoey's ears, drowning out everything except the sound of Chase's labored breathing as his mouth got closer and closer to her own.

The icing bowl was pressed tight between their bodies now as he had gravitated toward her, the only thing moving was his upper body as he leaned down, and Zoey thought she just might pass out if his lips didn't touch hers in the next heartbeat. His eyes never left hers, searching for any trace of anxiety or fear, but there was none; not one ounce of it clouded her mind.

As his lips grazed her cheek, she felt his warm breath against her, and she held perfectly still as those lips moved, painfully slow, toward her awaiting lips. She'd never wanted something more.

The front door banged open and Zoey jumped clear out of her skin, nearly dropping the bowl of icing before her fingers clutched it to her middle tightly. Chase spun on his heel, turning away from the door just as Shaun called out, "Merry Christmas ya filthy animals!"

Shaun was backing into the door hunched over, dragging a large laundry basket filled to the brim with wrapped presents. She hadn't witnessed the interaction between Zoey and Chase. Zoey blew out an unsteady breath, risking a glance over at Chase, who still had his back to them. He had set the uneaten cinnamon roll on the counter beside him and she could see the way his broad, hard back rose and fell with his uneven breathing.

Zoey flushed hot all over again. Chase had almost kissed her!

Tommy ran up to the door then, grating out irritably, "I told you to wait for me, I could have helped carry that." Shaun was still pulling the heavy, gift laden laundry basket by one handle through the kitchen. She straightened, letting out an exasperated huff and Zoey saw her roll her eyes as she placed her hands on her hips.

"I'm not helpless, Tommy," Shaun snapped, her tone laced with annoyance. Zoey raised her eyebrows, curious at whatever bug had gotten up both their butts this morning. "I have a broken pinky, not a broken wrist."

"You broke your pinky?" Zoey asked as she bent over to pick up the spoon she'd dropped earlier, noticing the small white and blue medical brace on Shaun's right pinky finger. Placing the spoon in the sink, she asked, "How'd you do that?"

Shaun raised her hand, as if inspecting it all over again and shrugged nonchalantly. "Meh, just got it caught at work. It's no biggie."

"It could have been your arm," Tommy snapped, crossing his arms over his muscled chest.

"Yeah, well, it wasn't!" Shaun snapped back, notching one hip out dramatically.

"You shouldn't be working on those cars when you're alone at the shop," Tommy grated, shifting from one foot to the other. Zoey watched out of the corner of her eye as Chase finally turned to face them all, after composing himself. Shaun's snort of derision brought her attention back to her friend.

"I have been working on *'those cars'* since I was twelve, Tommy. Since when does my career bother you so much?"

"Career?" Tommy laughed, and Zoey saw Shaun's face turn to stone as she stared at her fiancé. She was shocked at the way her brother was talking to Shaun. "You work in a mechanic shop."

"And I make damn good money doing it!" Shaun said quietly, seething. Zoey could tell by the slight trembling in Shaun's body that she was barely containing her anger. "Or are you just mad that I make more money than you?"

Tommy's brown eyes blazed with fury and he stomped through the kitchen past the three of them. Turning at the door, he sneered, "You're a real heartless bitch, you know that?"

"Whoa," Chase snapped at his best friend, his head swiveling sharply toward the shorter man. "You can be mad but you're not going to talk to her like that."

"Bite me," Tommy snarled before turning and heading up the stairs. His bedroom door slammed, and Zoey flinched at the sound. As far as she knew, Tommy had never spoken to Shaun that way, at least he better not have. He had been raised to be respectful and kind. Whatever was bothering him be damned, he knew better.

Shaun was still facing the doorway where he'd disappeared, staring blankly through the living room. Zoey touched her elbow and Shaun turned her head to look down at her, a half-smile, half-grimace pulling at her lips. "I shouldn't have said that; it was unfair."

"He'll calm down and then apologize," Zoey murmured, though she was angry at her brother. "I don't know what's gotten into him lately. He's been kind of a dick."

Shaun sank into one of the dining chairs and Chase stepped around them both to pour cups of coffee, handing one to Shaun, who thanked him with a sad smile. Zoey watched as he picked up his forgotten cinnamon roll, popping half of it into his mouth before his eyes met hers. She blushed and looked away quickly as he chewed.

"Free proposed to Jodi last night," Shaun said and smiled at the two of them then, and Zoey could see the happiness she felt for her sister in her sapphire eyes. "It was exactly the kind of proposal that Jodi deserved; sweet and romantic and intimate. Free is... so perfect for her." Then her shoulders dropped, and she took a sip of her coffee before staring into the mug morosely. "But then Tommy asked when we are going to get married, or at least start planning, and I said I'm not in a rush which made him angry. It's been... strained between us ever since."

Zoey turned toward the stove, picking up the bowl of icing and a clean spoon, drizzling the sugary confection over the now long cooled cinnamon rolls. Dishing one onto a small plate, she popped it into the microwave for a few seconds before placing it in front of Shaun, who smiled up at her before digging in gratefully. "These are your mom's recipe, aren't they?"

Zoey nodded, smiling, before glancing up at Chase, who had leaned his hips against the counter, holding his fresh cup of coffee in his hands, watching the two of them as they talked. His brows were furrowed, and she wondered briefly what he was thinking about to cause that look on his face.

Around a large bite of the cinnamon roll, Shaun said, "You guys are still more than welcome to come over for Christmas dinner. Mom is already planning on you guys being there." She swallowed and took a drink of her coffee before continuing, "Tommy will just have to get over this little PMS fit of his."

Licking her fingers noisily, she stood from the table and walked to the stove, dishing up another helping and carrying it to the microwave to heat it up. Her long, curly dark brown hair was pulled back into a loose braid that fell over her right shoulder, and tendrils that had come loose from the braid framed her face. Shaun then dished up another cinnamon roll, popping it in the microwave when hers was done, and then handed it to Zoey.

"I know you haven't had one yet," she said, forcing the plate into Zoey's hands. "Sit down, eat it. They're delicious."

Zoey did as she was told, sinking into the chair kitty-corner from Shaun and dug in, smiling when the familiar treat hit her taste buds. Grief assailed her for a moment, and she looked over at Chase, who smiled gently. She wondered if he could tell she was fighting that wave of sadness that crested over her, but then she smiled again. Of course, he could tell. He could always tell, somehow. He could read her better than anyone ever had.

When Shaun had finished her second cinnamon roll, she smacked her lips and sighed, then looked around. "Where's my girl?"

Zoey motioned with her chin toward the arched doorway to the living room. "Down for her nap—"

Shaun was already out of her seat, depositing the now empty plate into the sink, before striding toward the doorway. A second later, Zoey rolled her eyes when she heard Shaun wake Verity up by saying in a loud whisper, "Wake up my little elf, Auntie wants to get into some mischief on this Christmas morning."

THIRTY-THREE

Tommy remained sulking upstairs for over an hour, until Zoey marched up the steps and banged on the door until he opened it. When he did, she pointed one stern finger in his face and said, "Number one, if you *ever* talk to Shaun like that again I will personally kick your ass myself. Mom would be so disappointed in what happened downstairs, and you were raised better than that. Number two," she snapped, reaching forward with her other hand, slapping a Santa hat against his chest with her palm. He laughed, grabbing hold of the hat where it was still pressed to his chest, and then she dragged him out the door by the hand. Pushing him toward the stairs, she huffed, "I want to open presents! Now, get downstairs and stop being ornery! It's Christmas!"

Chase was walking around with Verity in his arms, bouncing her gently as they descended the stairs. Tommy walked over to where Shaun was sitting on the couch, bending at the waist and pressing his hands into the couch cushions on either side of her as he leaned in to press a hot, open-mouthed kiss to her pouting one. "I'm sorry. Will you forgive me?" Zoey heard him whisper against Shaun's mouth, though she had turned swiftly away from them at the start of the kiss. Zoey blushed furiously at the quiet rustling of clothing, and she could only imagine what the two of them were doing now.

When she risked a glance behind her, Shaun was stuffing the red Santa hat onto Tommy's head, then kissed him one more time before he straightened.

Chase moved around the living room to sink into the recliner chair, still holding Verity in one arm, and he placed a fresh, steaming mug of coffee on the end table next to him with his free hand. As Tommy disappeared into the kitchen to pour himself a cup of coffee, Zoey stepped toward the mantle and plucked the stockings hanging there off the hooks, passing them out to Shaun and Chase, placing Tommy's on the couch next to Shaun. She turned back to the last two, picking up Verity's 'Baby's 1st Christmas' stocking. She reached for hers but knew before she picked it up that it was empty.

A mini wave of grief settled over her before she pushed it away, turning and setting it down as she moved toward Chase and Verity.

Tommy came back into the living room, settling on the couch next to Shaun, his left arm draped over the back cushions along Shaun's shoulders.

Chase glanced up at her and smiled, picking up the royal blue stocking with white fur trimmed at the top. "You did not do stockings for all of us," he said in amazement. She smiled and shrugged. "Thank you."

Shaun and Tommy were already tearing into their stockings, unwrapping little gifts; lip balm, lotto tickets, their favorite candies, among other things. Chase set his aside, reaching for the little pink one that Zoey held. She handed it over, their fingers brushing lightly, and their eyes met briefly before he dropped his gaze to the baby in his lap.

Zoey sat on the edge of the coffee table directly in front of him, watching as he dug into the stocking, pulling out individually wrapped gifts and helping Verity tear the wrapping paper off. Rattles, a new pacifier, crinkle books, and baby snacks were all opened, slowly, but the excitement Verity showed at clutching the paper in her tiny fists was infectious, making the four adults laugh heartily.

When they had gotten through all of Verity's stocking stuffers, Shaun reached her hands out, muttering, "Gimme," and Chase chuckled and handed the baby over so he could reach down and pick up his own stocking to start opening the gifts inside.

After Chase had opened several items, including locally made beef jerky, a body spray that reminded Zoey of Chase, with hints of sandalwood and eucalyptus, he looked up at her with a wide smile, which made her voice falter as she said, "Umm, that body spray doubles as a deodorant..."

He looked up at her then, and her words trailed off at the intensity in his cobalt blue eyes.

"Are you telling me I stink?" he asked softly, teasing, and she laughed, rolling her eyes.

Tommy broke the moment when he stood, crossing to the Christmas tree and folding his legs beneath him as he sat in front of the pile of wrapped gifts, red Santa hat still perched on his head. As he began rifling through the presents, he passed gifts to each person, but Chase's eyes were still on hers. She finally broke away from his stare, standing and moving to the opposite corner of the couch from where Shaun and Verity were sitting, tucking her feet under her as she sat.

It didn't take long for all the gifts to be torn open, paper flying everywhere as Tommy and Shaun began shooting crumpled up balls of wrapping paper into the now empty laundry basket across the room. Exclamations of excitement and awe filled the small living room, and Zoey leaned back into the cushions of the couch, joy and contentment filling her chest at having the people she loved most here with her.

Verity began to fuss, her 'If-I-don't-get-fed-in-the-next-few-minutes-I'm-going-to-be-a-bear' fuss, and Zoey reached to take her from Shaun, standing. "I'll be back in a few, keep going," she said and skirted the living room, careful of the presents piled everywhere and balls of wrapping paper that had missed the laundry basket scattered on the floor.

Within minutes she was upstairs and had her clothing adjusted to allow Verity to latch, her fist thumping against her breast as she suckled eagerly. Letting her head fall back against the headrest of

197

the glider in the corner of her bedroom, she crossed one leg over the other and used the foot still on the ground to rock them gently.

A soft knock sounded on her door, and she raised her head to look over at the door, saying, "Yeah?"

The door cracked open just the slightest, just enough for her to see a sliver of Chase's body. He kept his head turned away, but spoke into the crack of the door so she could hear him, "Zoey..."

"You can come in, it's okay," she said gently, and she held her breath as he hesitated, and for a heartbeat she didn't think he would. But then the door pushed open wider, and he stepped inside, though he kept his gaze away from where she sat, Verity's head the only thing covering her naked breast.

He moved to sit down on the edge of the bed, keeping his back to her, and Zoey wanted to laugh at how stiff he was, but couldn't. He was in her room, just feet away from her. Her heart thudded in her chest as she watched his back, the muscles there rippling as he shifted his weight. The dark, nearly black hair on the back of his head looked soft to the touch, and Zoey wished she could reach out and touch it.

He took a deep breath and then turned his head so that she was watching him in profile, as he cleared his throat then and said gruffly, "Umm... about this morning..."

Embarrassment rolled like a wave over her body, making her flush hotly at the reminder of this morning. All of it.

"Don't worry about it," she whispered unevenly, her breath coming in short puffs. "Let's just forget it happened, okay?"

She watched as his back tensed, and she almost took the words back, but then he nodded stiffly and cleared his throat again, pushing himself to stand. "Right," he said roughly, crossing to the door. "I'll uhh... I'll see you back downstairs, Zoey."

"Okay," she whispered, but he was already out the door, pulling it closed behind him. Adjusting Verity to her other breast, she blew out an unsteady breath, letting her head once again fall to the rest against the cushion behind her.

This was going to be a long day.

THIRTY-FOUR

Zoey rejoined the three of them downstairs after feeding and changing Verity, coming down the stairs, her steps light. She didn't know what was going on between her and Chase, but whatever it was, she didn't want this new awkwardness to ruin the day.

By two in the afternoon, Shaun and Tommy had taken their leave, heading to Shaun's parents ranch home a few miles out of town. Shaun had pulled on her jacket, pulling her braid free, and said, "Mom will kill me if I don't get over there to help with dinner prep. Dad will have the game on, so feel free to come out if you'd like. Dinner is at five o'clock," before she and Tommy had walked out the door, hand in hand.

Zoey watched from the small window over the kitchen sink as they walked toward Tommy's truck. She blushed and turned away when he pushed her up against the metal side of the vehicle, pressing his body into hers as she wrapped her arms around his neck, kissing him. When she looked back, they had both climbed into the truck and were disappearing down the driveway.

Feeling hungry, Zoey placed a cutting board on the counter and crossed to the refrigerator and opened it, peering through the shelves. Plucking up one of the yellow bell peppers in the vegetable drawer, she made quick work of de-seeding it and cutting it into thick slices. Popping one in her mouth, she crunched on it as she walked to the arched doorway, calling to Chase, "Would you like a snack? I cut up a pepper if you want some."

When he didn't respond from where he was sitting in the recliner chair, she moved around to the side so she could ask again, but the words didn't leave her mouth.

Chase's head had lolled slightly to the side, his lips parted just a touch, and a moment later a soft snore left him. She giggled, shaking her head. Verity was snuggled into the crook of his elbow against his abdomen, her golden topped head resting against his chest, fast asleep as well.

Picking up one of the soft throw blankets on the back of the couch, she draped it over Chase's legs and lap, covering Verity up to her armpits. His chest rose and fell with his deep, even breathing. Her gaze traveled over his handsome features, and she shook her head again, a wry smile tugging at one corner of her mouth. That damn unruly lock of hair had fallen over his brow, as usual, and she hesitated only a fraction of a heartbeat before reaching out and carefully pushing it back. His hair was incredibly soft against her fingers, and she wished she could linger more, but didn't want to wake him. Tommy had turned the tv on to the pre-game show before he left, and Zoey reached for the remote, turning the volume down until it was just background noise.

Retreating to the kitchen to finish her snack, she leaned her hips against the counter while she ate. Chase and Verity were still sleeping when she finished, so she settled into one corner of the couch, pulled a blanket up under her chin, and was asleep minutes later.

THIRTY-FIVE

Chase woke slowly, and he yawned broadly, blinking his eyes open. The sky outside of the windows was dark, and he panicked, reaching for his phone to check the time. He shook his head when he remembered he didn't have to work that night. He must have slept hard.

Looking around, he realized Zoey must have taken Verity from him at some point, because the baby was no longer in his arms. He heard footsteps upstairs, then thirty seconds later watched as Zoey descended the stairs. She smiled at him when she saw him awake.

"Well hello sleepy head," she teased, walking around the living room. "I didn't want to wake you."

Chase chuckled, then yawned again, stretching his arms over his head. His body was stiff from sleeping in a recliner for several hours. "I wish you would have. I'm assuming you didn't go to Shaun's parents for dinner? I'm sorry I slept all of Christmas away."

She shrugged, scooping up the blanket that had been tossed aside on the couch, then folded it before laying it over the back. "It's okay, you obviously needed the sleep. Besides, they usually have the whole Kendall and Storm clans there, and it can be a little chaotic. I was okay just hanging out here. I fell asleep for a little bit, then watched *Elf* while you were sleeping."

"The Will Ferrell one?" he asked, and she nodded, grinning. She sat on the edge of the cushion, her knees angled toward him so that she faced him. Her hair had been pulled into a ponytail, and for a second the only thought he had was how he wanted to have that hair wrapped around his fist.

He shook away the thought, cursing the chubby he had begun to sport behind his pants.

"I let Shaun know we wouldn't be coming out, so she brought us dinner," she said, motioning toward the kitchen. "I don't know if she was expecting to feed an army or what, but there's way more food than two people should be able to eat."

Chase's stomach growled at the mention of food, and he smiled. "That sounds amazing. I'm starving." He stood, stretching again with a groan. "Where's Verity?"

"I put her to bed," she said, standing too. They walked together toward the kitchen, and she opened the refrigerator, pulling out several Tupperware containers filled to the brim of food. "We played hard today, so she was tired and cranky. I'm surprised she didn't wake you."

As Zoey prepped two plates of the holiday meal Shaun had sent over for them, Chase grabbed a glass of water, swallowing it down in one long pull. Once their plates were ready, she set them on the table.

"Do you want to watch another Christmas movie?" he asked, and she looked up at him. "I feel bad that I slept all day. Come out here and watch a movie with me. Please."

"Okay," Zoey said softly, and they picked up their plates, returning to the living room. They each took opposite ends of the couch, and together they pulled the long coffee table toward them. "What do you want to watch?"

"*Die Hard.*"

"*Die Hard*!" Zoey exclaimed with a surprised laugh, looking at him incredulously. "That is *not* a Christmas movie!"

Chase laughed, settling into the couch. "Of course it is! It's literally set on Christmas Eve!"

"That doesn't make it a Christmas movie," she laughed again, pulling the blanket she'd folded off the back of the couch once more, settling it over her lap and feet before picking up her plate.

"Well, what do you have in mind?" he asked, reaching for the remote. "I won't do *Polar Express*. I don't know why, but that movie just gives me the creeps."

"Oh my god, me too!" Zoey said, laughing. "Tom Hanks' animated character is *terrifying*. I had nightmares after I watched that movie for the first time!"

They bantered back and forth about which movie to watch, but ultimately settled on *Die Hard* after all. "See, there's a Christmas party. Christmas music. It's a Christmas movie."

Zoey rolled her eyes and stretched her legs out slightly, until her feet almost touched his hip. He glanced down at the shape of her legs beneath the blanket, and he patted his thighs. She looked over at him quizzically.

"Stretch your legs out. Put your feet in my lap," he said, patting his thigh again. "I won't touch."

Eyeing him warily, she finally relented, stretching her legs out so that her feet rested high on his thighs, dangerously close to his crotch. They remained that way for a better part of the movie, before she pulled them back and stood. "Shaun sent pie! I totally forgot about it!"

"You're holding out on me!" Chase laughed as she skipped to the kitchen, reaching for a tinfoil covered plate.

"Looks like she sent cherry, pecan, and blueberry," she called from the kitchen. "Which one would you like?"

"Pecan," he called back and within moments she was padding back around the living room, two plates of pie and a scoop of vanilla ice cream on each. She handed him the one with the pecan pie on it, then settled back into her corner of the couch as they dug into the pie. "This is homemade. I can tell."

She laughed, and he loved the sound. This was exactly how he wanted to spend Christmas. Just like this, with her.

Zoey set her plate aside, several bites left, and he clucked his tongue, extending his hand. "Give it here. We can't let that go to waste."

Rolling her eyes, she handed it over, and he polished off her piece of cherry pie as well as his own. She scooted down into the corner, resting her head on the arm of the couch, and without prompting, settled her feet back in his lap. He smiled to himself, then patted her ankle gently.

The movie ended and he nudged Zoey awake, who had fallen asleep with fifteen minutes left to go. She blinked over at him sleepily. "Go on up to bed. I'll clean up the kitchen."

She nodded, then stood, yawning. "Okay. Good night, Chase. Thank you for hanging out with me."

"Of course," he said softly as he watched her walk toward the stairs. "Merry Christmas, Zoey."

"Merry Christmas, Chase," she said around another yawn, and then she disappeared up the stairs.

Chase stood, carrying their empty pie plates to the kitchen, where he rinsed them. As he was placing them in the dishwasher, the door opened and Tommy walked in, none too steady on his feet. Chase heard a car pull out of the driveway and disappear down the street. He breathed a sigh of relief that Tommy had been smart enough not to drive home.

"Looks like you had some fun tonight," Chase said from where he stood at the kitchen sink. Leaning his hips back against it, he crossed his arms over his chest. "Glad you didn't drive home."

"Yeah, yeah, goody-two-shoes Manning," Tommy snapped, and Chase raised his eyebrows in surprise at the unmasked vitriol in the other man's voice. "You always were a buzzkill."

"What the hell has gotten into you, man?" Chase asked quietly, though an edge of annoyance had crept into his voice. "This isn't the Tommy I know."

"The Tommy you knew died when he had to watch his sister go through a rape trial and then bury his mom in the span of a couple months," Tommy muttered darkly, leaning his weight on the back of one of the dining chairs as he toed off his boots. Chase lowered his eyes guiltily. Tommy pointed toward the doorway and beyond. "You still haven't answered my question."

"You didn't ask a question, dickhead," Chase snapped dryly.

"Are you going to marry my sister or not?"

Chase's lips thinned and his heartbeat tripled its pace in his chest. "Not."

"Then why did you move in?" Tommy demanded in a loud whisper. "Why bother helping her?"

"What's so wrong with giving her the tools and confidence to take care of herself?" Chase retorted sharply. Their friendship had become strained in the weeks since he'd officially moved in. This absolutely insane idea that Tommy came up with had clearly become an obsession and was driving a wedge between them, and he hated it. He pointed a finger at Tommy, snapping, "And it was your idea for me to move in permanently. Don't get pissy with me for doing what you asked."

"Yeah, I thought that meant you were coming around to the other part as well," Tommy muttered.

Chase laughed humorlessly. "Tommy, you can't even say it out loud. You know this is wrong! She has had everything thrust at her without her consent. You can't ask me to do this to her. I won't. I care about her too much to do that."

"I'll find someone else," Tommy said, his voice deadly calm and quiet. Chase's head tipped back as if he'd been dealt a blow to the chin, and his lips parted in shock.

"This is archaic, Tommy," he murmured, using every ounce of control he possessed to remain calm. "You can't do this. This isn't the 1850's where you can trade a woman for a cow, you idiot. You're the one that said I was the only one you would trust her with, now you'll just sell her to the highest bidder?"

"I thought you'd come around to it. Clearly that's not the case," Tommy said quietly. "You underestimate my resolution to make sure she's taken care of. There are other men I know that have expressed interest in her."

His heart was pounding erratically in his chest at the thought of someone else putting their hands on her, touching her, kissing her. He shuddered at the thought of some other man rocking Verity to sleep before sliding into a bed with Zoey...

"Okay look," Chase snapped, uncrossing his arms and shoving the fingers of one hand through his hair roughly, pulling the strands away from his forehead jerkily. He felt physically sick to his stomach. "I'll... You can't do that. No one else, Tommy, please. Swear it."

Tommy must have seen the panic and then ultimately, the defeat in his eyes, because he nodded in agreement before exiting the kitchen. Chase stood there for what felt like an eternity, anxiety and self-loathing and fury at his friend for baiting him the way he had.

That self-loathing felt like a stone had been dropped into the pit of his stomach, but the thought of anyone else with Zoey made him want to beat his fists against a wall.

No one else would touch either of them.

Over his dead body.

THIRTY-SIX

Chase's feet pounded the pavement; his legs were on fire, but he didn't stop or even slow down.

He couldn't.

Because when he did, the conversation with Tommy from almost a week ago replayed in his mind, and he hated himself more each time.

He hated *Tommy* more each time.

Tommy played him; there was no other way to look at it. Tommy had known just what buttons to push to send Chase over the edge, to make the decision he had been teetering on for over a month.

Every time he looked at Zoey he felt ill. Self-loathing ate at him mercilessly.

That didn't stop Chase from fantasizing about her, though. Not in the slightest. Which only made the hate talk in his head that much worse.

She deserves better, the angel on his right shoulder urged. *Don't do this. You can't do this to her. She will never forgive you.*

But then, the little devil on his left would whisper, *I dare you to stand by and watch as some other man puts his hands on her. Touches her where you've only been dreaming of...* And Chase would grit his teeth and tell the little guy on his right to mind his own business.

He'd been a bear to be around for nearly a week, and he knew it. He was surly, grouchy, and downright unbearable to spend more than a few minutes with. This guilt and hatred for the situation consumed him.

Music blasted in his ears through the earbuds blue-toothed to his phone that was in his pocket, angry metal music doing little to drown out his thoughts.

It didn't help that he'd woken up in a cold sweat, his sheets drenched, his hair sticking to his forehead, the recurring nightmare made worse because it wasn't those two little girls locked helpless and alone in the back of that car, but Verity. Little golden curls sticking hotly to her head in the hot car as she screamed from being left alone after her mother was abducted. Abducted and tortured. And it wasn't the face of Holly Vines that he saw in the ditch when they finally found her, but Zoey's.

Zoey's lifeless, half naked body, battered and mutilated, dumped like trash after...

He'd jumped from the bed, long strides taking him to the bathroom just in time to vomit. His entire body convulsed with soul wracking trembling. He'd stood, rinsing his mouth at the sink, staring at his own gaunt reflection in the mirror. That vision, even though it was a dream, would haunt him for a long, long time. He hadn't been able to return to sleep.

Instead, he'd dressed for a run, heading out before four in the morning, and so far he'd completed nearly nine miles without turning around. It would be another nine back home, and he was sure his legs would give out on him before he made it back.

He knew Zoey was worried about him from the small, quick looks she sent his way through her lashes when she thought he wasn't paying attention. He'd begged off from the gym for the week, not sure he could manage the hour of one-on-one time with her while his mind was so at odds with itself.

He wanted her.

But he didn't *want* to want her.

He didn't want to hurt her, but knew if—or when—she found out about what he and Tommy had done, she would hate them both. And then where would he be?

Because at this point, he didn't just want her. He was worried he was feeling far more than that. And that scared the living hell out of him, too.

THIRTY-SEVEN

"Michigan law states that when a person is formally convicted of rape by a court of law, their rights to any child(ren) born of said rape are fully terminated and forfeit. Unfortunately, however, that doesn't extend to grandparents. They have what's called Grandparent's Rights," their lawyer, James Mallory said quietly, as if gauging Zoey and Tommy's reactions as he spoke. "We can fight it, but we need to look at the possibility that the judge *may* choose to grant visitation with the Patterson's." At Zoey's strangled cry, he hurried to continue, saying, "However it is slim and *if* the judge so chooses that option, it would more than likely be supervised visitations only, and for probably only an hour or two a week."

Tommy's hand had balled into a fist where it rested against his knee, and Zoey could see his other knee bouncing rapidly in agitation. He didn't like the conclusion any more than she did.

"So Zoey can just be forced to hand over her *infant* to some strangers? Parents of the man that drugged and ra—"

Zoey clutched a hand to her mouth to hold in the sob threatening to erupt from her. *This isn't happening,* she thought manically. *They can't do this.*

"I'm assuming the Patterson's attorney will say that they are upstanding individuals, well-liked in their community. We can do some digging, see if that's true. If there is anything they're hiding, I'll find it, and use it against them. *But,*" he warned, "their attorney will do the same for you, Zoey. Anything you're hiding, anything that makes you look like you're struggling to parent Verity properly, they will use against *you*, in return."

"Like what?" Zoey whispered, shocked. "I've never done anything! I— I've never been in trouble! And I'm a wonderful mother—"

Tears slid down her cheeks then, unable to stem them. Fear undulated over her. *What if they take her? What if they find something, anything, viable to take her from me?*

"Setting an example, being in a healthy, committed relationship, is a huge win on our side," James said. "Being a unified, family unit will look good to a judge."

"But I'm not ready to date," Zoey whispered, panic rising in her throat, making her voice tremble. "I'm in therapy dealing with everything—" she then raised her eyes to James' when he drew his lips into a small line, suddenly looking uncomfortable, as she breathed, "They will try to use me being in therapy against me, won't they?"

Nodding grudgingly, he said, "It is... very likely, yes. However, getting your therapist to act as a witness and testify to how well you're responding to it will be vital."

"So I'm just screwed any which way I look at it," she whispered despondently. She had walked into James' office feeling more confident than she was feeling now. "They're going to win, at least in some fashion."

"If their attorney can prove that they are good people, would it be so terrible to let your daughter have a relationship with her grandparents? It would be a stipulation that she is to have no contact with Robby whatsoever, and *if* they ever break that, it will be a violation of the agreement if that's what happens, and that will terminate their rights immediately," he said. Zoey raised angry eyes to his, ready to argue, but he continued gently, "Zoey, I know this is scary and not what you were expecting, and I'll admit it's not fair with how they're going about it. But as her mother, you can't make decisions solely based on how you feel, or how it affects you. What is best for *her*?"

"I don't like you right now," she whispered sullenly, and he chuckled, nodding.

"If you liked me one hundred percent of the time, I wouldn't be doing my job correctly," he said with a laugh. Tapping the papers in front of him, he continued, "They're going to push to have this go through mediation to avoid going to court. We can try to reason with them, give them crumbs to latch onto to see if they will bite, or we can drag this out and take it before a judge. Either way, it's not going to be easy, I need you to understand that."

"Will they bring up the—everything before?" Tommy asked, risking a glance at Zoey before changing his direction of words.

Again, James nodded glumly. "I'm afraid so. They will use whatever they can to discredit Zoey's character."

"This is bullshit!" Tommy finally snapped, standing and striding around the room angrily. "She already did all this, proved that what he did was the truth, why should she have to do this all over again! *She* was the victim, not him, not his parents, *her*!"

"You and I both know that, and the trial records will be a huge win in our favor," James said, eyeing Tommy as he paced around the office. "The video surveillance was crucial to our win last time, if necessary, we will pull it out of evidence and use it again."

Zoey hated the idea of that tape being played again. It was grainy and not great quality, but it was detailed enough to have been useful... When Robby had finished with her, leaving her in the back corner of the parking lot in the snow, he'd walked right into the building, straight toward the camera he hadn't realized was there.

"The first mediation isn't scheduled until the end of February, we have plenty of time," James said, straightening the file of papers on his desk in front of him, then he stood. "Try not to fret, that's what I'm here for."

He reached out a hand to Tommy, who took it in a firm shake. He then held his hand out in a fist toward Zoey as she stood, too, and she smiled slightly before bumping her fist against his, their version of a handshake. "Thank you, James," she said quietly, pulling her jacket on. "You've been wonderful, as always."

"I'm just doing my job," he said kindly, and Zoey was grateful that they had him on their side, again.

"We'll be in touch," Tommy said and ushered Zoey out the door after another round of good-byes. Without touching her, he led her through the lavish attorney's office and out to the snowy January afternoon. "We'll get through this, you know that, right?"

Nodding, she was focusing on her footing on the icy sidewalk when a flash of red and blue out of the corner of her eye caught her attention. She looked up and her heart started to thud in her chest as Chase waved at her from the interior of his squad car that had pulled up alongside them. He parked and climbed out, coming around the back of the vehicle to stand in front of both of them. Tommy had his hands shoved deep into the pockets of his winter coat, and Zoey was clutching the sides of her lapels over her chest to keep the snow from whipping against her neck.

"How did it go?" he asked, jerking his chin toward the office they had just left.

"Were you circling the building, waiting for us to come out?" Zoey asked with a smile, though her teeth were chattering from the cold.

"Maybe," he grinned, hunched into the upturned collar of his own patrol jacket against the wind and snow. "I didn't want to have to wait to find out what happened."

She heard a disgruntled snort come from Tommy, and she turned to glance at him curiously before returning her attention to Chase. "We're in for a long haul," was all she could manage as the fear choked her once more.

"We'll get through this," Chase murmured gently, stepping forward and bending his knees slightly to bring his face more level with hers. "Hey," he said, when she didn't raise her eyes to his. Lifting her gaze, she swallowed down her tears, as he continued, "I am not going to let anything happen to you or Verity. I promise."

Zoey had never wished for a hug more. She needed to feel his arms around her, reassuring her that she and her child were safe, that they always would be. But she knew Chase would not initiate it, and she wasn't entirely sure she would have the courage to do it herself.

He had been distant and grouchy all week, and she gnawed on her cheek for a moment before she broke. The tears she'd fought all morning slipped down her cheeks, and the relief at seeing him was enough to push her over the edge. As he started to straighten, she threw herself forward, wrapping her arms around his waist and pressing her face into his chest that was covered in layer upon layer of tactical gear, which meant it wasn't a very *comfortable* hug, but it was exactly what she needed. With tears still stinging her nose and slipping down her cheeks to freeze in the cold on her skin, she nestled her face in closer against the hard ridges of his tactical vest.

Even through the blustery cold, she could smell the body spray he'd used that morning before leaving, sandalwood and eucalyptus enveloping her senses and calming her in a way that she couldn't explain. When his arms circled around her, she tensed for a half of a heartbeat before sinking more fully into the embrace. She felt one of his hands stroking her hair that was flying around her head as she took a deep, shuddering breath in, holding it for five seconds, and then releasing it for a count of five.

He squeezed her gently, and she felt when he leaned down to murmur in her ear, "Inhale courage, exhale fear. God dammit I'm so proud of you, sweetheart."

And in that moment, she knew she had fallen completely and irrevocably in love with Chase Manning.

THIRTY-EIGHT

"I want to hear more about the meeting," Chase murmured close to her ear, and she nodded, but then her teeth started chattering again and he chuckled. She saw him glance over her shoulder at Tommy, who was still waiting nearby, and he said, "But later, okay? Let's get you in the car and out of the cold."

He walked them the short distance to her Subaru, and he opened the passenger door, letting her slide in before he closed it behind her. Tommy stepped around to the driver's side but didn't open the door right away. It sounded like Chase and Tommy were talking, but her teeth were chattering so loudly in her own head that she couldn't hear what they were saying. Reaching into her coat pocket, she pulled out her key and leaned over the console to stick the key in the ignition, starting it and allowing the heat to start warming the interior. But that meant that now she *really* couldn't hear what they were saying outside of the car.

Out the window, she watched as Chase's body went rigid, and peeking up at him, she saw his jaw was clenched tight, a muscle there jumping. He must have sensed her stare, because he glanced down at her, and then a smile tugged at his mouth and his eyes softened briefly before he nodded stiffly in reply to something that Tommy said. His eyes still on hers, she watched as he said, *"Okay"* and she knew whatever he had just agreed to was not something he wanted.

Tommy opened the door then, sliding in behind the wheel and Chase tapped his knuckle on her window once before he disappeared, heading back toward his patrol car. Tommy rubbed his hands together to warm them, adjusting the thermostat to max heat. He glanced over at her and she blushed, knowing what was coming.

"So... a hug, huh?" he asked nonchalantly as he put the car in gear and pulled away from the curb, pointing them in the direction of home. "That's kind of a big deal."

"Let's not make it a big deal," Zoey pleaded. "It... I don't even know how it happened. I just knew I needed a hug after that, and I feel safe with Chase." She blushed again, not ready to speak of the *other* feeling she'd finally admitted to herself. She sat back in the seat, the warmth from the blowers finally chasing away the chill enough for her to stop shivering.

She was in love with Chase.

Holy crap.

I'm in love with Chase. Now what?

"Is there... something going on between you two?" he asked, and again she blushed scarlet.

"No, of course not! That would be weird, he's your best friend..."

"Well, yeah," he said, shrugging as he turned a corner. "But, if there was, I'd be okay with it. Just so you know. I trust Chase. And I think you do, too." When she stared out the windshield, too embarrassed to speak, he continued, and she wished the floor would open up and swallow her whole, "You deserve to be in a good relationship after everything you've been through, Zoey. I think it would be good for both of you. And, just so you know, I wouldn't like, kick his ass or anything."

She was sure she was blushing a violent shade of vermillion to the roots of her golden blonde hair, and she was silent the rest of the way home, too caught up in everything Tommy had just said, what James had told them in the meeting, and finally acknowledging the feelings she'd been bottling up for weeks. *Was* she ready for a relationship finally? Was this really enough time to know if she was actually in love? A month and half?

Yes, it really was.

But... what if he doesn't feel the same?

She shook her head, smiling to herself just the slightest. She knew he felt *something* for her. She just wasn't sure what that something was yet. But she would find out.

Climbing out of the car when Tommy pulled into their driveway, she went inside, finding Shaun and

Verity watching an old episode of *Overhaulin'*, and Shaun was explaining how they were "absolutely destroying that classic" and how they "should be ashamed of themselves." Zoey laughed, because Verity looked entirely enthralled in what Shaun was saying, her big indigo eyes rapt on Shaun's face.

Shaun waved her off, knowing if Verity saw her she would throw a fit until she was picked up by Zoey, so she slipped up the stairs and into her bedroom to change out of the clothes she'd chosen to wear to the meeting with James. Pulling the dressier blouse than she would normally wear over her head, she hung it back in the closet, since she'd only worn if for a few hours. Peeling the dress slacks down her thighs, she folded them over the laundry basket in the corner, then faced the mirror in the opposite corner. Standing naked except for her bra and panties, she let herself look at her body, at how it had changed in the weeks of hard work she'd been putting in at the gym with Chase.

Chase. Would he like her body? Or would he think she was too soft around the middle still?

She banished the thought as soon as it started though, refusing to let her self-worth be determined by a man, even Chase, and whether he found her body attractive. She was soft and fleshy in more places than she'd been before her pregnancy, and though the weight loss had been an added bonus to the workouts she and Chase had been doing, she was more impressed by the definition that had begun to show in her arms, her back, her stomach.

She was *stronger* than she'd ever been, and *that* was enough.

Slipping into a tight pair of olive-green leggings that did wonders for her still jiggly thighs and leftover mommy tummy, she found her favorite gray sweater, the buttery soft material floating over her body in a caress. Pulling a brush through her wind-tousled waves, she touched up her make-up, applying a fresh coat of mascara, making her eyes pop. It would still be several hours before Chase would be home from his shift, but she wanted him to look his fill of her.

The words that James had said to them earlier came back to her again, and she stopped mid swipe of the mascara wand, her hand dipping slightly as she stared at her reflection.

What if... what if I can kill two birds with one stone?

Being in a healthy, stable relationship would look good for her when they go to court, because she knew damn well that mediation would never work between herself and the Patterson's.

So... what if...

Shaking her head, she snorted derisively at herself as she continued to swipe the mascara wand over her lashes. But that thought kept popping up, until she dropped the mascara tube onto the dresser and sank down onto the edge of her bed, letting the thoughts roll through her completely.

What if, and it's a big if... what if she and Chase were in a relationship? She trusted Chase more than probably anyone, in the short amount of time that they had really gotten to know each other. *And it wasn't like she was going to trick him into it, because she knew there was already something there.*

It still felt like trickery, though, and shame filled her. Chase was a genuinely good person. She couldn't trick Chase into a relationship with her to help win a court case.

But if they managed to get there on their own... That would be okay, right?

She gnawed on the inside of her cheek for a half a heartbeat before skipping from the bedroom and down the stairs. Finding the Bluetooth speaker she used to use a long time ago while she was cooking or cleaning, she hooked up her cellphone to it and scrolled until she found a playlist.

Setting it on the windowsill ledge, she hit play, and music filled the small kitchen as she started preparations for dinner: Chase's favorite.

Because the quickest way to a man's heart... is through his stomach.

THIRTY-NINE

She hugged me.

Nearly four hours later, and he was still trying to wrap his head around it. Zoey had reached out and *hugged* him. Full on *hugged him.* He didn't need to see the utter shock on Tommy's face to know just how big of a deal it was, because of course he knew. This was huge.

And he was so goddamned proud of her.

The hours had dragged by, his entire thought process derailed by a petite golden blonde with the prettiest indigo eyes he'd ever seen and the kindest heart of anyone he'd ever known. He willed the clock to move faster, to speed up so he could rush home. He needed to see her, even if that hug was the only one he'd get for a long while, he now knew what it felt like to hold her in his arms, and dammit all to hell but he liked it, a lot.

No, he more than liked it. He loved the feel of her against his body, her hair between his fingers, her hands pressing against his back. Even if it had

227

been through all the layers of his patrol gear, the feel of her against him was permanently seared into his brain for the remainder of his days. And even if it took forever, he wanted to do it again. And again.

Bouncing his left leg as he drove the short way home, he pulled into the driveway and cut the engine, though he didn't climb out as quickly as he thought he would have upon reaching home.

Tommy had given him a Cliff Note version of what the lawyer had said in their meeting. That the opposition would do whatever they could to malign her character, including the fact that she was a single mother. The lawyer had gone as far to tell her that being in a stable relationship would better her odds... and when they'd spoken over the top of Zoey's car after tucking her into it to stay warm, Tommy had said, "We can let it be *her* idea..." to which Chase had clenched his teeth together so tightly they'd ached. It was still deceitful, especially to manipulate her into believing that *she* came up with the idea.

And then he'd felt her eyes on him, glancing down through the slightly frosted window at her beautiful, brave face, and he'd nodded. Not because he agreed with what Tommy was saying, but because he knew they were well on their way there anyway. But if letting her come to the conclusion herself would get them there faster, with less chance of her finding out about the deal he'd made with her brother... he'd go along with it.

Because ultimately, he just wanted her to continue to bless him with those beaming smiles she'd recently started giving him.

Climbing out of the Rubicon, in a newfound hurry to get inside to her, he hurried up the stone path and let himself in through the door, stopping abruptly, stunned into speechlessness.

Justin Timberlake's 'Carry Out' played on an invisible speaker from somewhere in the kitchen, and Zoey was...dancing.

When Chase could finally pick his jaw up off the floor, he admitted with an internal grin that it was more of a slow sway of her hips to the music, but there she was, in the middle of the kitchen floor, moving and singing along to music. *Provocative* music.

And then the aromas wafting from the stove met his nostrils and he about started to salivate. Reaching out to place his hat on one of the hooks just inside the door, he shrugged out of his patrol jacket and hung that up as well, before stepping cautiously toward the stove.

"Is that... Scallops and risotto?" he asked in awe, looking over at her after taking in the sight before him.

Zoey graced him with that radiant smile and reached for her phone, hitting the buttons on the side to turn the music down so that it was just background noise. Then she nodded, stepping toward him where he was still half hunched over the stove. "Brown butter scallops, air fried Brussel Sprouts with a balsamic reduction drizzle, and parmesan risotto. I hope that's okay?"

"Zoey, I could kiss you right now," he murmured in a dazed laugh, looking back down at the delicious looking meal. When he realized what he'd said, his eyes flashed up to hers and he immediately said, "I just meant because it looks so good—"

"—I also paired it with a dry white wine, if you want that with it instead of a beer..." Zoey whispered, her voice trailing off toward the end, as if realizing what he'd said at the same time he did. She blushed, and he'd never seen anything as pretty when her cheeks turned that shade of pink.

They remained staring at each other for an extended heartbeat before she looked away, the tip of her tongue darting out to wet her lips, and he nearly groaned. She waved toward the arched doorway and said, "Go ahead and shower and change, I'll have this plated up when you're done."

"Yes, ma'am," he said and winked, then disappeared through the door and up the stairs. He shucked his uniform quickly, showering in record time before slinging a towel around his hips and nearly sprinting to the bedroom to pull on a pair of gray sweatpants. He pulled them off almost immediately and reached for a pair of jeans. She had gone through the trouble to make his favorite meal; he could at least get properly dressed for it.

He then pulled a navy-blue V neck shirt over his head, barely taking the time to ruffle the towel over his wet hair before going down to the kitchen.

Zoey had plated the meal and was in the process of taking the two plates to the table when he ducked in through the doorway. Her ass in the tight, olive green leggings made his mouth water just as much as the food did. When she turned, she smiled at him and pointed to the chair next to hers, "Come on, sit down while it's still hot."

He sank into the chair and realized that not one, but two wine glasses had been set on the table: another big step for his brave girl.

His brave girl? he asked himself as he scooted his chair slightly closer, watching her from the corner of his eye.

He sighed and let the inevitable thoughts parade through his brain.

Yes, his brave, wonderful girl. She was having her first alcoholic drink since the attack. Even if it was barely a two-ounce pour, it was another huge step for her today.

When had she stopped being Tommy's little sister and become just Zoey? No, when had she stopped being Tommy's little sister and became *his* Zoey? He wasn't sure when it happened, but it did help assuage some of the guilt he still felt for imagining her naked all the time.

His dick responded to that thought, and he shifted in his seat, clearing his throat awkwardly.

"This looks divine," he murmured unsteadily as he picked up his fork and suspended it over his plate, unsure what to taste first. "If this tastes half as good as it looks, I'll marry you tomorrow."

Zoey laughed, rolling her eyes at him. "You're an awful lot of talk tonight. First kissing, now marriage. I think you need to take me on a date first."

Is she...flirting with me?

Stabbing into one of the delicately browned scallops on his plate, he popped it into his mouth, his eyes nearly rolling into the back of his head. He nodded dumbly, looking at her directly, and after swallowing the delicious bite, said roughly, "Deal."

FORTY

Zoey could have sworn she stopped breathing after the outrageous flirt left her mouth. She couldn't believe she'd said that!

And then watching Chase's expression as he took a bite of the succulent seafood, he'd nearly sent her into a frenzy with the huskily spoken, "Deal."

He must be joking. There's no way he meant it. Right?

Right?

Lord she hoped he wasn't joking, because she wasn't sure her newly unpadlocked heart could take it if he was teasing her.

"Where's Tommy?" he asked before taking a bite of the creamy parmesan risotto, an audible moan escaping him this time. She beamed another smile at him, glad that he was enjoying it.

Tucking one strand of hair behind her ear, she took a bite of scallop and murmured, "He's at Shaun's for the night."

"Hence the scallops?" he asked, and she was surprised that he remembered that Tommy was allergic to shellfish.

"It was a big day, I wanted to celebrate and not let myself worry too much about the court proceedings, and since I can't do shellfish when he's here... Yeah, hence the scallops," she laughed. Reaching out, she took hold of the stem of the wineglass, bringing it to her lips to take a tiny sip. It was drier than she would have preferred before...but it complimented the seafood perfectly. And who else would she trust to have her first drink of alcohol with than Chase?

"I'd love to hear what the lawyer said today, but I understand if you don't want to talk about it right now," he murmured around another bite.

Zoey shrugged. "His honesty took me by surprise, though I'm not sure why. James Mallory has always been brutally honest with us about everything we were facing. We're in for a long fight, I think."

Chase nodded, resting his forearm on the edge of the table, and she knew he was watching her closely. "Is there anything we can do to help?"

Her eyes flashed up to his cobalt ones and she almost told him what James had said about relationships, but she just shook her head, dropping her eyes to her plate. "Just that they will try to malign my character in any way they can. James says we have a solid case, but that if it goes before a judge, he may decide on supervised visitation regardless of how strong our case is. And that I should be ready for anything."

The only real reason Zoey could come up with for not telling Chase about what James had suggested was the fact that she knew the kind of person Chase was... and if she mentioned it to him, he would do it in a heartbeat if he thought it would help her, help Verity.

And she wanted to know that whatever this was between them could be real.

When they'd finished the meal, Chase swallowed the last of his wine, hers was long gone—though she didn't feel the slightest buzzed, not surprising with how little she'd allowed herself to have—and he shooed her out of the kitchen, insisting that since she cooked, he would clean.

Zoey sank into one corner of the couch, watching him as he moved around the kitchen, rinsing dishes before stacking them in the dishwasher, cleaning the stovetop, and when he opened the refrigerator to put away the still half full bottle of wine, he audibly gasped, and Zoey knew he'd found dessert.

"Oreo-freaking-cheesecake?" he groaned, pulling the handmade dessert out and putting it on the counter. "I don't even care that I'm stuffed, I'm having a piece."

Zoey laughed, smiling over at him when he turned to give her a grin. "I'll take a sliver, too, please."

"I will dote on you hand and foot," he chuckled, dishing up two slices of the chocolate and cream cookie dessert before walking around the living room to bring her a small piece. "Your cheesecake, my lady."

He settled on the arm of the recliner, not even bothering to sit in the chair, digging into the sweet treat.

"Yeah, that settles it," he said after finishing the slice of decadent cheesecake. "I'm marrying you for sure."

Taking the last bite of her sliver, she then picked up the crumbled pieces of the crushed Oreo crust with her thumb, bringing it to her lips. She shook her head at him, laughing again. "If you keep saying that, I'm going to hold you to it," she teased lightly, though her heart was pounding. Where had this newfound boldness come from?

He raised his eyes to hers and once again those butterflies took flight in her belly, as he murmured, "Zoey, sweetheart, I'll let you hold anything you want to me."

The air fairly crackled between them, charged with tension and dare she say... arousal? Zoey jumped clear out of her seat when Verity let out a wail from upstairs where she'd been sleeping in her crib. Skirting around the edge of the chair where Chase was still perched, she practically threw her empty plate and fork into the sink before racing up the stairs, though it wasn't because of Verity's fussing... it was because she'd been half a second away from throwing herself into Chase's arms for the second time in one day.

FORTY-ONE

Zoey's boldness dissipated by the following morning, and she cringed at the memories from the night before. She didn't know how she was going to look Chase in the eye. What on earth had gotten into her?

Standing in the atrium of the gym, she fidgeted nervously with the strap of her gym bag that was slung across her chest as she waited for Chase to arrive. They had another lesson with Mike scheduled at 8:00. She pulled her phone out of her pocket, checking the time and also checking for any messages from Chase. It was 7:37pm, and usually if he was running late he would let her know.

The gym floor was bustling tonight, most of the machines in use and a steady flow of bodies from one part of the gym to the next. As comfortable as she had become in the gym with Chase, being there without him still made her nervous.

Checking her phone again, seeing a message that read:

On my way, I'm sorry I'm running late. Be there in ten minutes.

She chewed on her lip as she slipped the phone back into her pocket. Maybe she should have stayed in the car until he got there.

Then she straightened her shoulders and muttered to herself, "Stop being such a baby, Zoey. Go do your warmups so he doesn't have to wait on your slow ass."

She checked in at the front desk and then walked quickly through the busy gym to the locker rooms, where she shed her outer gear and changed her shoes. Bringing her 'emotional support' water bottle with her, she picked up one of the rolled up blue foam mats and spread it out on an empty stretch of floor, away from anyone else, and began her stretches.

She worked through a circuit of squats, mountain climbers, inchworms—which she had told Chase were the devil, to which he'd laughed out loud—and toe taps.

She was in the middle of her second set of mountain climbers, another warm up she hated with a passion, when she sensed someone step up beside her, then out of the corner of her eye she saw someone kneel next to her. Before she could turn her head, she heard an unfamiliar male voice say, "I was watching from over there, your form is all wrong, here—" just as she felt one hand on her back, pushing down to flatten the curve she'd inched her spine into, the other sliding on the back of her thigh, fingers curving in to the inside of her knee to move her legs wider.

Instantaneous panic undulated over her, and she dropped out of the mountain climber with a gasp, pulling away from the hands that were on her. *Pushing her toward the ground. Pulling her legs apart.*

Her vision narrowed and darkened; terror so thick in her veins she was sure she was going to black out. She was shaking so violently, she thought she may throw up.

She couldn't breathe. Her lungs were frozen, and panic continued to claw at her chest. She couldn't take a breath to save her life, and she twisted her head enough to look up into the unfamiliar face that was uncomfortably close to her own as he knelt beside her.

"I would highly suggest you get your fucking hands off her, right now," a deep, menacing voice growled from above her, and she was finally able to draw an unsteady breath in.

Chase! her mind screamed, but her vocal cords were useless.

He was here. Her unspoken protector.

The guy stood, backing away quickly at the pure venom in that hard voice, holding his hands up in innocence. "I was just trying to help," she heard him stammer, his voice breaking at what she assumed was nothing short of fury on Chase's face that she still couldn't see.

"I'm fairly certain that the first rule of gym etiquette is not to touch someone unless they say so," Chase snapped. She could see his sneaker clad feet as he moved closer to her, where she remained on her hands and knees, gulping in air now that her lungs had decided to work again. He knelt beside her, and she shrank away from him involuntarily, her body still shaking violently. He didn't reach for her, but murmured gently, "Breathe, sweetheart. Can you count them for me?"

She nodded stiffly, keeping her eyes on the floor between her hands. Breathing in for five seconds, she held it, then exhaled for five.

"Jeez, dramatic much?" the guy said, his voice snarky as he walked away, and she thought Chase might jump the guy, the tension rolling off his body palpable.

When at last she felt the dread leaving her body and her violent trembling slowed, she hung her head between her shoulders as tears stung her nose.

"May I?" he asked softly, reaching out one hand, and she shook her head. He respected her decision, lowering his hand away from her and simply sitting with her while she processed. "Are you okay?"

She nodded once, then shook her head. "I don't know," she whispered brokenly, her voice thick with unshed tears. She knew by the awkward silence around them that she had caused a scene, and had drawn quite the audience. Humiliation swamped her, choking her anew. "I want to go home. Please. Get me out of here."

"Okay, sweetheart," he murmured softly, no trace of judgment in his voice, which she was thankful for. "We can go. It's okay."

She stood, her legs shaky, and he walked with her to the locker rooms, where she quickly changed her shoes and put on her jacket. He met her just outside the door moments later, his own bag slung over his shoulder, and led her through the building and out the door.

"Where's your car?" he asked, and she pointed in the direction of her vehicle. He held out his hand and she dropped her keys into his palm, before he ushered her toward it. He opened the passenger door, and she climbed in.

But when she sank into the seat, her tremors started over and she was unable to stem the tears as sobs wracked her body. Chase had rushed around the hood of the car, climbing into the driver's seat. Starting the car, he adjusted the thermostat to combat the January cold. He sat next to her, half turned toward her, but she didn't look at him. Couldn't bring herself to look into his face as the anxiety washed over her, drowning her.

"I'm sorry," she whispered on a hiccup, swiping her hands over her cheeks to wipe away the torrent of tears. "I swear I'm trying."

"That bastard is lucky I didn't break his fucking hands," Chase murmured low. He was still half turned toward her, his right arm draped over the back of her seat, his hand dangling close to her shoulder, though he didn't touch her. "You're doing so great, Zoey. I'm sorry I wasn't here to stop that."

She hiccupped again and shook her head sadly. "I'm pathetic. Can't even do warmups without a babysitter."

Zoey peeked at him through her lashes and more tears fell at the look on his face. His hand was inches from her left shoulder, where it rested along the back of the seat, her head tilted back against the headrest behind her. His fingers moved, just the slightest, and she felt them graze her hair, twirling one blonde strand in his fingers. She hiccupped again but didn't shift away from his touch.

"You are not pathetic. I wouldn't say you're doing great if I didn't mean it," he said gently, reverently. Then, tilting his head to the side to peer at her more closely, he asked, "Is there anything I can do to help?"

She shook her head again, sniffling. Zoey took a deep, shuddering breath in, then let it out slowly. "I'm okay now. I'm sorry."

"Please stop apologizing," he said, continuing to twirl that single lock of hair in his fingers. She turned her head to face him more fully. "I made a promise to you, and I broke it."

"You couldn't have known," Zoey said in an effort to take away the haunted look on his face. She hated seeing it. "I thought I could get away with hiding in the corner to do my warmups while I waited for you to get there. I should have waited in the car."

"I shouldn't have been late," he said gruffly, his eyes sorrowful. "And you shouldn't have to worry about unwanted attention at the gym. If I had been here, he wouldn't have had the chance to get that close to you."

Zoey smiled sadly, casting her eyes down, staring at her clasped fingers in her lap. "I'm sorry you have to babysit me."

Chase shook his head then. "I don't think of it like that, Zoey. I hope you know that. I enjoy coming here with you."

She let one corner of her mouth lift in a wry smirk, looking at him out of the corner of her eyes. "Thank you for saying it, even if I don't necessarily believe you."

"I wouldn't have offered it if I didn't want to," he said earnestly, his eyes searching hers.

She nodded, though she dropped her gaze back to her lap, just now becoming acutely aware of what a mess she probably looked like. Embarrassed, and she swiped the heels of her hands over her face once more, scrubbing the tears away. "I'm sorry you didn't get your workout in because of me."

He shrugged, finally moving his arm from behind her and twisting so that he was sitting forward in his seat again. "I'm not worried about one workout, sweetheart. You are more important right now."

She blushed at his words, though she rolled her eyes. "Your flattery is unnecessary."

As he put the car into gear and pulled out of the parking lot, she settled into her seat, pulling the folds of her jacket around her chin. Chase noticed, and reached out to adjust the blowers, turning them toward her. "How's that?"

She nodded, smiling over at him. "Thank you, Chase."

Her gratitude was for more than just the heat in the car, and he knew it. When he looked over at her, he smiled gently. "You're welcome, sweetheart. Anytime."

She wondered just how much further she could fall for Chase Manning.

FORTY-TWO

"What about your Jeep?" Zoey asked as they pulled into the driveway at home.

Chase shrugged. "I'll go get it later, I'm not worried about it. It's locked. And, it's Petoskey."

He climbed out of the car and skirted the hood to come open her door. He offered her his hand to help her out, and she hesitated for only a moment before placing her right hand in his, letting him assist her out. As soon as she was standing, albeit a little shakily still, he dropped her hand, though he did walk behind her as they made their way to the door.

Tommy and Shaun were snuggled together on the couch, and Zoey could see the green and red lights of the baby monitor where it sat on the coffee table beside them. Zoey knew Verity would be in her crib fast asleep.

Chase took her gym bag and set it down and ducked his head to look at her. "Hey," he murmured, and she raised her eyes to his. "Why don't you go start a bath, okay? I can bring you a cup of tea."

She nodded, taking another deep, shuddering breath. "Okay. Thank you."

Zoey slipped up the stairs and into the bathroom, where she turned the light on and inspected the damage her crying had done to her face. She groaned. Her eyes were red-rimmed and her nose was pink at the end, and her mascara had left streaks down her cheeks. She blew out her breath and squeezed her eyes shut for just a moment before stepping over toward the tub, where she started the water to fill, squeezing out an extra dollop of bubble bath that immediately started to froth, and even sprinkled some lavender Epsom salts into the bottom of the tub to dissolve.

Next, she leaned over the sink and washed her face thoroughly, scrubbing all the dried tears and streaked makeup off her cheeks. Once that was done, she lit the handful of candles that she always kept in the bathroom for herself, then switched the overhead light off so that the only light in the small bathroom was that of the candlelight.

Stripping, she tossed her clothes into the hamper in the corner and then stepped into the hot water, lowering her body into it. The tub was deep enough that she could submerge up to her armpits, the frothy bubbled water covering her breasts. She turned the water off with her foot and leaned back against the sloped edge.

When a knock sounded on the door several minutes later, she called softly, "You can come in."

Chase's face appeared as the door cracked open, and as much as she wanted to hide away from his gaze, she didn't. Not that he could see anything through the thick layer of sudsy bubbles floating on top of the water, but just knowing she was naked underneath the cover of water made those butterflies come back.

He stepped into the dimly lit room, bringing her a steaming cup of tea. He set it on the wide ledge of the bathtub near her shoulder, keeping his eyes away from her as he straightened.

"Is there anything I can get you, Zoey?" he asked, his voice rough.

She meant to say no, but the words that came out instead were, "Will you sit with me? Please?"

She held her breath as her question registered to him, and his eyes flashed to hers briefly.

"In here? With you in the tub?" he asked, surprised.

Zoey let out a self-deprecating laugh and shook her head. "Yeah... Actually, don't worry about it, I don't know why I—"

"Let me change out of my gym clothes," he said huskily, and then he disappeared out the door, his footsteps fading down the hallway to his room. She barely dared to breathe while she waited, but just minutes passed before she heard his door open and close, and his steps as he drew nearer to the door, but then he passed by the door and she heard him take the stairs down, and she called herself every silly name she could think of. Thirty seconds later, she heard footsteps on the stairs again, and held her breath as he halted on the other side of the door.

"Are you sure, Zoey?" he asked.

"Yes," she heard herself whisper, then watched in the dim light of the candles as the door opened and he entered, keeping his eyes away from her form in the tub. He was carrying a beer in his hand. He set the bottle of beer on the wide edge of the tub next to her tea, then folded a towel, placing it on the floor before lowering his tall frame down to it. Leaning his back against the side of the tub, he stretched his legs out on the tiled floor, groaning as he shifted on his tailbone. She couldn't believe she was sitting inches away from him, naked, the only thing between them was water and frothy bubbles. She watched the back of his dark head as he rolled his shoulders, a motion he did quite often.

"Thank you."

He turned his head just slightly so that she could see him in profile, though he didn't look at her. "You have to stop thanking me."

She watched as he reached out and wrapped his fingers around the bottle of beer, then took a long pull of it, before setting it in his lap, both hands wrapped around the narrow bottle. She reached out of the water to take the cup of tea, bringing it to her lips. It was perfect.

"I don't think I'll stop thanking you any time soon," she said quietly into the dimly lit room. It was extremely intimate. "You're so amazing to me and Verity, Chase. I can't thank you enough for what you do."

He ducked his head, staring at his hands clasped in his lap around the bottle of beer. "I don't deserve your thanks, Zoey."

Zoey's eyebrows drew together. "What do you mean? You don't have to do what you do for me, for Verity. You're the most incredible person."

He turned so that she could see him in profile again and she watched as one corner of his mouth tilted up just the slightest. "I won't bore you with all the ways I'm not, sweetheart. I'm..." he trailed off, as if searching for the right word. "I'm incredibly selfish."

"That's a lie," Zoey said with a smile, shifting, making the water lap at the sides of the tub. "You're the least selfish person I know."

"I wish I could agree with you," Chase said quietly, then took another drink of the beer. He turned his shoulders so that he could look at her, his eyes meeting hers, and he murmured huskily, "I'm afraid where you and Verity are concerned, I've become extraordinarily selfish."

Zoey's mouth parted slightly, her heart thundering in her chest when his words registered. She opened her mouth to say something, though what she wasn't entirely sure, but they both heard Verity begin fussing from across the hallway.

He cleared his throat roughly before pushing himself to his feet. "I'll uh, go get her while you uhh—" he motioned with his hands vaguely and Zoey blushed hotly, then he was gone, closing the door behind him with a soft click.

FORTY-THREE

Stopping just outside the door, Chase leaned against the wall and let his head thump against it as he stared at the ceiling. What the hell had come over him? Why had he agreed to sit in that bathroom with her? And dammit all to hell, but his cock was stiff as a board after sitting so close to her being naked, that light, floral lavender and lilac scent of her assailing his senses and driving him insane.

The hot water had curled the tendrils of hair that had fallen out of the topknot she'd twisted her hair into, and though he'd only looked at her for the briefest of moments, his fingers had fairly ached at the need to reach out and tuck those strands behind her ear before leaning down and pressing his mouth to hers. He longed to know what she tasted like. Wanted to know what her body would feel like against his fingers. Fuck.

He tamped his desire down and heard the water sloshing as she stood to dry off. He stepped across the hall and opened her bedroom door, crossing the floor to reach down and pick Verity up from inside her crib as she let out a disgruntled wail. He recognized that cry and sympathized with the baby, murmuring against her temple, "I know, she's just getting dressed. She'll be right here."

He rocked her gently in his arms, bouncing slightly as he swayed, attempting to keep her distracted long enough for Zoey to get out of the bath. Again, his cock twitched at the thought of her standing naked, dripping wet just fifteen feet away. He heard the bathroom door open, and he turned toward the open bedroom doorway, and when she appeared, his good intentions went all to hell.

Zoey had pulled on her usual lightweight, dusty purple robe, though it clung to her damp skin and Chase's mouth went dry at the sight.

Lord he was in a heap of trouble. His cock twitched in appreciation, and he nearly groaned out loud.

Zoey padded toward him and reached for Verity, who had seen her mother and was now in full meltdown mode. As carefully as he could—because he was afraid if he touched her at this point he wouldn't stop until she had begged for him to touch her, to kiss her—he passed the baby over to her. Verity was hungry and angry, thumping her little fists against Zoey's chest as she quickly backed toward the glider chair in the corner. Her eyes didn't leave his in the dim room, only moonlight filtering in through the window, casting everything in a silvery glow.

She sat down, finally lowering her gaze to the hungry baby in her arms, and she didn't even hesitate before sliding one side of her robe off her shoulder, her perfectly round, creamy white breast on full display to him before Verity's head covered it, the sounds of her suckling filling the room as her indignant cries went silent.

Chase's dick was so hard he ached as he stared, unable to tear his eyes away, and unable to force his feet to move him out of the bedroom.

Instead, his traitorous feet took several steps forward to bring him to the side of her chair, and he watched in fascination as Verity suckled greedily. Zoey raised her eyes to his, slowly, and when her eyes met his, he was lost. Her lips were parted slightly, her breaths coming in soft, quick pants as she stared at him.

He reached his hand out, hesitating only a heartbeat before letting the knuckle of his index finger smooth over her temple and down the ridge of her cheekbone. She closed her eyes, letting her head tilt to the side slightly, as if searching for his touch.

The sound of two sets of footsteps coming up the stairs broke Chase out of his stupor and he took a step back. Shaun and Tommy disappeared into the bedroom, the door closing behind them.

Fuck he needed a shot.

"I'll uhh—" he stammered as he spun toward the door. "Good night, Zoey."

Pulling her bedroom door closed behind him as he left, he palmed his aching erection through the fabric of the sweatpants he'd changed into, grateful that his tight boxer-briefs minimized how much showed, though it was torture at the same time. He headed down the stairs and straight to the kitchen.

He reached up over the refrigerator and pulled down a bottle of whiskey he knew Tommy had stashed up there, then found a shot glass in the cupboard. He poured a hefty portion into the small glass and then tossed it back, grimacing as it went down. He rarely drank liquor, let alone did shots. This day was testing all of his willpower and good intentions.

Leaning his hips against the counter, he willed his body to relax. After what felt like an eternity, his aching erection went down to just a chubby, and he could deal with that.

Pouring a second shot, Chase had downed the whiskey when he heard Zoey come down the stairs. He turned his head as she walked in and called himself every filthy name he could think of. She was still wearing that thin purple robe—and nothing underneath it. The deep V of the folds of the robe sliced between the valley of her breasts and all he could think about was dropping to his knees and pressing a hot, open-mouthed kiss to the soft, bare skin there. Her legs and feet were bare as she entered. Her hair was still in the messy topknot from her bath, those tendrils that had escaped the topknot on her head framing her face. She carried her now empty tea mug to the sink, rinsing it. Chase tried not to stare at the curve of her bottom under the robe as she leaned over the sink. *Christ, she isn't wearing any underwear*, he thought on a groan. He was just about to pour a third shot when she turned to face him.

"Are you hungry?" she asked softly, hesitantly, wringing her hands in front of her nervously.

Lord was that a loaded question. Hungry for *her*. Hungry for the feel of her cheek on his fingers like it had been earlier. Hungry for a taste of her mouth beneath his.

But of course, he couldn't say any of those things.

"I thought you were going to bed?" he asked.

"You're the one that said good night to me, I thought you were going to bed," she said, tilting her head slightly to the side. Then she whispered, "I don't want to go to bed yet."

"Fuck," he groaned on a whisper, turning back to the bottle of whiskey and pouring that third shot, picking it up and tossing it back quickly. Then, he braced his palms on the edge of the countertop, gripping it until his knuckles turned white, hanging his head between his shoulders as he tried to breathe. His senses were on hyperdrive, and he heard when she stepped toward him, his back still to her. And then he felt the softest touch against his back, and his knees nearly buckled. She was touching him.

"Chase?" she asked softly, stepping closer. Her breathing was coming in soft, shallow pants, and it was doing nothing to help calm his rapidly fraying control. Her fingers trailed over the curve of his back, along his spine, and he twisted his neck to stare at her over the top of his left bicep, where she had stepped to his side.

"Zoey," he husked, "you aren't ready for this."

"I think I am," she whispered, and he squeezed his eyes shut before reopening them and pinning her with an intense stare.

"You've had a very emotional day. This isn't what you want," he whispered, nothing moving but his lips. Because if he did, he was going to kiss her. He was going to touch her. And even if she didn't know it, he knew she wasn't ready. "This is a trauma response, Zoey."

Zoey's brows furrowed and her lips parted, and he almost wished he could take it back when her hand lifted away from his back as if he'd burnt her. She stepped away, and he hated the hurt he saw clouding her eyes then.

"I'm an idiot, I'm sorry," she whispered. As he straightened, turning toward her, she bolted through the arched doorway and up the stairs. He didn't move until he heard her bedroom door close.

He proceeded to call himself every awful name he could think of.

FORTY-FOUR

"That's enough, Zoey," she heard Chase grunt from behind her. Instead of listening, she gritted her teeth and dipped into another weighted squat, her muscles burning as she rose back up. She saw his hands floating near the bar, ready to grab it, which made her even angrier, and she dipped again, heaving out a breath with the effort. "Zoey, stop, that's enough for this set."

But she shook her head and adjusted her footing and grip on the metal bar that rested on the back of her shoulders. She was angry with him. Angry with herself. And this was the only thing she could do to punish herself.

Keep going until she had no strength for anything. Until she could do nothing but fall into bed and pass out, so she didn't have to relive the rejection from the week before.

She'd been an absolute idiot to think she could ever be what Chase wanted. His rejection had stung, had embarrassed her to tears as she lay in her bed that night. She wouldn't make that same mistake again. Nope.

So she ducked again, lowering into a perfect squat even if her thighs shook and her back ached. As she came up struggling this time, she heard Chase mutter darkly from directly behind her, "God dammit, Zoey, would you stop? This is how you get hurt!"

Too late, she thought mulishly. *Should have stopped me from making an ass of myself. Practically threw myself at your stupid handsome face. That's what hurts.*

Before she could lower into another squat, he lifted the barbell off her shoulders, hauling it back into the cradle. With her hands still wrapped tightly around the bar and no warning, she lost her balance, stumbling backward with a disgruntled, "Hey!"

Because he had stepped forward to grab the barbell from her, as she stumbled back, her ass connected solidly with his front, and they both froze. Her breath sucked in like a vacuum, her arms still at ninety-degree angles, hands wrapped around the bar that now rested in the cradle and his front pressed firmly against the entire plane of her back. And her ass... well, it was planted firmly against Chase's lap.

She could feel his breath as it skittered in uneven puffs against the back of her neck. She expected him to pull away immediately, but neither of them moved except for her to straighten her back, allowing more of the expanse of her back to align with his chest. His hands moved then, sliding over her still clenched fingers, down her forearms until they curved around the underside of her arms.

Zoey was panting; not from her workout or even from the anger that she'd carried like a shield with her all week, but with arousal. She let her eyes drift closed, letting herself feel his hands on the bare skin of her arms. Slowly, achingly slowly, his fingers continued their path along her arms toward her shoulders, where he paused, and she nodded just slightly, and his hands slid down the slope of her ribcage to settle on the curve of her waist.

Her head dipped forward so that her chin nearly touched her chest, her breathing unsteady. Heat was coursing from the top of her head to her toes, and everywhere in between.

She finally pulled away from the heat of his front, dropping her arms to her sides as she turned to face him, raising her eyes to his.

The whole exchange couldn't have lasted more than a handful of heartbeats, but Zoey felt as if something snapped into place between them, this thing that they had both been skirting around for weeks.

Chase cleared his throat and pulled his gaze away from hers, glancing around the busy room. When he looked back down at her, she had dropped her gaze to her hands, rubbing a spot on her left palm where a blister had formed.

"Let's take a break," he murmured huskily, and she nodded. "There's a first aid kit at the front desk, they can give you something to cover that blister."

She didn't raise her eyes to his again before ducking beneath the bar and walking toward the front desk that sat at the front of the room. The attendant gave her a single-use antibiotic packet and a paper wrapped bandage. She pressed the bandage into place, rubbing her fingers along it to mold the adhesive to her palm, and thanked the woman behind the counter again. She turned and headed back through the maze of machines, scanning the faces around her for Chase.

She stopped short when she saw him.

Half laying atop a blonde woman, Zoey's hands clenched into fists at her sides when she recognized the woman as Shay. One of her shapely, tanned legs was thrown over Chase's shoulder as he pressed down, stretching her hamstring. Her face flamed a thousand shades of crimson, but she couldn't tear her eyes away as he leaned into the other woman, her back on the floor. That dark, unruly lock of hair fell over his brow as he pressed into her leg, and Shay reached up and brushed it back. It was... incredibly intimate.

Shay smiled coyly and then grit her teeth as he pushed again. Zoey was close enough now that she could hear as she murmured into his ear that was inches away from her lips, "So... does this mean you're coming over again later?"

Zoey's mouth fell open and her heart thundered in her ears, blocking everything else out. Shay raised her eyes to hers, a smug smile tugging at her lips, as she said, "Can we help you?"

Chase's gaze swung around, and she was frozen to the floor, entrapped in that electric blue gaze. His face fell the slightest, and he moved away from Shay, sitting back on his haunches, just as the mobility seemed to return to Zoey's body. She bolted.

Her face was flaming and she thought she just might throw up, so she dashed into the women's locker room, hiding in the farthest stall. She leaned back against the cool metal door.

Breathe.

She felt humiliation rise through her, choking her.

Breathe, dammit, she thought to herself angrily.

"Zoey," she heard him call into the locker room. She let the back of her head rest against the door at her back.

"Go away," she called back miserably, her throat tight. Mortification made her chest ache. Of course that was the type of woman he would be interested in. Tanned, toned, obnoxiously attractive. Not damaged goods, like she was.

"Zoey, please come out," he said from the doorway, his voice pleading.

"Go away," she repeated, harsher this time. "I'm going home."

"I'm sorry," she heard him say quietly. "I—"

But she didn't want to hear whatever he was going to say. Didn't want to hear about whatever went on between himself and the stunning blonde that seemed to always be there, oogling Chase every chance she got. He'd spotted for her several times, while Zoey was doing warmups or cool downs, the simple workouts that didn't require his assistance... or him being her babysitter.

"I don't care," she grated out and exited the stall, stalking toward him where he still stood just inside the doorway. She chucked her shoes off and threw them in her bag, shoving her feet into her boots and pulling on her jacket. She slung her bag over her shoulder and pushed past him.

"Zoey," Chase started, reaching for her, but she yanked her arm away before he could make contact, her eyes flashing up to his angrily.

"Don't touch me," she said through clenched teeth. She didn't know why she was so angry. It's not like anything had even happened between them. Even if the looks and touches they'd been sharing made her want more... made her want those lips to come down on hers in a fevered kiss—

Glaring up at him, she snapped, "I'm going home."

And she walked back through the maze of machines to the door, exiting out onto the snowy sidewalk.

FORTY-FIVE

By the time eight o'clock had rolled around that evening, Zoey had worked herself into a fine fit. She'd left dinner warming, assuming he'd be home shortly after seven, as he usually was when he worked dayshift, but as the minutes passed and finally reached eight, she was angry as a hornet. The least he could do was let her know he wasn't coming home for dinner!

Then she sighed, letting her own fork drop against the plate. What right did she have to expect any kind of communication regarding his social life? Clearly, she wasn't what he wanted, anyway.

Zoey picked at her food, not really interested in eating it now. Tommy had wolfed down two helpings in the time that Zoey had taken a handful of bites, in between feeding Verity spoons full of pureed sweet potato. She knew Shaun was watching her out of the corner of her eye, but was grateful that she never voiced her concerns.

Zoey was just clearing their plates from the table when the door opened and a flurry of snowflakes whipped in through the door as Chase entered, closing the door forcefully.

She spun around to find him shrugging out of his patrol jacket, and she glared at him as he hung it on the hook by the door, but his face was fierce as he stalked toward her.

"You. We need to talk," he growled as he stopped a foot away from her, his brows pulled down low over his blue eyes.

"Go to hell," she sneered, turning away from him and heading toward the sink. She was acutely aware of the extra pairs of eyes on them from the table as she picked up a dish towel, wringing it in between her trembling fingers.

"Nuh-uh. I let you get away with being a brat earlier, but we're going to have this conversation like adults," he gritted out through clenched teeth. He pointed toward the arched doorway and beyond to the stairs. "Now."

"A brat?" she exclaimed incredulously, her mouth falling open in fury.

He nodded his head once, succinctly.

"You don't get to talk to me like this—" Zoey seethed, and he glared down at her. Shaun had stood, clearly about to object, but he sliced his eyes toward the two still at the table and Shaun stayed silent. "Verity—"

He notched his head toward Shaun and Tommy. "They can watch her for ten minutes."

"I really don't appreciate—"

"I. Don't. Care," he snapped, each word clipped and curt, as he pointed toward the doorway. "I'm not going to say it again, Zoey. I will throw you over my shoulder and carry you out if necessary."

"You wouldn't dare," she whispered on a furious taunt, but then a tingle of fear skittered down her spine as his eyes darkened and he took one menacing step toward her. Fear, excitement—she didn't know what it was and she didn't know if she wanted to find out—washed over her and she stammered, "Okay! Fine."

Slamming the dish towel down onto the counter beside the sink, she marched through the doorway and turned to climb the stairs, her footfalls heavy with anger. She knew by the sound of his own booted footsteps that he followed close behind her. When she got to her bedroom, she walked in, Chase right on her heels. When she turned to glare at him, he shut the door with enough force that it startled her momentarily.

She swallowed through sudden panic, whispering, "Chase—"

"I want you to be quiet," he snapped, each word clipped. His electric blue eyes were alight as they met hers. She shivered, though the panic had faded when he didn't make another move toward her. Even as angry as he was—and she could tell he was *pissed*—she knew she was safe. This was Chase, after all. "I want you to shut that pretty mouth of yours and listen to me."

She opened her mouth to object out of spite, but the look he gave her was withering, and she shut her mouth with a click. She crossed her arms over her chest, notching one hip out. Waiting.

"What you heard today—" he started, and she opened her mouth again, but he glared at her until she rolled her eyes and stayed silent. "What Shay said... I haven't gone there in a long time, Zoey."

"I don't care," she said stiffly. "You're a grown man. You can diddle whoever you want."

"Diddle?" he asked, his eyes lightening just the slightest in amusement.

Zoey rolled her eyes in exasperation. "Why should I care what you do, Chase?"

"Why *do* you care?" he asked huskily, stepping forward once. Twice.

"I don't," Zoey lied, swallowing past the lump it caused. He towered over her now, stopping barely a foot from her. She glared up, a long way up, into his face.

"Liar," he breathed.

Dammit.

"What does it matter?" she snapped, shifting from one foot to the other.

"What does it matter?" he repeated, his voice a low, husky growl. It sent shivers down her entire body. "It matters, because *I* care. Because every single day that I spend with you, every single time I touch you, it makes me want more. It matters, because when that prick put his hands on you last week, I about went insane with not only fury, but jealousy. *It matters*, Zoey, because I have been telling myself not to... but for weeks I have been dying to know what it feels like to kiss you."

Zoey's breath hitched in her throat as she stared at him, then started again, choppy and uneven.

Not with fear. No, that's not what was making her heart hammer inside her chest as she looked up at him, at that devastatingly handsome face, into those intense blue eyes.

Desire curled around her, through her, making her cheeks feel flushed and her body feel like a livewire had been touched to her bare skin.

He stepped forward again, bringing them within inches of each other, her clothing rustling against the fabric of his uniform that he still wore. His breath puffed against her face as he stared down at her, his chest rising and falling with his own ragged breathing. He was so close, but his hands never moved, as always leaving the choice up to her.

Her eyes fell to his mouth, and she saw his jaw tighten slightly before she raised her eyes to his once more.

She nodded, just barely, and he groaned low in his throat before his head lowered to hers.

At the first touch of his lips to hers, Zoey gasped. It was like a match being set to kindling.

Feather light, just his lips brushing hers. Her eyes were open, wide as they stared into his. His breathing was ragged, as was her own, but still, he didn't press further.

Waiting for her.

Her hands moved of their own accord, rising to either side of his face, one sliding around the back of his neck, the other slipping through his shaggy hair. She tugged on the back of his neck, bringing his head down even as she raised on tiptoes to capture his lips more fully with her own.

Fire exploded inside her as his tongue met hers for the first time, stroking softly, tangling lightly. His lips moved over hers, never rough, always gentle. Zoey moaned into his mouth, and he chuckled breathlessly.

His hands slid around her waist to her back, but he quickly withdrew, whispering, "I'm sorry, I should have asked—"

But Zoey was shaking her head, pressing closer to him, aligning her body to his. Pressing her lips against his, she breathed brokenly, "It's okay. Please, don't stop."

Zoey sighed when his hands came back up to slide across her lower back, and she propelled forward another half step, bringing her front into direct contact with his, from chest to hips. His body curved around hers, their height difference only making it better as she clung to him as their kiss deepened, and a groan rumbled through his chest and into hers. She shivered at the sensation of feeling his chest rumble against her breasts. She kissed him again, deeply, hungrily, relishing the feel of his mouth on hers finally.

"God, I've wanted to do this for weeks," he breathed against her lips, his voice low, husky. When she adjusted her body against his again, pressing her hips against his, she sucked in her breath, and her eyes flew to his. His lips tilted at one corner in a wry smile, his fingers smoothing lightly over her back in soothing sweeps. "I can't help the effect you have on me, Zoey."

"I—I don't know that I'm ready for that, Chase," she whispered, embarrassed at the admission, and she lowered her gaze.

One hand left her back and reached up to tip her chin up gently, until she was looking at him again. "I'm not asking you to. I would never ask you to do something you're not ready for. You know that, right?"

She nodded, though her heart was hammering with anxiety. This was a lot to process all at once. Not that she hadn't been thinking about it for weeks... But this was different. This was real, tangible, not some pipe dream.

"May I kiss you again?" he asked quietly.

In answer, Zoey raised her lips to meet his as he lowered his head. He was infinitely gentle, his touch never heavy or threatening. Zoey hadn't been kissed like this... ever. Had never felt this all-encompassing, soul deep arousal that spiraled through her with every brush of his lips over hers, every slide of his fingers against her skin, every sweep of his tongue through her mouth.

"Zoey," he groaned then, dragging his lips from hers. He pressed his forehead against hers, rolling it there as he chuckled raggedly. "Holy hell, you're so sweet. You taste even better than I imagined." His fingers trailed over the soft skin at the crook of her neck and she shivered. "I don't want to stop kissing you, but I don't want to frighten you."

"You're not," she whispered, breathing against his lips even as he continued to roll his forehead across hers. "Please don't stop."

Chase growled and pressed his lips to hers once more, this kiss deeper than the others, hungrier, needier. She arched against him, her body screaming at her for more, more. To which he gladly obliged.

He towered over her, his hands once more at her back, holding her against him without being demanding or overpowering. Zoey's body was on fire. *More*, she cried internally. *I want more.*

"I want—" she started, but stopped, biting her lip.

"What do you want, sweetheart?" Chase whispered huskily, his lips trailing along her jaw, up to her temple. Zoey let her head fall back, giving him better access. "What do you want, Zoey? Tell me, I'll do anything."

"Will you... will you sit down?" she asked shyly. "I want to touch you."

He kissed her lips again before backing away, one of her hands lightly clasped in his, until the backs of his knees touched the edge of her mattress, and he sank down onto it. His knees spread, and she stepped forward until she stood between them. His mouth was now level with the base of her throat, and he leaned forward just slightly to press his lips to the heartbeat she knew was fluttering there. His fingers trailed over the slope of her hips, down to the outside of her thighs, but they didn't move any further.

Zoey's fingers fluttered over the hard ridges of his shoulders, trailing over the detailing on his uniform. She reached for his necktie and giggled when it unexpectedly popped off; she wasn't expecting a clip-on.

He shrugged, grinning at her. "It's for safety. A real necktie could be used to strangle us."

Zoey nodded soberly, an unwitting image of some faceless attacker using his own necktie to hurt him. She banished the thought, wanting to be present in this moment.

Her fingers continued their way down his front, releasing the first several buttons of his brown uniformed dress shirt. When the backs of her knuckles tickled the now bare skin just inside the folds of his shirt, he sucked in his breath, grinning wolfishly up at her.

His hands were still lightly resting on the backs of her thighs, though they did trail up and down several inches either way, making her squirm.

"Do you have anything on under this shirt?" she asked, pulling at the folds of his shirt to peer inside, but all she saw was tanned, bare flesh.

"Would you like me to take it off?" he asked softly, watching her.

"I don't know," she whispered. "Yes. No. I don't know!"

He chuckled, and she could feel it rumble through his chest where her fingers were still pressed against his skin at the base of his throat. "We take this as fast or as slow as you want, Zoey. I'm in no rush."

"Can I touch you if you take your shirt off?" she murmured, glancing at him through her lashes. "Or is that not fair?"

His hands left the backs of her thighs, and his fingers were already working on the remaining buttons down the front of his shirt. "You can touch anything and everything you want, Zoey. Learn my body. I want you comfortable with it. With me."

Oh, swoon.

How was he so freaking perfect?

Before she knew it, he was shrugging out of the dark brown shirt, and his upper body and abdomen were gloriously naked to her. She'd seen him in this state of undress many times over the last two months, but never this up close and personal.

And I get to touch.

Chase took her hands in his, bringing one, then the other to his lips, where he pressed a tender kiss to her fingers, before planting them, palms flat, against the slope of his chest.

His breathing was ragged, and she could see his chest rising and falling, feel it shuddering under her hands. She slipped one hand over the smooth expanse of his shoulder so that she could slide her fingers through the hair at the back of his head.

"I don't know if I want to keep touching you or keep kissing you," she whispered breathlessly.

"How about both?" he breathed against her lips, pressing light, sipping kisses there. "I am yours to do with whatever you want, sweetheart."

Zoey moaned and pressed her mouth to his more firmly, and within a heartbeat their mouths had melded, tongues tangling again. They kissed until they were both breathless, and Zoey's insides had been turned to mush.

She did what he said and splayed her hands wide, smoothing her palms over as much of his bare skin as she could. Her fingers learned the curvature of his pecs, strummed the muscles that bunched and flexed along his upper back and down the backs of his arms. He sucked in his breath on a shudder when her fingers flit over his hard abdomen, and they smiled against each other's lips.

"This is insane," she whispered. "I can't believe this is happening."

"Hmm," he hummed in agreement. "Is this okay?" he asked, spreading his large hands wide on the backs of her thighs again, squeezing lightly. She nodded, and the tingle that jolted through her body straight to her middle felt like an electric shock. His fingers were just inches from the cleft of her thighs, where she ached deliciously.

Their mouths fused again, and Chase growled low in his throat when she grew bold and slipped her tongue into his mouth to chase after his. He nipped at her bottom lip lightly, and she gasped as the sensation did wonderful things to her.

When his fingers trailed toward the inner curves of her thighs, she stiffened reflexively and he immediately dropped his hands, letting his arms fall to his sides, and she closed her eyes against the agony that crossed his face.

"I'm sorry," she whispered brokenly, tears stinging her nose.

"Don't," he murmured from where he sat, his chest heaving. "I told you not to apologize to me. Ever."

She took a small step forward, until the front of her thighs touched the insides of his. She reached for one of his hands, bringing it up to her mouth, where she pressed a kiss to the backs of his fingers. Whispering, she said, "I want you to touch me."

But he shook his head gently, letting one corner of his mouth tilt up marginally. "I want to touch you, too, sweetheart. But I don't want you shrinking away from me when I do."

The torment in those blue eyes that raised to hers was a testament to how much her mental and emotional well-being meant to him, how much it affected him. And how deeply he meant the words that he said. Tears shimmered in her eyes, and his other hand raised to swipe one that escaped down her cheek. He then leaned forward slowly, until his lips met hers once more, brushing softly.

Then, his breath ragged against her lips, he whispered huskily, "Because when I'm finally inside you, sweetheart, I will be the only man you think about."

FORTY-SIX

"I was about to come do a hand check," Shaun muttered dryly as Zoey and Chase came back down the stairs into the living room. She had taken the time to fix the makeup that had gotten smudged during their kiss while he had gone to his bedroom to change out of his uniform. Watching him walk out of her bedroom, his back bare down to the line of his pants around his hips was... enough to make her want to grab his hand and pull him back to her to keep doing what they'd been doing.

Zoey felt her face flame scarlet at Shaun's sly words, and she glanced first at Tommy, who was staring at Chase beneath lowered brows, and then over at Chase. He winked at her before coming around the couch and finally picking up the squealing, wriggling infant from the floor where she'd been playing with an assortment of baby toys on a blanket.

She watched as Chase raised his eyes to Tommy, and again that strained look passed between them.

Then again, she was sure Tommy knew exactly what had been going on upstairs... and even if he'd said he was okay with it, she was still his little sister, and Chase his best friend. Wasn't there some guy-code that made best friend's little sisters off limits?

She shook her head, not wanting to worry about that now. Because all she wanted to do was relive everything that had just transpired.

She'd kissed Chase. And Lordy was it amazing!

She watched as Chase held Verity high over his head, letting her kick and flail her arms wildly in the air. Her little shirt rode up where his hands held her beneath her arms, revealing a large chunk of belly, and he took advantage of it, lowering her so he could blow raspberries into it. Verity let out a scream of delight and fisted her little fingers into Chase's long hair in excitement.

He yelped, but chuckled, and within a heartbeat the infant had released her death grip so he could bring her back into the cradle of his arms. He lowered his tall frame into the recliner chair, turning Verity in his lap so that her back rested against his front. She was having none of it, as she twisted like a miniature crocodile, so that she could look up at him. He clasped her under her arms, pulling her up so that she was sitting in his lap, facing him. She clapped her chubby hands wildly and he leaned down to press a raspberry kiss to her neck, making her squeal another high-pitched giggle.

"Would you like me to warm up your dinner?" Zoey asked quietly from where she stood by the kitchen door. He turned his head from where he sat in the recliner to look at her. He smiled, and it made her stomach do flip flops crazily. The bastard knew it too, because his electric blue eyes darkened with desire as he stared at her.

"I could eat," he murmured, his voice thick.

Zoey swallowed hard, a blush tingeing her cheeks once more, before turning and fairly running through the arched doorway to the kitchen to escape those blue eyes.

She made a plate quickly, fingers fumbling. She brought it out to him where he still sat with Verity in his lap. Zoey could tell by the way Verity was beginning to arch her back that she was overly tired and ready for bed. Coming around to the front of Chase's chair, he took it with one hand, and she reached down to pick the baby up to free his other hand. The backs of her hands were pressed snugly against the hardness of his abdomen as she slid them between Verity's body and his, and she felt more than heard his sharp intake of breath at her touch.

Her eyes flew to his, their faces mere inches apart where she leaned over him to pick up the baby, and she was surprised at the urge to incline forward to press her lips to his again. And again.

Tommy coughed uncomfortably, making Zoey jump. She hurriedly pulled Verity away, straightening and slinking around the couch and disappearing up the stairs.

FORTY-SEVEN

Chase watched Zoey as she moved around the kitchen. After putting Verity to bed, she had come downstairs, her pretty indigo eyes finding his where he had moved to the couch, the longer sofa allowing him to stretch out now that Shaun and Tommy had left to her apartment for the night. She came over and picked up the now empty plate from the coffee table where he'd set it, and he made to stand, but she insisted that he stay where he was.

From where he was sitting on the couch in the living room, he could watch her while she cleaned up after dinner; the dinner he had interrupted and demanded she go upstairs with him to talk.

He chuckled to himself. They certainly hadn't done much talking.

He could tell things had finally shifted between them after that kiss. His dick woke up as he thought back to how good her mouth tasted; how soft her lips were against his own... Her eyes kept finding his as she moved around the kitchen, as if she couldn't *not* look at him.

They hadn't had the chance to talk about what had happened upstairs, or what it meant for them, but they would have time. All he knew was that he liked Zoey. He *liked her,* liked her. A lot. She had quickly become a vital part of his life. And lord did she do things to him, drove him damn near crazy. He wanted her, but more than that, he just wanted to be with her, every day.

He had known he hurt her feelings that night in the kitchen, knew she would see it as rejection. She had barely looked at him, barely spoke to him, all week. It was hell. As if all the other flashing neon signs that were making it glaringly obvious they were moving in this direction, her self-imposed absence in his day to day life over the last week had been nothing but torture. He'd *missed* her.

He'd been angry as hell at her by the time he'd pulled that damn barbell out of her hands—something he should have never done, for her safety and his own—but it had all disappeared when her body hauled up against his. He'd lost all train of thought except, *holy fuck.*

And then she'd seen him with Shay and he'd seen the hurt in her eyes, which killed him more than anything. He'd worked himself into a downright bear of a mood all day as he'd gone over what he was going to say to her when he got home, and the more he thought about it, the angrier he got. Until he'd slammed into the door, grateful to see a little bit of spark in those eyes finally, instead of that hollow, dejected sadness that had clung to her all week.

He loved when she was feisty. She was fighting, finally.

When Tommy had first come to him that night with that insane proposition, Chase had thought he was losing it. It was Zoey... he couldn't be with Zoey, definitely couldn't marry Zoey.

Now... it was all he thought about. The thought of her being with anyone else made his stomach churn. He wanted to be the one to take care of her, take care of Verity. He wanted, no, *he needed* to be the one that held her, kissed her, because she made him burn just as much as he now knew she did for him.

Perhaps it was his male vanity or some kind of he-man complex that made him want to beat his chest with his fists and roar, but he felt deep pleasure at knowing she felt safe around him; she didn't flinch at his touch—except when he touched the inside of her thighs, which he'd made a mental note to avoid in the future—but his chest puffed up with pride at how far she'd come from several months ago.

As if sensing his gaze, Zoey looked over at him and caught him staring. She blushed and dropped her eyes, but within a heartbeat had raised them back to his as she set the dish towel on the counter. His cock twitched at the hungry look in those indigo eyes.

She came toward him, walking around the room until she stood in front of him where he reclined in one corner of the couch. He rolled into more of a sitting position and extended his hand to her. Without hesitation she placed her hand in his, and he tugged her down to the couch beside him and she settled close to his side, touching from shoulders to hips to knees. She tucked her legs up beneath her, leaning more fully into his side, and that he-man urge to beat at his chest in triumph rose in him all over again.

Moving slowly, he raised his arm until it was draped over her shoulders, his left hand cupping the outside of her arm. Her hand came to rest on his thigh, and he nearly catapulted off the couch at the innocent but electrifying touch.

She looked up at him then and he reached across with his other hand, tipping her chin up with his forefinger and thumb on her chin, and he held her gaze so she would understand his intention as he lowered his mouth to hers. The hand on his thigh tightened, but her eyes slid shut and tilted her head and leaned into his kiss, her other hand splaying wide on his abdomen.

Their mouths melded, heads turning in opposite directions to allow the kiss to deepen. Chase's fingers slid from her chin to cup her jaw and she shivered, sighing against his mouth. His cock was rock hard behind the fly of his pants and he groaned deep in his chest. "You drive me crazy, Zoey."

He watched as worry flashed over her face as she pulled back slightly, and he immediately regretted what he'd said. "I'm sorry," she whispered, lowering her eyes. "I don't mean to—to tease you..."

Chase slid his fingers into her blonde hair, tipping her head back up so she was looking at him again. "That's not what I meant, I swear. We take this as slow as you want, I promise. I don't ever want you to feel pressure from me, sweetheart."

Zoey shifted on the couch beside him, blushing when she glanced down at his lap, at the obvious evidence of his own arousal. "I don't want you to think I'm doing it on purpose."

Chase grinned then, rubbing his thumb across her cheekbone lightly. "I'm sure you do it on purpose, just like I do this—" he kissed her thoroughly until they were both breathless, before continuing raggedly, "—on purpose, too. This... teasing... is normal, sweetheart. It's part of the foreplay in a relationship."

Zoey's indigo eyes went wide as she stared at him. "A relationship?" she whispered.

Chase smiled gently and nodded, though his heart was hammering in his chest. They hadn't talked about what any of this was... but it felt right. He nodded, murmuring softly, "I think so, don't you?"

"You—you would want that?" she asked in a shaky breath, her eyes still searching his. "With me?"

"Very much," he murmured honestly, his thumb still rubbing in small strokes on her cheek. "Would you want that with me?"

"Yes," she said with no hesitation, before she blushed and a shy smile pulled at her lips. She leaned forward, pressing her mouth to his in another kiss and he nearly lost it when she pushed her tongue into his mouth to reach for his. He growled his approval, meeting her kiss hungrily. She moaned against his mouth, her fingers fisting into the fabric of his shirt over his abdomen. Pulling away just far enough to catch her breath, she whispered, "I've been thinking about this for weeks, too, Chase."

"I tried not to," he said gruffly, spreading his fingers through the hair at the nape of her neck, letting his eyes rove over her face. "You're my best friend's little sister."

Zoey laughed, and his heart expanded exponentially. From this close, he could see how her eyes held little flecks of gold around the irises, that deep indigo blue with a darker blue ring around the outer edge. She had a smattering of freckles across the bridge of her nose that he hadn't noticed before. He wanted her to laugh again.

"Why is that funny?" he asked, leaning back slightly and grinning at her.

She smiled back, shrugging her shoulders. "I don't think you're going to have much of a fight from Tommy is all."

He swallowed hard, his heart thudding painfully in his chest. "What do you mean?"

Zoey laughed then, lowering her lashes over her eyes shyly. "He uhh— asked me if there was anything going on between us. I said no, because at the time, I didn't know what any of this was... but he told me he wouldn't kick your ass, if there was something between us."

He let out a deep breath, chuckling, though his gut tightened with guilt. "That's surprising. I thought he'd be against it."

"Oh, not at all," Zoey laughed, and that knife twisted in his stomach a little more. He hated this, but lord was this exactly where he wanted to be right now. "I think he was hoping it would happen."

Oh, sweetheart, if you only knew... but he shook the thought away. He didn't want to think about anything but the beauty in his arms right now. He pecked another kiss to her lips softly before tucking her into his side. He squeezed her shoulders gently and let his hand trail over the outside of her arm. She settled against him, resting her cheek on his chest, and he sucked in his breath when her fingers strummed along his abdomen through his shirt. He was still achingly hard behind the fly of his jeans. He leaned down and pressed a kiss to the top of her head and she snuggled deeper against him, and he smiled.

Flipping through the tv channels, he landed on a college basketball game and settled into the corner of the couch, content to have her close. His fingers continued to sweep over her arm, trailing from the tip of her shoulder to her elbow and back. After several minutes he glanced down to look at her and smiled when he realized she had fallen asleep, her breathing shallow and even. Dragging the blanket off the back of the couch behind them, he carefully spread it over her, then let his chin rest against the top of her head.

With her asleep against him, it wasn't long before he followed her into sleep.

FORTY-EIGHT

Zoey woke by slow degrees, stretching and then going completely still.

She was sleeping on someone. Her cheek pressed to a hard abdomen, her mouth inches away from a lap, her arm thrown across hard thighs that were stretched out alongside her. A hand was tangled in the hair at the back of her head and with every rise and fall of the abdomen beneath her cheek she heard a soft snore from above her.

The tv was still on, casting a blue glow through the otherwise dark living room, and the sound was muted. She licked her lips, swallowing hard as she realized just how close she was to Chase's lap... and the fly of his jeans.

Stretching again, she grimaced at how sore she was. Sleeping on a couch was not nearly as comfortable as a bed, and her back and hips were aching from the position. Garnering the courage to try and move, her breath halted when she felt the fingers in her hair moving, stroking softly, and it was then that she noticed the bulge that had begun to form behind the fly of his jeans, inches from her face. When she dared to breathe, her breaths came in quick, shallow pants.

Neither of them moved save the gentle stroking of his fingers through her hair, and with each passing second, she could feel herself growing more aroused at the simple, innocent touch. Her fingers smoothed over the fabric of his jeans on his lower thigh, just above his knee where her hand rested, and she felt more than heard his rough exhale of breath above her.

Raising her cheek from where she'd been resting, she turned her head to look up at him where he had slouched into the corner of the couch in his sleep, reclining so that he was laying nearly flat, making a human body pillow for her to rest more comfortably on. The dim blue glow of the tv illuminated his face, making his eyes look even more intensely blue than normal as he stared down at her. She rested her opposite cheek on his abdomen, her eyes roving over his face. Her eyes slid shut when his fingers continued their soothing stroking through her hair, massaging the back of her head softly, her lips parting slightly in a breathy moan.

Another growled groan rumbled out of him and she opened her eyes, meeting his intense gaze again. His breathing was becoming labored, his chest rising and falling rapidly, but he remained perfectly still other than that.

Rising up onto her elbow, his hand fell from where it had been sifting through her hair as she rested, half laying over his abdomen, her eyes still searching his. "Zoey..." she saw his lips form, and she didn't hesitate another heartbeat before leaning forward to press her mouth to his.

His answering growl of approval made her brave, and she moved closer, her hair falling over her shoulder to form a curtain on one side of their faces as they kissed. The hand that had previously been in her hair returned, sliding up the slope of her back, urging her closer gently. His other hand smoothed the curtain of hair back away from her face, twisting it through his fingers before cupping the back of her neck as their kiss deepened, mouths moving ravenously. Zoey moaned, clenching her thighs together tight. She was wet and aching.

Pushing her away gently, he sat up, pulling the edge of his shirt up until he could pull it over his head, tossing it away, before returning to his reclining position, this time naked from the waist up. Reaching for her hand, he dragged it to his mouth, where he pressed a hot, open-mouthed kiss to her wrist, and her pulse jumped at the contact, making her gasp.

His eyes were intense as he stared into her own, and he held her gaze as he moved her hand down to press it to his naked chest. "Touch me, please, Zoey."

Staring at him for a long heartbeat, she finally lowered her eyes to where her hand rested on the slope of his chest. His hand fell away from the back of hers as she trailed just the tips of her fingers across the hard expanse of chest laid bare for her.

His arms were muscular and toned, his soft, tanned skin looked soft to the touch, so she did, smoothing her palm over every inch she could reach. Her fingers slid down the valley of his abdominal muscles toward his belly button, though she didn't dare go further.

When he made a strangled sound in the back of his throat, she snatched her hand back and her eyes flew to his, just to be caught in those cobalt blue depths like an insect in a Venus fly trap. His hand came up and caught her behind the back of her neck, pulling her down toward his mouth. She fell forward, letting her hand catch her on the back of the couch as she leaned into his kiss. This kiss was hungry, carnal, and delicious. "Oh my god," she moaned, shifting against him, her body on fire. "I need..."

"What, sweetheart? What do you need?" he asked when she didn't continue, his voice rough with arousal. "Is this okay?"

She nodded frantically, her lips moving against his. "I don't know what I need," she moaned, frustrated. She was still so new to this. She knew she wanted something, something more. But she didn't know how to ask for it. "I wasn't expecting to... hurt."

Panic flashed in his eyes, and he pulled his hands away quickly, and she cried out at the loss. "I'm hurting you?" he asked, worried.

"No," she cried in a groan, rolling her forehead against his. "Chase, I want more."

He chuckled against her mouth then, lacing his fingers through her hair once more, pulling her mouth more firmly against his. "Ahhh," he murmured, nipping at her bottom lip lightly. "You've never been turned on like this, have you?"

Zoey shook her head, clenching her thighs tight again against the onslaught of arousal at his words. A blush fired through her, making her even hotter, and she fisted her fingers against the fabric covering the couch. "I want... something. I don't know how to do this..."

"Have you ever touched yourself, Zoey?" he asked against her mouth, and she thought she would evaporate on the spot with embarrassment. She remembered overhearing him in his room and flushed hotly at how she'd wanted to touch herself, too. She shook her head and a growl rumbled through him before he asked, "You've never had an orgasm, sweetheart?"

She shook her head again, embarrassment flooding her. She opened her eyes when she felt his fingers at her chin, his lips touching hers softly. He shifted on the couch, centering himself on the cushions, forcing her body over his. She gasped when she felt his hardness at her hip.

"Put one leg on this side of my hip," he murmured huskily, patting the other side of the couch. She stared down at him in shock and he grinned wolfishly before pecking another quick kiss to her surprised mouth. "If you want to, you can climb up. I won't hurt you, I promise, sweetheart. I just want to make you feel good."

She swallowed hard but did as he instructed, shifting so that she could swing one leg over both of his so that she was straddling his hips, her hands resting on his bare chest for balance. His hands rested on the couch, not touching her as she adjusted herself over him. Leaving her completely in control.

She gasped again when she felt his hardness at the apex of her thighs, terrifying and thrilling at the same time. He was panting beneath her, his chest rising and falling sharply with each harsh breath, his eyes intense as he stared up at her. She settled on him and cried out at the sensation, grinding slightly, before stopping abruptly, embarrassed again. She raised herself off of him and whispered, "I'm sorry—"

"Does it feel good to you, Zoey?" he asked, his voice low, strained. She nodded. "It does to me, too. You can do whatever you want to me. I told you I want you to learn my body. I want you comfortable with it, with me. Do whatever feels good, sweetheart."

His words were sexy, thrilling, and sweet. His hardness pressed against the junction of her thighs, through their clothing, and she rotated her hips, moaning quietly. She watched him beneath her, her mind hazy with arousal. She ached, down to her core. She'd had no idea desire could feel so painfully erotic. Apparently, she had a lot to learn.

He didn't touch her, instead left his hands clutched into fists at his sides, letting her make these discoveries on her own, letting her learn him in her own way. Leaning down, she kissed him, her tongue spiraling into his mouth, and she rocked over him. She gasped when he groaned fiercely beneath her, and the sound made her even more feral. She still didn't know what she wanted more of, but she knew she wanted something.

"Chase," she cried against his mouth, rotating her hips against his in an effort to appease the ache there, but it just made it worse. She was panting, her breathing harsh against his lips. "I don't... don't know what I need."

"Sit up, sweetheart," he whispered raggedly, and she did as he said, until she was sitting more firmly on the ridge behind his fly. He reached for one of her hands, bringing it to his lips and kissing it before moving it toward her, and she blushed furiously when she realized what he was suggesting she do. "Use me to make yourself come, Zoey. Touch yourself."

"I—I can't," she whispered brokenly, suddenly shy. But he held her hand at the waistband of her leggings, leaving the decision up to her. "I don't know what to do..."

"Do whatever feels good, sweetheart," he whispered huskily. "I want my brave girl to come for me, let me see it. Use my body to make yourself come, Zoey. Learn your body, too."

Sliding her hand into the waistband of her leggings, she closed her eyes when her fingers found her clit. She knew his eyes were on her, could feel it as her cheeks heated in another shy blush. But then she ground herself against him as she began to circle that little nub, moaning at how good it felt, and he groaned his approval beneath her, which made her braver. Why had she never done this before?

She opened her eyes, staring down at him as she moved herself over him, rubbing herself along the hard ridge between her thighs, all the while continuing to stroke and circle until her legs started to shake. Her hand reached for his, squeezing tight. She didn't know what she was building toward, but whatever it was, she wasn't going to stop until she got there. This felt too good.

"That's my girl," he whispered from beneath her and she gasped. "Keep going, sweetheart."

She was climbing, climbing toward a precipice, her entire body humming like an electric current was running through it. Grinding against him, she cried out as her body began to tighten and she stopped, worried she was going to do something wrong.

"Oh god, don't stop," Chase panted beneath her, and she resumed her manipulations against that little nub, quickly rising once again. "Go over, sweetheart. I've got you. I want you to feel so good all you can think about is this, about us."

"Oh!" she cried, throwing her head back when she reached that pinnacle, her body hurtling itself over that cliff to free fall into an intense, body shaking climax. "Chaaaase..." she moaned long and low, her entire body trembling and shaking as something inside her quivered uncontrollably and stars burst behind her tightly clenched eyes.

"Fuck," Chase moaned beneath her, raising his hips just the slightest to grind against her as she continued to move over him. Her chest was heaving as her sight returned and she sagged against him, pulling her hand out of her now drenched leggings. She raised her head from where she had pressed her forehead against his shoulder to catch her breath. His hands drifted over the curve of her back lightly and he turned his head to press his mouth to hers sweetly. "You did so good, sweetheart. That was beautiful to watch."

Zoey blushed, coming down off that high. She could still feel him hard against her and she made to move off of him as she whispered, "I'm sorry..."

He didn't let her move away from him though, his fingers trailing in soothing sweeps across her back as he chuckled raggedly. "Don't. This wasn't about me, sweetheart. This was all about you. How did that feel?"

She blushed again but smiled shyly. "I think I'd like to do that again."

He laughed, his teeth shining whitely against his face in the semi darkness of the room. "Good. I'd like that, too."

"I feel like I *should* be embarrassed... but it felt too good I don't even care," she whispered and blushed again when he chuckled. One of his hands came up and brushed the hair away from her face, tucking it behind her ear with his fingers. Resting her chin against his sternum, she gazed up at him as she whispered, "Is... is that what it's supposed to be like?"

Sweeping the rest of her hair over her shoulder with the back of his hand, he let his fingers trail over her now bare neck and curve of her shoulder, and she tilted her head in the opposite direction to allow him better access. He smiled at her and she saw that his eyes crinkled at the corners slightly when he did so. His other hand came up and combed through her hair and she sighed at how good it felt. She'd never had this kind of intimacy before and had not held out hope of ever getting to. She stayed quiet, enjoying his light touches while she waited for his response.

"Yes, sweetheart, that's what it's supposed to be like," he said gently, though she could see a hint of sadness in his eyes. "I hope to earn your trust enough to show you how much better it can be, too."

"It gets better than that?" she asked in awe, and knew her eyes must be as big as saucers.

He grinned at her, letting his thumb smooth over her cheek lightly. "Mmhmm. That was just a teaser, sweetheart." When Zoey's eyes widened, he chuckled, but his voice was soothing when he murmured, "We're not in a rush."

Fighting and losing the battle to a wide yawn, Zoey let her cheek rest against his chest. "I should go to bed, but I don't want to... I like laying here with you."

Chase shifted them so that she was lying to his side, his back pressed against the back cushions of the couch. "Turn over," he murmured gently, but she shook her head quickly, and he must have seen the momentary panic flash in her eyes. "I'm sorry, I just thought that it would be more comfortable for you."

Zoey tamped down the anxiety and shook her head again, leaning away on her elbow. "It's okay, I'm sorry." She grimaced when he glared at her for the apology. Taking a deep breath, she closed her eyes and whispered, "He... he did it from behind. I don't— I trust you, Chase... but I don't think I can have you behind me..."

"You don't have to explain," he said gently, sweeping his thumb over her cheek softly. She didn't know what had possessed her to tell him. She hadn't shared details of that night with anyone other than her therapist. She peeked at him from beneath her lashes shyly, and when her gaze met his, he said softly, "But thank you for trusting me enough to tell me."

Her heart melted at the sincerity in his voice, and she knew without a doubt she was falling even more in love with him. There was no stopping the rapid free-fall she was in now.

He dropped his hand from her face and reached for the blanket that had been pushed into the crease of the couch, holding it aloft. She settled in front of him, her cheek level with his chest, and he draped the blanket over them before wrapping his arm around her waist to keep her from falling off the edge of the couch.

For a year her response to physical touch had been pure terror; it felt strange to be in the circle of Chase's arms without that accompanying fear.

Instead, she felt incredibly safe and protected. She could hear the steady cadence of his heart beneath her ear, feel it beneath the palm she had resting against his chest. So much had changed in such a short amount of time, but it somehow felt right.

It felt *normal*.

And with that thought, she settled against him and closed her eyes, inhaling deeply the now familiar scent of sandalwood and eucalyptus as she drifted off to sleep.

FORTY-NINE

Chase somehow managed to disentangle himself from the jumble of limbs and blanket that he and Zoey were in without waking her, which was no small feat. Padding silently to the kitchen, he prepped the coffee to percolate and then headed up the stairs to his bedroom. Stretching his aching body, he groaned. The couch was far too short for his six foot five frame and made for a short night of sleep, but he would do it all over again if he could hold her like that every time.

Gathering his uniform pieces together, he laid them out on his bed before he slipped down the hall into the bathroom and started the shower. He'd overslept with no alarm set to wake him, so he had just enough time for a quick shower before he needed to be out the door, definitely no time for a run today.

He showered hastily before stepping out and drying with a towel, then slung it around his hips before slipping back out the door.

Stopping, he listened at the door of Zoey's room for any sign of Verity beginning to wake, but the room was silent. He continued down the hallway and into his bedroom, shucking the towel and quickly dressing in the uniform he'd laid out, glancing at the clock next to his bed.

Racing back out the door and down the stairs, he tiptoed through the living room as quietly as he could in his heavy work boots. He peered over the edge of the couch, smiling when he saw Zoey still sleeping soundly, curled into the blanket he'd covered her with when he'd gotten up. He checked the baby monitor next to her on the coffee table, the small green and red lights indicating it was powered on and working; she would hear Verity when she finally awoke, if she wasn't awake before then, though he hoped she took advantage of the weekend and slept in, at least a little. They were up late.

At that thought, he nearly groaned into the quiet, semi darkness of the room as he remembered how unbelievably gorgeous she had been sitting above him, on him, trusting him implicitly. How insanely sexy she had been as she made herself come with her fingers, his name on her lips...

Taking a deep, steadying breath in, he stepped into the kitchen and poured a hefty portion of coffee into a travel thermos. He slipped on his patrol jacket, then lifted his hat from the hook by the door before taking one last look toward Zoey sleeping on the couch.

By the time he made the short drive to the station, he had just enough time to rush into the building and clock in before the morning debriefing started. At six foot five, sneaking in was not really an option, but he tried his best to slink into the back, leaning back against the wall.

Sheriff Bradley eyed him stonily, but continued his morning debrief. His partner, Graham, snickered then coughed roughly to cover it, and Chase rolled his eyes.

It must have been an uneventful night shift, because the brief was short lived, and then they were dismissed. Graham stood, picking up his coffee cup and walking toward Chase, who pushed away from the wall.

Graham's blonde eyebrows went up in a silent question, one side of his mouth tipping in a smirk. Chase shook his head and motioned toward the door, exiting. The two headed toward their desks, which were just two small tables pushed together so that they faced each other when sitting at them. A desktop computer sat on the top of each one, and as Chase sat down, he wiggled the mouse enough to wake the screen up before typing in his credentials and logging into his system. A small filing cabinet sat beneath each of the desks, and he used his keys to unlock the top one, pulling out a file.

Graham sank into his chair, facing Chase, as he took another drink of his coffee. Stretching his legs out beneath the desk, he reclined on his spine, and Chase could feel the other man's green eyes on him as he studied the file in his hands. Without glancing up, he muttered darkly, "Whatever you're dying to say, just say it, Beckett."

"I don't have anything to say," Graham murmured, lifting the disposable coffee cup to his lips again. "You're just never late. Something going on?"

"I just overslept. I didn't have an alarm set," he admitted sheepishly. "I fell asleep on the couch."

"Hmmm," Graham murmured, his mouth twisting in another small smirk. He set his coffee down on the desk and sat up in his seat, leaning his forearms against the desk and whispering, "Does this have anything to do with a certain petite blonde you can't seem to stop texting all day?" Chase swallowed and swung his eyes to Graham's face. Graham grinned and nodded, leaning back once again. "I thought so. Y'all getting hot n heavy or what?"

Chase glared at his partner, anger flashing through him. "Don't talk about her like that. She's... not like that."

Graham's blonde brows rose again, this time in surprise. "So you're just walking around halfcocked all the time because you can't seal the deal? No wonder you're ornery."

Chase pointed one finger at the other man and snarled, "I told you not to talk about her that way. She's a sexual assault victim, jackass."

"Oh shit," Graham breathed, his green eyes lowering to his hands. "I didn't realize— Wait, I knew I recognized her... from the Chandler/Patterson case..."

Scrubbing his hand over his face, Chase shot his friend a look that silenced the other man. Then he sighed heavily before rolling his shoulders to release some of the built-up tension. He glanced over the desks at his friend and partner. "Yes. That's her. Her brother has been my best friend since middle school."

Graham laughed out loud then and muttered dryly, "Dude. You're falling for your best friend's little sister? Do you have a death wish?"

Chase lowered his gaze to the file on his desk, not really seeing what was on it. *Was he falling for Zoey?*

Shaking the thought away, he shrugged then said, "It's complicated."

"I'd say so," Graham said as he continued to chuckle. "I don't envy you, man. This is exactly why I'm still single. No-freaking-thank-you."

Chase glanced at the clock and sighed again; time to go. He'd been released from his Field Training Observation and finally had his own cruiser for patrol, but Graham would head out at the same time. If one of them ever needed backup, the other was only ever a few minutes out.

It was quiet, not much activity, which made the morning seem to stretch on interminably. Reaching for his phone while parked in a zone known for speeders, he typed a message to Zoey.

Good morning, beautiful. I hope
Verity let you sleep in a little.

He sent it, then set his phone down in the passenger seat beside him. Glancing through reports on his mobile laptop, he was surprised when a message came back just moments later.

> Good morning yourself. You know well enough Verity doesn't let me sleep in. She was a bear this morning.

He chuckled, getting ready to type a response, when another message came through.

> You snuck out early this morning...

Chase cringed internally. He should have at least woken her up to say good-bye before he left.

> I didn't want to wake you. I won't leave without a good-bye from now on, beautiful.

He didn't have to wait long for a response, and when he read it, his heart pitter pattered inside his chest.

> I'm going to hold you to that.

Chase chuckled and typed back:

I told you that you can hold whatever you want to me, sweetheart.
I hope last night didn't scare you.

The little message bubble popped up and a second later he read:

I'm a little embarrassed... but not scared, Chase. I trust you.

He groaned, that gut gnawing guilt eating at him again. If she knew anything, anything at all of what he and Tommy had been talking about, what had been decided behind her back... she wouldn't trust him. Not one bit.

So instead, he messaged back:

You have nothing to be embarrassed about, sweetheart. That was so sexy. Please remember that we take this at your pace. I don't want you to ever feel pressured from me. I mean it. You're in control.

It was a while before another message came through, and after a routine traffic stop, he checked it, smiling.

He typed up one last message and then sighed.

He was in so much trouble.

FIFTY

"Hi," Chase said as he came through the door, shutting it quickly behind him. Zoey looked over her shoulder from where she stood at the sink, rinsing dishes to place into the dishwasher.

"Hi," she said shyly, dropping her gaze from his. She'd had all day to think about her brazenness from the night before, and each time she remembered what they'd done—what she had done—her entire body ached with embarrassment. She had almost hoped to be cleaned up from dinner and hidden away in her room before Chase made it home from work, just to avoid having to look him in the eyes.

"How was your day?" he asked, shrugging out of his jacket and placing it and his hat on the hooks by the door.

"It was alright," Zoey said quietly, her voice cracking slightly. She cleared her throat and risked a glance over at him, but quickly dropped her eyes when they met his. "I had a flat tire after work, so I had to call Tommy and wait for him to come out and switch it out before I could make it home. Everything has been pushed back. Verity was a cranky mess by the time we got here."

"I'm sorry, I wish you would have called me. I would have come out to help," he said, stopping beside her at the sink, leaning his hips against the counter. "Is Verity teething again?"

"It's okay, it just made for a long night," Zoey murmured, her heart hammering in her throat having him so near. He smelled like eucalyptus and sandalwood, and even through her embarrassment, she wanted to reach out and touch him again. She shook her head slightly, continuing, "She might be, I'll have to check tomorrow. How was your day?"

She risked another glance over at him where he stood directly next to her, her face flaming when she saw him watching her closely.

"It was alright," he parroted her response quietly. Shifting, he bumped his shoulder against hers gently. "Are you okay, Zoey? I don't want you to be embarrassed about last night. Is that why you won't look at me?"

She nodded, keeping her eyes on the dishes in her hand. She'd rinsed it several times and had yet to place it in the dishwasher next to her. "I don't know what came over me."

She saw his hand reach out and a second later the plate she was holding was taken from her hands and set aside. With his other hand, he grabbed a dish towel from the counter and dried her hands, before setting it down and taking her hands in his, turning her to face him.

"Did you not like it, Zoey?" he asked gently, softly.

She squeezed her eyes shut tight, shaking her head slowly. "No... I definitely liked it."

"I did too," he said quietly. Tipping her face up with one finger under her chin, he smiled gently. "It was wonderful to watch."

Zoey groaned and made a face, though he didn't let her lower her face to hide again. "I just keep thinking about it... I've never been so embarrassed."

"There is nothing to be embarrassed about, Zoey, I promise. It was so hot," he said, his voice dropping. "I thoroughly enjoyed watching you take your pleasure. I look forward to being the one that makes you come apart."

"Oh god," she groaned again, pulling her hands from his to cover her face. "I can't believe I'm having this conversation with you. I can't believe I did that."

"It's just the start, sweetheart," he laughed, prying her hands away from her face gently, holding them hostage as he buckled his knees, bringing his face level with hers. "Do not be ashamed of anything that we do together. We will learn each other, okay?"

She nodded, making another face. "Okay."

He straightened to his full height, and Zoey squeezed his hands that still held hers captive. "Are you hungry? I saved a plate for you."

"Yes, thank you," he said, releasing her hands and stepping around her toward the refrigerator. Grabbing a beer and popping the tab open, he said over her shoulder, "I can get it though. Will you sit with me?"

She nodded, then swallowed hard when he set the beer aside and untucked his shirt from his slacks, lifting the hem enough to scratch at his stomach briefly. When she realized he caught her staring, he winked, and she blushed to the roots of her blonde hair all over again. "We will have plenty of time to play, sweetheart. Right now, I'm hungry for food."

She turned and opened the oven, where she'd left his dinner warming. She pulled it out with an oven mitt, taking it to the table. She set it down as he crossed the kitchen to grab a fork before sitting down, beer in hand.

Zoey sank into the chair kitty corner from him as he dug into the meal, a simple baked spaghetti with crunchy, buttery garlic bread. "I have fixings for a salad, if you'd like that, too."

"This is good, thank you," he said, reaching out a hand to stay her when she made to stand. Their eyes locked. "I'm sorry I was running late. I hate that you ate alone."

"It's okay," she said softly, leaning one elbow on the table, propping her cheek in her palm as she watched him eat. "I know what your job entails. I can't be upset with that."

"Thank you," he said and smiled. "I'm ready to get back into the gym tomorrow. I hope you're ready for a workout."

"Actually—" Zoey started, then stopped. Before she could chicken out or talk herself out of it, she said in a rush, "I want to start drills."

He looked up at her, his face going blank for a heartbeat. "What?"

Taking a deep breath in, she said, more slowly this time, "I want to start drills. Jui-Jitsu drills. I'm ready."

Chase set his fork down on his plate, leaning his forearms on the edge of the table, linking his fingers together, suspended over his half-eaten plate. His gaze was intense on hers, as if searching for any hesitation in her face. "Are you sure?"

"Yes," she said, her voice steady. She dropped her gaze then, continuing, "I don't want anyone else to do it, though. Just you. I trust you; I know you won't hurt me."

She saw his hand reach out to clasp her behind the neck, pulling her close, letting his lips press to hers for just a second in a quick kiss. "Have I told you how damn proud of you I am? You are the bravest woman I've ever met, Zoey."

She laughed then, shaking her head. "You keep saying that. I hope you know how much it means to me. It makes me kind of believe it."

"You should," he said, leaning back and picking up his fork once again. "I mean it." He took a bite, chewed, then swallowed, and followed it with a drink of his beer. "I'll talk to Mike tomorrow, see when we can start."

She nodded, smiling. "Okay. Thank you, Chase."

"At some point you have to stop thanking me," he murmured, leveling a stare at her. "I told you; there isn't much that I wouldn't do for you and that baby girl upstairs, Zoey. I hope you know that."

Zoey's heart expanded at his words, and she nodded slowly again. She was beginning to believe every word he said.

FIFTY-ONE

Zoey panted, chest heaving. Sweat coated her body, and one bead of sweat slid down from her forehead, tracking down her cheek.

Mike, the Jui-Jitsu instructor, was trying to kill her, she was sure of it.

She *really* disliked him at the moment as he grunted for her to keep going.

Pushing harder, she followed both Mike and Chase's movements, copying them. She refused to fall behind.

She understood what Chase had meant when he said Jui-Jitsu was going to be tough. She was *dying*.

These drills were no joke, she thought sourly.

Mike had them doing multiple different drills, all beginner moves, but they were different from the body strengthening workouts that she and Chase had been doing. They'd practiced 'break fall', 'shrimping', 'button scoot' and 'stand and base' all in succession, which Mike had said were basic maneuvers she needed to master. They would be running these for the first several sessions. They were all drills she could practice without a partner, which she was grateful for in their first session.

"You're doing great, Zoey," Chase said, out of breath, from several feet away, as he practiced the same moves, again and again.

Mike called out to them that they could break, and Zoey flopped to her back, arms flung out to the side, as she panted heavily. Chase lay on his back next to her, and he chuckled breathlessly as he turned his head to look at her. Touching his fingertips to hers where they were outstretched, he squeezed them lightly.

"You survived," he chuckled, and she squeezed his fingers back.

"I don't like Mike," she laughed, teasing the older gentleman that stood several feet away from them. "You're mean."

"You're going to hate me soon enough. I'll take the dislike for now," the instructor laughed in response, and she groaned.

"If this is just the beginning, I don't doubt that," she laughed lightly, still regaining her breath.

Mike had been kind enough to give personalized, private lessons for Zoey, as Chase had explained her situation. She wouldn't be doing the classic Jui-Jitsu lessons, the kind that students took to go to competitions with, but ones tailored for self-defense specifically.

"Do you want to see that hold break I was telling you about?" Chase asked, and she turned to look at him.

"Right now?" Zoey asked, her eyes going wide with panic.

"Mike and I can run through it, so you can see it in person," Chase said gently, squeezing her fingers that he still held. "For observation purposes only."

"You would do that?" she asked, awe tinging her voice.

"Of course," he said, shrugging his shoulders where they were still pressed flat to the cushioned mat beneath them. "You'd probably get a kick out of seeing Mike whoop my ass."

"You don't think you'd win?" she asked, raising her eyebrows in surprise.

He laughed out loud, looking over at the instructor. "Not a chance. He's a pro. Won all kinds of competitions and awards. I'm out of practice."

"You used to do Jui-Jitsu?" She was surprised, she hadn't known that.

"Not Jui-Jitsu exactly, but we have training similar to it," he said. "We spar every once in a while, to keep up on it."

"Are you ladies going to keep chit-chatting all night, or are we going to run these drills?" Mike asked, standing over them. His words were harsh, but his tone was light, and Chase laughed out loud.

"Yes," he said, quickly hopping to his feet. He stood over Zoey, one foot on either side of her legs, and extending his hand down to her. He cocked one eyebrow at her, and she smiled, reaching up and placing her hand in his. She rolled on her spine, sitting up, as he pulled her to her feet. His hands settled on the slope of her hips for a heartbeat, and he grinned at her. "Proud of you," he whispered, and she beamed up at him.

As Chase stepped back, he shook his body out, rolling his head across his shoulders, before facing Mike. To demonstrate, Chase pinned Mike to the ground, flat on his back. Chase's knees were on either side of the older man's hips, and his hands went to Mike's throat, making panic tighten Zoey's chest. But then Mike arrowed his hands into the gap between Chase's wrists, throwing his elbows out to break the chokehold. Fast as a viper strike, Mike's hands criss crossed over Chase's own throat, grabbing handfuls of Chase's shirt and pulling tight toward him, effectively cutting off Chase's air supply. Within seconds, Chase tapped out, but not before his face started turning red.

Chase laughed, taking a deep breath as he sat up. "I forgot how fast that works."

They ran through it several times, Mike talking Zoey through it as they demonstrated. Chase changed up how he'd try to pin him, but the older man's years of experience won out every time. They switched positions, showing Zoey that even though Chase's ability and technique may be out of practice, it was still effective.

It was terrifying and thrilling at the same time.

"Wanna try?" Mike asked, looking over at her.

"Oh no, not yet," Zoey said, shaking her head vehemently. "That was impressive though."

When their lesson was over, she and Chase walked out of the room together, heading back out to the main part of the gym. Chase stopped her before she walked into the locker room, his hand gentle on her elbow.

"Proud of you," he said again, and she smiled radiantly up at him. Leaning down, he pressed a kiss to her lips, then swatted her butt lightly and wrinkled his nose. "Go shower. You stink."

Zoey gasped in feigned outrage, laughing as he winked, then disappeared into the opposite locker room door.

FIFTY-TWO

Zoey sighed and rolled over in bed, picking up her phone and checking the time. 1:07am. She hadn't seen Chase that morning before he'd headed out for his run, having overslept her alarm, exhausted from the workout with Mike the night before. He had sent a brief message earlier in the evening stating that he wouldn't be home until late, but she hadn't realized just how late he'd meant. Disappointment had flooded her, and then self-doubt had taken over. Maybe... maybe she'd misread all of the signals he'd been giving her...

But then she shook her head. There was no misreading those signals. He wanted her, he had made that clear. He had said they were in a relationship... and she still got butterflies when she thought about what had happened nearly a week before. They hadn't gone that far again, but the kisses they shared always left her wanting more. The hard ridge behind his fly afterward was surely evidence that he wanted her just as badly.

A noise from outside startled her and she shivered, tucking the covers more securely under her chin.

Worry crept in then as she glanced at the clock again. Perhaps something had happened? Was he hurt? She picked up her phone and opened the message thread between herself and Chase.

Everything okay?

She almost hit send, but then deleted it. She clicked the side button to turn the screen off, dropping it back to the mattress next to her. She wouldn't bother him, especially if he was still at work. She rolled her eyes in the dark. She was already a worried, harping girlfriend. Good grief.

She shifted onto her side again, pulling the covers up to her chin. She hadn't been able to sleep at all, tossing and turning in the dark after putting Verity down for the night.

Zoey's senses were on hyperdrive.

Whatever voodoo magic he used on her had awakened something in her. Squeezing her thighs shut tight against the rush of desire that seemed to make her entire lower body ache whenever she thought about Chase, she bit her lip to keep from moaning out loud.

The house was quiet, Tommy had gone to Shaun's after work, having assumed that Chase would be back after his shift, but it had just been herself and Verity home all evening. It had been a while since she and Verity had been home alone all night. Either Tommy or Chase were usually there throughout the night.

She checked her phone again; 1:53am. Still no new messages, but she wasn't surprised. He probably thought she was asleep. She should be asleep. She closed her eyes, willing herself to fall asleep, knowing it was futile.

Instead, her mind went to Chase's hands, always so gentle and soft when they touched her. How he always asked her permission before placing those hands on her. Now, she imagined them on her, the way they had been yesterday when he'd kissed her so thoroughly, his fingers trailing along her back, how it had felt to have his palms cupping the backs of her thighs through her clothes. She imagined how they'd feel on her bare skin, cupping her breasts, her hips. She ached to run her hands over his body again. She wanted to know what he looked like naked, what he would feel like inside her...

Again, heat flashed over her and she moaned, burying her face in the pillow to stifle it so she didn't wake Verity across the room.

Part of her brain told her this was all happening too fast, but another part of her insisted that it felt right. Felt safe.

And part of her wanted to erase Robby from her memory, from her body.

Chase had told her that *this* is how it's supposed to be, that it gets better than this... She wanted to know just how much better. She wanted to—needed to—burn those old memories like a house going up in an inferno, until all that was left was ashes.

So she could replace them with something better. Chase's kisses had kindled a fire in her.

She wanted to see just how hot she could burn.

For him.

Breathing heavily, she rolled onto her back, letting her hand drift down her body. Lifting the hem of the soft sweater she was wearing, she let her fingers find her clit through her lacy panties, the only other item of clothing she was wearing. Her eyes slid closed, wishing it were Chase's fingers on her, instead of her own.

Zoey's eyes snapped open and she rolled over in bed, leaning up on her elbow to listen when she heard Chase's car pull into the driveway, the headlights shining briefly on the walls of her bedroom through the window as he pulled in and parked. She glanced at her phone again; 2:19am. She heard his car door close softly, and then heard his booted feet as he walked through the kitchen and up the stairs. He slowed coming down the hallway, moving quietly. She heard the bathroom door close, and then the shower turned on, and she couldn't help the flush of heat that spread across her body when she imagined him stripping his clothes off piece by piece until he stood naked. She rolled over again, clenching her thighs tightly together against the ache that she had been fighting.

The shower turned off several minutes later and she held her breath as he exited, padding lightly down the hall. He paused outside her door for several long heartbeats, and Zoey thought he would knock, but then he continued down the hall and she heard his bedroom door close. She released her breath that she hadn't realized she was holding. Her entire body was on fire.

Glancing through the darkness toward Verity's crib, she watched her sleeping soundly. Zoey sat up silently, her heart pounding. She slid her legs over the side of the bed, standing and slipping on silent feet to the door. She pulled it open without a sound, glancing once more at the sleeping baby, before closing the door behind her.

She fidgeted with the hem of the soft sweater she'd worn to bed, smoothing it over her bare thighs. She'd wanted to sleep in nothing but a brief, skimpy pair of lacy panties and the soft sweater, and the naughtiness of it made her blush.

Padding down the hall, she stopped outside of Chase's door, her hand poised to knock. Her heart was hammering in her chest, making her feel slightly lightheaded. She couldn't believe she was doing this. She gathered all the courage she had left in her and knocked lightly. She heard him cross the room and then a second later the door opened. Her mouth went dry when she realized he'd been in the process of pulling on a pair of sweatpants. They hung loosely on his hips, and his upper body was bare. His skin still glistened from his shower. She could smell his body wash, eucalyptus and sandalwood, and his hair was wet and tousled messily where he'd run the towel over it haphazardly.

One dim lamp had been turned on across the room next to the bed, casting the room in shadows.

"Zoey?" he asked softly. His electric blue eyes were intense as he stared down into her own. "Are you alright? Is something wrong?"

Zoey shook her head, her breathing quick and shallow. She dropped her gaze to his chest, letting her eyes slide over his naked skin. She only let her eyes flit down to that spot between his thighs for a heartbeat, but she could see that he was beginning to tent the fabric of his sweatpants. She blushed scarlet, raising her eyes back to his abdomen, a much safer zone.

She reached one trembling hand out, touching just her fingertips to his abs, rippled with hard earned muscle. He sucked in his breath and before she could react, he had caught her hand with his own, and her eyes flew back to his. She made to pull her hand away, but he flattened his palm over the back of hers, pressing her hand to his body, forcing her fingers to splay wide on the flat plane of his abdomen. His thumb stroked the back of her hand softly, his fingers covering hers, keeping her hand in place.

"Zoey..." he whispered huskily, his eyes never leaving hers, his thumb still trailing over the back of her hand. Her fingers flexed slightly, and she watched as his eyes drifted closed for the briefest of moments before they opened again, his blue gaze hot and hungry.

Zoey stepped forward, closing the distance between their bodies. Smoothing her palm up his abdomen and chest, she rested it over his sternum. She could feel his heart thundering beneath her palm and knew her own matched his in cadence. She licked her lips and watched as his eyes tracked the movement. She couldn't stop the blush that spread across her cheeks again.

"Zoey..." he whispered again, almost hesitantly, and she flexed her fingers where they were still covered by his.

"I... I don't know what I'm doing..." she whispered, blushing furiously as she lowered her eyes. "Obviously I've never... But I know I want this, Chase. I want you."

"Zoey, sweetheart—" he started, but she shook her head, raising her eyes to his.

"No," she whispered, stepping closer still. "Please don't tell me I'm not ready, or that I don't know what I'm asking for, or whatever other excuse you're trying to come up with." His brows were pulled low into a V, but his eyes were gentle as he stared at her. "I... I need this. I need you. Make me forget he ever touched me, Chase. Make me new."

The eyes that stared back at her were pained. He raised his other hand, slowly, so that she knew what he intended, and she sighed when his fingers grazed her cheekbone before letting his palm conform to her cheek. "I don't want to scare you."

"You won't," Zoey said gently, reaching up with her other hand to touch his bewhiskered chin. He hadn't shaved in several days, and she let her thumbnail scratch lightly against the growth there.

And because she was feeling more confident than ever, she inched her fingers around to the back of his neck and slid them into his hair, pulling his head down to hers. His mouth settled on her open one, and in an instant their tongues were tangling together, her sigh mingling with his groan. This kiss was needy, primal. She inched closer, pressing her body along his, reveling in the feel of his arousal. There was no fear; only desire to have this man make love to her filling her mind.

His hand released hers where it was still pressed against his chest, and he cupped her face with both hands as his mouth devoured hers. His kiss was both voracious and gentle at the same time. Heat flooded her lower body and she moaned into his mouth, which only made him kiss her harder. He pulled away, letting his head fall back over his shoulders as he sucked in lungful after lungful of air. Zoey pressed her forehead to his bare chest, sliding her hands across the slope of his ribcage as his fingers threaded through her hair at the back of her head. She swayed and his hips met her middle. She gasped, then settled against him more fully, and he growled deep in his chest.

"Fuck," Chase groaned into the darkness of the hallway behind her. "You're going to be the death of me."

Zoey smiled, pressing her lips to his bare chest in a kiss. His fingers were still threaded through her hair, holding her head still. He tipped her face up, lowering his mouth back to hers. He moved them inside just enough to close the bedroom door with a soft click.

At the sound of the door closing, Zoey's breath hitched in her chest. Pressing light, sipping kisses to her lips, she stared up into those blue eyes that were so intense on her own.

"Are you sure, Zoey?" he whispered. "We don't have to. I will wait as long as you need."

Zoey shook her head, spreading her fingers through his hair, holding his mouth to hers. "I'm sure. Please. Make me new."

Chase growled low in his throat then, nipping her bottom lip lightly, making her gasp. "You are... fuck," he growled on a breath. "You're perfect, Zoey."

And then he was kissing her again, his mouth melding with hers until she couldn't tell where she ended and he began. His hands never strayed from where they were threaded into her hair, but her hands roamed over his naked shoulders and chest, her fingers testing the ridges of his ribcage and the narrowness of his hips. When they broke apart to breathe, he pressed his forehead to hers, rolling it back and forth several times.

He slowly took several steps backward, drawing her with him, until the backs of his legs met the edge of his mattress, and he sat on the bed, drawing her between his spread thighs.

Zoey was acutely aware of her bare legs beneath the hem of the sweater, and she wanted his hands on them. "Touch me, please, Chase."

"Where, sweetheart?" he asked huskily against her mouth. "I want you to tell me exactly what you want. And if you don't like something—"

She shushed him by pressing her mouth to his again, sinking her tongue into his mouth and kissing him hungrily. Zoey spoke directly against his lips, "I want your hands on me. Everywhere."

He groaned and gathered her into his arms, his movements almost timid. He pulled her closer against him as their mouths melded again. Her arms settled across his shoulders, her fingers sinking into his hair. One of his hands slid down her back, over the curve of her bottom. His fingers trailed, feather light, over the bare skin on the back of her thigh and she sucked in her breath on a quiet moan.

"Yes, please," she breathed against his lips. His palm flattened against her skin, his fingers curving around the slope of her thigh, skimming against the tender skin on the inside of her thigh. She trembled, but not in fear. Desire coursed through her like a white water rapid, nearly carrying her away.

Tearing her mouth from his, she pulled her hands from his hair and settled them on either side of his face. "Before— before we do this. I need you to know something, Chase."

His hands curved around her waist, settling on her hips lightly, and he nodded, letting her know he was listening.

"This might change whether you want to do this or not," she whispered. "But you need to know."

"Did that bastard give you an STD?" Chase asked, his eyes going hard.

Zoey gasped, then laughed, shaking her head. "No, thank god." He nodded, his face relaxing. She trailed her fingertips over his dark eyebrows, tucking that errant lock of hair back into place off his forehead, and she let her lips tilt up just the slightest at the corners. "I think I've fallen in love with you."

FIFTY-THREE

There. She said it.

She knew she couldn't go through with this without being honest. He deserved to know that this was a big deal for her, something she was trusting him with implicitly, because she loved him. For her, there would be no casual hook ups. No, this was special. He was special. And he deserved to know the truth. No secrets.

She ducked her head, too shy to look him in the eye. One of his hands came up and tipped her chin up, and when her eyes met his again, there was a softness in them that she hadn't seen before. He leaned in and pressed his lips to hers softly, sweetly.

"Good," she heard him whisper against her lips. "Because I'm falling in love with you, too."

Tears stung her nose, but she didn't care as she draped her arms over his shoulders again, pulling him to her. They kissed until they were breathless again, and then Chase pushed her back slightly so he could stand.

"I'm going to take my pants off now," he warned her, and she nodded stiffly, keeping her eyes on his. Out of her peripheral vision she could see his arms move as his hands went to the waistband of his sweatpants, and then his shoulders bobbed as he hooked his thumbs into them and pushed them down. Never taking her eyes off his, she waited while he stepped out of them, and then he was fully naked in front of her. He grinned wolfishly at her. "Whenever you're ready, you can look, sweetheart. Whenever you're ready, you do whatever you want to do to me. I won't touch you until you ask me to."

And then Chase slowly lowered his tall frame to the bed beneath him until he was reclining on the pillows. One arm above his head, one at his side, lightly gripping the bedspread in his fingers, leaving her completely in control, which only made her love him even more fiercely.

Zoey lost the battle with her curious eyes, and they darted down to his lap.

Her mouth went dry.

His cock stood proud at the junction of his thighs, and when she stared at him, it twitched, and her gaze flew to his electric blue one. His lips were parted slightly, his breath coming in soft, quick pants that matched her own where she stood at the foot of the bed. It was... much larger than she had anticipated.

"You can do whatever you want to me, Zoey," he breathed. "Whatever you need. I am yours, sweetheart."

She watched his impossibly broad chest as it rose and fell with each of his breaths, his shoulder and arm muscles bunched beneath the smooth skin. His abdomen was the stuff fantasies were made of, and his long, hard thighs were dusted with dark hair. That impudent lock of hair that always fell over his brow was back, and Zoey ached to brush it back with her fingers.

Stepping closer, she met his gaze again as she reached beneath the hem of her shirt and hooked her fingers into the sides of her panties, shimmying them down her thighs until they dropped at her feet. His gaze darkened just the slightest, and when she looked down at the hardness between his legs, she licked her lips, and a tingle went up her spine when he groaned as he watched her.

She climbed onto the bed at his side, the mattress dipping beneath her knees as she knelt beside him. She ran the fingers of one hand up and over his chest, then back down his torso, stopping short before they reached the dark hair that housed his sex. Chase sucked in his breath as her fingers teased across his skin, lightly enough to tickle slightly. His electric blue eyes were alight with blue flame as he stared up at her.

Leaning down, she pressed a kiss to his mouth, lightly, brushing her lips back and forth again and again, exchanging breaths, before staying. The hand above his head gripped the headboard spindles, keeping his promise to only touch her if and when she asked. His tongue, however, speared into her mouth, reaching for her, tasting her, and she moaned at the liquid heat that drenched her between her already trembling thighs.

Placing one shaking hand on that incredibly broad chest, she shifted, lifting one leg over until she straddled him. Chase groaned, and the vibrations rumbled between her thighs as she settled upon him, north of his straining cock. She felt him, hard and urgent, pressing against her backside. But still, he didn't touch her, though that hand on the bed twitched slightly, inches from where her knee now pressed against his hip on the mattress.

"Whatever you need from me, it's yours," he murmured huskily, staring up at her from where he lay repose on the bed, letting her take her time. Letting her decide when, how, and where.

So Zoey flattened both of her palms against his chest, raising on her knees as she shifted backward. Chase's breath hissed in through gritted teeth at the first tentative probing of the broad head of his cock into her, and Zoey banished whatever remaining fear she'd been harboring as she slowly, inch by glorious inch, sank down onto him. Until she sat fully, until he was buried all the way inside her, until he was so deeply embedded in her that she threw her head back, letting her golden hair riot down her back at the ecstasy, even as she rolled her hips against him.

"Fuck," Chase hissed from between clenched teeth, and if Zoey didn't witness the softness in his eyes, the fierceness on his face would have terrified her. But those eyes, they were gentle, waiting. Waiting for her. Just like he promised.

Adjusting to the fullness of him, the length of him where he pressed so deeply, Zoey moaned on a broken breath.

Her body had gotten strong, the training they'd been doing changed her, strengthening her entire body, arms, back, core, and thighs. She raised herself up on those thighs, then sank down again fully, repeating the motion over and over even as his breath became choppy beneath her. That hand still clutched the headboard in a white-knuckle grip, the fingers of his other hand fisted in the bedsheet beneath them. He lifted his hips, just the slightest as she came back down, and Zoey cried out as she felt even more of him fill her.

In the back of her mind, she could almost imagine what her therapist would say to this new development. But she didn't care. She was being made new.

It was slow, probably painfully slow to him, as he panted beneath her, but he didn't rush her, not once. She bit her lip as she ground down onto him, and she felt more than heard the guttural growl as his own head thrashed against the pillow under it.

"Chase," she breathed, her body shaking. She needed his hands on her. "Touch me. Please."

"Where?" he panted, though his hands didn't move an inch. "Show me."

Continuing to move over him, drawing nearer to some precipice she wasn't sure she wanted yet, she reached for his hands with her own. At first, she twined their fingers together, holding tightly as she rode him, her head thrown back wildly again. She could feel his thighs under her trembling with the restraint of holding back for her. He tugged one of their clasped hands toward him, toward his mouth, where he pressed a hot, open-mouthed kiss to her knuckles.

"Ohmygod," she moaned, the sight of him beneath her so erotic, those bright, gentle eyes that were alight with desire. She brought his hand to her hip, placing his palm against her. Skimming under the loose sweater she still wore, she guided his hand up her side, her ribcage. The other hand she placed on the curve of her ass, and he squeezed lightly. The fingers that skimmed up her ribcage continued its ascent, until his finger tips grazed the underside of one of her breasts. Her breath hitched, and he stopped, withdrawing, but her hand stayed his, pressing him to her. He growled beneath her, and the sound was thrilling.

"Touch me, please," she whispered again brokenly even as she circled her hips on him.

Both hands slid beneath the softness of her sweater, the wide span of his fingers covering almost all of her ribcage. His touch was infinitely sweet, tentative, as they moved again to fully cup her breasts. Chase swore under his breath, his chest heaving beneath her.

And when his fingers found her already pebbled nipples and rolled them each between his thumb and forefinger, Zoey shattered with a harsh cry.

Release slammed through her, squeezing him like a fist inside her, her entire body shaking with the intensity of it. Chase's hands released her breasts, smoothing to span her ribcage, where he held her, his body bucking upward again and again until Zoey felt him come with a roar.

Zoey sagged against him, her thighs trembling, on fire, and his hands caught her, cradling her against his chest where she rested her flushed cheek against his bare skin. His heart hammered under her ear, and she panted against his skin, one palm flat against the other side of his chest. Chase gasped, his breathing ragged, against the top of her head, where he pressed a kiss to her hair. She felt his fingers trailing softly over her back, still beneath her sweater.

Zoey choked on a strangled laugh then, and he sucked in his breath at what it did to her body and his, still nestled inside hers. "Oh no," she whispered, her face flushing scarlet. Mortified, she leaned up and covered her breasts over the sweater, hiding the stains that had bloomed against the fabric. The intensity of her orgasm had triggered a let-down, and she was horrified that her body had reacted, until—

Chase pulled her hands away gently, staring at the spots that flowered there. "Is that why you didn't want to take this off?" he asked softly, raising his eyes to hers.

Zoey made a face, shrugging. "Partly. I was worried it would happen if you... if I... And I didn't want to—to gross you out— And my stomach is still soft—"

But then Zoey gasped, her words halting, as she felt him stirring inside her again, hardening, filling her once more. He groaned, arching his hips upward into her, sheathing himself fully again.

His blue eyes were alight with that same blue fire from moments ago, and his hands, ever tender and never rough, spanned her waist, settling on her hips, his thumbs cushioned by her stomach as he pushed upward into her.

"Does that—" he panted as he gyrated into her, making her moan, "—feel like I'm grossed out, Zoey?"

Zoey tossed her head, her golden hair cascading over her shoulders and down her back.

He sat up, hinged at the waist, all the while keeping her astride him, buried to the hilt inside her. Zoey moaned. His hands smoothed around to press lightly on her back beneath her shirt, keeping her close.

"You." He pressed a hot, open-mouthed kiss to her throat. "Are." One to her jaw. "Perfect." Her cheek. Sweeping his lips across hers, he breathed, "Will you take it off for me? Please?"

His blue eyes were so earnest as they searched hers, she nodded. Reaching for the hem, she lifted it over her head, letting it flutter to the floor beside the bed. She was now just as naked as he was, their bodies pressed together, chest to chest, belly to belly, his cock fully buried inside her. As her arms came back down, Chase's hands smoothed over her shoulders to cup the outside of her biceps, drawing them around his neck.

Zoey's fingers sank into the long hair that fell over his brow, pushing it back, and touched the short cut sides with tentative fingers even as his mouth melded with hers in a deep, languid kiss. His large, gentle hands smoothed over the nakedness of her bare back, pressing her close as they began to move again.

Using the arms draped over his shoulders as leverage, Zoey rode him, harder this time. Sweat shone on both their bodies as they strained together, their mingling moans of pleasure filling the room. Chase's hands drifted to her hips, where they gripped, tight enough to hold her as he pushed his hips upward into hers, again and again, until their breathing was ragged and Zoey thought her heart was going to pound out of her chest as that tumult built inside her again.

"Yes, Zoey," Chase panted against her lips as she rode him, her thighs on fire. "Come on, sweetheart."

"Chase!" Zoey sobbed, throwing her head back as she came hard again, gripping him tightly. His mouth found and loved her throat, the cradle of her neck, one hand pressed against the middle of her back, the other still gripping her hip. As her release rocketed through her, Chase bucked wildly beneath her, slamming to the hilt as he too came, his jaw clenching with the power of it even as he groaned throatily against the skin of her neck.

She had already been burnt to ashes; this time she would rise from them. New. With Chase at her side, as her friend, her protector. Her love.

When at last their bodies stopped shuddering and their breath had come back to somewhat normal, Chase laid back on the bed, bringing her with him, and then rolled them to their sides, pulling out of her finally with a broken groan. He pulled the sheet up over them, and she didn't hesitate when he silently asked if it was okay to pull her close against him.

Zoey hid her face against his chest, and she felt his finger smoothing the now sweat dampened hair away from her temples. He reached down and lightly tipped her chin up so she was looking up at him. He pressed his lips to hers in a featherlight kiss, and she sighed even as she settled fully into his embrace, the feeling of being safe for the first time in a long time slightly overwhelming. He tucked her against his side, and it wasn't long before her eyes closed in sleep.

FIFTY-FOUR

Chase remained awake for a long time after Zoey's soft, even breathing signaled that she had succumbed to sleep herself against him.

He was the lowest, vilest human to ever walk the earth. He didn't deserve the woman laying next to him, trusting him, *loving* him.

He hadn't lied, at least. What he'd told her was the truth; he *was* in love with her. Completely. Part of him had always loved her, just in a different way than he did now. He'd known for weeks that he was in jeopardy of losing his heart to her.

And then she'd shown up outside of his door and laid bare all her secrets, asked him to make her new... he was powerless against it. Not a force in the world could have stopped him from taking everything she was offering and giving him everything he had in return.

Everything except the truth... not the whole truth, anyway.

He was a complete and total jackass.

He snorted into the darkness that surrounded them, then held perfectly still as Zoey shifted against him before burrowing deeper into his side. Pussy whipped was the term that came to mind, and he snorted to himself again, the self-derision thick in his chest.

Her hand curved over his chest and she sighed in her sleep. Shifting slightly, he raised one hand to stroke over the hair that fell over her shoulder onto his, and then he leaned down and pressed a kiss to the top of her head. Because even though he hated the feeling of guilt that he couldn't shake, he knew he didn't want to let her go. Not now.

Not ever.

FIFTY-FIVE

Zoey woke by slow degrees, snuggled deeply into a downy soft comforter that was tucked around her shoulders. Blinking her eyes open, she frowned when she didn't immediately recognize the room. Sitting up, bringing the blanket with her against her chest, she glanced around the mostly dark room, the gray of very early morning filtering through the curtains across the room.

Chase's uniform was hanging on a hook on the back of the door, and she swung her gaze back around to the bed, then she remembered where she was: Chase's bed.

Memories from the night flooded her, and she flushed a thousand shades of red when she thought back on how she'd basically begged Chase to... *Oh god*, she thought with a groan, burying her face in her hands. She shifted in the bed and her breath hitched. Her body ached in ways she wasn't used to, which made her blush all the harder.

337

Looking around the room, she saw his uniform hanging on a hook on the back of the door, which had been pulled mostly closed, left open just a crack. The hallway beyond the door was dark, the house quiet.

Searching the floor for her discarded sweater and panties from the night before, she swung her legs over the edge of the bed and groaned at how sore her legs were. *What a workout,* she thought and smiled to herself. Pulling the sweater over her head, she shoved her arms in and picked up her underwear before crossing to the door and pulling it open.

She knew it was early enough that if she went into the bedroom now, Verity would inevitably wake, ready to nurse, so she continued to the bathroom, turning on the dim light and tossing her underwear into the laundry basket in the corner. Looking herself over in the mirror, she touched her slightly abraded lips from their heavy kisses and Chase's stubble. Her hair was a mess from Chase's hands, so she ran a hairbrush through it to get the tangles out, letting it fall over her shoulders once more.

She exited and continued down the hall to the stairs, taking them on nearly silent feet. The knowledge that she was naked beneath the sweater that barely hit high thigh made her feel naughty.

She could hear Chase moving around the kitchen before she made it to the bottom of the stairs and took the corner into the kitchen. He was bare chested, just a pair of gray sweatpants slung around his hips, and her mouth watered at the sight.

Chase was just placing the tea kettle on the stove when she entered, and he glanced at her over his shoulder when he heard her bare feet on the linoleum floor. He smiled at her and her heart stuttered, sending butterflies soaring through her midriff.

He truly was the most handsome man she'd ever seen.

And he was all hers.

"Good morning," he murmured quietly, his voice husky. He turned to face her, though he didn't move toward her.

She blushed again, tucking one side of her hair behind her ear before whispering, "Good morning." She crossed her arms over her middle, not feeling nearly as naughty as she had moments ago.

"I have your tea going, it should be ready in a few minutes," he said softly, turning to pick up his coffee cup from where it was set on the counter. He raised it to his lips, taking a sip before holding it in his large hand as he leaned against the counter.

She nodded, dropping her eyes from his and shifting from one foot to the other nervously. "Umm, thank you."

She watched as he set his coffee down and took the few steps toward her until they stood just a foot apart. "Zoey," she heard him murmur gently, but she didn't raise her eyes to his, her arms still wrapped around her middle. "Will you look at me, please?" When she finally brought her eyes to his, he reached out a hand and tucked the other side of her hair behind her ear, and she sighed at the contact. "Are you alright? Did I hurt you last night?"

"I'm..." she whispered, searching for the right words. She smiled shyly, lowering her lashes briefly. "I'm perfect, Chase. Though I still can't believe it happened."

"I can. We've been on our way here for a while," he whispered, and his hand slid to cup her jaw in his palm, tipping her chin up so she was looking at him fully. "You know that, right? Whatever this is... it's been inevitable, don't you think?"

His thumb was stroking along her cheekbone slowly, soothingly, as he spoke, his blue eyes intense as he stared down at her. She nodded her head and closed her eyes, tilting her cheek more fully into his palm, before reaching up and covering the back of his hand with hers. "Yes."

When she opened her eyes once more, those butterflies spiraled like crazy in her belly at the look on his face. His thumb continued to stroke her cheek, and then she heard him whisper reverently, "Marry me."

FIFTY-SIX

Zoey gasped, her heart hammering in her chest. There's no way she heard him correctly. She stared up into his face as if he'd grown wings or sprouted horns on his head. She shook her head in disbelief, her eyes wide.

"What?" she asked, and it came out a high squeak.

Chase smiled gently, his eyes soft. The tea kettle began to whistle, and he reached out to move it off the burner before letting that hand settle on her hip, his touch light, but the heat of it fairly burned her through the fabric of her sweater. His fingers stroked softly against her hip even as the thumb at her cheek continued to sweep across her skin, sending tingles through her entire body. "Marry me, Zoey," he repeated quietly.

"You've got to be joking," she whispered, her voice still coming out a higher pitch than normal.

Chase's eyebrows notched together slightly, though his eyes were soft with amusement as he said, "I don't typically go around proposing marriage as a joke, Zoey."

"You can't be serious, Chase," she whispered, her heart thundering in her chest.

"On the contrary; I've never been so sure of something in my life," he husked.

Zoey opened her mouth to speak, but nothing came out, so she closed it again with a click of her teeth. Trying again, she breathed, "Chase..."

"I realize that this has all happened fast," he said softly, his blue eyes searching hers as he spoke. "Believe me, I had no idea when I came back home that I'd fall for my best friend's sister. I've never fallen so hard or so fast in my life, Zoey."

"Really?" she whispered, her fingers tightening around his that were still holding her cheek.

Chase nodded, his eyes soft. "Irrevocably." His eyes dropped to where his thumb smoothed over the skin of her cheek and he murmured, "I don't have a ring—"

"I don't need a ring," Zoey whispered, and his gaze returned to hers.

"Is that a yes, then?" he asked quietly, his eyes searching hers intently.

"This is crazy," Zoey whispered dazedly, though her gaze never left his. Then, nodding slowly, she murmured breathlessly, "Yes, Chase."

"Then you'll have a ring," he stated simply, then grinned widely at her. She reciprocated his broad smile, then surprised herself by leaning up to press her mouth to his. His hand released her hip and those fingers sank into her hair, as he deepened their kiss. When he drew back, he pressed his forehead against hers and said, "I will protect you and that baby girl with my life, Zoey. I swear it."

She nodded brokenly, tears stinging her nose and filling her eyes at his ardent words. Her face barely moved from being held in his large hands, and her lips rubbed against his with the movement. Those tears spilled over her lashes and slid down her cheeks and her voice shook when she whispered, "I love you."

"I love you," he husked against her mouth. "I don't know when it happened, but it did."

"Tommy and Shaun are going to lose their minds," Zoey whispered dazedly. Chase laughed.

"I'll handle Tommy," Chase murmured, raising his head. Zoey pressed her cheek against his bare chest, wondering if Tommy had meant it when he'd said he was okay if something happened between them.

Sliding her arms around his bare torso, she trailed her fingers along the curve of his spine. His arms went around her too, and they swayed together in the early morning light that filtered in through the kitchen windows. She felt it when he rested his cheek against the top of her head, and she smiled, turning her face slightly to press a kiss to his chest before returning her cheek to resting there so she could listen to the steady cadence of his heart as it beat beneath her ear.

"I don't want to go to work," he murmured from above her, though she heard it more as it rumbled through his chest where her ear was still pressed to his chest. He tightened his hold around her lightly.

"I don't want to go either," she whispered. "I could stay this way all day."

She heard his chuckle as it rumbled through his chest and then her face was being tipped up again, his mouth finding hers in a hot, open-mouthed kiss. When they were both breathless again, he released her mouth and whispered huskily, "That's what the honeymoon is for."

Zoey let her hands drift down to settle on the curve of his ass, spreading her fingers over his taut buttocks, settling herself firmly against his front. He growled low in his throat, and those butterflies kamikazed in her stomach as his gaze darkened with desire.

"Did I create a sex monster?" Chase asked gruffly, grinding his hips into her front, making her gasp when she felt his hardness against her.

"No," Zoey said primly, though her lips twitched with a smile before Chase's mouth covered hers, effectively proving his point when she moaned and curved her body along his. "Chaaaase," she sighed breathily when he finally released her lips.

Chase chuckled against her lips, pecking quick, light kisses to her mouth. "You're going to be insatiable now, aren't you?" he teased.

"It's your fault," Zoey murmured, teasing too. "If you hadn't come home and been all sexy and so damn nice to me all the time..."

Chase laughed out loud, rocking them together as

they stood in the kitchen. "So women *do* like the nice guys?"

"I can't speak for the female population as a whole," she laughed, too. "I've never been one to fall for the bad-boy type myself."

"Hmm," Chase murmured, spreading his hands wide on her back, pulling her closer as he whispered, "funny that you fell for a cop then, huh?"

"Funny indeed," she whispered back, leaning up on her tiptoes to capture his mouth with hers again. The hands at her back bunched up the fabric of her sweater, and she shivered when the coolness of the air around them hit her exposed bottom as he inched the sweater up higher. One of his hands released the handful of fabric and smoothed over her bare ass cheek, palming it in his large hand, squeezing gently, and she moaned throatily against his mouth. "Ooohhhh."

The front door opened, and Zoey squeaked in alarm, pulling her mouth from his and yanking her arms from around his waist. Chase angled his body to hide her in front of him, glancing over his shoulder to see who had entered. She felt his muscles tense beneath the fingers that clutched his forearms. Peeking around Chase's arm, she blushed hotly when her eyes met Tommy's where he still stood just inside the door.

Zoey was mortified that she was still wearing nothing but her sweater, her legs bare from high thigh down to her toes, and Chase's entire upper body was bare, his gray sweatpants slung low around his hips. She knew it was plainly obvious what had just transpired, and she was worried how her brother was going to react to his best friend clearly making out with his half naked sister.

"Well, that didn't take long," Tommy said drolly after a long silence, and she wished the floor would open up and swallow her. "It's about time."

Had it been that obvious to everyone? she wondered, her face flaming again. Chase's body was still tense as he stood close to her, blocking her half naked body.

Tommy made his way toward the coffee maker, taking out a mug from the cupboard and pouring himself a steaming cup, keeping his back to them.

Zoey raised her eyes to Chase's, and he winked down at her. Leaning close, he whispered, "Why don't you go upstairs, I can bring you your tea when the water is reheated."

She nodded, blushing again. The water was most likely cold by now. "Don't let him bully you," she whispered back.

"I think we're safe," he whispered, pecking a kiss to her forehead. "Go on. I'll be right behind you."

Pulling at the hem of her sweater to cover more of her bare legs, she slunk to the arched doorway of the kitchen and hightailed it around the corner and up the stairs. Verity was still sleeping, thankfully, so Zoey stepped into the bathroom, turning the taps to get the shower to running. Within minutes the small room was filled with steam, and she pulled the sweater over her head, letting it drop into the same laundry basket she'd tossed her panties in earlier. Stepping beneath the wonderfully hot spray, she sighed when the soothing heat spread over her muscles.

A quiet knock sounded on the door and she halted in lathering shampoo into her wet hair to call softly, "Yes?"

"It's just me," she heard Chase say as the door opened just a hair. "I have your tea."

"Oh, thank you," she said through the shower curtain. "Can you set it on the sink for me?"

"Sure," he said, and she heard his footsteps on the tile floor as he came into the bathroom, then the soft clink of the porcelain mug on the edge of the sink. "It's here when you're ready for it."

"Thank you," she whispered, her breathing coming in short, soft puffs. She heard his footsteps as he headed back to the door, but she called softly, "Chase?"

"Yeah, sweetheart?" he asked, and she could hear that he had stopped at the door.

"Be safe," she said quietly. "Come home to me, please."

She heard his striding footsteps a half a heartbeat before the curtain opened and she squeaked in surprise. He leaned in and pressed a kiss to her shocked mouth, sending his tongue swirling into it. One hand came up to steady herself against his chest and he sucked in his breath at the water that ran down his chest and abdomen at her touch. He nipped her lower lip once, making her gasp, and then soothed it with a gentle kiss before pulling back.

"I'll see you after work, sweetheart. Give my sunshine a kiss for me when she wakes up," he said, and then he was gone, sliding the shower curtain closed. She knew when he exited the bathroom, the door closing with a soft click.

Her heart hammered in her chest, the only other sound in the room was the steady beat of the water as it rained down on her.

FIFTY-SEVEN

Tommy was still in the kitchen, seated in one of the dining chairs at the table when Chase came back down the stairs ten minutes later, dressed in his uniform. He crossed to the coffee maker, pouring himself a cup. The silence in the room other than the sound of his booted footfalls and the quiet sloshing of the coffee as he poured it was deafening.

Keeping his back to his friend, he tugged at his collar, then slipped the first button through the loop at his throat, taking a deep breath.

"I asked her to marry me this morning. She said yes," he said quietly, his voice rough. He cleared his throat.

He saw Tommy's head nod out of his peripheral vision, and he swallowed past a lump in his throat. His joy from the night and morning spent with Zoey had dissipated when Tommy had walked in the door, a cruel reminder that this wasn't real. Not entirely.

"Good," Tommy said and that gut gnawing guilt tore at him all the more fiercely, making his stomach churn. A crushing wave of claustrophobia hit him, and he needed to escape the confines of the small kitchen and his best friend's presence.

Turning on his booted heel, he made his way to the coat hooks, pulling on his patrol jacket and hat, before slamming out the front door.

Snow drifted down, blanketing everything in fluffy white, and he used the snowbrush from his car to brush off the snow that covered his car, then did the same for Zoey's, so it would be ready for her when she came out with Verity.

He made the drive to the station, his thoughts convoluted. He was still processing what had transpired in the last six hours. He felt like he'd missed a step and was still gaining his footing again, his entire world rocked by the memories of the way her body had felt wrapped around his, those little noises she made when he'd pressed deep, how blindly she trusted him with her body as she fell apart in his arms, trusting that he'd be there to catch her.

And he'd proposed. He'd actually proposed marriage to Zoey. She'd said yes. His chest felt light as he thought of the beaming smile she'd graced him with. He would do anything to make her dazzle him with that smile every day for the rest of his life.

Walking in, he said hello to Rosie as he passed, making his way to the small conference room where they would have their morning debrief. Graham was already there, leaning back in one of the chairs, his long legs stretched out in front of him, ankles crossed. His eyes were closed, a travel mug of coffee resting on his abdomen, folded between his hands.

"Long night?" Chase asked as he tapped his toe against the bottom of one of Graham's boots as he passed, sinking down into another chair nearby.

Graham peeled one eye open, glancing at him out of the corner of that open eye, before letting his lid drop back down. He shrugged his shoulders, shifting lower into his seat as he grumbled, "Mom had a rough night, we were at the hospital until about four am."

"Hope she's okay," Chase murmured, taking a drink of his own coffee.

Again, Graham's shoulders raised and dropped. "She tripped over her dog while letting him out last night. She's got a couple cracked ribs, but I think her pride is more bruised than anything else. I just didn't get a whole lot of sleep. Those damn waiting room chairs are uncomfortable as fuck." Then, opening one eye again, he eyed Chase sideways. "You alright? I know that accident had you out late."

"Yeah, fine," Chase said, shifting in his seat. "It wasn't pretty. That snow we got was brutal, made clean up a bitch. Just idiot drivers that don't know how to slow down on snowy roads."

"I saw the kid the paramedics brought in while I was there with Mom. He looked pretty banged up," Graham said, finally opening both eyes and sitting up slightly in his seat as more deputies filed into the room, taking seats or leaning against the walls.

Chase nodded, remembering the scene from the night before. "He's lucky he spun out into a ditch and not into oncoming traffic. It could have been far worse than it was. I hope he takes driving in a snowstorm a little more seriously from here out."

"Mmm," Graham hummed in agreement. "Sometimes it takes an accident like that to wake them up."

"It shouldn't be like that," Chase muttered. "It shouldn't take almost dying to appreciate the time you've got."

"You're very philosophical this morning," Graham snorted, pulling his legs in and sitting up straight in his chair.

Chase sighed heavily, shoving his fingers through his hair, raking the longer strands away from his forehead. He admitted to himself that what happened last night with Zoey had done something to him. He'd never felt like this for anyone, and it scared the hell out of him. Whether Tommy's proposition had been the start of everything or not, what he'd said to Zoey that morning was the absolute truth; they had been on their way to this moment for a while. From the moment he'd seen her in her bedroom that first night back, holding Verity as she'd nursed, he'd been gobsmacked, and every day since then had only been a stepping stone to where they were now.

Though guilt still lingered, he let it slip away. Because they *had* been inevitable. And he wouldn't let a single day go without appreciating what he'd been given.

FIFTY-EIGHT

Zoey was just pulling dinner from the oven when Chase came in through the door at seven-thirty that evening, and she smiled shyly over at him as he closed the door.

Without breaking his stride or stopping to take off his patrol jacket, he came toward her. She set the baking dish on the stove and turned toward him, her eyes wide, a half a heartbeat before his arms went around her and his head lowered to hers. She gasped, taken by surprise, as she met his kiss.

When he finally pulled back, he chuckled, glancing at her hands, which still had oven mitts on them. She laughed, embarrassed, and slid them off before setting them on the counter beside them. She looked back up at him, her eyes scanning his face.

"Hi," he said gruffly, those blue eyes of his intense as he stared at her.

"Hi," she parroted, smiling again. "How was your day?"

"Long," he said, one side of his mouth tilting up slightly. "I thought about you all day."

"You did?" she asked, her voice a husky whisper.

He nodded. "Hold on," he said then, turning back toward the door. He unzipped his patrol jacket and shrugged out of it, hanging it on one of the hooks, then hung up his hat. Turning back to her, he stepped forward. She'd never seen him with such anxious energy, like he couldn't stand still. He reached for her hands and she let him take them into his hands, shivering at the coolness of them from being outside in the cold. Butterflies had long since taken flight in her belly, her heart racing in her chest.

"What is going on with you?" she asked lightly, smiling up at him. She gasped audibly when he dropped to one knee in front of her, her hands still clasped in his. "Chase..."

"I know you already said yes, but I wanted to do this the right way," he said softly, his voice steady. "I know this has all been a whirlwind, Zoey. I know how crazy it all seems. But I realized today I don't want to take one single day with you and Verity for granted. Marry me in two weeks, Zoey. I want nothing more than to spend the rest of my life with you, and I want that life to start as soon as possible. Tell me you want that, too."

One of his hands released hers and he dug into his pocket, pulling out a small square box. Glancing down, he opened it, then brought his eyes back to hers. Nestled in the velvet lining was a ring with a sparkling diamond, two smaller diamonds settled on the band to either side.

"When did you have time to do this?" Zoey asked, her voice coming out slightly squeaky. He grinned up at her and the force of it nearly made her knees buckle. Damn was he handsome!

"I went shopping on my lunch break," he admitted, and she laughed. "You didn't answer my question, Zoey."

"Two weeks?" she asked, her eyes wide, though a smile still pulled at her lips. "This is insane, Chase, you realize that, don't you?"

He tugged her hand forward, placing a kiss to the knuckles of her left hand. "Is it though?"

"We don't even know if we would be good together in a relationship," Zoey whispered.

"Isn't that what we've been doing for weeks, even if we didn't realize it?" he asked, and she laughed again. "Marry me in two weeks, Zoey. It's the earliest my parents could make it."

"You already told your parents!" Zoey shrieked with another laugh. "Chase!"

He shrugged, grinning sheepishly. "I was excited. They're thrilled, by the way."

"*This is crazy*," she breathed again, shaking her head. Then, she nodded, laughing again. "Okay, why not. Let's get married in two weeks, you crazy person."

Chase beamed a grin up at her, sliding the sparkling ring onto the third finger of her left hand, then squeezed it before rising to his feet in one fluid motion. His large hands spanned across either side of her jaw as he pulled her face to his for another deep, scorching kiss. "I love you."

"I love you, too," Zoey whispered against his lips, laughing as unshed tears made her nose tingle. "You've lost your damn mind, but I love you anyway."

He chuckled too, and the sound was a balm to her nerves. His arms went around her again, holding her against his chest gently as they swayed together in the middle of the kitchen floor.

The door opened and Zoey turned to look, just as Shaun and Tommy came in, kicking snow off their shoes. Shaun stopped moving as her gaze fell on them, Chase's arms still locked around her, and Tommy ran into Shaun from behind, knocking her off balance.

"Umm," Shaun said, her eyes ping-ponging rapidly from Zoey's face to Chase's, then back again. "Hi... what's goin' on guys?"

Chase squeezed his arms around Zoey lightly and he dropped a kiss to the top of her head, making Shaun's eyes widen even more. Zoey laughed then, worried her friend's eyes just may bug out of her head.

Extricating herself from Chase's arms, she slid her hand into one of his. "Hi. Umm, we have news."

Shaun's eyes dropped to their clasped hands, spying the glittering diamond on her finger, and her jaw fell open in shock. *"Holy shit, no way!"*

Shaun rushed forward, tugging Zoey into a hug, making her laugh. When she leaned back, she laughed harder when she saw tears shimmering in her friend's blue eyes. "Why are you crying?" Zoey exclaimed.

"This is just the best news," Shaun stammered, swiping at her eyes roughly. "You've deserved to be happy for so long. This is just so great!"

She turned to Chase, hugging him hard, making him chuckle, too. He patted her back awkwardly, then Zoey watched as his eyes met Tommy's over Shaun's shoulder as she pulled away. Shaun tugged Zoey's hand forward so she could take a good look at the ring, saying how beautiful it was. Zoey nodded, though her attention was on Chase and Tommy, as a silent conversation passed between them.

Tommy looked at her then, and he stepped forward, but stopped short. Smiling, she wrapped her arms around his waist and hugged tight, the first hug they'd shared in over a year.

When they pulled apart, he swiped at his eyes, grumbling something about dust in his eyes, which made her nose tingle again with tears. He extended his hand to Chase, who took it in a firm shake. "Welcome to the family."

Chase nodded, glancing down at her again, as the two released their handshake. "Glad to be a part of it."

"Ohmygod this calls for champagne," Shaun stammered, turning in a full circle, as if she didn't know which direction to move first. "Do we still have any bottles left from New Year's Eve?"

"I think so," Tommy said, moving toward the refrigerator. Opening it, he pulled out a chilled bottle of champagne. "Glasses?"

Shaun searched the cupboards, pulling down two champagne flutes. "The guys will have to use whisky glasses," she said, placing two crystal highball glasses next to the stemmed flutes.

"Isn't anyone hungry?" Zoey asked, laughing.

"Starving," Chase murmured as he leaned in close, close enough for his breath to fan the shell of her ear. She shivered, her body instantly on high alert as his fingers grazed the lower part of her back through her shirt.

"I meant for food," she whispered, turning her face up to look at him.

"Yeah, that too," he whispered back, winking at her.

"You're incorrigible," she teased lightly.

Zoey plated dinner as Shaun popped the cork of the champagne, and within minutes the four of them were seated at the dining table. They clinked glasses lightly, and Shaun murmured, "Congratulations you guys. This is so exciting!"

Digging into the meal, Shaun went through a round of twenty questions, wanting in on all the details. Chase just shrugged and said simply, "I've loved Zoey for a long time. Just in a different way now, I guess. I realized I couldn't imagine a life with anyone else. And we decided we don't want to wait."

Zoey smiled over at him, her heart nearly bursting at his words. He reached out and squeezed her hand, the one that now had that sparkling ring on it.

Shaun nodded around a bite of her food. Tommy was quiet as he ate, listening. "Don't want to wait?" Shaun asked after she swallowed.

"Are you guys free in two weeks?" Zoey asked shyly, looking at both Shaun and Tommy. Shaun's eyebrows shot up, but Tommy's face remained impassive. She wondered if he wasn't as amiable to this as he had originally said, but then shook the thought away. It didn't matter if he didn't like it. They were getting married. She loved Chase, and he loved her. That's all that mattered.

"What? Two weeks?" Shaun stammered incredulously. "That's not enough time to plan! Even Jodi couldn't pull that off!"

Zoey shrugged, looking over at Chase. "I don't think we're going to do anything extravagant. Probably just go to the courthouse."

"Absolutely not," Shaun said, affronted. "We can pull together something small and intimate without it being a courthouse wedding. Are you pregnant?"

Zoey blushed to the roots of her hair, swallowing hard around a bite of her food. She avoided her brother's eyes. "No!"

"For not wanting to plan your own wedding you sure are invested in planning theirs," Tommy muttered, and Shaun shot him a sour look.

"Don't start," Shaun said curtly. "This isn't about us. Tonight is about Zoey and Chase."

Tommy grumbled something unintelligible into his plate, but Shaun ignored him, turning back to Zoey. "We don't have much time, but I'm sure if we ask Jodi to help, we can swing something in two weeks."

"Shaun, just give us a few days to breathe," Zoey laughed, glancing over at Chase again nervously. "It literally just happened."

Shaun nodded again, taking a drink of her champagne. Zoey could fairly see the wheels turning in her best friend's head.

As soon as they had finished their meal, Shaun shooed Zoey and Chase out of the kitchen after refilling both their champagne glasses. "Go on lovebirds, we'll clean up."

Chase took Zoey's hand in his, leading her up the stairs. When she stopped at her bedroom door, he halted, turning to look at her. She dropped her eyes to the floor, shifting nervously from one foot to the other.

"What are you doing?" he asked softly, his eyebrows dipping into a V.

"I... I thought we were going to bed... I didn't know if—" she stammered quietly, and then his finger tipped her chin up. He smiled.

"You do realize there will be no more sleeping separately, right?" he asked quietly, his voice a low rumble. It made her shiver. His head dipped until he could press his lips against the corner of her mouth, brushing softly, teasing. Her lips parted, her breaths coming in short, quick puffs. "Do you understand, Zoey? I want you in my bed, sweetheart."

She nodded, just barely, causing his lips to brush along her cheek. A deep hum of approval thrummed through his chest and it made her knees go weak.

Backing toward the door of his bedroom at the end of the hall, he pushed it open, drawing her with him. The only light that guided them was the silver moonlight that filtered in through the window. Chase set his whisky glass of champagne on the bedside table, then took her stemmed flute from her hand, setting it aside as well, before sliding his hands around her waist, settling them on the curve of her back. Wrapping her arms around him, she stood on tip toe as she reached for his mouth with her own.

Zoey's fingers fisted into the fabric of his patrol shirt that he still wore, using it as a handhold to pull him closer. He chuckled in the darkness and it sent shivers down her body. Pulling her hands away from him, she reached for the buttons of his shirt, slipping them through the holes quickly, until she reached the bottom. He'd already untucked the shirt from his pants, and she slid her hands up his abdomen, over his pecks, and to his shoulders, where she pushed the shirt down his arms, letting it fall to the floor. Leaning forward, she pressed her lips to the center of his chest, where she could feel his heart hammering. He groaned, sinking his fingers into her hair, holding her head still as her lips flit over his skin.

Her fingers shook slightly as she reached for his belt, and her fingertips brushed the hard abs just above the waistline of his pants, making him suck in his breath. His fingers tightened in her hair and she gasped. He loosened his grip immediately, but she just looked up at him and whispered, "I liked that."

The blue fire that lit his eyes was going to burn her to ashes. A growl rumbled from his chest and he dropped his mouth to hers quickly, kissing her ravenously even as her fingers continued to work at his belt, button, and then zipper of his pants. He rocked his hips into her hand when she palmed him through the fabric of his underwear, a rough snarl escaping him. "*Fuck*."

His hands left her hair, dropping to the hem of her shirt. Gripping it, he pulled it up and over her head, letting it drop to the floor with his. His fingers went to the clasp of her bra between her shoulder blades, unhooking it deftly, and a heartbeat later that too fell to the floor, leaving her upper body as naked as his.

Sliding his hands, palm flat, into the waist of her leggings at her back, he palmed her ass cheeks in both hands, squeezing lightly. She panted against his mouth. "I thought about this all day."

"Hmmm?" he murmured, his lips trailing over hers as he dragged her leggings and underwear down over the curve of her ass, pushing them down her thighs. He dropped to his knees in front of her, dragging them the rest of the way down her legs until she could step out of them. His mouth found her stomach, pressing hot, open-mouthed kisses to the soft, still fleshy curve of her stomach. She burned with embarrassment, self-conscious of how soft she still was, but his large hands spanned her waist, his thumbs sinking into the cushion of her belly as his tongue did wicked, wicked things to her. Her hands fell to his head, tunneling her fingers through his hair, holding him to her as she cried out softly. "You've been thinking about this, sweetheart? What have you been thinking about? Because I know what I was fantasizing about all day."

"I want you inside me," she whispered brokenly, her fingers tightening in his hair. "I want to feel you again."

Backing her up until her legs bumped into the edge of the mattress, she sat down, but then his hand came up, pressing against her stomach until she lowered her back to the bed, and she gasped when he spread her knees to kneel between them.

"Chase...?" she breathed heavily, watching him as he stared down at her from his spot between her legs. She was achingly bare to him, and she blushed hard.

Trailing his fingers along the smoothness of her thigh where it was draped over the edge of the bed, she breathed raggedly when those fingers grazed the lips of her sex. "Is this okay, sweetheart? Can I touch you here?"

"Yes," she cried, undulating her hips into his hand. "Yes, please."

His finger sank into her then, and her eyes slid shut as she bit her lower lip to keep from moaning loudly. He moved in and out of her, twisting his finger, hitting that hidden spot deep inside, making her legs shake. "You are so unbelievably beautiful, Zoey. I love how much you love me touching you."

He was drawing her closer to that edge with every thrust of his finger, and then she bucked her hips when she felt him add another finger, stretching her. "Ooohhh," she moaned, her head thrown back as his thumb circled her clit, and then she was burning up, her entire body on fire as she came around his fingers. "Chase!"

"Yes, sweetheart. Come all over my fingers," he groaned from where he knelt between her spread thighs, still pumping his fingers in and out of her as the walls of her pussy clenched around them. "That's it, Zoey. So sexy."

As the last pulses of her climax edged away, she gasped into the darkness, opening her eyes and searching his out. His chest heaved like a bellows as he stared down at her body where his fingers were still buried inside her. He looked like he wanted to devour her.

Dragging his fingers out of her, she shuddered, a breathy sigh breaking past her lips, and he grinned up at her darkly. Turning slightly, he reached for the whisky glass of champagne, bringing it to his lips and taking a drink before raising it over her body. She gasped in a shocked breath when he slowly poured some of the cold, bubbly liquid over her stomach, abdomen, and in the valley between her breasts. Her nipples peaked into hard nubs at the shock of cold.

Standing, he levered himself above her on his arms, lowering his mouth to her body to sip up the rivulets of champagne that snaked across her skin, some of them sliding down her sides and up her chest toward her neck. He licked and kissed every inch of her skin that the effervescent alcohol had touched, making her writhe because the only thing that touched her was his lips, his teeth. His lips closed around one of her nipples, sucking softly, and she panicked, raising her hands to his hair and pulling his head up.

"I want to taste you," he grated out, his head lowering back to wrap around her nipple again. His tongue flicked over it, again and again, and she cried out, feeling the tug deep inside her at the same time. "You taste so good. I love watching you nurse Verity. I hope to watch you do the same for a baby in the future, Zoey."

"You want a baby with me?" she asked brokenly, her head thrashing on the bedspread beneath her. "Oh god, Chase, please."

"Mmmm," he murmured on a low hum. "I think I would very much like to put a baby in you at some point, sweetheart."

"Chase," she cried, tugging at his head as he dipped again to take the other nipple into his mouth. "Please. I want you inside me."

Standing, he pushed his pants and boxer briefs down his thighs until he stood naked in front of her. She reached for him, but he held his weight off her, his hands supporting him over her. Her legs were still draped over the edge of the bed, her hips barely on the mattress. Reaching between their bodies with one hand, she watched as he stroked his rock-hard cock in his hand before bringing the rounded head to her entrance.

"I'm so terrified I'm going to scare you," he whispered brokenly as just the tip of his cock sank into her. She moaned, wrapping her legs around his hips, trying to pull him in deeper, but he was strong and held back. His hand came back up to fist into the comforter on the side of her head, still holding himself off her.

"You won't," she cried, undulating her hips, still trying to get more of him. Her hands spread over his sides, her fingers trailing each rib. "Please, I want to feel you against me."

He eased into her, inch by inch, until his hips sat flush against hers. He ground his hips in a circular motion and Zoey's eyelids fluttered at the pleasure it induced.

Chase finally lowered his body closer to hers, leaning on one forearm that was pressed into the mattress next to her shoulder, so that half of his body rested against her. Reaching up with the other hand, he slid his hand to cup the side of her jaw, his thumb stroking her cheekbone as his fingers sank into her hair behind her ear. Her hand came up to cover his as he began to move, withdrawing from her body nearly to the tip before thrusting back in. Her legs were still wrapped around his hips, the bottoms of her feet pressing into the backs of his thighs.

They remained locked like that as he continued to withdraw and then sink back into her, over and over again, their bodies moving together, their breaths harsh as their mouths met in hungry, passionate kisses.

Zoey's head fell back against the mattress, her mouth falling away from his as she opened her mouth in a silent cry. He pumped into her, his mouth dropping to the curve of her throat. "There you go," he growled hoarsely. "Come for me, Zoey. Jesus fuck, let me feel you come."

He angled his hips, driving into her deeper, higher, and she began to shake as fireworks exploded inside her, around her, her skin tingling as if thousands of little sparks were zinging over her body. The hand still grasping her jaw forced her head back toward his, and he covered her mouth with his own, muffling the sharp cry that made to escape her throat as she came hard around him.

His movements became more erratic, his hips thrusting wildly into hers, and she knew he wasn't far behind her. As her body continued to tremble and her pussy clenched in aftershocks around his cock, she felt his breath hitch and his body went taut, those fingers at her jaw and in her hair tightening as he growled through his own release. Zoey moaned as she felt every throb of his cock, felt the heat of his seed as he emptied deep inside her.

Zoey couldn't help the breathy little laugh that escaped her as they panted together. He raised his head from where he'd buried it in her neck as he came, his brow glistening with sweat. "What's so funny?" he asked breathlessly.

"I don't think it's going to take long for you to put a baby in me, Chase," she laughed, touching her fingers to his forehead, pushing that errant lock of hair back.

Pressing his lips to hers, his fingers strummed along the column of her throat. He murmured against her lips, making her shiver, "We can keep practicing, just in case."

FIFTY-NINE

The pitiful wailing from the infant as they pulled her out of the sweat-drenched car seat was heartbreaking. Her golden curls lay flat to her head, her tiny face mottled from crying. The report had come in that a woman had been taken from this parking lot. The person that witnessed it had tried to follow while on the phone but had lost sight of the vehicle.

A woman had called in that she'd found an infant alone in a car. By the time Chase and his partner had shown up, the woman was beside herself.

"What kind of parent leaves their baby in a car?" the woman screeched to his partner as Chase cradled the infant close. Her indigo eyes were traumatized, and she hiccupped as she continued to wail.

Chase barked over his shoulder none too kindly, "The mother was abducted. She must have locked the baby in the car to keep them from getting her, too." The woman's teeth clicked shut, and Chase's lips thinned. Nosy bitch.

They did a cursory check for any identification in the vehicle, finding the registration. That was when the call came in and Chase's blood ran cold.

The infant was handed off to a CPS officer and Chase was in his patrol car, driving the half mile to the scene that had just been reported.

As he climbed out of his car, he carefully picked his way down the steep embankment of the ditch, where a body had been found. A white shirt had been torn to shreds off her torso, and she was naked from the waist down. Beaten and bloody, she had suffered at the hands of the monster that had done this.

But as Chase got closer, his heart began to pound out of his chest and he whispered, "No. No!" Dropping to his knees, he forgot everything about leaving the body as it was, rolling her over to stare down at her beautiful, now battered face. Her caramel blonde hair was tangled and blood soaked. "Fuck. Zoey! No!"

Hands gripped his shoulders and he tore away from them, gathering her into his arms as he rocked her, petting her hair away from her too-still face, her indigo eyes open and unseeing. An agonized roar threatened to tear from his chest as he felt his world, his heart, shattering to pieces.

"Chase, wake up..."

Chase bolted upright, gasping in air as he blinked open his eyes. The darkness of the room felt claustrophobic, as did the sheets tangled around his legs. His chest heaved like a bellows and he shuddered when he felt a soft, warm hand against his shoulder.

Turning his head, he stared into those indigo eyes as she whispered, "It's okay. It's just a dream."

Scrubbing his hands over his face, he sucked in shuddering breaths before reaching for her. Pulling her into his lap, he buried his face in the curve of her neck, inhaling deeply the soft lilac scent of her skin. His arms folded around her as hers went around his neck, holding him to her.

"Can you tell me what this nightmare is? This is the third time this week," she whispered as her fingers strummed through his hair. His heart still hammered inside his chest, but the anxiety had started to dissipate at her gentle, soothing touches. He pressed his lips to her neck.

"I had this case, back in Detroit. A woman was abducted from a grocery store parking lot," he whispered huskily, his throat closing over the words. "She had two little girls that we found locked in her car, before we found her..." He swallowed hard as she continued to smooth her fingers over his hair, touching his back, then sliding back up again. "It was always the same, up until a few weeks ago."

"What changed?" she whispered in the dark, and he squeezed her tighter as that anxiety returned.

"I see Verity in the car. I see you..." he whispered, his voice breaking on the last word. He felt her breath stall in her chest pressed so close to his, and his hands spread wide on her back, holding her closer. Taking a deep breath, he admitted brokenly, "It... it haunts me, Zoey. The thought of losing you... it does something to me. I can't bear the thought of it."

"I'm not going anywhere," she whispered back, searching for his mouth with her own. His heart tugged at the soft, sipping kisses she pressed to his lips. "I'm not going anywhere, I promise. Nothing is going to happen to me. To Verity."

"What if I can't protect you?" he breathed, finally admitting his greatest fear. The reason he'd never had any pull to start a lasting relationship with anyone before. "What if I can't protect you when you need me the most?"

"That's not going to happen," Zoey whispered, twisting in his arms so that she could place one leg on either side of his hips, her knees pressed into the mattress as she cupped his jaw with both of her hands, raising his chin so that his eyes met hers. "That's not going to happen, Chase."

His fingers clenched and unclenched against the smooth nakedness of her back, her bare chest pressed close to his.

Their mouths came together then and it wasn't long before she was lowering herself onto his stiffening cock as their breaths mingled together. Twisting them abruptly, he pressed her back into the mattress, his body covering hers as he moved inside her. Her fingers cupped his jaw as he pumped into her over and over, never letting him draw more than a few inches away from her, her mouth repeatedly finding his in the dark.

Fear and love battled within him. He knew he'd never fallen so hard or so fast for anyone in his entire life. He'd made a point to avoid this kind of all-encompassing, soul deep emotional connection with anyone.

"I'm right here," she whispered brokenly as he continued to move in her, and he knew she was getting close when her breaths became erratic against his mouth. "I'm not going anywhere, my love. Oh Chase..." she moaned then, and he picked up his pace, slamming his hips into hers and grinding them in a circular motion. His orgasm was tightening at his spine, drawing his balls tight, but he needed to feel her come around him, first.

"Come on, sweetheart," he growled against her mouth. "Let me feel you. I need to feel you."

Her back bowed and he felt her thighs tremble where they were pressed tight against the outside of his hips just as she squeezed the life out of him. She let out an almost silent, keening cry against his mouth and he lost it, slamming into her before he exploded inside her, his orgasm sending his heat deep with spine tingling pulses.

He lowered his forehead to her shoulder as he panted raggedly, their bodies still coming down. Rolling them to their sides, he remained locked inside her, not willing to leave the snug warmth that surrounded him just yet.

She said she wouldn't leave and that she wouldn't go anywhere.

He doubted that would still hold true if she ever found out the truth, of how he had manipulated her. Holding her close, he closed his eyes tight against the ugly truth, his best kept secret.

SIXTY

With Shaun and Jodi's help, it didn't take long to plan a small, intimate wedding for the second weekend of February. Chase procured a marriage license from the county courthouse that would be valid for thirty days. Jodi, Shaun's sister, secured a private room at the historical Perry Hotel in town, where Zoey and Chase would be married in front of a beautiful Victorian fireplace, and afterwards they would have an intimate dinner with their closest family and friends.

The guest list was minimal, immediate family and close friends only, which Zoey was ecstatic about. Chase's parents, Caren and Bruce, were making the trip North the following week and would be in town from Friday evening to Sunday. Chase said they were looking forward to seeing Zoey again and welcoming her to the family. His sisters were making the trip as well, though only staying for the ceremony and reception.

Shaun had insisted on taking Zoey shopping for a dress, after seeing the dismal options in Zoey's closet. "You are *not* wearing *beige*," Shaun had said in horror when Zoey had shown her what she was thinking, which had made Zoey laugh.

Details were finalized quickly, making Zoey's head spin.

Lying in bed several nights later, her body draped over Chase's after another mind-altering orgasm brought on by his magic fingers and dick, Zoey lifted her head to rest her chin on his chest, looking up at him. He stroked through her hair as it fell over her naked shoulders.

"Are you sure about this?" she asked softly, trailing her finger over his sternum. "You don't think this is insane?"

Chase smiled, and it never failed to send those butterflies on a kamikaze mission in her stomach. "I am totally sure about this. Are you getting cold feet?"

"No," Zoey said softly, slowly. Turning her head to press her cheek against his chest, she listened to his heart beating as she stared up at him. His fingers trailed over her brow, touching her eyebrows, down her temple, tucking her hair behind her ear. "I just worry that you're going to regret diving into this as fast as we have. We didn't really test the waters first."

He leaned forward and pressed a kiss to her forehead. "I'm sure, Zoey. I told you; I can't imagine my life without you or Verity. I meant it."

She nodded, closing her eyes as she listened to the steady cadence of his heart beneath her ear.

"Are you ready for your partnered drill tomorrow?" he asked quietly. Keeping her eyes closed, she shrugged. "You don't have to do it if you're not ready, Zoey. You know that."

"I know," she said softly. "I think I'm ready. I can't keep putting it off."

"You're going to do amazing," he said confidently, strumming his fingers along the curve of her spine, making her body break out in goosebumps. "And you know all you have to do is tap out and I'll stop. I promise you."

Opening her eyes to meet his, she whispered, "I love you."

"I love you, too," he murmured in return, then shifted so he could tuck her front against his, their legs intertwining beneath the covers. "Proud of you."

Zoey smiled, her lips moving against the smooth skin of his chest as she settled in deeper before sleep claimed her.

SIXTY-ONE

Chase handed Zoey a small, plastic object, and she raised her eyes to his in confusion.

"They're airpods," he explained. "Bluetooth connected to my phone. I have something for you to listen to while we get ready."

"Okay..." she said warily, taking the small earphones out of the case. Before she could insert them into her ears, he ducked his head and kissed her, clasping her face between both of his large hands.

"I am right here. You are not alone, and you are not in danger. I will not let anyone, or anything hurt you. Tell me you know that," he said earnestly, his eyes searching hers deeply. She nodded, but his lips thinned, and he shook his head. "I need to hear you say the words, Zoey."

"You are here. I am not alone. I am not in danger. You will not let anyone, or anything hurt me," she repeated, her lips trembling just the slightest on the last word.

"Good," he whispered roughly, then pressed his forehead against hers. "I love you."

"I love you, too," she whispered back, and then he released her, stepping back. Mike instructed them to run through warm up drills, and Chase nodded toward the airpods still in her hands. She inserted them and a few seconds later, *Carrie Underwood's* "The Champion" came on in her ears, and she closed her eyes. She had heard the song for the first time the week before and had cried after listening to it. She'd put it on repeat, letting the words wash over her, sink into her, then lift her up. She knew there were other songs he'd found for her on this playlist. Other songs that had brought her much needed strength and confidence coming into the new partnered drills they'd started.

He tapped her on the shoulder, and she pulled one of the earbuds out so she could hear him. "That playlist will play on repeat until you are done, if you want." Tears stung her nose and she took a deep, steadying breath in. "You've got this. Eyes on me."

Replacing the earbud, they worked through their warmups. Once they were ready, Chase motioned for her to get into position. She took another breath before lowering herself down until she was flat on her back, repose. She swallowed hard and let the words in her ears give her strength as Chase straddled her hips, his knees on either side of her. They had practiced this part at home while they lay in bed, him straddling her from above to get her used to it, but they were usually naked and doing deliciously wicked things to each other. Mike had had them run through the rest of it so many times the session before she knew exactly what Chase would do, and she knew exactly what she needed to do. Staring up into the blue eyes of the man she loved and trusted above all others, he raised his eyebrows in silent question. She nodded, and he mouthed the words, 'I love you'. She nodded again.

She could feel her heart pick up pace, hammering so hard against her chest and in her throat that she thought it would pound its way out of her chest before too long. But her mind was clear, no anxiety riddled her or blackened her vision.

...I am invincible, unbreakable, unstoppable, unshakable... the music pounded through the earbuds, drowning out everything else. She could do this. She *would* do this.

Ava Max's "Kings and Queens" started loudly in her ears *...to all the queens who are fighting alone, baby you're not dancin' on your own.* And Zoey nodded once more at Chase. She was not alone.

From her right, she saw Mike slap the mat, signaling for them to begin. Chase's hands shot out, encircling her throat none too gently, and she made an arrow with her hands, shooting them upward between his forearms, at the same time throwing her elbows out with all her might, breaking his hold. She'd told him not to go easy on her; she wouldn't learn if he coddled her through it, and his strength nearly overpowered her, which just spurred her on even more. Striking upward in an X, she crossed her arms across his own throat, grabbing hold of the sides of his shirt and pulling forward, making him lose his balance and pitch forward. He caught himself on his hands as she tightened her hold, and he tapped out a heartbeat later.

She released the hold she had on him immediately and he sat back, sucking in deep breaths. His face was pink from lack of oxygen, and he grinned widely down at her. She beamed up at him at the same time he took both of her hands in his, squeezing tightly.

Taking one airpod out, Mike gave her praise and asked if she wanted to run it again. She nodded, then replaced the airpod in her ear.

They ran it several times, each time making Chase come at her from a slightly different angle, so she could learn how to defend from multiple different attacks. By the end of their lesson, Zoey's body was sore, but she had never felt more elated. Adrenaline coursed through her.

Pulling the earbuds out of her ears and tossing them away, Chase then tugged her to her feet, crushing her to him in a tight hug, lifting her clear off her feet. He buried his face in the crook of her shoulder as she wrapped her arms around his neck as her body began to shake in earnest.

Dropping to his knees with her in front of him, he planted both hands on either side of her face, bringing her forehead to his as tears slid down her cheeks.

"I am so goddamn proud of you," he whispered brokenly, his voice rough with emotion as he rolled his forehead across hers again and again. His thumbs

swiped at her tears before his lips sipped at hers gently, sweetly. "You brave, beautiful woman. Look at all that you can do. Look at all that you have overcome, Zoey. *You are amazing.*"

Zoey hiccupped, her fingers clutching at the hands still holding her face. "You are here," she whispered, the words breaking as she stared into his eyes. "I am not alone."

"Never, Zoey," he whispered reverently. "Never again."

SIXTY-TWO

Chase watched Zoey out of the corner of his eye as he drove them home from the gym, worried about how quiet she was. He was terrified he'd set her mental health backward too many steps with their partnered drills, because she was lost in thought as she stared out the car window.

Reaching out a hand, he gently twined his fingers with hers, bringing her hand to his mouth and pressing a soft kiss to the back of it. She looked over at him, smiling, and he breathed a sigh of relief at the warmth in her eyes.

He pulled them into the driveway and led her into the house. It was late, their lessons with Mike were always later in the evenings, which meant by the time they got home Shaun and Tommy had already put Verity to bed. The two of them were asleep together on the couch, folded around each other, and Chase took Zoey's hand in his and led her up the stairs as quietly as they could.

He stepped into the bathroom, turning on the light, then walked forward until he reached the shower, turning the taps to start the water running. Zoey still seemed a little spaced out, and he needed to bring her back.

As the shower's steam began to fill the small bathroom, he turned toward Zoey, hooking his thumb under her chin until she looked up at him. "Proud of you," he whispered again, and she nodded. "Get undressed and we will take a shower, okay?"

She nodded again, and again he was worried he'd pushed her too far. She stripped, as if on autopilot, dropping her workout clothes into the laundry basket in the corner, and he did the same, until they were both naked. He pulled the shower curtain aside, taking Zoey's hand and helping her step in, following behind her. Directing her under the showers warm spray, he was pleased to see some of the tension drain from her shoulders as she ducked her head under the water.

Turning her around, he picked up her shampoo and let a dollop fill his palm, before reaching up and slowly, methodically, working it into a lather in her hair. She moaned as his fingers massaged her head and the back of her neck as he worked the shampoo in, and his cock twitched at the sound. He placed his hands on her shoulders then, turning her again so they could rinse the suds from her hair. He paid the same attention while sliding the conditioner through her wet strands before methodically rinsing that as well. Reaching behind her, he picked up the purple loofa that hung from one of the hooks on the wall, working her lilac and lavender scented body wash into it before dragging it over her back, over her shoulders, down her arms, each rounded curve of her ass, the backs of her legs. Then he turned her, paying the same homage to her front as he had her back. Soaping her chest, over each breast, which made his cock harden further, down her abdomen, her hips, her thighs, between them.

Zoey clutched at his shoulders as he dropped to one knee in front of her to get her calves, and a throaty moan escaped her. Chase's breathing was becoming labored as he fought to hold onto his control. This was supposed to be about her, taking care of her, not sex. But goddamn if she didn't stop making that sexy noise, it wasn't going to matter.

He stood, then pushed her back slightly so the water could wash away the suds he'd lathered over every inch of her body. She stared up at him, her lips parted slightly, her breathing just as ragged as his own. He dropped the loofa to the floor of the shower, reaching for her at the same time she reached for him, his mouth crashing down onto hers fiercely.

"Make love to me," she begged against his lips when she pulled away enough to breathe. "I need you. Remind me... Remind me it's just us. Always us."

Hooking his hands around the backs of her thighs, he growled fiercely as he lifted her, pressing her back against the cool wall of the shower. She gasped at the shock of cold, and he grinned as his teeth nipped at her bottom lip. He shifted so that he held her with one of his arms beneath her ass, his other tangling into her hair, pulling her head back so that he could bury his mouth against her throat.

Her arms went around his shoulders, holding herself up even as he shifted again, lining up his cock to her sweet pussy and then driving deep in one long thrust. She cried out, her head thrown back against the tiled wall as he moved inside her, her thighs squeezing his hips, her fingers tight in his hair. He growled low in his throat again, loving the ferocity she was showing as she moved with him.

"*Fuck*, you take me so well," he ground out, pulling his face from her throat to kiss her hard, their mouths mating just as fiercely as their bodies. Words tumbled out of him, rough and dirty and fraught with emotion. "My beautiful, brave girl. Feel how well we fit together. Like you were made for me. Only me, Zoey. Just you and me, from here out."

Zoey kissed him, her fingers scrabbling at his shoulders as she moved over him, her body taking him as deep as he could go.

Growling, fierce possessiveness rearing up in him, he fisted his fingers in her hair, tugging her face toward his and breathing raggedly, "Say it, Zoey. Say it's just you and me. This pussy belongs to me and only me."

"Yes," she sobbed against his mouth. "Yes, Chase, it's just us. Just you and me."

He knew she was close, her body tightening around his, and the muscles of her thighs around his hips began to shake. "That's it, sweetheart. Come for me."

Chase's breath stalled when he felt her begin to shudder violently, and then clamped his mouth over hers as she let out a soft cry as she came hard around him. His orgasm was spiraling around his spine, building as he continued to pump into her hard, rougher than he'd been with her before. Releasing her hair, he slapped his palm against the tile wall as his body jerked with the force of his release, and he groaned hoarsely as his cock emptied inside her tight, sweet body.

"What do you do to me?" he asked in a broken whisper, panting into her shoulder. His legs shook, and his arms felt like jelly as he carefully set Zoey down on her feet. She swayed unsteadily, and she giggled. The sound tugged at his heart. "I just wanted to take care of you."

"You did," she teased, reaching up and scratching her fingernails across the stubble of several days' worth of growth left on his cheeks and jaw. He captured her hand in his, holding her palm against his cheek. He never wanted this to end.

SIXTY-THREE

The morning of February thirteenth dawned cold, but rays of sunlight filtered in through the window as Zoey woke.

I'm getting married today.

She stretched in her bed, the first time she'd slept in it in two weeks, since she and Chase had agreed to sleep separately last night before the wedding. She also wouldn't see him until it was time.

A knock sounded on her door, and she sat up, looking over at a still sleeping Verity. The door opened, and Shaun stuck her head in, doing a silent squee of excitement to see that Zoey was awake.

Zoey tossed her legs over the edge of the bed and stood, padding quickly over to the door and exiting with Shaun. In the hallway, she and Shaun did a little jig, then hugged quickly.

"Okay, so we've got a big day," Shaun murmured quietly as the two of them headed down the stairs to the kitchen. "The guys are already out of the house, Chase left for his run and then said he and Tommy would go hang out at his buddy Graham's house until it was time to go to the venue."

As Zoey walked into the kitchen, her jaw dropped. A beautiful bouquet of flowers in varying shades of purple sat in a vase on the table and a small card sat in front of them. "Chase had those sent over."

Zoey reached for the card, reading his handwritten note:

I can't wait to marry you today. See you at 2,

xoxo Chase

"Jodi will be over in a couple hours to help with hair and make-up," Shaun said and poured Zoey her tea, which had just started to whistle from the stove. "Your dad will meet us at the venue at one thirty. I have Mom bringing breakfast over, and she's going to take care of Verity while we get ready."

"I can cook," Zoey said, turning toward the refrigerator, but Shaun yanked her to a stop by the back of her shirt.

"Nuh-uh," Shaun said, clucking her tongue. "Not today. You're going to sit down and get pampered."

Zoey laughed, too giddy to argue. "Okay."

The morning flew by quicker than Zoey could have imagined. Serenity Kendall, Shaun and Jodi's mom, came by with a tray of fresh fruit and bagels, though Zoey's stomach was in knots, so she only nibbled. Seren was happy to take Verity, saying over her shoulder that she was waiting patiently to become a grandma, to which Shaun rolled her eyes. Jodi arrived around eleven in the morning, deftly applying make-up to Zoey's face and curling her hair into soft waves, then pinning it into a half updo, tendrils left to frame her face.

Before she knew it, they were loading into the cars and shuttling to the venue, where they had a room reserved to finish getting ready. She thought she saw Chase's dark head as she ascended the stairs, but when she looked again, he was gone.

In the bridal suite, she was zippered into her dress that she and Shaun had gone shopping for the week before, luckily finding an off the rack sample that fit to perfection with no needed alterations, and as a bonus it was on sale because it had been discontinued.

Staring at herself in the tall mirror in the room, she once again admired the dress she'd chosen. The silhouette was a simple sheath that fit closer to her body but floated easily without clinging. The neckline was modest without being matronly, curving from one shoulder to the other just below her collarbones. The long, delicate lace sleeves fit snugly to her arms down to her wrists, and a single, thin string ran from one shoulder across her back to the other, holding the back together above the dramatic open back that left her bare from the top of her shoulders to the lower part of her back. She blushed, once again fantasizing about the feel of Chase's fingers against her bare skin. It was simple and stunning. She hoped Chase thought so, too.

Shaun stepped out of the bathroom, dressed in her chosen maid of honor dress. It, too, was simple, a sheath silhouette with a hem that hit just below her knees. It had a cowl neckline that draped over Shaun's generous chest, the straps spaghetti thin and criss crossed over her back. The color was a rich, amethyst purple. She'd pinned her curls up in a loose French twist, and her make-up was beautiful but understated.

Seren had dressed Verity in her flower girl dress, a light shade of lilac, and had pinned a flower clip into her blonde curls.

Jodi handed her a small bouquet of white roses and greenery, saying softly, "Are you ready?"

Zoey nodded and said, "Yes!"

Jodi laughed and Shaun stepped forward, extending her hand, which Zoey took, squeezing it tightly. "Thank you for being here."

"I wouldn't have missed it," Shaun whispered, and Zoey could hear the emotion in her friend's voice. "Let's go get you married!"

They would be meeting in front of the old, Victorian style fireplace in the front room that had been reserved for them. Her father, looking handsome in a simple gray suit, a purple tie at his throat, met them at the bottom of the stairs. He offered his elbow, and she took it with no hesitation, smiling over at him. His brown eyes grew misty, and he patted her elbow gently. "Your mom would be so proud of you, baby girl. I wish she was here to see you."

Zoey blinked rapidly to stop the tears that rushed to her eyes, taking a deep breath. "I love you, Dad."

They made their way to the doors that led to the small room they would be married in, which were closed, blocking her view of the room within. The guest list had remained small. Chase's parents and three sisters, who Zoey remembered from school, were all present. She, Shaun, and Bree, his youngest sister, had graduated together. Graham, Chase's partner from work, had joined as well. Serenity and Levi Kendall were there, and Zoey was grateful. Clara, a friend from work, had been invited, too. Instead of an aisle and chairs lined up on either side, they had requested the guests sit at the tables since there were so few of them.

As the doors opened, Shaun stepped inside ahead of Zoey and Thom, going to her seat beside Tommy, who looked handsome, though uncomfortable in his dress slacks and button-down shirt. He'd forgone a tie, but she wasn't surprised. She smiled over at him as she and Thom made their way forward.

She finally let her gaze find Chase's, and she nearly stumbled when her eyes connected with his.

I really am the luckiest woman, she thought dazedly as they made the short walk to where he stood in front of the blazing fireplace. He wore a simple black suit, a white button-down shirt beneath it, and had found a tie that she knew would match the violet/indigo of her eyes perfectly.

He smiled at her, and her heart very nearly thundered out of her chest as she came to a stop in front of him. His eyes left hers long enough to meet Thom's, and they shook hands before her father took his seat at the table with Tommy and Shaun. Their officiant addressed their guests, reciting words of love and commitment, but Zoey didn't hear any of them as she stared up into Chase's eyes.

She passed her small bouquet off to Shaun, then Chase took both of her hands in his, squeezing her fingers gently, and she did the same in return. They recited the quick vows they'd agreed on, promising themselves to the other through sickness and health, good times and bad, and promising to love, honor, and cherish each other.

When the officiant asked for the rings, Shaun and Tommy stood, handing off the rings to Zoey and Chase.

"With this ring, I give you my heart. I promise that from this day forward, you will never walk alone, may my heart be your shelter, and my arms be your home," Chase said steadily as he pushed her three stone engagement ring, along with a band of tiny sapphires onto her finger.

Tears stung her nose and she inhaled deeply to steady herself. "I give you this ring to wear with love and joy. As a ring has no end, neither shall my love for you. I choose you to be my husband this day and forevermore." She slid the simple white gold band onto his finger, and her heart expanded, loving the way it looked on his hand.

Zoey lost track of everything else the officiant was saying, as Chase's fingers tightened on hers, his smile wide and breathtaking. She didn't even hear the man say "You may kiss the bride" before Chase's hands had dropped hers and had enveloped her face in his palms, leaning down to kiss her thoroughly.

Eventually her ears stopped ringing and she could hear the applause from their guests, and quiet weeping from Serenity and Caren. Verity had remained content through the ceremony, but now let out an indignant wail at being kept from her and Chase for so long.

He chuckled against Zoey's mouth, making her belly do flip flops, then pecked one more kiss to her lips before they turned together to the small crowd. He stepped forward, taking Verity from Seren, and Zoey wasn't sure her heart could hold anymore love for the two people standing next to her.

They made their rounds, saying hello to those that had come to celebrate with them as a smartly dressed waiter came in with a tray of crystal champagne flutes filled to the brim. Chase kept her hand grasped firmly in his as they made their way around the room. She shook hands with everyone, but was thankful no one leaned in for a hug except Caren and Bree, who she hugged back with one arm.

Their dinner was beautifully plated and absolutely delicious. After the wait staff had cleared the heavy porcelain plates from the tables, the photographer that Jodi had hired asked them to step over to their small, two-tiered wedding cake. Zoey held the fork aloft, waiting as Chase dug a small bite on a fork as well. They fed each other the decadent cake, the lemon filling the perfect mix of tart and sweet.

When Verity began to fuss, Chase leaned down and pressed a kiss to Zoey's mouth before handing her the baby. "I'll just be a few," she said and he nodded, at the same time lifting his champagne glass to his lips.

"Take your time," he said and smiled, then she and Shaun disappeared out of the room, taking the stairs up to their private suite to nurse.

Shaun unzipped the back of Zoey's dress enough to let her pull one arm free, lowering the bodice below her breast to let Verity latch greedily.

"I think that went really well," Shaun said and sat on the edge of the bed, bringing her glass of champagne to her lips. "You're glowing."

Zoey smiled happily, leaning her head back against the worn wood of the Victorian style rocking chair that she sat in. "I'm just... content. Blissfully, wholly content."

"I had hoped that all those secret little looks you guys would sneak at each other would turn into something," Shaun laughed. Pinching her brows together, she murmured, "Although I am slightly surprised Tommy was as amiable to this as he has been. I thought for sure he'd lose it."

Zoey laughed. "To tell you the truth, I think Tommy was relieved."

"What makes you say that?" Shaun asked.

She shrugged. "Just a feeling. I think he's relieved to finally be off the 'Zoey Babysitter' hook."

"I don't think that's it," Shaun said, taking another drink of her champagne as Zoey adjusted Verity to the other breast. "I think he likes that Chase is a cop. That he feels like Chase can protect you better than anyone else." She shrugged then. "I'm just happy to see you happy. You deserve it, Zoey."

Zoey nodded, smiling. "I've never trusted someone as irrevocably as I trust Chase. There's just... something about him. He feels like home."

Shaun's eyes misted and Zoey smiled again, as her best friend whispered, "Come on, let's get back downstairs if Verity is finished."

Zoey handed her Verity, who had grown sleepy, and she slid her arms back into the sleeves of her gown before Shaun deftly zippered her back into it. Zoey squeezed Shaun's fingers and murmured, her nose stinging with unshed tears, "I love you."

Shaun rolled her eyes and said, "Yeah, I love you, too. You're all weepy. I still think you're pregnant. Let's go."

SIXTY-FOUR

Chase had left the wedding guests in the private room that they'd rented to find the bar. He needed something stronger than champagne and hadn't seen the waiter in some time. After asking the smartly dressed bartender for a bourbon, the gentleman had waved him off with a smile when he'd held out cash. "On the house, congratulations, sir."

Raising the glass in thanks, he wandered back toward the room, but detoured into what looked like a study. It was blessedly empty. Walls lined with mahogany bookshelves filled with books covered three walls, and a fireplace roared on the fourth. Stepping over to it, he stared into the flames for a long time. His thoughts were once again convoluted, a jumbled, gut-wrenching mess. He was out of his mind with happiness. Contentedness that blanketed him whenever he watched Zoey; his *wife*.

What had he done? he asked himself, letting his chin drop forward.

He stood alone in front of that fireplace for a while before he heard footsteps behind him, and he turned to find Tommy standing several feet away from him. He took another drink of the bourbon in his hand, praying that Tommy would just stay silent. He had no such luck.

"Thank you," he heard from behind him then, and he felt anger fill his chest. This was *wrong*.

"Don't."

"What?" Tommy asked from where he stood.

"Just don't say anything. I don't need to feel anymore guilty about this than I already do," Chase muttered darkly. "I didn't do it for you."

"Does she suspect anything?" Tommy asked, and Chase's head whipped around to glare at the other man.

"I'm not talking about this with you. I will take care of her and Verity with everything I have. But from now on, this is between me and *my wife*," he said, his voice low and ominous. "Right now, our friendship is tenuous at best, Tommy. She is mine to protect. Even if it's from you. You got what you wanted; this... *bargain* you and I have made. I married her. Now leave it be."

A soft gasp ricocheted through the otherwise silent room, the only other sound the crackling of the fire beside him. Chase's heart sank into his stomach as he and Tommy both turned, his eyes finding her indigo gaze from just inside the door, the tears in her eyes and the heartbreaking look of betrayal on her face making his chest tighten.

Fuck.

SIXTY-FIVE

"Zoey, sweetheart—" Chase said, reaching for her, but she recoiled as if she'd been burned.

"Don't touch me!" she cried softly, heartache radiating off of her in waves. She felt faint, like she was going to collapse at any second, her heart was pounding so hard in her chest. This wasn't happening. This wasn't real. It couldn't be. It had to be some twisted nightmare.

"Zoey, please—" he began again, his electric blue eyes tormented as he stepped toward her again. Zoey backed away another step, glancing behind her to make sure no one else was nearby. She closed the door behind her, closing the three of them in. No one else needed to hear this. No one else needed to be witness to her world shattering at her feet.

Tommy stepped forward this time, but Zoey held up her hand to stop him from coming any closer. "Zoey, this isn't what it sounds like—"

"This isn't what it sounds like?" she asked, her voice coming out much stronger than she felt.

"Because *it sounds like* you two made some kind of deal." Her eyes sliced over to Chase's, and she saw the guilt on his face before she swallowed hard. "Did you marry me because he asked you to?"

Chase opened his mouth, but Tommy spoke. "Zoey, I just wanted you and Verity safe, taken care of."

Zoey squeezed her eyes shut for a half a heartbeat before opening them. Her eyes met Chase's and she repeated, "Did you only marry me because he asked you to?"

Tommy made to speak again, and Zoey clenched her fists at her sides, her arms ramrod straight, as she snarled, "I'm not talking to you!"

Tommy closed his mouth, looking sheepishly down at the floor. Turning her eyes back to Chase's, she struggled to keep her breathing steady. Her hands trembled at her sides as she waited for him to speak.

"Chase."

"It started out that way," he finally whispered, and her breath exited her lungs in an audible *whoosh*. Reaching out a hand, she clutched the back of a tufted chair to steady herself even as her knees threatened to buckle beneath her. He made another step toward her, and she held her other hand out to stop him. He halted several feet away from her. "But that's not why I married you, Zoey. I fell in love with you—"

A vicious laugh escaped her throat as she looked up at him, pressing her hand to her stomach, as if to hold in the dying butterflies that threatened to escape. She didn't know what to believe. Everything he'd ever said to her was a lie.

And she had been the fool that believed every word.

He'd manipulated her in the worst way possible.

"Is that why you came back?" she whispered. "Has—has this been your plan all along?"

"No," Chase murmured, shaking his head. "I came back for exactly the reasons I said. It wasn't until that night in the hallway—"

Zoey's eyes widened and Tommy spoke then, making her slice her eyes to his. "I needed you to be safe, Zoey. I needed to know you were taken care of, protected."

Zoey gasped out another derisive laugh, as she asked, "What about what *I wanted*? What about what *I* needed?" When Tommy's eyes dropped to the floor again, she shook her head in disbelief. "You're both no better than Robby."

Tommy's head snapped up and he ground out, "That's not fair."

What little control she had left snapped, and she shouted, "No, what *you* did was *not fair*!" she shouted, aiming accusing fingers at the both of them. "Robby took my body, took my own physical autonomy away from me, took away the feeling that my body was my own. What you did... you took something so much more valuable! You had *no right*! No right to take this choice away from me! *How dare you*!"

"And you—" Zoey seethed, turning on Chase, her eyes fairly glittering with fire, "—you *lied* to me. Robby raped my body, stole my peace, took it all by force. At least with him I *knew* what was happening and could try to fight! You... you actively deceived me, let me believe you weren't going to hurt me, take from me, anything that I wasn't ready or willing to give. But you *lied*," she snarled the word through clenched teeth as tears finally began to fall. She could see the tears in his own eyes, but she didn't care, not one bit, for his pain when he hadn't cared how much this would destroy her. "I let you into my life, into my daughter's life, into *my body*—" her voice cracked on the words, a single tear sliding down her husband's cheek, "—but you tricked me into all of it. I blindly handed you my trust, my child, my *love*—"

Chase's chest heaved as another tear slid down his face, her own unchecked as they fell in rivulets down her cheeks, dripping off her chin.

She wrapped her arms around herself tightly. "I want you to go. Both of you. Get your things and get out of the house, or I will."

"Zoey, no—" Chase whispered, stumbling toward her a step.

"Don't. Touch. Me." The ice in Zoey's words made him pause. Just as she knew he would, as he always respected her personal space, he didn't make another move toward her. She'd never seen him look as broken as he did now, standing in front of her. It matched the way she felt inside. "If you both won't leave, I will go stay with Shaun. We can have this annulled."

"Please don't," Chase whispered brokenly, and the pain in his voice was almost her undoing. Almost. "I love you so much."

"I can't believe a word coming out of your mouth," she whispered. "Everything you said to me was a lie."

"No," Chase said emphatically, slicing his hands across his body. "That's not true. I meant every single word, Zoey. You have every right to be upset with me, I deserve that." She stared into his handsome face, her eyes never leaving his as he whispered, "You said you wouldn't leave. You promised."

"Don't do that. This is unforgivable, Chase!" she cried, more tears sliding down her cheeks. She ached to be in his arms, ached to hear his heart beating against her ear, to feel those arms as they held her close. But it had all been a ruse. None of it was real. Her heartache made her tongue sharp as a dagger, and she punched it in deep, giving it a twist, wanting to hurt him as badly as she was hurting now. "You took that 'serve and protect' oath a little too seriously, don't you think?"

She knew she had cut him to the quick when his head snapped back as if he'd taken a physical hit. But she steeled herself against the agony she saw cross his features, instantly regretting her hateful words, but too proud to take them back.

Unable to bear the haunted expression on her husband's face for another second, she turned toward the door and opened it. Glancing back one last time at the man that had shattered her heart into pieces, she hiccupped a sob before exiting the room, closing the door softly behind her. Shaun found her almost immediately, her smile disappearing when she saw the tears streaming down her face. Shaun whisked her away up the stairs, barely making it to the private suite before she collapsed into her best friend's arms as the gut-wrenching sobs overtook her.

SIXTY-SIX

Chase walked out of the study as if he were a zombie. His feet felt leaden, his chest was on fire, and he felt like he could throw up. He watched as Shaun whisked Zoey away, up the stairs, heard the way Zoey was trying to hold in her tears as the two disappeared out of sight.

He made his way back to the reception room and thanked everyone for coming, his mind and motions on autopilot. He watched Tommy drain two glasses of whisky as he saw the last of their guests out, coming up with a lame excuse as to why Zoey wasn't there with him to bid farewell to their guests.

Shaun came down some time later and he braced for what was coming. The look on her face was fierce.

But she bypassed him completely, heading straight for Tommy, who had just finished off a third glass of whisky.

The crack of her palm against his cheek was *loud*, and Chase winced. He could tell just by the sound of it that it had to hurt. Tommy's head whipped to the side, but he didn't react.

"You bastard," Shaun seethed. "You absolute fucking *bastard!*"

She spun on him then, and Chase dropped his chin to his chest. She took two striding steps toward him and shoved the heels of her hands into his chest, hard. He stumbled back a half step. "How dare you do this to her. Both of you!"

"I know," he whispered brokenly, scrubbing one hand over his face. "I fucking know, Shaun. Fuck. I'm sorry."

"She's a fucking mess up there," Shaun seethed, then shook her head, turning back toward Tommy. "You had no right to do this to her."

"I wanted her taken care of," Tommy gritted out, pointing his finger toward the stairs. "Why am I the bad guy for that? I'd do it all over again."

"Do you even hear yourself?" Shaun gasped in outrage.

Chase sank into one of the empty chairs at a table, spreading his knees and letting his elbows rest on them, burying his face in his hands, letting their argument fade into the background. He wanted to go up and see her. To hold her. Make her see how much he loved her. How much he needed her. He couldn't do this life without her, now that he knew what life could be like with her by his side.

But then he remembered the devastation on her face, and he couldn't move. Couldn't take the steps to take him up the stairs. Because everything that she felt was valid. It hadn't been his intention to trick her, but ultimately, that's what he and Tommy had done. He had taken her choice away just as surely as that bastard Robby had. Only this time, it wasn't just her body that had been used against her will, but her heart.

And he couldn't forgive himself for that. Just as he knew she couldn't either.

He raised his head from his hands when he heard Tommy shout, "I don't care that it wasn't up to her. I would do it again in a heartbeat. I'd do it for you, too."

"You won't have the chance," she seethed. Pulling the ring from her left hand, she threw it at Tommy's chest. He fumbled for it, finally grasping it as she snarled, "I will not marry someone that I can't trust, Tommy. And I don't trust you."

Chase hung his head as Shaun stormed out of the room, leaving Tommy standing in the middle of the floor, staring after her.

How had this day gone so downhill so quickly? This was supposed to be the happiest day of his life. It had somehow turned into the worst.

SIXTY-SEVEN

When Zoey pulled into the driveway the following morning, she was grateful that neither Tommy nor Chase's vehicles were in the driveway. Serenity had taken Verity for the night, as she and Chase should have been on their honeymoon for the rest of the weekend. She had no idea where either man were, and she didn't care. As long as they didn't show up at the house while she was packing a bag for herself and for Verity to take over to Shaun's, she didn't much care where they were or what they were doing. She would be out of the house long enough for them to get their stuff and leave. She had not wavered on that.

But when she walked in the door, she saw the bouquet of flowers that Chase had sent over the morning before, and tears threatened to spill down her cheeks again. Her head ached terribly, and her eyes were puffy from crying the night before, so she fought them back with all her might.

Tossing the bouquet into the garbage, she ripped the card with Chase's handwritten note into pieces, throwing it away as well. Then she trudged up the stairs with the bag that had been packed for their short honeymoon, repacking it with normal clothes and pajamas. She had not made a decision about what she and Chase were going to do, but she knew she needed time to process. She was hurt; *really* hurt, by what she had learned the night before.

She was just exiting the bedroom after piling a few things into the bag for Verity when she heard the front door close and then heavy, hurried footsteps through the kitchen and up the stairs.

Chase rounded the corner of the stairs and stopped, his breathing ragged, like he'd sprinted the whole way.

"Hi," he whispered raggedly, and Zoey's breath hitched in her throat as she took a shuddering breath, her eyes cataloging his face.

"Hi," she breathed back, though neither of them made any move toward the other.

"I saw your car," he said, motioning with his hand toward the front of the house.

She nodded, gripping the strap of the duffel bag tighter in her fingers, if only to keep from reaching for him. "I was getting some things. I'm going to stay at Shaun's."

"Zoey," he whispered, his shoulders sagging. He took one step toward her, then stopped. "I'm sorry. I never meant for this to happen."

"You never meant for me to find out," Zoey countered, and he dropped his gaze guiltily. She shifted from one foot to the other as tears stung her nose again. Blinking rapidly, she whispered, "You said we had been on our way here for a while. That was after you two had already made your deal? Did you even mean it? Or was it a way to get me to agree to what came next?"

"I meant every word, Zoey," he murmured. "If your brother had not come to me with that proposition, I have every confidence that we would still have gotten to where we were. I was already falling in love with you."

"Stop," Zoey cried, the tears overflowing her eyes and sliding down her cheeks. She swiped at them angrily. "Please don't try to manipulate my feelings more. I'm already so confused."

"I don't ever want you to feel that way, sweetheart. I am so sorry that I've put these doubts in your mind," Chase whispered brokenly. "I swear it's the truth."

"I need time," Zoey hiccupped on a sob, her fingers coming up to clamp over her mouth as more threatened to spill out of her. "Please give that to me, Chase. I can't... I don't know what to trust right now."

Chase stepped forward again, until only a foot separated them. She refused to lift her gaze to his, knowing if she did, she would be helpless against those blue depths. She watched as he lifted a hand, and she let his fingers sift through her hair that hung over her shoulders. He leaned down, pressing his forehead to hers. Her fingers ached to reach out, to twine into the fabric of the shirt that covered his chest, but she didn't.

Rolling his forehead across hers gently, he whispered beseechingly, "I will give you time, sweetheart. I've never been able to deny you what you want, what you need. I want you to know that you can trust me. You know it in here," he said, placing his palm flat on her chest, where her heart pounded erratically in her chest at the contact. "I know you do. I know how much I fucked up, how much I hurt you, and I don't blame you in the slightest for having these doubts." He took a breath in, and she saw him squeeze his eyes shut tightly. "Take your time, sweetheart. But please—Zoey, *come back to me*."

A strangled sob broke from her, and she almost tilted her face to touch her lips to his, but again, she resisted.

He released her then, stepping back away from her, and she was unsuccessful at stopping the series of sobs that shook her body as she moved past him, nearly tripping down the stairs through the haze of her tears.

SIXTY-EIGHT

The two weeks that followed were the most miserable of Chase's life, by far. He had gathered just enough of his belongings to make it a few weeks staying at Graham's, while he gave Zoey the time and space she had asked for.

He hated every second of it.

It felt like all the joy had been sucked out of his life. He missed Zoey, he missed Verity. So much that it ached in his chest constantly. There was no sunshine without her, without the two of them. Everything was gray and dull.

Each night, he made sure to drive past the house, just to calm his own fears now that she was in the house by herself every night. He wasn't sure where Tommy had gone, but he knew he hadn't been back to the house. He also knew he wasn't staying at Shaun's.

He sat in his cruiser and watched as she and Shaun entered the lawyer's office for her mediation with the Patterson's. He hated that he wasn't in there with her. He had texted her that morning.

Good luck today. Please let me
know if there's anything I can
do to help. You know I'm always
here. You're not alone.

He had waited what felt like forever for her reply. When it came, it did little to alleviate the hollowness in his chest.

Ok. Thanks.

He'd left it at that, and watched as an hour later they emerged, her face tear streaked and her body shaking. He'd nearly jumped out of his car to go to her but had held back. If she needed him, she would tell him.

But nothing ever came.

Several days later, a wicked, early March snowstorm blew in from over the lake, dumping the northwestern region of Michigan with nearly two feet of snow. He had just finished a call, helping a teen unbury her car from a shallow ditch after she'd tried to stop at a stop sign, but had ended up sliding into the ditch instead, when a call for another auto accident came through. He finished up with the teen, making sure she was fine, though shaken up. He let her off with a warning and a cautionary word to slow down before walking back to his cruiser. He had just slid back behind the wheel when his phone starting ringing. He picked it up, surprised to see Graham's name on the screen as he answered it.

"Manning," he said into the phone.

"You need to get to the hospital," he heard Graham say, and he knew with the intensity in his partner's voice that it was serious, and he wasn't going to like what came next.

"Who?" he asked, barely daring to breathe as he buckled his seat belt in a hurry, then flipped his lights on as he pulled away from the side of the road.

"Chase, it's Zoey," Graham said softly, and he felt like his heart was going to sink all the way through his body. Pure panic engulfed him as he put on his siren. "She was in an accident. They're taking her via ambulance now. It doesn't look good."

"Fuck!" Chase shouted, driving as quickly as the shitty roads would allow him to. "Verity?" he asked.

"She wasn't in the car," he heard Graham say, and he breathed a momentary sigh of relief. "Don't worry about the rest of the shift. Just get to the hospital."

"Thank you," he murmured, his heart clogging his throat. They hung up, and he swerved slightly as he pulled into the hospital parking lot, driving up the ramp to the emergency department doors. The ambulance was already there, and he could tell they'd already taken her inside. He parked off to the side and bolted toward the doors, which swished open much too slowly. He sent a prayer up as he skidded to a halt at the front desk.

"Zoey Chandler, err, Manning," he barked, bracing his hands on the counter. "Where is she?"

The nurse behind the reception desk stood, pressing the button to the side to open the door that led into the emergency room. "Back here. Deputy Beckett told us you would be arriving."

"Is she okay?" he asked as he stepped through the gurney-wide door. Another nurse found him then, leading him back around the corner and down a hallway. "Is she okay?" he repeated.

"She's stable," the nurse said, stopping at a door. She touched his sleeve. "She's unconscious."

He pushed inside the heavy door, coming to a sudden halt when he found her surrounded by several nurses and a doctor. She was repose on the gurney; her eyes closed. One nurse was working on getting an IV inserted in her arm, another checking vitals. Blood seeped down her temple and cheek from a gash on her forehead, and her left arm was bent at a stomach-churning angle.

He stumbled forward, and one of the nurses turned to tell him to get back, but he shouldered his way closer, stopping so he stood near the head of the gurney as the hospital personnel worked over her.

"Are you family?" one nurse asked, eyeing him.

"Husband," was all he managed to croak out. Christ, she was so pale. The nurse seemed pacified and let him stay. When they started to wheel her out of the room, Chase followed. "Where are you taking her?"

"CT scan, then X-Rays," the nurse said. "We need to assess the damage to her arm, and determine if she has a concussion."

He nodded, following as far as they would let him go. He was sick to his stomach as he waited, pacing the hall outside of the rooms as they ran multiple tests. When they wheeled her back out and toward the room she'd been in before, he was right behind them. He reached out and clasped her hand on her non-injured arm, squeezing gently. Her fingers were like ice in his.

"Can she have a blanket?" he asked, and one nurse nodded before leaving the room. She came back a minute later with one of those blankets that they keep heated, and he spread it over her legs, going as high as her chest. Her breathing was steady, but shallow.

"We're going to wait for those results and the X-Rays to come back," the doctor said kindly, placing his hand on Chase's shoulder as he stood next to the bed, staring down into her pale face. "She's stable, and not in any immediate danger. She may wake up any time. If she does, press the call button. We don't want her moving her arm."

Then it was just the two of them, the last nurse that exited pulling the door closed behind her. Chase sank into one of the uncomfortable vinyl chairs, pulling it up close beside the bed. Bracing his elbows on the bed next to her hip, he clasped her right hand between both of his, bringing it to his lips as tears stung his nose, making his eyes water. He pressed her chilled fingers to his mouth as he stared into her face.

"I'm right here, sweetheart," he whispered against her fingers. "You can wake up anytime. Open those eyes and come back to me. Please."

SIXTY-NINE

Her head was pounding abominably, and her mouth felt like it had been stuffed full of cotton balls. The rhythmic beeping of machines around her felt like jackhammers inside her skull.

Opening her eyes felt like a herculean feat, and she blinked against the too bright light above her.

As she made to lift her hand to bring it to her forehead, she let out a sharp cry at the searing pain that knifed through her arm.

"Don't move, sweetheart," she heard from her right, and she twisted her head just enough to look in the direction of his voice. Her chest tightened and tears threatened. Chase. "Just hold still, okay?" she saw his arm reach next to her, hitting the little call button on the paddle connected to her bed. She focused her eyes on him as he dropped to his knees beside her, his elbows coming to rest on the hospital bed next to her. One of his hands came up and smoothed over her forehead as his eyes covered every inch of her face before coming back to hers.

His brows pulled together into a V and he picked up her hand with his, bringing it to his lips. "Hi, sweetheart," he mumbled against the backs of her knuckles. "God, it's so good to see those eyes."

Zoey swallowed, opening her mouth just as two nurses filed into the room. Panic undulated over her, and she squeezed Chase's hand as he made to stand. He squeezed them back and remained where he was, refusing to move away from her even as the nurses fussed over her.

"Hi," one said gently, leaning close. "Can you tell me your last name and date of birth?"

"Manning," Zoey whispered through parched lips. "Ten-nineteen."

"Great," the nurse said, smiling. "Do you know what happened?"

Zoey swallowed, trying to lick her lips. "Deer."

Chase squeezed her hand and looked up at the nurse, "Can she have a little water?"

"I don't see why a couple sips wouldn't hurt," she said, turning with an already made-up cup of ice water with a bendy straw. "Just little sips, though. You got banged up pretty good," the nurse continued as Zoey took a few sips of the ice-cold beverage. "You hit a deer?"

Zoey shook her head, though the action made her head pound. She groaned at the pain. "I missed it. Hit a tree."

"You have a concussion and a wound on your forehead that's been stitched up. You may have a scar, but Dr. Cavanaugh did his best to keep it minimal. You also fractured your radius and ulna. You're in a brace for now until the swelling comes down a little, then you'll have to have an orthopedic surgeon go in and put those back together," she said gently. "You'll probably be here until tomorrow."

Zoey nodded, just slightly, but she wasn't listening. Her eyes had sought out Chase again, and she noticed the dark circles under his eyes.

"How long have I been out?" she asked, her voice still coming out hoarse.

He squeezed her fingers again and said, "Since last night. About fourteen hours."

"You haven't slept," she whispered, untangling her fingers from his to reach up and tuck that favorite errant strand of dark hair away from his forehead. He wore his uniform, though it looked deeply wrinkled. He turned his face into her palm, nuzzling it with his nose before settling his cheek into it. Her fingers trailed over his heavily bewhiskered cheek. "Chase."

She didn't notice when the nurses took their leave. She didn't see anything but the face of the man still kneeling beside her, as his hand came up and covered the back of hers, holding her palm to his cheek. She watched as tears misted his cobalt blue eyes, and he whispered, "I've been waiting for you to wake up. I didn't want to miss seeing you open those eyes and look at me, sweetheart." Then he cleared his throat and his other hand reached up to tuck her hair behind her ear, careful not to graze the bandage on her forehead. "God, I was so scared, Zoey. When I got that call—" his words broke off and he turned his face once more into her palm, where she felt his lips press a kiss. He turned back to her, keeping her hand pressed to his cheek as he whispered huskily, emotion making his voice rough, "I'm so sorry, Zoey. For doing what I did. I have no excuse and I don't expect your forgiveness. All I can say is that I plead temporary insanity; my love for you made me so incredibly selfish."

Tears slid out of the corner of her eyes, tracking down her cheek. She scratched at his bewhiskered cheek with her fingernails as he continued.

"I want you to come back to me," he whispered, his own tears overflowing and falling down his cheeks. "Let me come home. Be my wife, sweetheart. My life is so gray without you in it. I can't stand it. You took all the sunshine with you. I love you."

"I love you," she whispered back, curling her fingers up into his hair behind his ear. "I want to be your wife, Chase. Come home. Please."

Chase raised from his knees so that he could lean over her. He pressed his mouth to hers, his hands cupping either side of her face. "I love you so much," he whispered against her lips. "Don't you ever scare me like this again."

A soft, half laugh escaped her lips still pressed against his. "I'm sorry. I won't do this again." Then, she asked, "Who has Verity?"

"Shaun," he said, still stroking her cheeks gently. He pressed his forehead to the unbandaged side of hers, rolling carefully. "I can't wait to get you home, sweetheart."

"I can't wait to get *you* home," she whispered. "I've missed you."

"We have all the time in the world," he murmured. "Because I'm not letting you go again. And I plan on putting a baby in you as soon as I can."

Zoey laughed out loud this time, kissing him again. "We're pretty good at practicing. I'm sure it won't take long."

"See? Insatiable," he whispered, teasing lightly, as she gazed up at him.

"Your fault," she teased back. She'd missed his smile so much.

"Damn right," he murmured. Then he smoothed both hands over her hair, once again letting his eyes rove over her entire face, and she knew it was as if he was making sure she was whole, and safe. "I love you. My beautiful, strong girl."

"Your wife," Zoey corrected quietly.

He grinned. "My wife," he repeated, and she smiled radiantly up at him as his mouth met hers again.

All would be well. Because she had Chase. Her fierce protector. Her best friend. Her love.

EPILOGUE

"Hurry, the candle is melting!" Zoey called, laughing. Chase rushed forward, carrying Verity. He sat down on one side of the picnic table, balancing Verity in his lap. He held her little hands in his, her fingers wrapped around his forefingers to keep them away from the singular flame that sat atop the miniature cake that Zoey placed in front of them.

Her arm twinged slightly, though it was brief. It had been four months since her accident. Her arm had healed, though the pins and rods that held the two broken bones back together still ached every once in a while. She had a nearly invisible scar along her hairline on the left side of her forehead, though she didn't mind. Chase kissed it regularly, letting his lips linger there, as if to remind himself of how he'd almost lost her.

Verity babbled excitedly, bouncing in Chase's lap as Zoey and Chase began singing a very off-tune rendition of Happy Birthday to the one-year-old. Her golden curls now reached her shoulders and

Zoey had pinned it back with twin matching bows, making pigtails.

Zoey and Chase both leaned forward to blow out the single candle, and her eyes locked with his. Letting go of one of Verity's hands, he reached up, threading his fingers through the loose waves at the back of her neck and pulling her mouth down to his for a scorching, open-mouthed kiss. Zoey moaned into his mouth before a little fist beat at her chest, and she backed away, laughing. Chase's eyes were alight with that same fire she felt, too.

Pulling the candle out of the cake, she slid it forward so that Verity could sink her fingers into it. Coming away with handfuls of icing, she shoved first one fist, then the other into her mouth. Chase laughed, adjusting her on his lap so she could better reach her treat, which she attacked with gusto. Zoey wished Tommy were here to celebrate, but it had been nearly two months since she'd seen him. Chase said he had traveled downstate somewhere, though neither of them were entirely sure where. He would text or call periodically, but it had been weeks since she'd even had that much communication with him. She knew he was struggling through the breakup with Shaun, and at the urging of her therapist, she was letting him grieve and heal in his own way, even if it hurt her to witness.

Zoey and Chase laughed as Verity attacked the cake for several minutes, then Zoey took her from Chase and the two of them disappeared into the house to wipe Verity down of the frosting and cake smeared between her fingers and all over her face and the front of her dress.

Tugging the surprise t-shirt over Verity's head, she whispered into Verity's ear, "Okay, this is your big part."

Setting her down on the ground as she walked back out the door toward Chase, Verity toddled over to him, hands raised with a squeal.

Chase scooped her up, flinging her high in the air before catching her. Zoey smiled, leaning against the picnic table as she watched them.

"Did you show Daddy your new shirt?" Zoey crooned to Verity, though she was speaking to Chase, too.

Chase's eyebrows came together as a look of confusion crossed his features, before setting her down. Kneeling in front of her, he proceeded to hold her arms out wide so he could read the words on Verity's shirt. His eyes sliced up to hers, his mouth dropping open as he whispered, "You are not."

Zoey nodded, unable to stop the beaming smile or the tears that sprang to her eyes. He stood, his eyes dropping to her stomach a half a second before he reached out and hauled her into his arms, crushing her to him as he spun them around once. She laughed, placing her hands on either side of his handsome face as he set her back down, his hands sliding to span across her stomach reverently.

"My baby is in there?" he whispered as he stared down at his hands.

She nodded again, smiling radiantly, dropping her hands to cover his where they stroked over her abdomen. "Your baby is in there."

"I love you so much," he growled, dropping his mouth to hers fiercely. When they broke apart to breathe, he sank to his knees in front of her. Verity had toddled to the side of them to play in the newly constructed sandbox Chase had built for her. Raising her shirt, he pressed his mouth to her stomach, below her belly button. "I cannot wait to see this belly round with my baby."

Zoey laughed, sinking her fingers into his dark hair. "I told you it wouldn't take long."

"I've been practicing," he murmured against her skin, making goosebumps break out over her. "I want to take you inside right now and practice some more."

"Then I guess it's a good thing that Norma and John are on their way here to pick up Verity for a couple hours," Zoey whispered in a breathy sigh as his tongue started doing deliciously filthy things to her. During their mediations, Zoey had gotten to know the Patterson's. They just wanted to know their only grandchild, and as James had said, what was so bad about that? They had agreed to two-hours of supervised visitation each week, but they had recently amended it to allow them to have unsupervised time with her. They planned to take her to the park today to celebrate her first birthday and would bring her back before dinner. Verity adored them and vice-versa, and that was all Zoey could have hoped for.

Zoey's head tipped back as Chase distracted her with his wicked tongue, her fingers tunneling into his hair to hold him to her.

"If there was a way to get you pregnant again, I'd do it," he murmured hotly, spreading his hands wide over the curves of her ass and pulling her closer. "I'd put another baby in you right now."

Pulling on his hair lightly, she brought his head away from her skin until he looked up at her. "One at a time, please," she teased.

"No promises on the next one," he growled as he stood, pulling her into his arms and kissing her until she was breathless. "I love you."

"I love you," she whispered back. "More than yesterday, not as much as tomorrow."

"We have a lifetime of tomorrow's," he whispered. "And we'll face them all together, sweetheart. You and me. Together."

She liked the sound of that.

ACKNOWLEDGMENTS

First off, WOW!! I cannot believe that we are here at the end of my second novel! What an adventure this has been, and I truly feel so blessed to be doing what I love! Thank you all for your continued love and support throughout this journey!

Mom, you were my first and always my biggest fan, and the best proofreader around. Without your love and support this wouldn't have been possible! You knew when I was fifteen that I would be here one day, even when I doubted it myself. On to book three already! I love you!

Nick, thank you for letting me hide away at my desk for hours—and sometimes days—on end. Thank you for messaging me that my breakfast, lunch, or dinner was waiting for me when I was ready for it, because you knew I wouldn't even think about eating (thank you, Chef). Thank you for your unwavering support, faith, and enthusiasm for this passion of mine. Without you and the love you give me, I wouldn't have started writing again. Without your support, I wouldn't be able to do this fulltime. You are my biggest cheerleader, my love. You are my forever Prince Charming. I love you!

Erin. Sissy. You are the best big sister a girl could ask for. You and that amazing group of ladies in NC have been such a blessing and the best cheerleaders! "Oh, Danielle Baker? Yeah, that's my sister!" I love you, Sissy!

Haley and Kim; Thank you to these wonderful fellow authors that I have had the pleasure of being on this journey with! Haley, thank you for always being a critical and willing sounding board, and the Tessa to my Jodi! Kim, I'm so glad I met you and feel fortunate to be traversing this new journey with you! Thank you, ladies! I can't wait for our coffee dates!

Stasha, you told me almost twenty years ago that you would edit for me when I was ready. I can't believe we finished book two! Thank you for being there through the very rough first draft all those years ago, to the newly polished draft we finished. Thank you for helping me get here and believing in me that I could!

To CP, THANK YOU for trusting in my totally random, weird AF text late at night requesting to talk to your husband... and to Mike, thank you a million times for your unbelievable patience with me and my seemingly unending questions regarding police work!

Katia, Tania, and the team with Miblart, thank you for the wonderful cover art, you took exactly what was in my mind and made it come to life! I look forward to what we can come up with for my future works!

To all the people that are not named but have beta read, listened to me venting or joined in my excitement over each new milestone, and all those that have rooted for me in this scary and enthralling journey, thank you! I wouldn't be here without you!

Lastly, to all my readers old and new, this has only been possible because of the love and support you've shown me and these characters. I hope you love reading their story as much as I've loved writing it. It was as emotional for me to write as it was to read. Zoey and Chase have a special place in my heart. I look forward to introducing you to MANY more in the future! Thank you!

MEET THE AUTHOR!

Danielle Baker, romance author of *Love Unbound* and *Best Kept Secrets*, was born and raised in the beautiful city of Petoskey, nestled on the crystalline shores of Lake Michigan. She is married to the love of her life, Nicholas, and they have four children between them. Danielle's love of writing began while she was in high school. She wrote a slew of short stories and had written three novels by the time she graduated. Life got busy and writing was put on hold for many years while she started her family. At the urging of her mother, sister, and husband, Danielle was given the boost she needed to "get back in the saddle" and keep reaching for her lifelong dream of becoming a published author. When Danielle isn't working, writing, or spending time with her family, she can be found with a cup of coffee in one hand and a book in the other.

She looked up, her eyes meeting the intense grey-blue gaze the same color as storm clouds from across the lavishly decorated event tent. The man was quite possibly the most handsome man she'd ever seen in her life. The candles lit throughout the space and on all the white linen covered tables cast flickering shadows to dancing everywhere, picking up highlights in his dark-blonde hair and casting half of his impossibly handsome face in shadow.

His suit was fit snugly to his body, grey dress slacks that delineated his long legs and left little to the imagination at the apex of his thighs. A matching grey, slim cut suit vest was buttoned closed over a black dress shirt, showing off his impressive upper body even though he was covered up to his neck. The material of the black dress shirt stretched across his shoulders and over his biceps as his arm relaxed as he lowered if from taking a swallow of his drink. The forest green necktie that all the other members of the groom's party wore had been loosened at his neck, and the top button of the black dress shirt had been unbuttoned. The sleeves of the shirt had been rolled to his forearms, and the candlelight shone on sun-bleached arm hair that dusted deeply tanned skin. His fingers were long, nearly wrapping around the highball glass in his hand.

She swallowed hard, her entire body completely still as he raised the glass of amber liquid in silent salutation before bringing it to his lips again. All the while, those storm-cloud, grey-blue eyes never left hers.

And she felt it all the way to her toes. Among other places.

Which just pissed her off, honestly. Who the hell was this guy?

Hardening her gaze, she stared at the obnoxiously handsome stranger across the room until he dropped his eyes, though she knew the second he raised them back to her, her entire body going hot. She refused to look over in his direction again. She wouldn't give him the satisfaction of seeing how his attention affected her.

Not that she was affected by that tall, brooding, insanely attractive specimen of man...

Her body disagreed otherwise; her heart hammered in her chest, making her breathing much more labored than walking across a room should entail, and her nipples were damn near begging for him to look at the them, the way they were peaked beneath the corseted bodice of her dress. Hopefully he couldn't see...

Her sister found her then, and she leaned down and hissed, "Who is that?"

Her sister just smiled knowingly and leaned closer to whisper, "That is Free's cousin, Kasey."

"He seems like an ass."

Her sister admonished her, but she wasn't listening, and she made a disgruntled sound in the back of her throat. "He's cocky and it's damned irritating, the way he keeps looking at me."

"Then maybe you shouldn't have worn that dress," her sister teased, winking.

She rolled her eyes and brushed her long hair over her shoulder, taking a deep sip of her champagne. The dress she'd worn was perhaps a little over-the-top sexy, but how often did a girl get to dress up and make jaws drop? Could she really be upset with the poor sucker for being pulled into her like a personified version of a Venus Fly Trap?

Tommy would be there soon anyway, so the poor guy would get the hint soon enough, if he hadn't already.

But as the evening wore on, he clearly wasn't getting the hint. Those thundercloud grey-blue eyes followed her wherever she went. As she stepped to the bar to get another glass of champagne, she knew how good the backs of her legs looked as she walked in her sky-high heels. Feeling devious, she put an extra little sway in her hips as she moved across the floor. When she glanced through her lashes at him, she was perversely delighted that it hadn't gone unnoticed. Ha. Poor sucker. Eat your heart out.

She was approached by a young blonde who asked her to dance, which she accepted with a grin. He was boyishly cute, though she admitted to herself he reminded her too much of her own little brother for her to consider him attractive in that sense. He was stiff as he stood with his arms around her lightly, and she wanted to laugh. It reminded her of those awkward middle school dances.

The blonde kid's eyes went up when something caught his attention over her shoulder, and then the sexiest, smoothest southern drawl she'd ever heard hit her full in the belly, making her knees turn into jelly. The younger kid dropped his arms from around her waist, stepping back as the owner of that voice came into view, and she stiffened immediately when she realized it was Mr. Storm-Cloud-Eyes from across the room. He held out one of those outrageously sexy hands and murmured low, "I believe this dance belongs to me."

She couldn't say no without creating a scene, and not wanting to do that to the bride and groom, she had no other choice but to accept. Setting her hand—dammit why was she shaking—in his, she sucked in her breath at the electricity that arched between them at the contact.

Her eyes flushed up—way up, Christ was he tall— to connect with his just as his other hand slid around her waist, pulling her close against the hardness of his body. His hard thighs brushed against her bare ones, his hips aligned with hers, and he brought her in close enough for her breasts to come to a rest against his broad chest. If her nipples weren't trying to get his attention before, well, they sure as hell were now.

And dammit if he wasn't the single most attractive man she'd ever laid eyes on, especially up close.

Mr. Tall-Blonde-and-Sexy moved them across the dancefloor, swaying effortlessly while keeping her effectively trapped inside the circle of his arms. Every time they moved, his thigh would press between hers and her breath would catch. What was wrong with her?!

Pump the brakes, woman!

"I have a Tommy," she blurted out, then could have kicked herself, turning a vicious shade of red in embarrassment. "I mean, I have a boyfriend. Tommy."

Her teeth gnashed together when she heard it— no, she felt it as it rumbled against her breasts that were pressed so close to his chest—as he laughed at her. The fucker was laughing at her!

"Mmmm," he murmured low, so low that it too, vibrated into her chest, making her nipples tingle. This was not going well. "Is that why you won't look at me? Because you have a 'Tommy'?"

Annoyance flashed through her and she stiffened her body slightly against his. "I've barely noticed you."

He leaned closer then, dropping his head so that his mouth was just breaths away from her ear, and he murmured in that slow, sexy drawl, "That's not what your body is saying, darlin'."

She spluttered in indignation and made to pull away, but his arm tightened just the slightest around her waist, his hand capturing hers more fully, and at the way his fingers spread wide across the lower portion of her back, she was struggling to remember why she was pulling away. Shit, she was struggling to remember how to breathe.

"And if your 'Tommy' were doing his job properly, your body wouldn't be so hungry for mine right now," he continued, his voice barely above a whisper. At the same time his words registered, his palm pressed against her lower back, bringing her firmly against his hips, and she felt his hard length press into her middle. She gasped in shock, at his words, at his boldness, at the feel of him hard against her. His nose nudged her temple, his lips moving against her high cheekbone, directly next to her ear, and it made goosebumps flash across her entire body. "I'd love to get my mouth on those pierced nipples you think you're hiding beneath that dress. I'll bet he doesn't even play with them. Hmm? Does he make you come? Or do you fake it to make him feel better about himself? I guarantee you wouldn't have to fake it for me, darlin'. Your body knows it, too."

This time the gasp that escaped her was a confusing mix of arousal and outrage, and she pushed against his chest hard enough to force him to let her go or cause a scene. Her eyes went wide when she caught sight of a sandy blonde head across the room, his brown eyes fixed on her and the man that had been holding her entirely too close. What was worse, this jackass had probably known all along Tommy was standing there watching. And for how long? What had he seen?

"Fuck you," she snapped heatedly, risking one last look up into those eyes before she turned on her high heels and walked off the dance floor, leaving him standing there in the middle of the room.

Striding toward Tommy, she slid her arms around his shoulders and leaned into him for a deep kiss, sinking her tongue into his mouth. He kissed her back, wrapping his arms around her waist possessively. This kiss was so different than all their other kisses. This was heady, primal, and she felt it all the way down into her belly. An approving growl rumbled through *his chest into hers as he curved his tall frame around her, pulling her even deeper into the kiss. His hips pressed into hers, and a gasp tore through her at how hard he was against her. Her body was on fire.*

Pulling away to breathe, she raised her eyes to his. But they weren't the soft, honey brown she was expecting. Instead, she was caught in that storm-cloud, grey-blue gaze that could only belong to one man... Mr. Steal-Your-Girl Kasey.

Shauntelle Kendall woke with a start, her body jerking like she'd been about to fall in her sleep. Her eyes adjusted slowly to the inky darkness of the room while her heart hammered out a heavy cadence in her chest. Her body was flushed, tingling all over, her lower body aching with a need that would not be soothed.

Sitting up, she scrubbed her hands over her face, pushing the long braid she kept her hair in at night over her shoulder. The sheet was a tangled mess around her long legs, and she struggled in the dark to extricate herself from them. Swinging her legs over the edge of the bed, she stood, crossing the room to the door, unmindful that she was in nothing but a pair of skimpy boy-short underwear and a loose fitted men's t-shirt.

Padding down the short hallway to the bathroom, she stepped inside and flipped the light on, staring at her reflection in the sudden brightness of the room.

It was the same dream. Over and over again. For months. She grunted at her reflection as she splashed cold water on her face and corrected herself: *a year.* It had been a year of this stupid dream.

And it was always Kasey that she was kissing, not Tommy. Tommy, *her boyfriend. Her fiancé.*

Then, hanging her head sadly, she sighed and corrected herself again: *no, her ex-fiancé.*

Grabbing the hand towel hanging next to the sink, she blew out a heavy breath, forcing the thoughts away. She couldn't think about that right now. It had been seven months since they'd split, but the pain still lanced through her from time to time.

Leaving the bathroom, she made her way into the tiny kitchen, prepping a large pot of coffee to percolate. She added an extra scoop of grounds just for a little extra kick, then switched the toggle to turn it on. When the little red light didn't come on and the usual gurgling sound of the water beginning to run didn't sound off, she swore under her breath and checked to make sure it was plugged in and that the breaker hadn't been flipped. She unplugged it and plugged it into a different outlet, but nothing happened.

"Dammit," Shaun muttered sourly, letting her shoulders drop in defeat. She had made the mistake of choosing the least expensive coffee maker she could find at the time, and it was living up to its cheap ticket price. Her sister Jodi had told her to splurge on a better quality one, but Shaun was stubborn.

She could just hear Jodi saying "I told you so" and grimaced.

It was going to be a rough morning if there was no coffee. Murder seemed highly probable.

Making her way back to her bedroom, she dressed quickly, shoving her legs into the same tight jeans she'd worn the day before that were still in a heap on the floor. Pulling the loose t-shirt over her head, she tossed it into the laundry basket in the corner of the room. She rummaged through the dresser until she found a sports bra and squeezed into it, adjusting her breasts in the tight confines of the material. Tugging on a lightweight, long-sleeved hoodie, she grabbed up a Detroit Tigers baseball cap and put it on her head to contain the flyway's that had escaped her braid throughout the night.

As she drove, the sky began to lighten on the horizon, painting the sky with golden light, which highlighted the leaves that were in full autumn color. Everything was bathed in deep reds, bright oranges, and golden yellows of mid-October in northern Michigan.

A new coffee maker was on her list to buy today—the only item on her list—but this was an emergency situation, so gas station coffee would have to do for now.

Pulling into her favorite gas station convenience store, she climbed out of the truck and headed inside. As the door shut, she heard a car horn blast from the road.

"Hiya Frank," she called, and he grumbled a curt hello back. She grinned; Frank was a grumpy old coot and had been the night cashier here for ages.

Pursing her lips, she eeny-meeny-miney-moe'd which basic convenient store coffee blend to choose, settling on a dark roast that looked like it had been left to sit for a while, which meant it would be a little burnt and strong as hell. She poured a large cup full and brought it to her lips, her entire body wiggling with anticipation at the first sip. It burned her tongue, and she hissed in pain before taking another hedonistic sip.

Shaun reached for a lid and capped it carefully, cautious not to let any of the precious liquid slosh over the edge of the cup, then turned to head toward the cashier counter.

She was brought up short when she ran headlong into a tall, unyielding body, and she watched in dismay as her coffee fell from her fingers, the Styrofoam cracking down the side of the cup as it crashed to floor. The lid flew off, sending hot coffee splashing all over the tiled floor and soaking her shoes and the bottom of her jeans, as well as sloshing over a pair of well-worn work boots that were standing *far* too close.

"Oh you have got to be shitting me—" she snapped in annoyance, the scathing retort falling off her lips before she could stop it, because honestly, *who stands that close to someone else?!* Planting her hands on her hips and raising her eyes to the face of the man she'd run into, her eyes went wide, and she shook her head in disbelief.

She had rotten luck this morning, but *this?* This was just not fair.

"No. Nope," she muttered darkly, backing away as she growled in exasperation. "*You.*"